UNEARTHING
THE
GUARDIAN

For Tim

UNEARTHING
THE
GUARDIAN

A Novel

J.A. Guenther

Chapter

I

Danielle Sawyer sat, legs stretched out in front of her in a plush chaise lounge in her small home office listening intently to the voice coming from her headphones. She paused the recording, backed it up a bit, and listened again. After a long moment she hit pause again and began to type. After a while, she again hit play and this time she typed as she listened, translating the Spanish recording into English as she went. Today was a good day because the material she was translating was actually of interest to her. The process was the same regardless but the work was only as interesting as the material being translated, and some projects, like medical transcripts or educational lectures, were as interesting as watching paint dry. Today's project, however, was an article for an online news source and dealt with the impact of the Mexican drug cartels on NAFTA in general and on the automotive industry in particular. Although she had spent years living out east, Danielle had been born and raised in Detroit, the "Motor City," and had grown up surrounded by the auto industry. For her, automotive work was a return to her roots.

The interviewer in the piece was speaking with executives from each of the American auto manufacturers, previously known as the "Big 3." The first executive spoke of trailers full of component parts that had been hijacked by armed thugs during a border crossing. The second complained that it was harder and harder to convince their American executives to accept foreign work assignments in Mexico because of the ever-present threat of kidnappings and violence from the cartels. The last to be interviewed was the senior vice-president of North American Purchasing for the firm now known in Detroit simply as "Government Motors," since being bailed out and essentially bought up by the US government. As the new interview began, Danielle spaced down in her translation and began a new paragraph. She noted the speaker's name as Matthew Miller. Although clearly an American, he was speaking in Spanish as he responded to the Mexican interviewer's questions. She listened for a few moments more, paused the recording, and typed out a brief translation of the question being asked.

Before resuming the recording, she removed her headphones, stood up from her chaise and headed to the kitchen to turn on her electric tea kettle. She was greeted almost immediately by Gordie, her black lab. While working, she was always careful to lock him out of the office because the dog possessed such an enormous amount of energy that he seemed almost incapable of sitting still. She took a moment to rub his round belly while waiting for her tea water to boil and again after she put the tea bag in. After their brief visit she returned, tea in hand, to the office and closed the door behind her, locking him out. She felt a brief twinge of guilt as she heard the clicking of his nails on the hardwood, pacing back and forth in front of the door. She picked up her headphones and popped them back on, silencing the clicking nails outside.

Once again she hit play and the broken Spanish of Mr. Matthew Miller resumed.

"Aunque los costos bajos del labor en México son atractivos," said Miller.

"Although the low labor costs in Mexico are attractive," typed Danielle.

"Hay siempre costos adicionales en seguridad para proteger nuestros empleados y nuestros camiones contra la violencia de los carteles," he concluded.

"There are always additional costs in security to protect our workers and our trucks from the violence of the cartels," she concluded.

"Seek him out," the voice said, this time in perfect English.

Danielle sat for a moment, her hands still poised over the keyboard, momentarily confused by the sudden linguistic shift. She clicked the rewind icon and played the recording back again. Again she listened to Mr. Miller lament the high costs of security in Mexico. He began to elaborate on the challenge of protecting their investments in machinery and component parts only this time the recording continued in the same broken Spanish. She shook her head and laughed at herself, taking a sip of her tea. She began again to type her translation.

"Seek him out" the voice came again, this time over top of the Spanish recording but still in the same voice, as though Matthew Miller were interrupting his own interview. She hit pause, took off her headphones and picked up her cell phone. She hit a speed dial number and before long a deep, masculine voice answered.

"Morning, Tom, it's Dani. How are you?" She asked, listening to, but not really hearing, his response. "Look, I wanted to ask if you intended for me to include the voice-over stuff in my translation. I'm not sure what it's about and being that it's already in English, I just wasn't sure what you wanted me to do with it?"

"What are you talking about?" said Tom, sounding amused and wondering to himself if perhaps his translator had been nipping at the tequila.

"The voice-over bit that you added to the interview, where Miller is telling the interviewer to seek someone out? What's that about? What do you want me to do with that?" she tried again.

"Dani, I don't know what you're talking about," Tom's amusement had turned to concern. "There's no voice-over anything on that recording, just business as usual."

"Well, Tom, I'm telling you that there's a voice-over on it. Maybe you didn't intend it, maybe your file became corrupted when you sent it over or something but it's definitely there. I haven't even finished listening to it but already there've been two spots where an English-speaking Miller starts up about looking for somebody."

"Shit, that's all I need," barked Tom into the phone. "Well, can you send it back to me and I'll see if I can get one of the sound guys to fix it?"

"Look, it's not a big deal. I don't need to do anything with it, I can work around it. I was just asking in case you wanted me to address it somehow in the translation," said Dani.

"I'm not worried about you! I need that recording for the piece. We need the audio for the story too. Do me a favor, just send it back and I'll have them clean it up. I'll send it back over to you afterward, OK?"

"OK, sure, whatever you want. I'll send it back to you this morning. Let me know when you want me to take another look at it, OK?" she paused, listening. "OK, I'll talk to you later. Bye."

Danielle hung up and turned back to her computer. She saved her translation file, closed off the original, replied to Tom's e-mail and attached the file she'd been listening to, sending it back for his review.

With that done, she found herself with a free afternoon. She curled up on the comfy chaise, pulled a throw off the back cushion down onto her legs and began again to sip her tea. The room was small and very warm and soon her eyelids began to droop. She felt herself sliding into the downy comfort of the chaise's thick cushions, sliding into the deep blackness of sleep like a turtle slipping under the water's surface.

The dream came to her in an odd way. Unlike most of her dreams, in which she felt like an active participant, in this dream she felt like an observer. As though she were watching her dream played before her on a newsreel. She found herself back on Woodward Avenue, not far from the home where she grew up. In front of her stood a group of kids only one of whom she recognized. Her closest childhood friend, Nora Fontana, stood with two brunet boys in front of a bright orange car, talking to a third boy and a chubby man with a beard. The chubby man appeared to be in his early twenties and was standing by the third boy, who was blond, rail thin, and looked to be about sixteen. One of the two brunet boys with Nora seemed to be arguing with the other. He was heavily freckled, holding a skateboard, and seemed to be eleven or twelve years old.

"Oh c'mon," he was saying, "don't you want to be in a commercial? He said he'd have us back before the street lights come on so your mom won't even find out!"

"And what if they *do* pick us for the commercial?" he argued back, "She'll find out for sure!"

"Well, yeah, but by then you'll be in a commercial," he exclaimed, as though no further explanation were required. "What's she going to say?"

"I don't know, Jimmy," the boy hesitated. "Mom told me not to go with strangers ..."

"Look, Jimmy, if they don't want to go, just leave 'em," said the blond boy. "It's less competition for us at the audition!"

The young, dark-haired boy named Jimmy waved good-bye to his friends and followed the blond boy and the bearded man into the orange car. The car was neither a sports car nor a true sedan. She'd never seen one like it before and couldn't have identified the make or model. As it pulled away, an inexplicable panic swept over Danielle. She wanted instantly and desperately to get young Jimmy out of that car. She tried to yell to him but found that she had no voice. Like a member of the audience, she realized that she had no influence over the characters in the play. She was sure that Nora, who was older than the two boys, would step in. Dani couldn't tell for certain but Nora seemed to be at least sixteen in the dream, almost as near in age to the chubby bearded man as to the two boys. Why wasn't she saying anything? Helplessly, she watched young Jimmy buckle himself into the backseat. She felt as though the car might explode and consume his small body in flames.

The car did not explode, however. It drove off without incident and Nora and the other boy turned and started walking toward home. They didn't seem to notice Danielle standing there. She attempted to speak to them but couldn't. She tried to follow them but found that she was walking through thick sand that swallowed her feet every time she took a step. A distant voice came to her clearly and persistently insisting that she "Seek him out! Seek him out! Seek him out!" But she didn't know how.

Jerking awake, Danielle found herself covered in sweat, her heart beating wildly in her chest. She barely had a moment to recover before her cell phone began to ring. She stared at it a moment, her sleepy eyes struggling to focus on the caller ID. She cleared her throat then answered the call.

"Danielle Sawyer," she said, trying not to sound as though she'd just woken up.

"Danielle, this is Tom. Is everything OK?"

"Hey Tom, yes, I'm fine. What's up?" She tried to keep her voice calm even though her heart was still pounding from the dream.

"I've got my sound guy here and we're listening to the audio from that automotive piece you were working on. Where did you say you were when you heard the voice-over stuff?"

"It was when Matthew Miller was talking. The first time I heard it he was talking about the increased security they needed to protect their trucks and then I heard it again a little later during the same interview."

"And you're sure about that? It wasn't maybe some place further on into the piece?"

"No, I'm sure. It was Miller. I recognized the voice. It was his voice on the voice-over. Can he fix it?" Danielle asked, wondering if she might be able to resume her translation yet this afternoon and glancing at her watch.

"Well, that's just it. There's nothing to fix. We've listened to that interview three times. There's no voice-over on that recording. It's just Miller going on about the cartels and component parts and whatever. It's the interview, that's it." She could hear in Tom's voice that he was confused, but trying to give her the benefit of the doubt. "Did you have the TV on in the background while you were working or any chance you were picking up some other signal or something?"

"I don't ..." Danielle hesitated, stood up and walked to her office door. Cracking it open she peered down the hall into her living room. The TV in the other room was, in fact, on. It was often Danielle's habit to let the TV run while she was in the house alone. It kept her company and made the house seem less empty. She felt a crimson wave of embarrassment flood into her cheeks. She closed the door as quietly as possible and turned her attention back to the phone. "Now that I think about it, Tom, maybe there was another voice. I'm, um, right by a window over here. Maybe there was someone talking outside. Why don't you send that back over and I'll try it again?" Danielle felt that blaming a noisy, albeit fictitious, neighbor was less embarrassing than admitting she'd overheard her own television. "OK, I'll get that translation back to you just as soon as I possibly can. OK ... yep, thanks. Talk to you soon."

She hung up the phone, picked up her empty mug and headed out of the office and down the hall, followed closely by Gordie. She paused in the living room to turn off the TV and then proceeded into the kitchen and set her mug down in the sink. She made herself a sandwich, tossed Gordie a piece of lunchmeat, and sat down at the table to eat. As she did, her mind wandered back to the dream she'd had. She wondered why of all people she'd dreamed of Nora. They hadn't seen each other in months. In the dream Nora had appeared exactly as she had when she was a teenager. It was incredible to Danielle that she could have recalled Nora's teenage appearance with such clarity. It was the mid-'70s and Nora had worn her hair feathered back like the rest of the teenagers at that time. Her skin was deeply tanned from lying in the sun and her gray-blue eyes were rimmed with thick, black lashes.

Danielle thought about the boy named Jimmy. She was sure she didn't know him and yet, for some reason, he'd seemed very familiar to her. She tried to remember the boys that Nora had hung out with around that time but Nora had always been a beautiful, popular girl and Danielle was several years her junior. At that time, she was still more interested in dolls than boys, so the names and faces of Nora's young admirers were a little hazy to her even then, much less thirty-some years later.

She walked her empty plate over to the sink and then turned back to her office. By the time she sat back down at her computer, she had a message waiting from Tom. She opened the attachment and resumed her translation. This time, she heard only Miller's lengthy Spanish explanation of the dangers of the Mexican drug cartels with no additional commentary from the TV or her fictitious neighbor.

By half past five that evening, Danielle had completed the translation and returned the finished product to Tom. She stood, stretched and decided to take her chunky, hyper dog for a walk. She opened the office door and allowed Gordie to wander into the room, sniffing for crumbs and wagging his tail so enthusiastically that it propelled his body into a sidewinding, undulating motion, like a fat snake moving through a river.

"Hey there, Chunky Monkey Butt," she greeted him, rubbing his broad back, "ready to take me for a walk?" As soon as the word "walk" escaped her lips, Gordie was ready. He immediately ran for the side door, bowing as though asking permission to play, his tail flying fiercely back and forth. "Hold on, hold on," she muttered, searching through the closet in the office. "I need to find my shoes." From the chaise, her cell phone began to ring.

"Danielle Sawyer," she said, bringing the phone to her ear with one hand as she continued the search for her shoes with the other.

"Geoffrey Williams," responded the voice on the other end.

Danielle stopped her search and gave the caller her full attention, a broad grin breaking across her face. "Well hello there, Mr. Williams. What are you up to?"

"Well, I can tell you what I'm *not* up to and that is my workout. It's what I should be up to but I just can't seem to find the energy today, you? What mischief did you get yourself into today?"

"I was just about to take my paunchy pooch out for a walk. Care to join us? You could call it your workout and kill two birds with one stone," she said playfully, anxious for the company.

"Yeah, alright," he said slowly. "Give me about twenty minutes and I'll be over there."

"Gordie's already jumping on my door. Give us twenty minutes and *we'll* be over *there*. You are home, aren't you?"

"Yep, you're on. See you then," he said and clicked the phone off.

After another extensive search through the messy closet, Dani had her shoes on and joined Gordie at the side door. "C'mon, Gordito," she said to him with a bow, "let's go pick up the other lazy bones and get ourselves some exercise, whaddya think?" She asked, as she opened the side door and braced herself against the pulling, rushing enthusiasm of her canine companion. Gordie pulled his owner along out of their own subdivision and down the block, past the scary, bouncing Rottweiler on the corner, who always motivated them both to move just a bit faster, and into town. Just past the Catholic church, the pair cut through the cemetery and re-emerged on River Drive. They followed it around the curve of a small lake. On the opposite side of the lake, they made a left down Harris Street and came to a rustic, neat home at the edge of the cul-de-sac. The home, like many in the area, had once been a summer cottage for some lucky urban family but had long since graduated from summer retreat to permanent residence. The structure was a small craftsman bungalow with a low-pitched, gabled roof, and a wide, unenclosed eave overhang. The porch was flanked with thick, square pillars and the landscaping was masculine but neat. In front of the porch were a row of boxwood shrubs, which Dani referred to as "bachelor bushes," because they were the typical male substitute for a real garden. It was the sort of plant that was better trimmed with a power tool than a pair of gardening shears.

She did her best to reel Gordie in, like an oversized trout, and then climbed the porch steps. Just as she raised her hand to knock, the door flew open and Geoff came out, greeting Gordie first and then reaching past him to give Dani a hug. "Wow, you're quick! It only took you about 15 minutes," he said, grinning broadly and looking genuinely impressed.

"Well, if it had been up to me, I'd have taken my time but Gordie had other plans," she shrugged.

"Ah, I see! So you're just along for the ride then?" he teased.

"Exactly! You think I'm joking but I promise I'm not!"

"No, I believe you. I've seen him in action. When are you going to start training him? He's a smart dog; he just needs an owner that doesn't let him get away with murder."

"If you think he's so smart, why don't you train him for me?" she replied, knowing the comment would prompt a change of subject.

"So what did you do today?" Geoff asked, ignoring the request.

"Oh, I worked on an automotive translation for most of the day but I had a break around lunch time and I took a nap. I had the weirdest dream," she began. "It was about Nora Fontana. Have you talked to her lately?"

"No, not really, we swapped an e-mail or two near the holidays last year but that was the last time I heard from her. What happened in the dream?"

"Well, it wasn't so much what happened, it was more when it happened. In my dream, she was just a kid, like maybe sixteen years old and in it we were back on Woodward, like when we were growing up," Dani paused for a reaction, but Geoff just watched her steadily, waiting for her to continue. "Don't you think that's odd?"

"No, why? You knew her then, right? So your mind was just playing with a memory or something," he shrugged.

"Well, not a memory. I'm sure I never witnessed before what I saw in the dream. She was with a bunch of other kids that I didn't recognize talking to some guy about shooting a commercial. One of the guys was trying to persuade the kids to go with him and I don't know why, but I was terrified for them. I was sure in the dream that something really bad was going to happen if they got in that car. One of them eventually did but nothing really happened. I'm not sure I even know what I thought might happen. It was just a sort of blind panic that I felt. The guy was a fat, bearded man, like maybe early twenties. I didn't recognize him."

"Oh, you're remembering that whole mess with the Guardian murders," he said, nodding solemnly. "I'm surprised she talked to you about that. I've never been able to get her to talk about it."

"The what?" she asked, caught completely off guard. "What are you talking about? She never mentioned anything like that to me."

"Well she must have if you dreamed about it. You must have just forgotten. There was this guy in the metro area—well, I say this guy but they never caught the person so I guess we don't know if it was a guy …"

"I know about the Guardian Murderer," she interrupted. "I grew up right in the middle of it, how could I not know about it? My mother barely let us leave the house for more than a year, but I'm sure I'd have remembered it if Nora had been involved with any of that!" She shook her head and glanced at the ground, trying to remember if she'd ever heard Nora mention anything about the infamous murderer known as the Guardian.

"Well I don't know if I'd say that she was 'involved' with it exactly but she dated the younger brother of one of the suspects and the cops interviewed her because she'd been around him during that time—the suspect, I mean. But the scene in your dream—that was the last time Jimmy Prince was seen alive. He was last seen getting into a bright orange car with two of the suspects. They told a group of kids that there were some people looking for kids to be in a commercial. That's how they lured him into the car. It was all very suspicious at the time and one of the guys was a known pedophile—the guy with the beard," Geoff shook his head again, staring down at the dog, who was busy sniffing a squirrel carcass on the road. "That was the brother of the guy Nora was dating."

"Oh my God! How could I not have known this about her? And how could I possibly have dreamt about something I never knew? She dated the brother of a known pedophile? I don't get it though. If they know all this and the guy was on record as a pedophile, how did they not catch him?"

Dani jerked at Gordie's chain, pulling him away from the rotting rodent.

"Well, OK. I say he was a 'known' pedophile but what I mean is, he'd been arrested for it before but the family was well off—*very* well off, so nothing ever stuck. I don't think Nora knew anything about it. The father was apparently not someone you messed with and from what she told me after the fact, she always thought the brother was a weird guy but the dad kept a tight leash on him. She thought he was weird but I think she just didn't want to believe he could be *that* weird. Do you know what I mean?" Geoff stared out over the lake as they made their way around it. His eyes were ice blue and might have appeared cold against his pale skin and white blond hair, if not for his warm smile and friendly demeanor.

"I still can't believe I never knew this about her. How'd you find out? Was your dad involved in the case at all?" Dani knew that Geoff's dad was a retired cop but couldn't remember for which county.

"No, dad was in Howell. Those murders happened in the next county over. Well, actually, I think they involved more than one county but neither were in my dad's jurisdiction. He knew about them, of course, cops talk and it was all over the news at the time. Did you know Jimmy Prince?" Geoff asked with that peculiar tone people get when presented with the rare opportunity to associate themselves with a famous tragedy, but from a safe distance.

"No, I never knew any of the kids that went missing. I was a bit younger than his target victim though. As I recall, they were all in their teens or tweens and I was like eight or nine when that was going on. I knew Nora but only through my older brother at that point. She actually used to babysit for us younger kids when mom went to the store. So she knew Jimmy Prince?" Dani thought about the freckled boy from her dream.

"Nora used to babysit you?" Geoff laughed at the thought. "I never realized that she was that much older than we are."

"Well, she's not really. Like I said, she's my older brother's age. I think she was a year ahead of him in school. Nora lived right nearby and mom was good friends with Mrs. Fontana. She knew that if there were ever any problems, Nora could just call home and have her mom come over. It was a safe neighborhood. That's what freaked everyone out so much. Hell, I think one of those kids was abducted from *Belle Mead*. You can't get much safer than that! If one of those kids could go missing, no one was safe and all the parents knew it!" Dani paused to let Gordie lift his leg on a nearby tree.

"Yeah, I remember that. I was a little young for that too and, like I said, we weren't in the same county but none of that mattered. My parents kept me inside all the same. I can't remember what the guy's alibi was or how he managed to get off the hook. You should talk to Nora. She might be willing to tell you. You have to understand, that whole experience really freaked her out. Can you imagine coming that close to a serial killer?"

"So she's sure the brother did it? What made her think so?" Dani was still trying to remember if Nora had ever mentioned any of this to her.

"I think she believes he did it but she's never told me why or what she knew about it. She only mentioned to me that she'd dated the brother, who was a couple years older than she was, and that the father was someone you wouldn't mess with," he concluded. "That's why I was surprised that you got her to talk about it."

"But I didn't," Dani protested. "I'm telling you, she never mentioned a word of any of this to me!"

"She must have. At some point, you must have read about Jimmy Prince being picked up by those guys and your subconscious remembered her knowing the brother so it put her together with him in your dream." Geoff sounded sensible enough to almost convince her. If only she could allow herself to be convinced. These odd coincidences had become all too common in her life since moving back to Michigan.

As they arrived back at Geoff's house, Dani gave him a hug and she and Gordie set off alone back up Harris and around the lake. As they walked, she thought about her life in Virginia and the voices that had filled her head since her decision to leave that life. She wondered how far she'd have to run to put them all to rest. She thought about the PTSD diagnosis that she'd heard more than once but wondered what Jimmy Prince could possibly have in common with everything she'd left behind or, for that matter, with the other voices she'd been hearing. Whatever the cause, she knew how people would react if they knew what was going on inside her head. As much as she wanted to tell Nora about the dream, she wasn't sure that she was ready to open that particular can of worms.

Chapter

II

Sitting at her cubicle, Danielle had just finished responding to her first e-mails of the day when a pretty, blond coworker in military fatigues came running over to her.

"Dani, have you seen what's going on in New York?" she asked, her voice tinged with panic but also a sort-of morbid fascination. "It's like something out of an Arnold Schwarzenegger movie!"

"What are you talking about?"

"Come look, they've set up a TV over on Stacy's desk," she responded, turning around and returning in the direction from which she'd come.

As she hurried back, Dani looked past her at the monitor on Stacy's desk. The words "Breaking News—New York" appeared in a red box at the bottom of the screen and above it the World Trade Center towers were billowing black smoke into the sky. In that instant she heard a deafening boom from the direction of the corridor just outside her office and the building began to shake horribly followed closely by the whoosh of a fireball barreling like a bright orange freight train through the center of the office. She watched helplessly as the pretty blond was consumed by the flames. Danielle was thrown back against the far wall of the office like a rag doll in a wind tunnel; her burned body fell hard to the floor. When she regained consciousness, her world had been thrown into smoky black disarray. With every breath, she felt as though she were breathing the flames directly into her body so she did her very best not to breathe at all. She crawled along the hard floor, not knowing where she was or where she was going. As she crawled, she thought about her nieces and nephews, thought about her parents and her friends back in Michigan. As she crawled, she thought about all the people and places that she was certain she'd never see again. She reached out her hand to pull herself further along the floor and touched what she believed was another human hand. She grasped the hand, held onto it and pulled it closer, hoping to either save or be saved. In her dazed state, she didn't understand at first why the hand offered no resistance. Not that she expected a struggle, but the hand came with her so willingly, it was as though the hand's owner had no free will at all. In a heartbeat she realized why—the hand's owner lay 10 feet away, dead. Repulsed, she tossed the dismembered limb away and began again to crawl.

From somewhere far, far away, Dani saw daylight and could hear voices. She began to crawl painfully toward that light, shoving aside bodies and pieces of bodies and rubble of every kind as she went. The faces and voices of her family flooded one by one through her mind as she crawled. The flames ate away at her lungs and the thick, black smoke made her blind—blind to everything except that slight sliver of daylight. As she approached it, she heard a voice and a hand was offered to her through the darkness. As she reached up, she saw her skin, hanging from her bone and muscle like wax dripping from a candle. She tried to take the hand but each time she tried, she found it to be just out of reach. From behind her, the flames licked at her boots, creeping ever closer to her flesh. In a panic, she tried over and over again to reach the elusive, outstretched hand only to have it slip away. The voice was calling for her. The words came to her as though through a long tunnel but the hand remained out of reach.

Danielle bolted awake, covered in sweat, coughing because she could still feel the heat and black smoke in her lungs. Her hands were shaking as she reached across the bed table and switched on the light. She found herself back in her quiet Michigan home. Gordie stared at her from his place at the foot of the bed then stood, turned a few circles and settled back down to sleep. For a moment longer she sat trembling under the thick comforter. She turned her hands over in front of her and looked at the scars that ran across them like roadmaps. She was fortunate. She had instinctively covered her face with her hands when the fireball passed, so the scars on her face were a great deal less noticeable, especially under her makeup. She sat in her quiet room thinking about Stacy and Kimberly, the pretty blond who had once been her officemate at the Pentagon. She thought about all the others who had not made it out alive. She thought about John, the kind man who had pulled her from the smoke and flames on that horrible September morning. She thought about the dismembered hand and all the body parts that littered the gruesome scene. She shook her head, as though trying to shake the memories out through her ears. She glanced at the clock—3:15 a.m. Still, she knew that sleep was a lost cause, at least for this night. She left Gordie to his pleasant dreams and walked downstairs. She felt the cool chill of the finished hardwood floors on her bare feet and immediately wished she'd remembered to put on socks. She curled up on the couch and pulled her laptop off the coffee table. Wrapping herself in a down throw, she switched on the computer and pulled up a blank e-mail template. After filling in the destination, she tabbed down to the subject line and paused for a long moment. Finally, she shrugged and typed simply "Lunch?" She tabbed down to the body of the e-mail and began to type.

> *Hello Nora,*
>
> *Hope all's well with you. I was talking to Geoff Williams the other day and your name came up. He suggested that you might be able to answer some questions about a dream that I recently had. I know that sounds weird and it probably shouldn't matter anyways. It was only a dream after all but for some reason, this one has stuck with me. Any chance we could have lunch sometime this week? I'd love to just pick your brain about it.*
>
> > *Looking forward to seeing you soon.*
> > *Take Care,*
> > *Dani*

She hit the send button and was very surprised when only a few minutes later, a response came back. She opened the e-mail and began to read:

> *Hey Girl!!*
>
> *What in the world are you doing up this late? I thought it was just me and the donut bakers up at this hour—hahaha! It's perfect though, I could use someone to talk to. So tell me about this dream! Did it by any chance involve a hot, male swimsuit model?*
>
> *By the way, can we switch to IM?*
>
> > *Nora*

Dani switched to IM and began her response:

"Hey Crazy Lady! I had another one of my nightmares about the attack. The anniversary always brings it back up again. I couldn't get back to sleep after that. What about you? Why so late? No, unfortunately, there were no hot guys in my dream. It took place back when we were kids. I think one of the kids in the dream was Jimmy Prince. Did you know him?"

Dani hit enter and waited for a response. Several times she saw Nora begin and then erase a message. After a very long pause, an answer finally came back.

"Why would you dream about Jimmy Prince?"

It seemed like an odd question, as though she had any choice in the matter.

"I don't know," she wrote, "guess I just needed a break from dreaming about terrorist attacks. Did you know him?"

This time the response came more quickly:

"Not really, I don't really want to talk about it. There was nothing I could have done. Wait, what was your dream about exactly? What happened?"

Dani took a deep breath and wrote out her dream with as much detail as she could remember and hit send. It was another long moment before Nora began to type and another long moment after that before the response popped up in front of Dani.

"That's not what happened. Nobody ever saw Jimmy get in the car. A witness only saw him talking to someone matching Craig's description. The other guy with him may have been that weird little friend of his, Michael. I wasn't the witness. That was some woman who had been shopping at a store nearby. They assume that at some point, Jimmy must have gotten into the car. That day, I was with Craig's brother. I only knew Craig and Michael through him. The thing about Jimmy speaking to them by the car was all over the news at the time. You must have heard that on the news.

Dani read the response once and then again. In an odd way, she felt relieved. She didn't actually remember hearing those details before on the news. She was, after all, just a young child when that story would have been reported but she had to concede that perhaps she'd been in the room when her mother or someone older was listening to the story and that it may well have seeped into her subconscious as a result. What she still didn't understand was why now— so many years later—would she dream about it? And why would her dream have involved Nora?

"Why on earth would I dream about that now?" she asked Nora, as though it were a question she could actually answer.

"I don't know. Maybe it's like you said, maybe your mind needed the distraction. Have you ever thought of seeing someone about the attack? That was a horrible thing to live through, there's no shame in it if you need some help putting it behind you."

"Oh, believe me, I've seen people. We all did. They had so many shrinks and grief counselors meeting with us after that. There was no escaping it. No offense meant to anyone, but that just wasn't for me," she responded.

Dani thought for a moment about all the counselors and their many, many diagnoses and suggestions. They all tried to make her remember the experience but the truth was, she couldn't. She'd heard many witness accounts about the attacks during all the media coverage over the years and she knew what she was told of her medical condition and of her rescue that day from those who were involved. Her own true memories of the actual event, however, were few and far between. She clearly remembered Kimberly telling her about the attacks in New York and she remembered a brief glimpse of the smoking towers on the TV. She wanted desperately to believe that she really hadn't seen Kim being consumed by the fire but she was pretty sure that she had. It was when the shock wave blew her against the wall that her memories became sketchy. Everything from that moment until the time she woke up in the hospital bed days later was a blur. She had memories but she could no longer tell if they were her own or if they were planted in her mind by others and by her own nightmarish imagination.

"Hey, you still there??" A message popped up from Nora. As she read it, she realized that it was not the only message awaiting a response. She toggled up to read the earlier note:

"I'm sorry to hear that you're still having nightmares about it," wrote Nora. "I'm up because my noisy neighbor upstairs is tap dancing in his kitchen or something and I couldn't sleep through it!"

"Your noisy neighbor upstairs? I thought you were living in your boyfriend's house now, or is he the noisy neighbor?" Dani grinned at the idea of Nora's boyfriend tap dancing in the kitchen at 3 A.M.

"Good Lord, Girl! We've *got* to get together. It's been too long. I moved out of Steve's place last month. Now I'm in this little apartment with leaking pipes and a loud, tap dancing neighbor – LOL! Well, OK, maybe he's not actually tap dancing, I don't know, but it sure sounds like it!"

She missed Nora. She had such a crazy sense of humor. She was always good for a laugh and these days, Dani was in desperate need of one.

"S'okay, let's get together! Are you free for lunch tomorrow (or shall I say, later today)? My treat!" Dani responded, feeling suddenly very anxious to see her old friend.

"You're on! Could you pick me up from work at noon? There's a great pizza place right down the street from my office. We could go there!"

"See you at noon!! Totally looking forward to it!"

"Me too," wrote Nora, "for now though, I think I'm going to take another stab at sleeping. The tap dancer seems to have tired himself out!"

Dani smiled as she closed out the IM and pulled up a search engine. In the search box she typed "PTSD" + "hearing voices." Reluctantly, she hit enter. Immediately her reluctance was justified as the very first article she found spoke about "positive psychotic" episodes associated with hearing voices as a symptom of PTSD. The circumstances and symptoms were unnervingly similar to her own. She bookmarked the article then moved to the next. Unfortunately, each article proved more distressing than the last with words like "Schizophrenia" and "Brain Disorder" being commonplace among them. She was anxious to know if there could be any other—less terrifying—explanation. She removed the "PTSD" component of her search and began again. In one of the articles, the author rephrased the term, "hearing voices" to "auditory hallucinations." This sounded less psychotic to Dani so she again revised her search term. She found, however, that she didn't care for the term "hallucination" either so once again she revised her search term. This time she typed in "auditory stimuli." This brought up one article that immediately grabbed her attention.

The headline read, "Clairaudience: Are you crazy if you hear voices?" Dani clicked on the article and skimmed through it. Next, she revised her search term yet again, this time she typed in "Clairaudience." The next article she read spoke to the phenomenon of hearing voices as a component of psychic ability or paranormal perception. To Dani, this sounded every bit as crazy and terrifying as potentially being schizophrenic and even the article acknowledged that the two were remarkably similar. The article concluded that "Clairaudience is distinguished from the voices heard by the mentally ill when they reveal information that could not be available to the clairaudient person by normal means." Included in the article was a link to a contact at a parapsychology research laboratory that was apparently affiliated with a reputable university. This brief glimpse of credibility made Dani feel more hopeful. The contact name was Dr. Erwin Meier. Dani went to her in-box, copied the address and began a new e-mail:

> *Good Morning Dr. Meier,*
>
> *I am writing to you because I have read online information regarding your research into the phenomenon of clairaudience and am very interested in learning more. Could you please tell me if it's possible for anyone to experience this phenomenon? Is it possible to have it occur later in life if it was not previously present?*

Dani paused, debating whether or not to mention the PTSD or her experience at the Pentagon. She decided that to do so might create a bias in his response and so she did not include this information.

> *I appreciate any assistance you might be able to offer,* she concluded.
>
> *Kind Regards,*
> *Danielle Sawyer*

She held her breath and hit send. With that, she put the computer away and got up to take her shower and begin her day.

Unfortunately, she had a truly boring morning on the docket. She spent hours on a tedious legal translation. The case involved a trademark infringement between a Mexican pharmaceutical company and a similar company in the United States. Finally, at about 11:00, she saved her work, logged off, and grabbed her purse. She pushed past Gordie and slipped out the side door. The warm fall sun hit her face and lifted her spirits. The drive to Nora's office was a pleasant one because the tree-lined streets offered a beautiful pallet of late-blooming flowers and early-turning leaves. She had her favorite music cranked up, and the weather was still mild enough to crack open the windows and let the warm breeze blow away the last remnants of the nightmares she'd been having. She let her mind wander to a more carefree, happy place. It was so pleasant, in fact, that she was a little disappointed when Nora's building came into view. Not that she wasn't looking forward to seeing her old friend but she knew that the sight of her would bring back poor Jimmy and the panic that she'd felt as he'd disappeared from view.

At exactly noon, she pulled into the lot, lined by bright gingko trees, and steered her black Tiguan in front of the massive brown brick building's entrance. For a moment she wondered if she should ask for Nora at reception or just try her cell and see if she could come out. Before she could decide, however, she saw Nora striding toward her, waving and smiling her friendly, toothy grin. Nora had always been a striking woman and wherever she went, men turned to watch her walk by. Today was no exception. Dani had to laugh when a group of large-bellied businessmen nearly knocked each other over to clear her path and then stood, transfixed, to watch her walk by. She was tall at about 5'10", blond and curvaceous with flawless, tanned skin and expertly applied makeup. She had a wonderful sense for which colors best suited her features and her wardrobe choices were fearless but flattering.

Nora inspired jealousy in a lot of women but not Dani. Perhaps it was because they'd known each other since before such things mattered; but to Dani, Nora had always just been her funny, goofy friend. She popped the lock and Nora climbed in through the passenger door. They hugged briefly and then Dani said, "OK, so where's this great pizza place?" On Nora's instruction, she took a right onto Hamlin out of Auburn Hills and down into nearby Rochester Hills. They made a left onto South Adams and pulled into a busy city center filled with upscale shops and Italian restaurants. On the corner of Adams and Butler they pulled into a tiny, crowded lot.

Inside, a young hostess greeted them and showed them to a small table at the far end of the restaurant. They sat down and for a long moment, their normally constant conversation hit a snag. Dani knew she had to bring the conversation to the subject of Jimmy but was unsure how best to do so. She was even more reluctant to bring up the voices in her head or her search for an explanation and yet, at the same time, she had to acknowledge that Nora was one of the few people she knew who might actually listen with an open mind to that particular conversation. She'd always been a bit on the edge when it came to her ideas and, if nothing else, always struck Dani as somewhat of a free spirit. As hesitant as she was about it, she was anxious for someone—anyone—in whom she could confide. Still, she was terrified of being taken for a nut case by one of her oldest friends. As she tried to come up with something to say, the waitress saved her the trouble. They placed their order and handed back the menus.

"So did you ever manage to get any sleep last night?"

"Not really," Dani replied. "Although, to be fair, I didn't really try. After all the nightmares, I kind of just gave up sleep as a bad investment and started working on my translation."

"Really? What are you translating now?" she asked, clearly hoping to steer the conversation to a happier subject.

"Well, this morning I've just been working on a medical case, very dull. Yesterday I was doing some automotive work. That was more interesting," she said, trying to decide whether to elaborate on her experience from the day before. She took a deep breath, "In fact, I had kind of a weird experience with that." She paused for a moment, staring down at her plate.

"Yeah?" Nora said slowly, "How so?" Dani could feel her eyes watching her closely.

"Well, I had my headphones on and I was listening to an interview. During the interview, I could swear I heard another voice." She paused again but continued looking at her plate. She frowned briefly then corrected herself, "Well, actually, it was the same voice but it was a separate conversation."

"A separate conversation?"

"Yeah, I mean like the same guy talking about two different things in the same interview, at the same time." Dani continued, briefly glancing at Nora before returning her eyes to the plate.

"At the same time? You mean like a voice-over on the recording or something?"

"Well, yeah, sort of. That's what I thought it was at first too. But the guy who sent me the tape said there was no voice-over on it. He even had his audio guy check for one. All he could hear was the interview—the one, normal voice track," Dani explained, trying to keep her voice steady.

"And what did the voice-over say when you heard it?"

To Dani's relief, Nora's tone seemed genuinely curious, rather than judgmental. She wasn't looking at her like a nut case. She was looking at her as though she had no doubt as to the truth of the voice-over and wanted only to know more about the content of its conversation. Dani looked up at her now, anxious to hear her opinion. "It said, 'seek him out'," she replied, and waited for her reaction.

"Seek who out?" she asked immediately.

"That's the question, isn't it?" she responded. "I really have no idea."

"Well, what was he talking about in the interview and who was it being interviewed?"

"The interview was nothing. It was NAFTA stuff, about the drug cartels."

"So you think you're supposed to track someone in a drug cartel?"

Dani laughed before she could stop herself, then felt bad for laughing at her friend, "Jeez, I hope not! If that's what the voice is after, it's going to have to find another translator." She smiled and shook her head. Happily, Nora didn't seem to mind that Dani found her question funny.

"Well that's a relief. So who then? Who was the person being interviewed?"

"Nobody really, some automotive big shot. His name was Mueller, I think," Dani frowned trying hard to remember the name. "No, I don't think that was it, but it was like that and I think his first name was with an M … Michael? Or maybe Martin?"

"Matthew Miller?" Nora asked, sounding horrified.

"Yeah, right! How in the hell did you know that?" Dani asked, sounding both impressed and completely freaked out.

"That's the brother!" she exclaimed, as though that answered everything.

"The brother? Whose brother? What are you talking about?"

"Craig and Matt—the guys I told you about—their names were Craig and Matthew *Miller!* I dated Matt and Craig was his brother, the guy that they thought took Jimmy. Their dad was a big shot in the automotive industry—I can't remember his exact position—but he was really wealthy and there was a whole big story about how he paid off his son's victims not to say anything. He was protected, of course, by a whole bunch of high-priced lawyers and cover stories but that was the speculation at the time. That his son was abusing all these kids, all these young boys, and his dad was spending the family fortune trying to cover it all up. Matt must have followed him into automotive. It wouldn't surprise me; he had all kinds of upper level connections. I can't believe this is all coming up again!" Nora seemed to have drifted away from the conversation and into her own, terrifying past.

"That was the man's name. Now I don't know, maybe it's a common name or something. I have to admit, this is all getting very creepy. Whoever he is, he's working for an American OEM." Dani began to wish she'd never begun this conversation.

"It's him," she said, sounding as though she'd already drawn her own conclusion. "I'm sure it's him. They couldn't arrest his brother and they couldn't prove the father's connection to anything. Why would you pull me back into this? Why couldn't you leave this alone?" She was glaring at Dani and seemed near tears.

"Me?" Dani was stunned and hurt by the accusation. "What are you talking about? I'm not trying to pull you back into anything. I'd have gladly left it alone if it hadn't come through my headphones and into my dreams!"

Nora sat staring at her for a moment, tears slipped down her cheeks and she glanced from her friend down to her empty plate and finally off into the distance. "I'm sorry," she said at last. "I didn't mean to accuse you of anything. I just don't like being asked to think about that time in my life."

"What made them think that the father had been paying people off?" Dani asked, hesitant to upset her friend further but now curious beyond control.

"Because of his job, he used to move the family around. There were some cops out east who had a theory and they were reportedly talking to the cops here in Detroit, sharing information. They had an open case. There was a Latino teenager in the Bronx who had complained about a young guy molesting him. He led them to Craig, Matt's brother, and the police picked up Craig for questioning but then a witness claims she saw a black limo pull up in front of the Latino kid's house and Craig's father—his name was Victor, I think—stepped out to talk to the kid's mom. After that, the charges were dropped and the whole thing just went away." Nora seemed completely lost in thought now and her voice grew softer and softer, as though she were just talking to herself.

"This all happened before I knew Matt and I didn't find out about any of it until years after I'd stopped dating him. I read about it in the newspapers like everyone else. But the cops in the Bronx saw the story of what was going on in Detroit. The papers published a sketch of a guy matching Craig's description from the woman who had seen him talking to Jimmy in the parking lot. So the East Coast cops called our cops and they picked Craig up. But nothing ever stuck here either. His old man always managed to pay somebody off or threaten just the right person. If that family knows anything, it's how to keep people quiet!" Nora's tone was bitter as the tears continued to stream down her face. She used her napkin to dab them away.

"That's horrible!" Dani replied, playing with the straw in her glass. "I can't believe that a mother would just allow her kid's well-being to be *purchased* that way!"

"Well," Nora began, sounding more like she was returning to the present, "they were broke and the kid was still alive and at least physically unharmed ..." Her argument was weak and she knew it so she took it no further. She looked across the table and simply shrugged.

"Still, it's an innocent kid. Who would allow an innocent kid to suffer—to be abused like that just for profit?" Dani shifted the plates to make room for the pizza that was being placed before them while waiting for Nora to chime in on the issue. She did not. Dani glanced at her. She was shifting uneasily in her chair, looking down at the pizza on the table.

"I'm sure his mom has had to live with her decisions," she said finally. "It couldn't have been an easy decision and I'm sure she did what she thought she needed to do at the time. But some decisions, I'm sure, are harder to live with than others." Her voice grew quiet and she seemed to be drifting into her own thoughts again.

"Did you ever meet Matt's father?"

She glanced up at Dani and took a sip of her soda, as though trying to clear her thoughts. "Yeah, a few times," she said at last. "He scared the hell out of me. I think a lot of people felt that way about him. I know Matt did. He was really tall—towered above most people—wore thick glasses and had a booming, loud voice. From what Matt told me, he had a temper like a tornado. It could spring up out of nowhere, destroy everything in its path and then just go away again. Matt had scars—physical scars—from where his father had knocked him around over the years. He hated him but more than that, he feared him. You could see it whenever they were in the same room together. There was a horrible history there, I'm sure of it, but he never talked about it. Whenever his father entered a room, Matt left it and just as quick as he could. He told me he wanted to give his father as few opportunities as possible to talk to him." Nora seemed more animated now, more like herself.

Dani was relieved. "He never threatened you or anything, did he?"

"Me? No. I was nothing to Mr. Miller. I was his son's most recent bimbo and that was it," she said with a touch of bitterness creeping back into her voice. "Looking back on it now, that wasn't too far from the truth."

Dani grimaced. "Hey, easy now, that's my friend you're talking about."

Nora smiled gratefully, "Well, I'm not proud of it now but I was taken in by their lifestyle. At the time, I think I convinced myself that I was in love with him but the truth is that I was dazzled by Matt's home and the limos and the yacht—the whole lifestyle. It was a sort of wealth that I'd never seen before. They lived on a private road in the wealthiest part of Belle Mead. You couldn't even call it a home, that wouldn't do it justice. It was an estate or a manor, something bigger than a home," she laughed at her own attempt to describe it. "It had a big wrought iron fence that surrounded the house and property and the fence was surrounded by big plants and trees that blocked the view from the street. They were all about maintaining privacy and keeping the rest of the world out," she said. "You had to go up a long, winding drive before you even saw the house come into view.

"I remember the first time Matt took me there, I was absolutely amazed that a single family would be living in a building that size. It looked like one of those royal estates you see on TV. Like something a Duke and Duchess would live in but, in this case, the young Duke was a pedophile!" she said sarcastically. "They even had a courtyard with a big fountain just in front of the house. It would have looked really pretentious for a smaller home but their house was big enough to make it work."

"Do you remember what it was like on the inside?"

"Yeah," she continued, "on the inside it was even more beautiful. There was a huge entryway with a sweeping spiral staircase that went up and off to the left. The stairs were gleaming white marble with a very intricate wrought iron railing that curved up the staircase and extended down the hall and along the second floor balcony. The marble columns that supported the stairs and balcony formed archways into the living room and kitchen. I remember the entryway also had this massive chandelier overhead and the floor in the entryway was an elaborate marble mosaic. I've never seen so much marble in a private residence before and they had staff that kept it meticulously polished so that the glare off the marble and the chandelier was almost blinding when you first walked in. The one wall in the living room was floor to ceiling windows with the most beautiful silk window treatments that I'd ever seen. Everything was very tastefully decorated—professionally done, no doubt— and the ceilings were at least twenty feet high. The kitchen was amazing! It had an enormous island in the center and a marble bar that encircled half the room. Supporting the bar were marble statues of lions, which might have looked gaudy but the colors throughout the whole house were very warm and neutral so it was regal looking, but definitely not gaudy. Matt told me once that he'd gotten into trouble as a kid for painting a mustache on one of the marble lions," she smiled at the memory.

Nora paused to take a sip of her soda. Despite the many years that had passed, it was obvious that she still vaguely missed her slim connection to the wealth and power of the Miller family. "The game room always freaked me out," she continued, "I hated that room! The father had been a hunter and he mounted all the creepy heads on the wall in the game room. It wasn't just the regular assortment of Michigan deer, either. He went hunting all over the world so there were heads from gazelles and lions and bulls—all kinds of very creepy heads all over that room!"

"So someone living in that house might have had easy access to a shotgun?"

Nora became suddenly silent. "Yeah, why?" she asked, her voice a whisper.

"Didn't one of the victims of the Guardian die of a shotgun blast to the face?"

"Yeah," Nora replied in the same frightened whisper. "Matt and Craig both knew how to shoot and the old man kept a whole cabinet full of guns in the game room. I don't think he even locked it. But let's face it; a shotgun's not hard to come by in a hunter's paradise like Michigan!"

"Do you know if the cops ever checked any of them to see if they could find the murder weapon?" Dani suspected she knew the answer already but couldn't stop herself from asking the question.

Nora snorted derisively. "You kidding me? Do you know what kind of shit storm they'd have faced from every high-priced lawyer in the country if they'd ever had the nerve to step one foot inside Victor Miller's beautiful home? They wouldn't dare!" she laughed bitterly and took a bite of her pizza.

"I thought as much. Did the police do *anything* when they were given reason to suspect Craig Miller?"

"I don't honestly know," replied Nora quietly. "Matt and I split up shortly after they found Jimmy's body."

Dani debated for a moment whether to take it any further and again, her curiosity won out. "Did you split up *because* they found Jimmy's body?"

Nora kept her head down but gave a sideways glance at her friend. "No," she said unconvincingly. "I think it's a bit more accurate to say that I became increasingly uncomfortable with his family and with his lifestyle. It just wasn't really me."

"Thank goodness," Dani added with a smile that she hoped would convey her support but it seemed to make Nora feel worse. "You don't regret giving him up, do you?"

"Well, he'd have given me up eventually anyway," Nora replied, leaving Dani wanting for an actual answer to her question, but she decided just to let it lie.

After they'd finished their lunch and Dani had dropped Nora off at her office, she headed back to her own home office where, unfortunately, she was met with a full afternoon of the most tedious translation work she could imagine. She spent the entire afternoon translating the medical records of Hispanic patients in a local hospital for their Spanish-speaking doctors back home. Throughout the day the one thing that peaked her interest was whether or not she'd receive a response from Dr. Meier. Finally, at about 6:00 in the evening, her patience was rewarded.

> *Good Evening Ms. Sawyer,* he wrote.
>
> *Thank you for your interest in our work. I will tell you first and foremost that clairaudience is a complicated topic and one not easily summarized in an e-mail correspondence. As you may know, the auditory stimuli associated with clairaudience can have any number of origins, most of which have*

nothing to do with parapsychology and all of which should be thoroughly examined before a conclusion of clairaudience is established.

Dani snorted, "You may be a psycho if ..." she said to herself.

That said, the good doctor continued, *I have attached here a schedule of our current lecture series. I would highly recommend any of my esteemed colleagues involved in the series and am certain you would find the information useful.*

Kind Regards,
Dr. Erwin A. Meier

Dani opened the attachment and discovered that the following week there would be a lecture given at a nearby college on parapsychological phenomena pursuant to near-death experiences. Dani registered immediately on the included web address and then, reluctantly, returned her attention to the piles of medical transcripts still to be translated.

Chapter
III

Looking out across the lawn, Dani could see a vast ocean extending beyond the rocky cliff side at the edge of the property. Its deep blue waters glistened in the warm sun, making it shine like a sapphire. She stood on the cool, stone patio of a beautiful villa. Hanging from the balcony above were bougainvillea vines that tumbled down and hung over the patio in a raucous range of colors. The flowers were surrounded by a thick cloak of lush, green leaves. As Dani passed under them, she marveled up at the dappled sunlight streaming through the blanket of flowers, their strong perfume filling her senses.

At the end of the lawn, she came to stone stairs, chiseled into the cliff side that led down to a small landing formed naturally by the surface of the cliff. On the landing, however, were two structures that were clearly *not* natural. Formed of carved, polished, white marble and attached to the face of the cliff by their wrists were two large, hand-shaped chaise lounges, the palms of which were curved inward toward the center, providing the seating surface. When seen together from the top of the stairs, the two lounges seemed to be on the verge of scooping water from the sea below, as though it were a giant wash basin.

As she descended the stairs, clutching the wrought iron railing nervously, she noticed that seated on the far bench in the lotus position was a pole thin wisp of a man. As she approached the empty chaise nearest the stairs, he gazed up at her and motioned for her to sit down. She did, then gazed at him for a long moment, taking in the odd essence of the man. He was clearly Asian but she wasn't sure of his exact country of origin and felt, for some inexplicable reason, that it would be rude to ask. He wore a white silk tunic and pants with an olive green wrap draped over his right shoulder, extending down his torso and tied at his waist. On his head, he wore a scarf covering his hair and over that, a jaunty, wide-brimmed hat made from the same drab green silk as the wrap and banded in beige. His ancient skin was as discolored and wrinkled as a well-used map. A sparse, white beard hung from his chin and between his stained but otherwise healthy teeth, he clenched a cigarette. With this, Dani finally found her voice.

"Don't you know those things will kill you?"

"Don't you know I've been dead for six centuries?" he asked, as he withdrew the cigarette, holding it between his thumb and forefinger. "What harm could a little cigarette do?"

Dani seemed startled. "You have? Then how are you here?" she asked, suppressing an urge to giggle.

"You tell me," the old monk said, discarding the cigarette with a flick and smiling amiably. "You're the one who brought me here."

"Me?" she shot back, now smiling in return. "How could I have? I don't even know who you are!"

"Of course you do, Danielle," he insisted. "True, you don't know my face and I've never before shared with you my name—which, incidentally, is Kōbō—but you have known me all your life. I am within you, guiding you. I am that little voice that steers you back when you fall off course. I loan you my strength when you find that you have none of your own and I give you sight when you're in the dark."

"Oh *come onnnnn!*" she laughed, nearly sliding off the palm of her hand seat. "Isn't this all just a little too fantastic? Are you going to pull out a magic wand next and conjure up a boat to sail over the water?"

Kōbō continued to gaze at her, his warm brown eyes amused by her analogy. "Do I look like a wizard to you?" he asked at last. She seemed to consider the question for a moment but offered no reply so he tried again, "Have you ever seen a monk wave a magic wand?"

This point she had to concede. "No," she replied, "I have not."

He smiled triumphantly and looked out over the blue sea. "This is truly beautiful," he said after a long moment. "I love what you've done with the place."

She could only laugh and shake her head, "Come again?"

"This magnificent villa," he said in reply. "It is your creation and it makes me feel truly fortunate to be assisting you through this life."

"You feel fortunate to help someone who is so imaginative?"

"No," he replied, "I feel fortunate to live in such a lovely villa! Compared to this, the monastery was a dump!" He smiled his wise grin.

Dani laughed and shook her head again.

"So why have you arranged for us to meet, at long last?" His tone became more somber and he gazed at her intently, awaiting a response.

"Me?" she asked, feeling very confused. "I didn't arrange for us to meet," she replied. "I thought you did."

"I live within you, remember? So if I did, you did," he replied gently. "Your mind created this beautiful sanctuary and called me to it. Your mind brought you here. There must be a reason. Think now, why are we here?"

"This is a dream!" Dani exclaimed, understanding and relief finally flooding over her at once.

"To you, it would seem so, yes," replied Kōbō.

"Wait, does that mean it is or it isn't?"

"To you, it would seem so," he repeated.

She raised a brow at him and then continued. "So why would I call you here? That's the question, isn't it?" she asked, more to herself than to him. "Why do you think I called you here?"

"Ah-ah," he replied, waving his finger at her reproachfully, "that's cheating!"

She scowled at him then tried again. "Well, I guess I'm worried about my dreams. This being another classic example," she said, unable to hide the bite in her tone.

"What's so bad about your dreams?" he said simply. "Is my company so unpleasant?"

She shrugged and felt guilty for a moment, believing she'd hurt his feelings. He read her thoughts though and gave her a playful wink.

Leaning back against the chaise, she thought about her recent dreams. "No," she began, and gazed out again at the glistening waters of the sea. "No, you're not unpleasant at all. This is by far the most pleasant dream I've had in a very long time. I'm worried though that my dreams mean I'm crazy," she sighed, relieved to have finally said it. "That I'm crazy—psychotic or schizophrenic like all those websites imply."

Kōbō snorted derisively. "So many idle minds dreaming up so many terrible scenarios," he said quietly. "You're not crazy," he continued, "trust me."

"You're telling me that I should trust the ancient monk who shows up on a big stone hand in my dream when he tells me that I'm not crazy?"

He smiled his warm, reassuring grin. "Yes. You're fine. All creatures in this life possess intuition, instinct. When young penguins inexplicably find their way to a generations-old breeding ground despite having never been there before in their lives, people call it instinct but for some reason they conclude that instinct in a fellow human being must be fanciful nonsense," the monk shook his head sadly. "They mock those who listen to the same inner voice that has been guiding the world for centuries. Is it any wonder humanity is such a mess now?"

Dani nodded. "So you don't think I'm nuts when I dream about things that have happened that I couldn't possibly have known about before? Like Nora's ties to Jimmy Prince?"

"I believe your inner voice is telling you what you need to know for your journey, just as it showed you the way to safety during that terrible attack," he said quietly.

"But that's different, I'd worked in that building for years, I knew my way around," Dani argued.

"But the hole in the wall through which they pulled you to safety, that had never before existed. You couldn't possibly have known where it was and yet you crawled to it," he countered.

"I saw the light," she responded.

"Through the blackest smoke and eyes singed by fire, you were shown the light, yes," he concluded.

She looked at him for a long moment, comprehension creeping in. "Why weren't the others shown the same light?"

"Their journey was down a different path."

"Wasn't it sort of the end of their journey?" she asked, sounding bitter.

"You think so? Wait and see," he said in a playful tone.

Dani wasn't sure why but she took comfort in that. "How did you die?" she asked, wondering for a moment if that was considered a rude question to ask a dead person and hoping that it was not.

"Ah," he shrugged, "it was so long ago. Who remembers these things? You should get going. You'll be late for your lecture," he smiled once more and then was gone.

Dani awoke with the warm autumn sunshine peeking through her silver, silk drapes. She felt calm and more relaxed than she had felt in a very long time. She slipped out of bed and headed down to shower, looking forward to the upcoming lecture.

Chapter
IV

As Dani pulled into the parking lot at the small community college where the lecture was being held, she turned off the car and sat staring at the building. Despite her morning enthusiasm, she now felt terrified at the prospect of walking into this lecture. She imagined a room of soothsayers in multi-colored silk robes like modern-day gypsies. She imagined crystal balls and tarot cards and she did not want to be associated with any of it. "Well, you came all the way out here," she said aloud to herself, "you might as well go in and do what you came to do." She released her safety belt, took a deep breath and swung open the door.

She arrived at the small, gray classroom but lingered outside, peering in at the other attendees. The speaker was a short, plump woman in gray slacks and an ivory twinset who was pacing in front of the desk as the audience streamed in and got settled. Already seated were a handful of young people with backpacks in jeans and sneakers, their gazes fixed steadily on their smartphones, earbuds firmly in place. Mixed among them were a few others nearer to her own age, looking uncomfortable and out of place. There were also a few individuals who looked like they were associated with the college or perhaps with the speaker and who seemed to be there more in a professional capacity. Even though she did not see a single gypsy, Dani still could not convince herself to enter the room. She couldn't figure out why. She was normally a confident, self-assured woman and she had certainly handled more terrifying situations than some psychic lecture. For the life of her, she could not understand why this situation had her feeling so completely unnerved.

"Not going in?" asked a young redhead who had been quietly observing her from the other side of the hallway.

"I'm umm, not sure this is the room I need," Dani lied.

She smiled in a conspiratorial way. "I know what you mean," she said simply.

Dani turned her gaze from the redhead to the classroom and back again to the redhead. She wished she'd go away. She was uncomfortable enough already without having to explain herself to some nosy stranger.

The young woman was still staring at her intently. Dani shifted her weight uneasily. She wanted to go but now felt as though she'd be allowing the woman to chase her away. She felt stupid and was getting more and more annoyed by the minute. As she turned to leave, the redhead spoke again.

"This lecture is for people who have had near-death experiences. Is that the lecture you were looking for?"

Dani turned slowly back to the young woman but did not respond. She shot another uneasy glance at the classroom as the plump woman in gray slacks looked at the pair in the hallway and then began to walk toward the still open doorway. For a nervous moment, Dani felt sure that the woman was coming over to persuade her to come into the room. Instead, she nodded slightly to the redhead and pulled the door shut, leaving the two ladies alone in the otherwise empty corridor. Dani felt a wave of relief flood over her, as though she'd just been granted a stay of execution.

"Thanks," Dani responded at last to the redhead, "I guess that wasn't my lecture after all. I should get going." Again she turned to leave and again the young woman spoke.

"Have you ever had one?"

"Sorry?"

"A near-death experience, have you ever had one?" she asked again.

Dani stared at her for a long moment. "Yes," she said at last. "Yes, I have."

"And the experience left you," she paused for a moment, searching for the right word, "scarred?"

"I have scars on my hands and body," she explained, raising her palms to show her, "and some on my face but the makeup hides most of those."

"I wasn't talking about the physical scars," the young woman responded seriously. "I'm talking about the scars no one else can see. Nightmares?"

Dani nodded stiffly.

"Replaying it over and over in your head, during those quiet moments when your mind wanders?"

She nodded again.

"Do you hear voices in your head?" The girl stared at her intently, her green-blue eyes measuring Dani's reaction.

Slowly, ever so slightly, Dani nodded again. She felt terrified. She felt exposed. She felt *judged.*

"What are they telling you?"

"Well, they're not telling me to kill anyone with an ax if that's what you're worried about," she snapped defensively.

"I didn't think they were," she said quietly. "My voices have never harmed another living soul and they've never suggested that I should either."

Dani stood for a moment in stunned silence. "You hear voices too?"

"Yes," she replied simply.

"Did you have a near-death experience?"

"No," she replied, "for me, it's a family thing. I've heard the voices all my life but then so do all the women in my family. Well, on my mother's side anyway," she corrected herself.

"A family thing?" Dani asked in disbelief.

"Yes, it's pretty widely acknowledged in certain circles that psychic ability is a genetic trait. Well, except in cases like yours where some medical trauma triggers it later in life."

"A genetic trait?" she repeated, still feeling a little like she'd just fallen down the rabbit hole.

"Yes, like being left handed or the ability to roll your tongue."

"And you've heard voices all your life?"

"Yes, well, you hear them early on but it takes practice to really understand what they're trying to tell you. It's like being a translator."

"I am a translator."

"Are you really?" the young woman asked, sounding surprised.

"Shouldn't you know that already? I mean, if you're a psychic?"

"See? That's what I mean right there. It's not like they tell you everything that might ever become relevant in your life. I'm sometimes really amazed—and even kind of pissed off—about the things they *don't* mention. If, for example, I wanted you to show up at the movie theater at 4:00 on Friday. I'd just tell you, 'show up at the movie theater on Friday'. Simple enough, right? But now you have to imagine that I don't speak your language. Say I speak Russian and you don't speak Russian. Do you speak Russian, by the way?"

"I do, yes," Dani responded.

"OK, so what language *don't* you speak?"

"Swahili."

The redhead gave her an odd look and then continued, "OK, so let's say that I only speak *Swahili*," she emphasized the word as though it were completely ridiculous to be having a conversation about Swahili, "and you don't. Because really, who speaks Swahili anyway?"

"About five million Africans."

She rolled her eyes. "And we need to find a way to communicate that we're to meet at the theater on Friday at 4 P.M.," she continued, as though she had not been interrupted. "Instead of trying to tell you where to meet me, I might show you a picture of a local movie theater or I might show you images from the movie we plan to see or," she continued, "I might show you a physical location at which there happens to be a movie theater. And to demonstrate 4 P.M., I might show you the face of a watch with the hands at 4:00."

"So you're saying that your voices don't just talk to you. They show you pictures as well?"

"Well sure," she seemed surprised by the question. "How long ago was this near-death experience of yours?"

"It was in 2001. To be exact, it was on September eleventh of that year."

The young woman's eyes grew wide. "I understand," she said quietly. "The twin towers?" she asked.

"The Pentagon," Dani responded.

"And they've been talking to you ever since?"

"No," she said firmly. Then, as though thinking better of it, "Well, I guess I don't really know. I don't know if I even really believe in this sort of thing."

"I understand," she said, "but you should know that the voices will continue, even if you choose not to acknowledge them. It's like gravity. Whether you believe in it or not, you will feel its effects."

"I'm sorry," said Dani. "I hope I didn't offend you."

"You didn't," the young woman answered truthfully. "But I'm going to tell you in all honesty that until you come to terms with who you are now and with the change that's happened in your life, your guides will never be able to effectively communicate with you. More important," she continued, "you'll never really be at peace with them. You have to understand that once that speaker has been turned on, you can't really turn it off. Alcohol helps numb it, but it's no solution really. If you're going to hear them either way, wouldn't you rather be able to understand their meaning? Wouldn't you rather know what they're trying to tell you?"

That's the question, isn't it? Dani thought. Do I want to know about some murdered kid? What's the point if there's nothing that can even be done to help?

As if reading her thoughts, the young woman said, "It's not always clear to me what they hope to accomplish with the messages they send but I have learned to trust them. You have to trust that they know more about the situation than you do and that they're leading you where you need to go."

"But there is no '*they*'," she said, feeling frustrated by the whole bizarre conversation. "'They' only exist in *my* head so how am I supposed to know their judgment from my own?"

"Like I said, it takes practice. I'm Faye Carlyle, by the way." She extended her hand and Dani shook it. She opened her purse, pulled out a pen and an old receipt and jotted something down. Handing it to Dani she said, "If you're ever in the mood to practice, just let me know. I'll be happy to show you how." Dani hesitated just a moment then accepted the receipt with Faye's number on the back.

"I will," she said. "Thank you."

Faye smiled at her and then walked away.

Chapter
V

Dani awoke to the bright sunshine streaming through her window. It was a chilly Saturday morning and she was slow to rise. At last, she flung back her warm down comforter, slipped on a pair of soft, chenille socks, and followed Gordie downstairs. As they entered the kitchen, he ran, as usual, straight to the French doors that led into the backyard. She let him out and watched as he ran over to the neighbor's fence and greeted their Jack Russell Terrier, Barney, who was out playing in his own yard. Within moments, the two dogs were racing back and forth along the fence line. Because of his much longer legs, it was hardly a fair competition but every few minutes, the larger dog would slow enough to allow the smaller to catch up and the two would again run along together. Dani stood there watching for a moment before turning back into the house. She crossed through the kitchen into the living room and out the front door where the morning paper was waiting for her on the porch. She bent down, picked it up, and returned to the kitchen, where she deposited it on the table, slipped it out of the plastic wrap, flipped it open, and began to skim through the articles on the front page.

She turned on the electric tea kettle and when it clicked off, Dani grabbed her favorite mug from the cupboard, tossed in a teabag, poured the water, and returned to the table. As it steeped, she flipped the page and what she saw next made her feel as though she'd been punched in the chest. For a moment, she couldn't breathe. She only stared down at the paper. There, staring back up at her, was the boy of her dreams. From the freckled face to the stick-straight brown hair, she recognized the face of Jimmy Prince immediately. The headline read, "Frustrated Father Speaks Out."

Dani sipped her tea and began to read. The article was an interview with Lawrence Prince, Jimmy's father, who spoke of spending $12,000 to obtain thousands of pages of police records in an attempt to reignite the investigation. He spoke of elected officials who refused to meet with him and detectives who no longer returned his calls. He spoke about Craig Miller and his firm conviction that Miller was somehow involved in his son's murder. The article also described, to Dani's horror and surprise, how Craig Miller had killed himself the year after Jimmy's murder. She finished reading the article and immediately took her tea and the paper into the office where she settled into her favorite chaise, pulled her laptop off the desk and pulled up a search engine. She entered the terms "Craig Miller," "The Guardian," and "Suicide." Taking another sip of her tea and a deep, fortifying breath, Dani began to read.

Six hours and two cups of tea later, she felt mentally exhausted and morally outraged. Article after excruciating article detailed a laundry list of missed opportunities and botched leads. There were only two reasonable conclusions that could be drawn by any thinking adult after reading the background information on this case. The first was that

Craig Miller was a pedophile and a sociopath. The second was that no one wanted to acknowledge the first. At least, thought Dani, no one connected to law enforcement.

One name in particular, Carla Hopper, appeared over and over again in the background information of the case. It was a name that seemed very familiar to Dani. She pulled up a new tab and entered just that name. In an instant she realized why the name seemed so familiar. Carla Hopper was the current county prosecutor who had inherited the decades old case upon her election. She was also personally and professionally connected to top executives at all three of the domestic auto manufacturers, as well as to the Miller family. These were people who could undoubtedly impact the political aspirations of a local politician, for better or for worse.

Dani stood, stretched, and then reached for her cell. Hitting a speed dial button, she wandered into the bathroom and glanced in the mirror as the line began to ring. In her reflection, she could see that her hair was sticking up at odd angles and that her mascara from the previous day was now smeared over her eyes, giving her the appearance of an exhausted raccoon.

"Hey! What's up, Buttercup?" answered a warm, friendly voice on the other end of the phone.

"Hey you," she replied with a smile. "I don't suppose you have time for supper tonight? My treat?"

"Well, I'm in Novi at the moment but I should be back up that way by around 6:00. Want to meet at The Biscuit?"

"Sounds great! I'll see you there," Dani replied, then hung up.

She took a quick shower, dried and styled her pixie-short, russet hair, and spent about twenty minutes applying her makeup, taking special care, as she always did, to conceal the scars. She dressed in khaki trousers, a cream-colored cashmere turtleneck and a tweed sports jacket that brought out the color of her chestnut eyes. She brought a bottle of perfume up to the level of her chest, sprayed it into the air and then twirled through the mist like a ballroom dancer. As she walked back downstairs, she headed first to the cupboard where the dog food was kept, scooped some out, dumped it into a metal bowl on the floor at her feet, and then stood back as Gordie rushed forward to give the full bowl his bouncing, slobbering approval.

At ten minutes to six, she pulled out of her drive and drove into the small, downtown district of Fenton that was known locally as Dibbleville, a carryover from the town's original founding. At the heart of the Dibbleville district was The English Biscuit, a trendy restaurant that had only recently been renovated to include an ultra-modern addition that did not, in any way at all, match the original modest structure of the very same building. The combination gave the odd impression of a trendy nightclub that for reasons unknown had been attached by one wall to a family farmhouse. Appearances aside, it offered an inventive and varied menu and was one of the few spots in the small town that could make such a claim. Dani parked on the one-way street at the back of the building and then walked around front. Entering, she saw Geoff already seated, a newspaper and beer sitting in front of him on the small table. He rose to greet her as she approached, giving her a quick hug and gesturing to the open seat opposite his own.

"So how've you been? To what do I owe the honor of the invitation?"

"To the fact that I really want to bend your ear. Hope you don't mind?"

"Not at all, I'll take any opportunity for a free meal." He smiled at her playfully, his ice blue eyes lighting up.

"Good choice on the restaurant, by the way. I haven't been here in ages!" She smiled as the waiter came over and took her drink order.

"So what did you need to talk about?"

"In a nutshell? The Guardian," she replied. "Actually, more the investigation than the murderer. First of all, did you know that Craig Miller killed himself?"

"Who?" he asked, looking alarmed.

"Craig Miller," she replied and then remembered that she had not recently briefed Geoff on all she had learned. "Oh, that's right! You don't know! Craig Miller is the brother of the guy that Nora was dating, the one she suspected of being involved in the Guardian murders."

"Oh, right," he said, a note of recognition coming into his voice. "And he killed himself?"

"Yeah, so I guess you didn't know, eh?"

"No, it's funny, as terrified as everyone was back then, I can't say that I ever knew what finally happened. How'd he do it?"

"Rifle to the face," she said flatly.

"Yuck, that paints quite a picture, eh?"

"Yeah, also kind of screams guilty, doesn't it?"

"When did he do that?"

"November 1978," she replied.

"And when was the last kid murdered?"

"March 1977"

"It would explain why the murders stopped, wouldn't it? Maybe he did the world a favor and killed himself before he could kill anyone else."

"Yeah, maybe," Dani replied, inserting a straw into the drink that the waiter had brought over. They paused their conversation long enough to order and then Dani said, "The thing that really bothers me is everything that happened before Jimmy was even taken. Craig Miller was arrested for pedophilia. You knew that right? He was arrested and they let him go!"

"Yeah, I did hear something about that but I guess I wasn't sure of the details."

"The cops picked up an accomplice of his, a guy named George Grey. The two of them had been molesting little boys at a youth outreach center. Grey implicated Miller so they picked him up. He—Grey that is—claimed that Miller had confessed to killing the first of the Guardian victims, I think it was the little Stevens boy. The cops couldn't get Miller to admit to that but they did get him to admit to the pedophilia. He admitted to specific details about his activities with Grey and these little boys they'd abused."

"Wow," Geoff said with a shake of his head. "I guess I didn't realize he'd confessed to it. How in the hell did he walk away from that without jail time?"

"Good question!" snapped Dani, as though Geoff were somehow personally responsible. "Sorry," she added quickly. "I've been reading about this all day long and I'm a bit wound up just now."

"I see that," he said softly. "Do you think maybe you should take a little break from thinking about this?" He put a hand over hers, his expression dark with concern.

"I'm OK," she reassured him, pulling her hand away. "It seems to me that people have gone quite long enough putting this on the back burner. To answer your question, his bail—which was originally set at $75,000—was inexplicably reduced to $1,000 and he got probation. His accomplice on the other hand," she paused for a moment to steady her own voice, "got a $75,000 bond and life in prison for the very same crimes!"

"How is that even possible?"

"Did I mention that Miller's father was very wealthy and *very* well connected?" Dani countered.

"Do you really think that's it? I mean, to ignore children being snatched off the street and murdered in order to protect some automotive executive? I can't see someone doing that."

"No, but that's not exactly what I'm suggesting," said Dani, shaking her head and lowering her voice. "What they let slide, at least initially, was a pedophilia charge. Young boys who had been molested but lived to tell the tale. Who knows what kind of arrangement the father made to bring that about? There's at least one other account of the father paying off a child's own parents to keep quiet. Nora told me about it. Let's imagine for a moment that he did something similar to that in this case. He paid off the witnesses and the family, maybe he even paid off the cops and judges and the whole thing goes away—until his son uses his new found freedom to start killing kids. Now, it's not about protecting the predator or the wealthy father or even the kids. Now it's about protecting themselves from their own mistakes, because if it ever comes out that they had the opportunity to stop this guy before he killed anyone—that they could have saved the life of even one child and chose not to do so because it might have embarrassed a wealthy family—how could they justify that?" Dani stopped speaking for a moment as the waiter arrived with their food. "How do you even begin to live with yourself again after you admit to that truth?" she resumed, once he had gone. "And it's not just the cops and the politicians who would have to live with it. This guy wasn't born a monster, he became one and it took him years and years to get there. How many people along the way might have stopped that progression were it not for the father's deep pockets and their own selfish motives?" As she spoke, Dani stabbed at her steak as though it had done her some grave, personal injustice.

"Are we talking about anyone in particular?" he asked, watching for Dani's reaction.

"We're talking about everyone. Everyone who knew this guy during all those transitional moments that turned him into a monster. Everyone who ever knew that he was a danger and who pretended not to see. Everyone who ever sat quietly by and watched as the father paid off the cops and witnesses and who knows who else. Everyone who could have come forward early in the investigation and still hasn't nearly forty years later!" Dani stared down at her mutilated steak. "This man had a mother, a father, a brother, friends, neighbors. These victims were kept hostage for days, sometimes even weeks, before he killed them. You can't tell me that no one knew or had any reason to suspect anything. Even Nora ..." Dani stopped speaking, as though she couldn't muster the courage to complete the thought.

"Even Nora what? Did she tell you something? Did she know something about this?"

Dani glanced up at him, her chestnut eyes dark and sad. "I'm not sure what she knows but I'm sure she knows something. You should see her when the topic comes up, Geoff. I know Nora. I know her expressions and her moods but I've never seen her like this. Just the mention of the name—you can tell—something about that family, that time in her life. It's like she's put it away on a shelf in the darkest corner of her mind and she wants it to stay there. I think that she believes that if she doesn't think about it, if she doesn't acknowledge it, then maybe it didn't really happen."

"Maybe *what* didn't really happen though? Who knows what she really knew or when?"

Dani looked at him for a long, serious moment. "Only *she* does," she said at last. "And maybe that's exactly the problem," her gaze fell back to her plate. "Maybe she didn't come forward and could have or maybe she even allowed herself to be bought off, the way so many others seem to have done." Dani's voice had fallen to a shameful whisper and she couldn't bring herself to look at her friend anymore. She was now speaking quietly to her side salad.

"I could never believe that of Nora," Geoff said stiffly. "I'm surprised that you could."

"Don't get me wrong," Dani said quickly. "I'm not suggesting some back alley transaction where Nora accepted an envelope full of cash from the father in return for her silence about a known crime. What I'm suggesting is that she was enjoying her connection to the wealth and influence of that family. She enjoyed visiting her boyfriend at his mansion in Belle Mead. She enjoyed the limos and the parties and the attention that comes with such an association. Maybe she had her suspicions and just didn't want to risk losing her relationship to the family in order to investigate them."

"That wouldn't make her a criminal," Geoff said, his voice still sounding stiff and cold.

"No," Dani said gently, "it wouldn't. It would make her as human as any other teenage girl who fell in love with a rich boy. But depending on what she knew and when she knew it, it might make her guilty of keeping that family's secrets at the expense of a young boy's life. If that were your reality, how would it make you feel?"

"You think she knew he'd abducted those kids and didn't tell anyone?" Geoff said, his voice softer now.

"No," she began, "I mean, I don't know. I don't know what she knew or when she knew it and the problem is, if she tells me then she has to admit it to herself and I don't think she's ready to do that, even after all these years. When she and I talked about it, she shut down every time I got close to the issue. The truth—*her* truth—is buried deep and it's pretty obvious that she wants it to stay that way."

"I can understand that," Geoff said. "Maybe you should just let sleeping dogs lie. It was nearly forty years ago. Why force her to relive it all now? Craig Miller's dead. I suspect the father's dead too."

"Miller's father, yes. But Jimmy Prince's father is still alive. So are the fathers of the other victims. Don't they deserve the truth? Shouldn't someone—anyone—be speaking for the kids who lost their lives so that the Miller family wouldn't have to suffer the indignity of the truth? The cops won't do it, the politicians won't do it, Miller's friends and family members won't do it. I just feel like these kids deserve to have a voice," Dani concluded, sounding sad and defeated.

"What I don't understand," Geoff said gently, "is why you feel you should be that voice? What does Jimmy Prince have to do with you?"

Dani couldn't bring herself to tell him about her nightmares or the voices in her head. So instead she said, "Why *don't* you feel like I should be? Like we all should be? Doesn't it bother you that everyone is turning a blind eye to what the politicians and police have done in this case—or more to the point—what they *haven't* done? Don't Jimmy and the others deserve to have their story told?"

"You found all this on the Internet, right?" Geoff argued. "Seems to me that the story is out there. Craig Miller is dead. He can't stand trial now. If it was him, he got away with it. Criminal ties are like marriage—'til death do us part. Perhaps it's not fair, but it's the truth."

"Right but the crooked cops, politicians, and accomplices aren't dead."

"But to convict any of them, you need to prove the culpability of Craig Miller in the crime and their culpability in knowingly covering it up. If he wasn't a criminal, then they weren't criminals," Geoff shot back.

"Are you going to say that no one could prove bribery or obstruction of justice—something?" Dani fought to control the volume of her end of the conversation.

"Proving bribery nearly forty years later would be just about impossible, especially if the payout were something that was difficult to quantify—like a promotion or political favors. Obstruction of justice, maybe, but again, that much time can wash away a lot of sins." As the waiter came to collect their plates, Geoff stared pensively at Dani. When he'd left Geoff said, "Maybe it's time that we speak to my father. Personally, I think you should let this drop but if you're bound and determined to pursue it, you should at least have some idea of what you can hope to accomplish."

Dani smiled gratefully. "I really appreciate it, Geoff, really."

"Don't thank me yet," he replied as he took out his cell phone and dialed his father. "We're a long way from proving anything."

Dani didn't care. In a case where no one seemed willing to do anything, she rejoiced at even this small step forward. As he began to speak, Dani excused herself to the ladies room. When she returned, Geoff was returning his cell phone to his coat pocket. "Dad's home now," he said, "do you have time to head over there for a bit?"

"Sure," she responded without hesitation. "Do you want to take my car?"

"Well, considering I walked here, I guess we'd better." Dani opened the little leather binder that had been left by the waiter and added her credit card to it. After only a moment more he came back around to collect it. When he returned it a few minutes later, Dani pulled out the bill summary, calculated a generous tip, signed, and returned the paper to the binder and her credit card to her purse.

"Let's go," she said, and the pair of them left the restaurant.

The car ride over had been quiet and calm, each retreating into their own thoughts but now, as they turned down the quiet, tree-lined street where Geoff had grown up, Dani began to feel oddly nervous at the prospect of meeting his parents. Although they'd known each other for longer than either of them cared to admit, she had never had the occasion to meet his family and felt surprised now by how little she really knew about the man seated beside her.

She snuck a sideways glance at him, as he stared out his window at the surrounding houses. He was tall and slim with high cheekbones and a sharp jaw. His ice blue eyes were friendly and inquisitive and his soft blond hair was blowing in the breeze coming from the open window beside him. It seemed to Dani that he'd neglected to shave that morning and the strawberry blond stubble gave him a rugged appearance that was very flattering. He wore a thick, fleece sweatshirt and well-worn, faded jeans.

"Take the next left," he said, interrupting her thoughts.

Reluctantly, Dani returned her eyes to the road.

"It's the light blue house on the right once you make the turn."

She noticed a tension growing in his voice and wondered why. She knew that Geoff was particularly close to his mother, who had once battled Hodgkin's lymphoma and won. She knew Geoff well enough to know that his mother was the heart and soul of their family. She also knew that he had one sister who lived somewhere out of state, although she didn't know where. All she knew about his father, however, was that he was a retired police officer and that he and his son had always had what Geoff referred to as a "complicated" relationship. Remembering that, she began to understand the source of the growing tension.

As they pulled into the drive, Dani noticed that the garage door was open and that just beyond it, a very large man stood towering over a Harley-Davidson motorcycle. When they entered the garage, he smiled warmly and extended his hand toward Dani.

"Dad," began Geoff, "this is Danielle Sawyer. Dani," he continued, "this is my father, Paul Williams."

"It's nice to meet you, Mr. Williams."

"Please," he said, "call me Paul. Do you prefer Dani or Danielle?"

"Dani's fine."

"It doesn't bother you that it's a boy's name?"

"How can that be?" she asked with a grin, "It's my name, isn't it? Do I look like a boy to you?" It was a line that Dani had spoken so many times in her life that she was now able to deliver it with just enough sarcastic sting to force a change of subject, while still appearing friendly and unperturbed.

Paul threw his hands up in mock surrender. "OK, you got me there," he said. "It's nice to finally meet you. I've heard a lot about you over the years."

"Same here," she lied.

"I was very sorry to hear about your injuries on 9/11," he said solemnly. "But Geoff tells me you've healed up nicely and that you've put it all behind you now, right?"

For a split second, Dani thought about her nightmares and about the scars on her hands. "Yep, all behind me," she lied again.

As Paul wiped down the bike, he motioned for Geoff and Dani to take a seat. Across from the bike was a brown twill couch that looked as though it had also survived the Guardian murders of the late '70s. Stuffing peeped out of the corners and the brown fabric wasn't quite dark enough to cover the myriad of stains it had collected through the years. None of that bothered Dani though, as she flopped down next to Geoff, and she soon realized that it was still a very comfortable couch. In fact, the only thing she did not enjoy about sitting on the couch was that she now had to crane her neck that much further to speak to Geoff's dad. He stood easily 6'5" tall, perhaps more. His hair was sandy blond streaked heavily with gray. His eyes were the color of a deep ocean and his skin was tanned, as though he'd spent most of the summer on a boat, or perhaps on his motorcycle. His face was friendly but his skin was weathered. Dani could find no trace of a family resemblance between father and son.

"So Geoff mentioned on the phone that you had some questions about law enforcement?" he asked, still wiping invisible dirt from the pristinely clean bike.

Dani gave a sideways glance at Geoff, who was staring off in the direction of the front yard. "Yes, well," she stammered, "about law enforcement in general and about the Guardian murders in particular."

Paul's face grew dark and his smile faded. "The Guardian murders, eh?" he shook his head grimly. "That was a terrible time for Detroit. I haven't thought about that in years. Parents locked their kids up for the better part of a year while that was going on. Remember that, Geoff?" he asked, still looking at the bike. Geoff nodded but said nothing and so his father continued, "The shame of it was, they never did catch the guy. The murders just stopped and then so did the investigation. Well, I suppose you wouldn't get anyone involved in the investigation to admit that, of course. They'd tell you that they're still looking into it and it's still an open case, blah, blah, blah but without a fresh lead, it might as well be a closed case."

"Did you know any of the police who worked on it?" Dani asked.

Paul looked up as though surprised to find her still sitting there. "No," he said with a shrug, "I really only knew the guys in my own precinct and a few guys from Wayne County that rode bikes as well. What would make you curious about the Guardian murders after so many years?"

Dani ignored the question. "Were you surprised that it didn't get solved? I mean, there was an awful lot of attention surrounding the investigation and then everything just stopped. Isn't that unusual?"

"Well, what's *usual* in a case like that? It's horrible to say it like this but in the case of a serial killer, you almost have to hope he keeps on killing until he leaves enough of a trail to find him. It's not like a typical murder. In a typical murder, the killer knows the victim. There's some reason that he killed that particular victim. It's that line of reasoning that's going to help the cops figure out what happened. But with a serial killer—some nut who's out there just killing for the sake of killing—there is no reasoning with that." He stopped wiping down the bike and pulled up a stool, sitting opposite the couch. "In a case like that, you have to hope he gets sloppy and leaves a clue. In the case of the Guardian, he left those kids spotless. That's how they came up with the nickname. When he dumped the bodies their clothes were clean, they'd been scrubbed down and re-dressed, nails cleaned—like he was their Guardian and had been taking care of them. It was a sick nickname," he said, a look of disgust on his face. "I can only imagine how the parents felt about that, but what can you do? The press has a way of coming up with these things. Apparently, nicknames sell papers when there's a serial killer loose. There was even evidence that the killer took the title in stride. With the last boy, the mom said something in the press about her son's favorite type of fast food and sure enough, when they recovered the body and performed the autopsy, they found that food still in his stomach. The killer had fed him his favorite food right before he smothered the poor kid. As a dad, it made me sick. We all wanted to get that bastard in the worst way."

"They weren't actually *all* cleaned up though, were they? Wasn't one of the victim's shot in the face?" Dani asked, although she already knew the answer. "Why do you suppose he did that?"

Paul looked at her for a long moment. "Yes," he replied, "the one little girl had been shot but the body was still cleaned up. The clothes had been washed and pressed, same as the other victims. I'm sure it was to destroy any evidence. Some of the cops I worked with even thought the killer might be a cop. It seemed to be someone who knew something about law enforcement."

"I thought he shot her at the scene, right? So did he clean her clothes and re-dress her while she was still alive?"

"It would seem so, yes. The theory at the time was that he'd tried to smother her, same as the others, and that he took her for dead—she must have passed out and been unconscious. So he cleaned her unconscious body and re-dressed her but then she started to wake up at the dump site. Just as he was dumping her, he realized that she was not dead. I believe he shot her in a panic. He'd very unwisely chosen to dump her body just down the street from a police station so shooting her right there was a big risk. I'm sure it wasn't planned on his part. That was a knee jerk reaction to an unforeseen circumstance, I'm sure of it."

"What an idiot!" Geoff murmured, shaking his head.

"The serial killers sometimes like to taunt the cops. Like I said, with no reasoning behind a murder and no killer-to-victim connection, they can be damned near impossible to catch and the killers know it. So they can get pretty brazen. Look at this case, all the evidence suggests that he shot the poor girl just yards from the police station and still, they didn't catch him."

"How is that even possible?" Dani asked in frank disbelief.

"There were a lot of things about that case that seemed impossible."

"What else?" Geoff asked, finally pulling his attention back to the conversation.

His father ignored the question. "Why do you want to know about the Guardian murders now?" he asked Danielle.

"There was an article in the paper today," she said simply, "and it's just got me thinking about it. I remember growing up while that was going on. Like you said to Geoff, all the kids were locked away for the better part of a year. I just find it interesting that after all that panic—after all the attention that was paid to it at the time—and nothing ever really came from it. Do you think that there's a chance that there's still someone out there, alive, who knows what really happened to those kids?"

"Any cop will tell you that just because no one has come forward, doesn't mean no one knows," he answered grimly. "I'm sure there's still someone out there who knows something or who could at least provide a new lead. But if they weren't inclined to talk more than thirty years ago, they're sure not going to be inclined to talk now."

"Have you ever heard of Craig Miller?" Dani asked, her gaze fixed on Paul's face, watching for his reaction.

"The rich kid they suspected in those crimes?" he looked up at Dani, "Yeah, I've heard of him."

"Do you think he did it?"

"Do I think he did it?" he seemed to be considering the question. "Well, let's say that if he didn't, I think he knew who did. I'm not sure it was just one person. In fact you'd have a hard time convincing me that it was. Miller was barely more than a kid himself. I think he was mid-twenties when that was going on. The Guardian kept the kids for a long time. The one girl was missing for more than two weeks. To keep a twelve-year-old kid hostage for two weeks, you'd really need at least one more person—one person to keep an eye on her while the other person went out for supplies. You'd also need a very out-of-the-way spot—some place very private where a family member wouldn't just happen to stumble upon the child. Miller's family had a lot of money and more than one property. As I recall, they had a cottage up north somewhere. I know there was some speculation that he'd taken the kids up there but no one could ever prove it. Last but not least, you'd need self-control and maturity to keep a kid hostage for that long. An impulsive twenty-something pedophile who can't even molest kids without being caught and charged is certainly not mature enough to kidnap them, hold them for weeks, rape them, suffocate them, clean them up and dump them without assistance and without getting caught."

"Did the police ever search that other location? The cottage up north?"

"Not during the active part of the investigation. They may have in the years that followed but I couldn't tell you for certain and even if they had, by that point, there would almost certainly be nothing to find. You could check the vents maybe but I don't see them doing that at this point. Miller's father proved one thing, he was very good at covering the boy's tracks. Before he died—the dad, I mean—he had all kinds of paperwork destroyed, even Craig's birth certificate."

"I read about that too. No need to destroy everything unless you have something to hide, right?"

"Well, not necessarily," Paul replied. "You have to remember that he was a very private businessman and even the appearance of impropriety or any possibility of litigation might cause a guy like that to run to his shredder."

"Yeah but we're not talking about dubious tax documents or old receipts. We're talking about his son's birth certificate! You don't think that's kind of odd?"

"The birth certificate of a son who committed suicide by sticking a gun between his eyes. For a family like that, a suicide alone would be an embarrassment, much less the suicide of a son accused of pedophilia."

"A son who admitted to pedophilia," she corrected him.

He shrugged. "Either way, both the father and the son are dead now."

"And you don't think there's *any* way to prove what really happened?"

"Not unless you can speak to the dead!" he replied.

Chapter
VI

Since meeting with Paul Williams, his words had been nagging at Dani, "Not unless you can speak to the dead." The notion was ludicrous, wasn't it? Nobody could speak to the dead. Her logical mind was sure of it. But if the voices in her head weren't coming from ghosts, then what? She remembered with a shudder all of the articles about psychosis and schizophrenia. "Great," she said aloud to no one, "I'm either crazy or hearing from ghosts. Six of one, half dozen of the other and now I'm talking to myself!"

She shook her head in disgust and returned her attention to the faded receipt sitting on the desk in front of her. She'd been staring at it for nearly an hour but had yet to pick it up, as though it were contaminated by a highly contagious, potentially deadly virus. She pushed her chair back, stood and went into the kitchen to brew a cup of tea. Gordie joined her, as he always did when she entered the kitchen for any reason. Whether she was preparing a spinach salad or filet mignon, he stared at her with the same slobbering fascination. Today, it was the hot water that she poured into her tea mug that left him enthralled. She bobbed the tea bag around briefly, added the milk and sugar and stood blowing on the hot tea as she stared back at him.

"If I call this woman," she asked, "does it mean I've completely lost my marbles?"

Gordie cocked his head to one side, lifted his ears inquisitively and sniffed the air in the direction of her tea cup.

"Thanks, that's very helpful," she teased. She picked up her mug, gave him a quick scratch on the back and returned to the office, where she resumed her vigil of staring down at the toxic receipt. Finally she set the cup aside, picked up her cell, and dialed. She prayed for an answering machine, or better yet a wrong number. No such luck. Faye picked up on the second ring.

"Hello?"

For a moment she held her breath and said nothing.

"Hello? Anyone there?" the voice came again.

If she were really psychic, she wouldn't need to ask, Dani thought. "Uh, hello," she stammered into the phone. "Sorry, I hope I'm not disturbing you. This is Dani Sawyer. We met at the umm … at the college, remember?" She felt like an idiot and thought briefly about hanging up, but was sure that her number had already been captured by caller ID—too late to back out now, she decided.

"Of course! Nice to hear from you. How are you?" She spoke as if they'd known each other for years.

"I'm fine thanks. You?" Dani wished she'd never called.

"Good! So have you decided to start listening to the voices in your head?" Her tone made Dani feel as though she were being mocked and this annoyed her even more.

"Could we not call it that, please?" She tried unsuccessfully to keep the irritation out of her voice.

"We could, but it wouldn't make it any less true. It's like AA, Dani. The first step is admitting you have a problem.

Practice it with me, 'Hello, my name is Danielle and I'm a psychic.'"

Now Dani was quite sure she was being mocked. "Maybe this was a mistake," she said, ready to hang up, caller ID or no.

"Maybe," she said, "but there must be some reason that you called me today instead of last week or not at all. Want to tell me about that first? You can still decide to hang up later."

Dani hesitated but did not hang up. "These voices," she said at last, "can they be controlled?"

"Controlled?"

"Yes. If they're a part of me like rolling my tongue or being left handed then can I control them as if they were a part of me?"

"What I said was that the ability to *receive* the messages is as genetic as being left handed. The voices are not a part of you. You're just the receiver. The broadcast system is not within you and no, it cannot be controlled, at least not to the extent that I think you'd prefer. You can, however, learn to adjust the volume."

"Can I decide to turn it off?"

"No—not really, not completely. If they have something that they feel you need to know, they will transmit the message. What you choose to do with that message is up to you. What I can teach you are some basic techniques that will help you meet the voice on the other side of the transmitter and that will direct the incoming messages in a way that will help clarify their intent for you. Plus, you'll be able to become more in control of how and when the messages come across. It takes time and practice but I think you'll find it worth your while."

Dani braced herself for the price of the scam. "And how much do these *lessons* cost then?"

"We can order takeout, your treat! Do you want to meet at my place or should I come to yours? Where do you live, by the way?"

It was one thing to talk on the phone but to have this complete stranger come to her house? She wasn't prepared for that. "I'd prefer to meet at a café or something. I *will* treat though."

"I understand what you're feeling, Dani, but trust me, a café is no good. This sort of connection requires quiet. It requires privacy and it requires a little trust. If you're not ready to trust me, I don't think this will work. Here's my advice, from what you're telling me, it sounds like your guides are already trying to reach out to you. Before you go to bed tonight, take a warm bath. Take a warm bath and then lie down in a quiet, dark room. Concentrate on your breathing. Take deep, steady breaths and try to clear your mind completely. Instead of lying in bed thinking about all your problems or the bills you've yet to pay or the phone calls you've yet to return, just lay there quietly and think about walking in a dark forest or along a sunny beach. Don't do anything on that beach, just walk and enjoy the view. Try to see it in your mind. You'll probably just fall asleep and if you do, that's OK. They may come to you in a dream if you doze off. The object is to keep your mind clear and open for any message they may wish to send."

"They?"

"Your guides—think of them as your translators on the other side. Other people who have already passed on want to communicate with you but can't speak your language so they speak to your guides and your guides speak to you."

"I thought I was the translator? I thought that was the whole point."

"You translate from your guides to other people here who need to receive the messages. Say Mrs. Smith, who passed away last spring, wants to tell her daughter, who is still among the living, that she shouldn't worry and everything will work out for the best. She'll communicate through your guide on her side, then trusts you to pass it to her daughter."

"Why doesn't the guide just give it to the daughter? Or better yet, why doesn't Mrs. Smith just give it to her daughter directly? Why all the hoops to jump through?" Dani asked, with a bit more bite in her tone than she had intended.

"Not everyone has an ear for this particular language," Faye replied gently. "Why do your Russian clients need you? Why don't they just deliver their messages personally to their English-speaking friends? The answer is, they can't and neither can Mrs. Smith. This ability is a rare gift. Not everyone believes it exists but it does, I promise you, and it has been given to you. Now it's your responsibility to put it to good use."

"My *responsibility*? Who are you to decide what responsibility I should be given? Or that I should have to take on any additional responsibility at all? Isn't it enough that I was nearly roasted alive that day? Now I have to be haunted by these voices in my head and it's my *responsibility* to pass along their messages? Who are you to decide that?" Dani felt a sort of inexplicable fury growing in her chest.

"I haven't decided anything. Are you a religious person, Dani?"

"I don't go to church if that's what you mean."

"That's not what I mean actually. I mean, do you believe in God?"

Dani thought about it for a moment before she said, "I've read the bible and I admire Jesus Christ for the man that he was. I think he sets a good example for us all. If that makes me religious then I guess I'm religious."

"I haven't given you this gift, Dani, He has. He just sent me along to help you figure out what to do with it."

Dani was silent for another very long moment. "So what should I expect to hear?" she asked grudgingly. The whole idea that she should lie awake waiting for a spirit guide "transmitter" to send her messages made her cringe.

"Anything they want to tell you. Try not to look for a certain message. Just take whatever they'll give you gratefully. Remember, they're trying to help. If you do dream, write down whatever you can remember as soon as you awake. Try and remember every detail, no matter how small. They say the devil's in the details. From a spirit point of view, that's probably not the right message to send; but it is true that even small details can be very important so as you're dreaming, try and force your sleeping mind to seek out the details."

"And then?"

"And then call me when you're ready to talk again. This is a journey, not a destination. If you're not ready to trust me now then we'll have to wait until you are."

"I'm sorry, it's not that I don't trust you ..." she began.

"Yes, it is and that's OK. I get it. But it really is best if we don't begin until you're ready. So call me when you're ready." With that the phone went dead. Dani stared at it for a moment longer before setting it down.

Gordie had joined her in the office and was now curled up at her feet. She reached down and, as she did, he rolled over on his back and exposed his belly to her, then waited. "Just lie there and wait, eh?" she said to him. "Seems you're already taking Faye's advice!" She glanced at the clock on the wall—10:22. "Shall I draw a hot bath?" At the mention of the word "bath," he gave her a mistrusting look, rolled back onto his feet and ran out of the office and down the hall. "Turncoat," she murmured, then walked out of the office and down the hall to the bathroom.

After pulling a fluffy, cotton towel and some lavender bath salts from the linen closet, she bent over the tub and adjusted the faucet until a warm, steady flow was pouring into the tub. She put the stopper in place and walked out of the bathroom and upstairs to her bedroom. She pulled a white, terry cloth robe out of her closet and returned to the bathroom. After checking the temperature of the water again, she began to undress. As the water flowed into the tub, she sprinkled the lavender over it and took deep breaths, pulling the efflorescent mist deep into her lungs before lowering herself into the hot water.

She sat upright and motionless for a moment while her body adjusted to the temperature, then slid down below the water's surface to soak her hair. She held her breath for a moment and floated beneath the water's shallow surface, which muffled the click, click, clicking of nails on the hardwood. She used her toes to twist off the faucet knobs and then lay silently with her ears under the water's surface. After a few moments, she sat up again and glanced out the open door. Gordie had taken up a position just beyond it in the hall at a safe distance from the evil bath tub. He sat stock still and looked like a black, furry sphinx. Over the years, the fine hairs around the front of his muzzle had grown white and they made him appear as though he had a white mustache and goatee. As she looked at him, he tilted his head in question but did not come any closer. Dani turned her attention back to the tub. She stared at her scarred hands, the fingertips of which were already beginning to prune slightly. She ran them down her thighs, over her calves and stretched herself out, grabbing her ankles for a moment, the warm water relaxing her muscles. She released her ankles, sat up and stared down at her body. Although the muscles of her legs were still tight and sculpted, the skin over them bore similar scars to the ones on her hands. The surgeons had done their best to return to her what the fire had stolen away but she knew that her body would never—could never—be as it had once been. She'd come to terms with that truth long ago, but to want to sit in a bath tub, staring at the evidence—she'd have to be masochistic. Pulling the stopper out with her toe, she stood and stepped out of the tub, dried herself and slipped on the soft robe. She wrapped it tight around her slim waist and cinched it closed.

Stepping in front of the medicine cabinet, she opened it, pulled out a small tube of moisturizer and squirted some into the palm of her hand. She returned the tube to the cabinet, closed the mirrored door and rubbed the crème between her palms. She rubbed it first onto her face and then onto her hands and forearms. Afterward, she stood in front of the mirror for a long moment staring back at her reflection. She tried to remember how her bare face had looked before that awful day in the Pentagon but she could not. She'd lived her life with the firm belief that no good could come from looking back. Life lie in front of her and what was gone, was gone. She could not, therefore, understand why the ghost of Jimmy Prince held such a fascination for her. She could never bring him back, she knew that. So what did she hope to accomplish?

She clicked off the light and stepped out into the chilly hallway. She walked down the hall and into the office to retrieve her cell phone, which doubled as her alarm clock in the morning. She found it sitting atop the newspaper, which was still open to the article about the search for Jimmy's killer. Next to Jimmy's picture was that of another Prince, the elder Prince. The sad, mournful expression on the face of Lawrence Prince provided the answer to the question Dani had just been posing to herself. This poor man, she thought, has been stuck in his own hellish past—in Jimmy's hellish past—for nearly forty years. In his eyes she could see that there could be no peace for him until someone pulled him free from that hell. "And the truth shall set you free," she said aloud to the photo.

Chapter
VII

Still holding the article and the cell phone, she climbed the stairs to her bedroom. Once inside, she set them both down on her nightstand and switched on the nearby lamp. She set the alarm on her cell and plugged it into the charger. Finally, she slipped out of her robe and under her thick, down comforter. Perhaps, she thought, I should be dressed for this. For an insane moment, she wondered whether her spirit guides would know if she were coming to them naked. She then wondered if her guide would be a man or a woman. "Get a grip," she said to herself, but then slipped out of bed and pulled on a nightshirt, just in case.

She returned to the bed, switched off the lamp and lay in the darkness. She tried to remember what Faye had told her to do, "think about walking in a dark forest or along a sunny beach …" she thought. A beach just didn't seem right for the occasion. Something about a dark forest seemed more appropriate, like venturing into the scary unknown. She closed her eyes and tried to imagine herself walking through a dark forest. She wondered if it should be a rainforest or a deciduous forest. Clear your mind, she commanded herself.

She'd never been to the rainforest so she decided that a deciduous forest made more sense. She pictured herself in a dark, deciduous forest, walking through the trees. For a moment she pictured herself in the same nightshirt that she'd just pulled out of her dresser but then realized that no one in Michigan would walk through a dark forest in pajamas and bare feet because you'd be stabbed by the pine needles. Wait, she thought, were there pine trees in a deciduous forest? Or was that a coniferous forest? She'd never been able to keep them straight. Well, either way, she thought, she'd never go hiking in any kind of forest in her bare feet and a nightshirt, so she adjusted the image accordingly. Hiking boots, jeans, a warm sweatshirt—that seems about right, she thought. She then imagined that she could hear a nearby stream cutting through the forest, the water rippling down over the stones beside the trail. The thought of the stream, however, made her realize that she'd failed to use the facilities before heading off to bed. "Dammit!" she snarled. She slipped out of the covers, down the stairs, across the hall and into the bathroom. Moments later, she retraced her steps and slipped back into bed, ready to explore another, perhaps drier, area in the forest. "This has got to be the stupidest thing I've ever done," she said bitterly into the darkness.

She closed her eyes and imagined herself back in the forest. The leaves on the trees were painted in bright autumn colors and the sun poked through the canopy, adding intermittent splashes of light to the undergrowth. She imagined a cool breeze on her face, and soon she began to feel very sleepy. She walked along the dirt path, looking at the trees but trying to keep her mind free from distractions. After a while, she began to wonder if she was dreaming or still just imagining the forest. Then she wondered if there was really a difference between the two. While her mind lingered drowsily over this question, she was startled to find a deer standing in front of her on the path.

She couldn't recall thinking of a deer and so had to conclude that she was now dreaming, her unconscious mind taking over the imagery. She took a step closer to the young doe but it did not run away. She came nearly close enough to reach out and touch it but as she attempted to do so, the doe turned and began walking further up the path. It wasn't running, it didn't seem to want to flee, it was as though the deer had decided to take a walk with her. Where it went, she followed.

The two walked together down the dirt path and over a slight rise in the landscape until the growth became so thick that the path became lost in it. The deer too disappeared into the thick growth and Dani felt an unexpected panic rising in her chest. She picked her way through the thick growth, looking for any trace of the deer. There was none. Vines and branches encircled her and held her back. She shoved ahead with all her weight and then, in an instant, the resistance was gone and she fell forward down stone steps that were carved into the side of a steep cliff.

Terrified, she clung to the railing until she'd recovered her balance. She looked back. The forest was gone and she was once again in front of the magnificent villa. She could feel the hard, dry stone under her bare feet. The hiking boots were gone, the jeans and sweatshirt were gone—replaced by her gauzy cotton nightshirt. She was relieved she'd put it on before going to bed. She turned back in the direction of the cliff side and stared out over the crystal clear sea. Feeling his eyes upon her, she turned to find Kōbō smiling up at her from his hand bench down on the stone landing.

Odd as it seemed, she felt relieved to see him. He was a friendly face in the middle of a scary new experience. He was dressed just the same in his jaunty hat and white, silk tunic.

"Please," he said, "won't you join me?" He smiled broadly and gestured to the bench opposite his own. Dani returned his grin, took the remaining steps two at a time and soon sat opposite the old monk on the marble hand statue.

"I don't really understand what happened," she began. "I was in the middle of a forest following this deer and then poof! I was here!"

"Aren't dreams wonderful?" he asked.

"They are, aren't they? Especially when they bring me to a place like this. I love it here." Dani felt light and euphoric. It was the first time in days that she'd allowed herself to forget about the Guardian and the dead children. She felt calm and at peace.

"The question, though, is why were you in that dark forest?"

"I'd rather not tell you. You'll think I'm nuts." She looked at her bare feet resting on the warm sandstone.

"You're afraid the dead monk who talks to you in your dreams will think you're nuts? I am you. If you're nuts, then I'm nuts. Please tell me, what were you doing in that dark forest?"

"If you're me, then you must know," she shot back with a mischievous grin. "It's a long story but the truth of it is, I was looking for a guide." As she spoke, she looked down at the stones beneath her feet and outlined one with the tip of her toe.

"A forest guide? Like a ranger?"

Dani looked up to find him smiling in mild amusement, laughing at his own joke. "No," she returned his smile, "not a forest ranger. Another kind of guide, I don't know what kind of guide." Her voice trailed off and she looked back down at her feet. "Faye told me to do it, so I did it."

"Ah," he said, "the problem is, you mentioned Faye to me, but you never mentioned me to Faye."

For an absurd moment, she was worried that she'd hurt his feelings by not talking about him to her friends. "What does *that* mean?" she asked. "I haven't told Faye any of my dreams. We're not that close really."

"Why would you take her advice if you're not really that close?"

"I thought that if I followed her advice, she'd be able to help me with a problem. But she said that I didn't trust her and that until I can trust her, I should sit in a dark room and think about a forest." Dani looked back up at him. "That didn't come out exactly right. Dreams have a way of becoming really confusing if you stay in them too long, have you ever noticed that?"

"I have," he agreed. "My advice is that you go back to Faye and tell her about this dream. It's just a strange dream, after all. What could it hurt to trust her with it?"

"I suppose you're right." She looked out over the cliff side at the bright blue sea beyond and then back at the hand opposite her own. Only then did she realize that she was alone and the monk had gone. She looked back up the staircase and, at the top, she noticed that the doe had returned and was standing there, staring down at her.

She climbed the stairs and as she approached the top, the doe began to walk. As Dani followed, the villa once again became a dark forest, but she could no longer control what she was wearing. She was walking over the rough trails, littered with pine needles and acorns and thorns that poked into her sensitive feet. The path was so dark that she could not see the branches to avoid them, and they hit her face hard as she advanced. She could no longer see the doe ahead and began to feel that she was being pursued. She was frightened and despite the dark woods and thorny path, she began to run.

She ran as if her life depended on it and until her feet and legs ached. Hungry snarls approached her through the trees. The panic rose through her chest and wrapped itself around her throat. She ran blindly to escape something or someone that she could not see. As she ran, the branches tore at her nightshirt. Half-naked, terrified, and running blindly through a thick forest, she searched in vain for the doe or a road or any sign of civilization.

Up ahead, she thought she could see sunlight. She ran faster, the thin branches whipping over her skin, leaving red welts on tender, bare flesh. She ran as fast as she could for that little slice of light and as she approached it, she burst out of the forest and onto a narrow runway. The rough trail changed in a heartbeat to pressed gravel beneath her feet. Beyond the landing strip, Dani could see only sand and water. While she stood there, a pack of coyotes broke through the trees immediately behind her, snarling and baring their teeth. Dani's heart was pounding wildly in her chest. She walked back over the gravel and onto the narrow beach, beyond which stretched an enormous body of water. When she reached the water's edge, the pack rounded on her, and she fell backward into the water in a futile attempt at escape. She heard the roar of an engine and one of the coyotes threw its head back and let out an unearthly howl that made her skin crawl. Overhead, a small plane circled the runway, as though preparing to land. Dani waved up at it frantically, never taking her eyes off the coyotes as they crept closer and closer to where she stood.

Dani bolted awake, drenched in sweat. Her room was dark and quiet. She clicked on her light, reached into the drawer of her nightstand and pulled out a pen and a small notebook. With as much detail as she could remember, she wrote down the dream. Then she got up, pulled her white robe on over her cotton nightshirt and pulled back her drapes. The morning sun flooded her room and chased away the last remnants of the nightmare.

As she started for the door, she noticed that Gordie, most unusually, did not move from his spot on the bed. He regarded her sleepily, stood, turned twice, and then lay back on the bed as if to continue sleeping. It was not until she walked into the kitchen and began moving pots around that his curiosity overtook him and he decided to investigate. She was grateful for the company. She made herself a bowl of oatmeal and then put a scoop of dog food into his metal dish on the floor. They ate together in silence and when they were done, she opened the French doors into the backyard and followed him out.

She took a seat on the steps and watched Gordie sniffing for squirrels near the back fence. She thought about the dream and the panic she'd felt as she was running through the woods. Ten minutes later, she stood and went back into the house, leaving Gordie to the hunt.

She dressed, styled her hair, applied her makeup and then picked up her cell. This time, she did not hesitate to dial. Faye picked up on the first ring.

"Well?" she asked. "How'd it go?"

"I had a horrible nightmare and just as you asked, I wrote down as much detail as I could remember. I tried to imagine the forest like you said but I dozed off and then the dream changed."

"It's OK," Faye assured her. "You saw what they wanted you to see. Was there anyone else in the dream? Did you speak to anyone?"

"No, not really, just Kōbō but he doesn't have anything to do with …" she hesitated, wondering if she should explain about the voice in her head and the boy of her dreams.

She decided against it. "He's got nothing to do with this," she said simply.

"What makes you so sure?" she asked, but did not wait for a response. "Who is Kōbō? What do you know about him?"

"He's nobody," Dani assured her. "He's popped up in my dreams before but he's just that—a dream."

"You don't know that," she persisted. "Tell me everything that happened last night from the time you hung up with me," she commanded. "Tell me everything, including everything you know about this Kōbō."

Dani recounted the night's events, reading from her notes when necessary and including as much detail as she could remember. She also told her about the first dream she'd had in which Kōbō had introduced himself to her. "So that's everything. It was terrifying toward the end but I can't say that I met any guides or that I was given any great insight."

"Oh come on!" she exclaimed, sounding exasperated. "What does he have to do? Smack you over the head with a sledge hammer?"

Dani began to pace. "What's that supposed to mean?"

"It seems pretty obvious to me that Kōbō is your guide. If you had really created him from your own mind and if you really believed him to be insignificant, he—which is to say you—would never have told you to tell me about him. Because you believed him to be insignificant! So why tell anyone about him if he were insignificant?"

"This conversation is starting to give me a headache," Dani complained.

"You approached him through the woods because I told you to," Faye continued, ignoring her. "But why he chose to return you to the woods—especially in such a frightening way, is another thing. He must have something he wants you to see there."

"Something he wants me to see where? It was a *dream*!"

"Did you notice anything special about the woods or the runway? Anything that might tell you where you were?"

"You think it's an actual location somewhere? That it really exists?"

"I do," Faye said. "And it's probably some place nearby or some place that maybe you know from your own past. He's trying to lead you somewhere. So think, Dani, did you see anything that might give away the location of the woods or of that airstrip?"

"I really don't think so," she said. "I was running the whole time. I was being chased. I wasn't looking for signs and, honestly, I had no reason to think I'd find one. It was just wilderness all around."

"What about when you were facing the airstrip? The plane maybe? Was there writing on the plane?"

"There may have been but I didn't … I can't remember that. I don't think I really ever saw it in the dream. I was more focused on the doe and the coyotes. Do you think the doe means anything? I felt like I was supposed to follow her."

"You *were* supposed to follow her. But I think that's where her function ended," Faye explained. "I think that's why she disappeared. This is going to be tough for you to understand but I think the doe was also a guide, just like Kōbō. I think her one and only function was to direct you through the scenes that Kōbō wanted you to see. So you believe the coyotes were pursuing you in your dream?"

"Yes, I'm sure of it. Faye, I think …" Dani began, then paused, still debating.

Faye waited a moment before speaking, "Is there something else?"

Dani took a deep breath. "There is. I think you have to know about Jimmy. Something's telling me that he's the reason I'm seeing Kōbō. I think the forest has something to do with Jimmy." Faye said nothing, but waited for her to continue. "It all started with a voice and a dream." She recounted to Faye the incident with the voice-over on the recording and the dream with Nora and young Jimmy. Faye sat quiet and attentive on the other side of the phone as Dani spoke.

When she was done, Faye thought for a long moment and then said, "I'm glad you decided to tell me about your dream. I think you're right. I think he is the reason for these most recent messages, although I don't think that he's the reason for your abilities and I'm sure that helping Jimmy won't make them go away."

Dani hadn't realized that she'd held out any such hope but when Faye said that, disappointment stabbed through her chest like a knife. "I never thought it would," Dani lied.

Faye ignored that and said, "I think it's very significant that Nora knows that family. Whether she wants it or not, you have to bring her into this."

"You can lead a horse to water ..." Dani began.

"And you *must* make her drink it," Faye finished for her. "She may be able to identify that airstrip or the woods. They showed it—all of it—to you for a reason. You can't pretend not to know about Nora any more than you can allow her to pretend not to know that family. You cannot ignore your truth any more than you can allow Nora to ignore hers."

Dani saw at once that she was right. Nora hadn't asked to become involved in the crimes of a pedophile any more than

Dani had asked for the voices in her head, yet here they both were. "I'll speak to Nora again today," Dani said quietly.

"Any reason to believe that there were actual coyotes involved in anything related to Jimmy Prince?"

"No, I don't think so, although the Millers' home up north was supposed to have been in a very secluded, wooded area so I guess it's not impossible."

"Not impossible but not likely," she added. "That bit of information seems so incongruous to the rest of it, I believe it's meant to be taken symbolically."

"Symbolically?" Dani asked, already feeling frustrated at having yet another puzzle to solve.

"Yes, remember what I told you about their ability to communicate? Sometimes they have to show you images to get you to a particular concept. Although what that concept is, I couldn't tell you. Maybe only that there was a predator. I think that's where the coyotes come in."

"Why would Kōbō want me to run naked through a forest at all?" Dani felt that this whole experiment had gone wildly off course and she was wondering for probably the one hundredth time if perhaps Faye were just some sort of scam artist. The bullet through that theory, however, was that she had yet to ask Dani for anything.

"I believe, he was probably trying to convey part of the message or an actual experience in the life of someone else." Faye hesitated and then said, "This type of translation requires more of a commitment than taking words from one language and putting them into the next. It's important that you understand that. You must always remember that the people who are trying to get their message across sometimes have very painful memories that need to be conveyed to put their message in its proper context. Sometimes those experiences are coming from individuals who can show you only what they know and who are perhaps struggling to explain it to you in a language that you can understand. That's why you must accept any information that they want to share and you must do it gratefully and with an open mind—because they're going to great lengths to impart that information to you."

For the message to make sense, though, we need to put it in better context. You need to think about that dream, look for a context for it in your own life. Why would he have shown you that? Are there people or places or circumstances that you recognize or that you can relate back to the dream? I wouldn't read too much into the villa. He's come to you from the villa twice and I believe that's just sort of a neutral space in the dream world where you can go to be safe and where he can present himself to you."

"This is so stupid," Dani snapped. "If I can sit on that stupid hand statue and speak to him, why doesn't he just tell me what he wants?"

"I'm afraid it's not that simple," Faye said gently. "You have to remember that Kōbō is merely a translator, like yourself. He can only relate to you what others say to him. The spirits who give him the information may not have all the answers, so they show you what they can. Other spirits may know the full truth but only show you what they want you to see for reasons of their own. Spirits on the other side retain some measure of their old personalities. They're individuals, just like you and I. Some are more trusting than others, some are more manipulative than others. Some are older, some are younger. Sometimes the spirit is that of a young child and you must see the world through his eyes, and many times, a child's view lacks the clarity of an adult view. It would be impossible for a child to relate an adult idea in an adult context because his life experience wouldn't give him enough perspective. When that happens, it will be incumbent upon you and Kōbō to try to understand that message using the language of a child."

"I feel like I'm trying to translate a language before I even know the vocabulary. How am I supposed to do that?"

"The vocabulary will come to you in time. It will develop slowly between guides, like Kōbō, and yourself. You should be prepared for a language of symbols, rather than spoken words. For example, if my guides want me to understand that someone has been murdered, they will show me a bottle of poison. It appears as a small, black bottle with a skull and crossbones on it, like you would see in a child's cartoon. It doesn't tell me that the person was poisoned necessarily, which is what I thought at first. It tells me the person was murdered. They may have been shot or stabbed, doesn't matter. The bottle of poison carried in the hands of someone means that person was murdered. If a person appears to me holding a dead house plant, it means they died of natural causes."

"Why doesn't your guide just tell you, 'Hey, this guy was murdered'? For that matter, why can't they tell you who did it and when?" Dani asked incredulously.

"Why doesn't your Russian guy just speak English?" Faye asked sharply. "Because he can't, that's why. You first learn his language, then you understand his message, right?"

"Right," Dani replied rather meekly.

"So please stop arguing with the logic and do as you're told! Listen to what they're trying to communicate, try and figure out where that airstrip is and look for how this dream fits into your life now. They've shown it to you, specifically, for a reason. You're in a position to help this spirit but first you have to understand what you're being shown."

"I understand," she said with a repentant tone

"Call me if you need me," Faye replied.

"I will. Thanks," she said. With that, the line went dead. Dani looked at her phone for a long moment and then said aloud to the silent house, "No time like the present." She took a deep breath and dialed.

Chapter
VIII

Nora picked up on the third ring. "Hello?" she answered, her voice heavy with sleep.

Dani had not thought to consider the time. She glanced at her watch and realized that she was calling people at half past eight on a Saturday morning. Should she hang up and call back later? Too late now, she thought.

"Hello?" the sleepy voice came again, sounding irritated, "Is there someone there?"

"Hi, Nora," she began apologetically, "I'm so sorry to wake you. I didn't realize how early it was."

"Dani?" she asked. "Is that you?" The irritation was not completely gone from her voice but it had softened into the polite sort that people save for misguided children or senile adults. "What's up?"

"Nora, I'm sorry. Why don't I call you back later? I really didn't mean to wake you."

"Forget about it," Nora insisted, still sounding annoyed despite her claims of forgiveness. "I'm up now, might as well start my day."

Dani was certain that she could not have chosen a worse beginning for this conversation but could see no other option but to continue, and so she did. "I need to ask you some more questions about Matthew Miller and his family." On the other end of the phone, she heard Nora groan.

"Not this again!" she nearly growled. "Dani, I told you already. I don't want to talk about it."

"I know you don't, Nora, and I wouldn't ask if it weren't really, truly important. But it is and so you must. Please, I really need your help."

"Why? What's so important?"

"Jimmy Prince, he's important. So is his family and the other victims and all of their families. They're all very important. They're every bit as important and more than the Miller family reputation."

"I don't give a shit about the Miller family's reputation and you know it, so don't lay that on me." Nora's voice had gone far beyond annoyance now, well into hurt and shame and rage.

"I know that," said Dani, her voice nearly a whisper. "Which is why I don't understand what's stopping you from the truth."

That was a lie. Dani did understand. It was shame stopping her. Shame that she had not acted then, so many years ago, when it may have helped more, when it may have saved lives. Shame that she ever considered the Miller family's reputation and her own selfish interests before considering little Jimmy Prince and all the others. Shame that she had allowed the beast to take the easy way out before acting to stop him. She understood her friend's shame but could do nothing to spare her from it now and so she lied and waited for a response.

"What good would it do?" she said at last, a hint of despair in the question. "They're dead. The victims, that monster, they're all dead. What does any of it matter?"

"The victims' families aren't dead," Dani said gently. "And there may be other still-living victims, who are maybe too afraid to come forward. Who knows if the guy acted alone? Maybe his accomplices are still out there and alive. Maybe the accomplices have left more victims. Someone needs to put an end to it!"

"But I don't know anything, not really—nothing really useful." Something in her voice left Dani unconvinced.

"Why don't you let me be the judge of that? Tell me, do you know if the Millers had a private plane?"

"Yeah, I think so," she said hesitantly. "Well, I know they had at least one because I flew in it a few times. They may have had another one too. There was a bigger one that the dad used when he traveled for business, but I don't know if that one belonged to the family or if it maybe belonged to the company he worked for, not sure."

"What kind of plane was the smaller one? Do you remember?"

"Well, I know it was a Cessna because they always referred to it as "the Cessna," but I don't know anything more than that. That is to say, I don't know specifically what kind of Cessna it was."

"Do you know where they kept it?"

"They flew it out of Pontiac the times when I flew with them. I remember because I'd never known there was an airport in Pontiac before then. It was a small thing, nothing like Metro airport."

Dani's heart began to pound as images from her nightmare raced through her mind. "Was there an airstrip surrounded by a forest?"

"A *forest?*" Nora sounded incredulous, "In Pontiac? No, of course not. It was surrounded by the city of Pontiac, and a few open fields and abandoned lots." Dani's heart sank.

"Where did you fly, those times you went out on the plane?" she asked.

"Once we flew to Mackinac Island," she said. "Several times we flew to their cabin up north."

Dani felt hopeful again. "Up north? Where exactly up north? Were there woods near their cabin?"

"Were there woods up north?" she repeated the question as though she hadn't heard her right. "Dani, what's gotten into you? Haven't you ever been in northern Michigan? Of course there were woods! That's all they've got up there."

"Where was their cabin, Nora? Do you remember?"

"That fanny place," she said, offering no further explanation.

Dani gave a quizzical look on the other end of the phone. "Sorry?"

"You know, the fanny place. My aunt had a cottage up there too. We went when we were kids and used to giggle about the name," she seemed to be searching for the word.

"Oh!" Dani said laughing. "Fanny Lake! Their cabin was near Fanny Lake?"

"Right, right on the lake there. It wasn't what you and I think of as a cabin. It certainly wasn't like my aunt's cottage. It was on the lake but surrounded by woods on all the other sides so it was remote and really beautiful. It was made out of stained timber, you know how they do sometimes, trying to make it look like a real log cabin or whatever but the back had windows three stories high in the shape of big arches so that in the living room, the natural light flooded in from outside. There was a deck off the second floor in the front that was fantastic in the summer for barbecues. The front porch was screened in and led off onto a stone path through some tall trees and down to the dock. They had their own, private dock, of course, with a speed boat that we used to use for water skiing. It had a four-car garage and a circular drive that led down to the main road. It was beautiful up there," her voice sounded wistful and sad.

"And when you landed near Fanny Lake, was the airstrip in the woods?" Dani asked, anxious to put a stop to the nostalgia.

"The airstrip?" she asked, her voice still distant. "What is it with you and airstrips today? You mean the airport? Well, first of all, I don't think we landed right near Fanny Lake. Honestly, I can't remember where it was but it was a full, regular airport and no, it wasn't in the woods. It was in the middle of some fields. Who puts an airport in the middle of the woods? Wouldn't you hit the trees with the plane if you did that?"

"Well, it wasn't exactly an airport, just a strip and there was a little gap between the strip and the woods," Dani mumbled more to herself than to Nora. She felt a wave of disappointment and, more than anything, frustration. "I don't understand," she complained, "I thought you said that everything was near the woods up there?"

"OK. You got me," she replied, "everything except the airport where we landed." Dani seemed not to hear her. "Dani, you still there?"

"Yes," she snapped. "Yes, I'm still here."

"I don't get it. Why do you sound so annoyed? Why does it matter if the airport was in the woods or not?"

"It's a long story."

Dani heard movement on the line as her friend sat up, "I don't have to be anywhere and I love a good story," she replied. "Plus, I need to understand why this is so important to you."

"I don't know, Nora. It's ..." she hesitated, searching for a way to explain. "It's maybe a little crazy. I don't want you to think that I'm crazy."

Nora laughed lightly, "I think you're running that risk either way. At least if you tell me then I'll understand what's making you crazy."

"Let me ask you this," she began, "do you believe in psychics?"

Nora laughed, "What are you? Some kind of psychic now? Are you going to read me some tea leaves or something?"

Dani sat silently, waiting for the truth to catch up.

"Dani?" she asked, her voice becoming more serious. "You don't really think you're a psychic, do you?"

"I don't know," she said honestly, "but I know a psychic who seems to think that I am."

"Well yeah, but psychics are all crazy, right? So you can't trust them," she laughed. "Seriously though, what makes you think the person telling you you're a psychic is an actual psychic? Did she ever predict anything that you know of?"

"I don't think it works like that. Don't ask me why but I don't think so. It's not about telling the future. It's about a connection to the past. It's about connecting with the people who have gone before us. They're the ones talking to me about this. They showed me an airstrip, near some woods. I think Jimmy was chased through those woods."

"You saw Jimmy being chased through the woods?" Nora's voice sounded suddenly frightened and childish.

"Do you know if he was chased through the woods? Do you remember any airstrip near some woods? Did you ever see the brother with children? Maybe up at the cabin?"

Nora was silent for a very long moment. Dani knew she was struggling with something and so waited quietly. "Maybe I should come over there and talk," she said at last.

"I'll be waiting whenever you get here."

"I have to get dressed. I'll be over in a few hours," she said before hanging up.

Dani dressed herself in faded jeans and a soft cotton t-shirt. She ran a brush through her hair but skipped the makeup. Nora knew all her scars and with her, there was no need to hide them. She went into the kitchen and made up a plate of sandwiches, a bowl of tortilla chips and some guacamole. Next, she pulled out the blender, some fresh strawberries, tequila, and some margarita mix. She blended up a batch of strong margaritas and stuck them in the freezer. As she did, she noticed a tube of frozen cookie dough. She pulled it out, sliced it apart, and popped the cut cookies into the oven. As the timer on the oven chimed, she saw Nora's car pull into her drive. She opened the side door for her.

"Perfect timing!" she called to her, as she watched her slam the car door. "The cookies are just coming out of the oven."

"Cookies?" she called back. "Chocolate chip?"

"What else? Nice to see you!" She gave her friend a quick hug and stepped aside to let her in. Nora was also in jeans with a striped blue and white top that looked vaguely nautical. Unlike Dani, Nora had taken the time to do her makeup, as Dani had known she would. She didn't have any scars to hide but she took great pride in her beautiful, meticulous appearance.

As Nora took a seat and set down her large, leather bag, Dani pulled out a tray, took the cookies out of the oven and scooped them from the pan to the tray. She clicked off the oven and brought the tray over to the table, setting it next to the chips and guacamole. The women took a cookie and looked at each other in silence as they ate. After the second cookie, Dani said, "I made some margaritas. You interested?"

Nora raised an eyebrow and flashed a mischievous grin. Dani stepped to the freezer, pulled out the margarita pitcher and poured two tumblers full, she handed one to Nora and took her seat again. She snagged a third cookie off the tray and asked, "So what can you tell me about Jimmy and the cabin up north?"

Nora took a long drink of the margarita and set it back on the table. "I can't be sure it was Jimmy Prince but I did see Craig with some kids up there. I'd heard some talk about the pedophilia charge. His dad was furious about that but …" she shook her head in what seemed like frustration. "I remember thinking that was wrong even then. Who gets angry over bailing out their kid from a pedophilia charge?" Dani was confused at first but she did not interrupt. "I mean horrified, appalled, heartbroken—that's what you're supposed to feel, right? But angry? He acted like Craig had smashed up the family car or something, like it was a traffic ticket," Nora took another long drink of the margarita and reached across the table for the pitcher and a refill.

"Anyway, I didn't know exactly what had happened but I knew that he'd been busted for messing with little boys and that he wasn't supposed to be around them anymore. There was some kind of restraining order or legal thing that was supposed to have prevented him from being around kids. Matt and I had driven up to the cabin that weekend to …" she paused and glanced up at Dani's curious expression before she continued, "… to be alone. We'd been dating for a while and I was thinking of … but I didn't," she insisted.

"I believe you," Dani offered quickly. "What does that have to do with Craig and the boys?"

"Well that's just it. We got up there and the cabin wasn't empty. Craig was up there with Michael and some other guy I didn't recognize and two or three young boys. One of them may have been Jimmy, that was around the time that he was missing, but I don't know for sure. I only know that when we opened the cabin door, Craig and his friends were already in the living room with pizza, beer, pop, and these boys. There was porn on the television and Matt flipped out. He told me to go back to the car and he stayed in the cabin yelling at Craig, threatening to tell their dad. As I left the house, I heard Matt threaten to tell the cops and have him re-arrested. Looking back on it now, I know he never would have, but I was young and I guess I wanted to believe that he was a better kind of guy. Maybe Matt hoped he was that kind of guy too, I don't know." She seemed very sad as she emptied her second margarita. "He made all kinds of threats but he didn't get them out of there. We didn't take the kids back with us or anything. We should have taken them back with us." Tears began to stream down her face and she clutched the cold glass as if holding on for dear life.

"When he came back to the car, I told him we should call for help. Nobody had cell phones back then, not like today, but there was a public phone in town. I told him we should call. I made him take me to a store in town where I knew there was a phone. I even called and connected but he'd followed me to the phone. When he realized that I was serious, that I was really placing the call, he came up behind me and kept pushing me to hang up. I didn't know the address of the house, I'd never paid attention." The tears were flowing now and her hands trembled around the drink. "I begged him to tell me, to let me tell them. I asked him why he'd allowed me to call if he wasn't going to allow me to tell them what was happening. That's when he pulled the receiver out of my hand and hung it up. He pulled me out of the store and we turned right around and headed home. He wouldn't talk about it, wouldn't let me question him on it. I know he was horrified by it. I know in my heart that somewhere inside him, he wanted to pull those boys out of that house. *I* wanted to pull those boys out of the house, Dani, you have to believe me. Leaving that house then was the last thing I wanted to do, please believe me!" She wept until she couldn't catch her breath, her eyes pleading with her friend for understanding and forgiveness.

"Honey, I know. I know you wanted to save those kids. You were a kid yourself and in a situation that was way over your head."

"I was a kid?" she said bitterly. "They were the kids! They needed someone to protect them and we just turned around and went home! How could we have done that, Dani? What were we thinking? We should have pulled them out, driven them straight to the police. We should have saved those kids!"

"You *were* a kid," Dani insisted, "but you're not now and it's not too late to do the right thing for those families, Nora. They deserve closure. They deserve justice. You can give them that, at least."

"But *how?*" Nora pleaded. She seemed desperate, desperate for relief from the guilt and shame that she'd kept bottled up for so long.

"By going to the police now. Tell them everything that you know about the Millers—everything that you saw then."

Her expression changed into something Dani didn't quite recognize. Was it fear? Or maybe disbelief? "Dani, how can you still be so naive? Do you really think the cops *didn't* know? How many times had they given him probation for molesting children? How could the cops not have been involved if they knew what he was, if he had *admitted* to what he was and he still wasn't thrown in prison?" She reached again for the margarita pitcher and poured more into her tumbler. "If they wouldn't fight for those kids then, do you really think they'll fight for them now? Do you really not understand the power and wealth of the Miller family even now?" She took another long drink from the tumbler and stared solemnly at the table in front of her.

For the briefest moment, Dani felt abashed; but then the anger returned. "Bullshit," she shot back. "That's just an excuse to quit. You cannot tell me that every cop everywhere is exactly the same or that defeat is a certainty. There must be some cop or lawyer or judge somewhere out there who is also a parent and can understand what must be done. Did you ever even try? Have you ever spoken to the victims' families or to their lawyers? To the feds or maybe the press? People need to get pissed off about this. If enough people get pissed off, the roaches will be forced out of hiding," she insisted.

"You're being naive," Nora repeated.

"Have you ever even spoken to Geoff's dad?"

"Geoff?" she asked, confused. "Geoff Williams? What does he have to do with this?"

"His dad's a retired cop. He might be able to help."

"Oh yes, and I'm sure he'd just love to have this mess dumped in his lap," Nora picked at a cookie as she spoke.

"We have to start somewhere, Nora. If he doesn't want to be involved, he can just say so. Otherwise, maybe he can help."

"Even if he was to tell us where to go with the story, it's still my word against Matt's and he'll just deny the whole incident."

"Maybe, Dani conceded. "Or maybe he will prove to be a better man than he was a kid. Maybe he'll stand up now and do what he should have done all those years ago."

Nora snorted and shot her a look.

"OK, maybe not but maybe your information will reignite the investigation. Maybe if we could just get one honest cop to take a fresh look at the evidence, we could do something for the families of these victims."

Nora finally looked up and met her eyes. "Tell me who to talk to and I'll talk," she said, tears streaming down her face.

Dani smiled, "Let's start with what you know. So you saw him with kids that once at the cabin. Was there any other time or did you ever hear him talking about kids on any other occasion? Did he ever have kids on the plane?"

Nora thought about the question for a long moment. "He used to take the plane to an island," she said, taking another cookie from the tray and breaking it into smaller pieces as she spoke.

"What island?" Dani asked.

"To be honest, I'm not sure. They always just referred to it as 'the island.' They talked about some kind of camp up there."

"A camp? Like a summer camp you mean? Or was it more like a campground for vacationers?"

Nora looked at her plate as though she might find the answer written there. "I don't know. I'd just sometimes hear him talking about visiting the camp or flying into the camp and I knew that when he talked about the camp, he was planning to fly into that island. Matt knew about the island but he never flew there, not that I know of anyway. It was just Craig and his group of friends."

"Did you ever ask Matt about it?" Dani asked, pouring herself a second drink.

"Yes, but I could tell he didn't really want to talk about it. He'd always change the subject pretty quickly. The whole family was very hush, hush about everything Craig did. He'd had so many problems with the law that everybody kind of treated him like he was infected with something contagious. If they didn't have to interact with him, they didn't. I understood why but looking back on it now, that probably just gave him free reign to do whatever he wanted to, especially when you think about how much money the family had."

"Did he ever take kids up to the island?" Dani held her breath as she waited for Nora to respond.

"I never saw him take kids up there but …" Nora took a bite of her cookie and it seemed to Dani that she took much longer than necessary to chew.

"But what?" Dani demanded.

She swallowed hard and said, "Well, I'm pretty sure I heard him refer to it as a youth camp once," her eyes met Dani's. "He'd been busted for something similar once before, for running a camp or a shelter or something for underprivileged kids and then molesting the boys who came to it, but I'm sure they wouldn't legally have allowed him to do it again after he'd already been arrested once. Besides, when he said it, it sounded like he was joking." Her voice became a whisper, "I wanted to believe it was a joke," she said, more to herself than to Dani.

"So this youth camp was on an island. But you don't know which island?" Dani's expression grew dark as she thought about the many dead ends in this case.

"That's right but they flew the plane to it so it must have been some place where you could land a plane."

"We know you can fly a plane onto Mackinac," Dani put in. "Could they have been flying into Mackinac?"

"Possibly," she conceded, "but I don't think so. When they went into Mackinac, they usually just referred to it as Mackinac and anyways, they didn't like Mackinac. They said it was too touristy. I think the camp was on one of the less-populated islands."

Dani nodded. "That would make sense, wouldn't it? No ideas which one? I imagine Drummond would have been pretty isolated then. Even now it's mostly wilderness. Was it maybe Drummond Island?"

Nora simply shrugged. "Dani, I wish I could help honestly I do but I don't remember. I don't know if I ever knew. One of his dad's business associates, Arthur somebody-or-other used to fly up there too. In fact, I think he actually owned a place on the island."

"What makes you think that?" asked Dani curiously.

"They used to ask him about staying up there, as though it were up to him to allow them to do it. Maybe he was actually the owner of the camp. I'm not sure."

"And you don't know his last name?" she tried again.

"No, sorry."

"That's OK," Dani replied, trying to sound as upbeat as possible. "I'm sure we can figure that out somehow. Is there anything else that you can remember about Sir Arthur No Name?"

Nora gave her a tired grin. "Well, one thing I do remember is that he was supposed to be even wealthier than the Millers. In fact, I remember Matt saying that his name had even appeared on one of those 'world's richest' lists."

"You mean like in a magazine?"

"Yeah, some financial magazine that ranked that sort of thing every year. His fortune made the Miller's money look like chump change and it was what Matt used to refer to as 'old money'. He was a trust fund guy, the money had apparently been in his family for generations and I guess he lived very comfortably just off the interest.

"And this guy hung around with a known pedophile like Craig Miller?" Dani was dumbfounded. "Why would he risk his family's reputation on a guy like that?"

"Honestly, I don't think he worried about it. With money like that ..." she let the thought trail off.

"With money like that what?"

"They didn't have to worry about it. I wish it weren't true but people like that lead a consequence-free life. He wasn't in the public eye, the money he was spending had been earned generations before by some long-dead relative and his only focus in life was to enjoy himself and spend it. What does a guy like that care about family reputation?" Her tone was more than a little bitter.

"Anything else that you can remember?" Dani asked gently.

Nora's eyes were puffy and swollen, her once perfect makeup was a ruin of mascara and rouge smeared across her cheeks. She was surrounded by the ghosts of her past now and seemed not even to hear the question.

Dani rose to clear the plates. "Why don't we give this a rest? Want to see if we can find a movie on pay-per-view and maybe take the margaritas into the living room? I could use another myself."

Nora looked up gratefully. "You're on!" As she rose, she opened the door to the garden and Gordie trotted in happily. He joined them on the sofa for the latest romcom and when it was over, he followed Dani upstairs to bed. They left Nora snoring loudly under a blanket on the couch.

Chapter IX

Dani felt a warm breeze flowing over the cliff and the little hairs on the back of her neck stood up, though not from the breeze. She felt the sensation of being watched. She turned to find Kōbō standing behind her near the stairs leading down to their cliff side landing.

"Well hello there," she greeted him as the old friend he had become. "Where have you been?"

Kōbō returned her smile and came forward to take his customary seat opposite her own. "I thought perhaps you could use some time to sort through some things, to adjust a bit before we visited again," he replied, smoothing his white, silk trousers as he took his seat.

"That was nice of you. I needed it," she said truthfully. "And you've brought me back here now, why?" she asked, although she was sure that she already knew what his answer would be.

"To watch home movies," he replied, flashing his stained teeth as he smiled.

"Home movies?" She had to laugh. "OK, I was not expecting that. I'll give you this, Kōbō, visiting with you is never boring."

He seemed pleased with himself. "Why be boring?" He smiled his broad, brown grin again. He pulled a remote out from the sleeve of his tunic and pointed it at the broad cliff side next to the stairs then pressed a button.

As he did, Dani could hear the sound of an old projector click on somewhere in the distance and the slow churn of film advancing through it. In the blink of an eye, she found herself seated in a darkened viewing room. Kōbō had vanished. The marble chaises had been replaced by cushioned cinema chairs. She was alone in the room. On the screen in front of her, white scratches and dots flashed across a blackened screen as the film advanced in the unseen projector. As her eyes adjusted to the dark room, the image of a boy who was perhaps eight or nine years old appeared on the screen. Holding his hand was a tall, thin man in dark slacks, a white, short-sleeved oxford shirt, and horn-rimmed spectacles. His hair was dark, closely cropped, and parted to one side. Hanging from the collar of his white shirt was a thin, black necktie. She returned her gaze to the boy. In his free hand, he was holding an ice cream cone that was clearly melting faster than he could eat it, the cream drizzling in sticky, sweet streams over his fingers. The boy also had closely cropped hair but with a cowlick at the crown that made it stand up defiantly. He had freckles on his face and his ears protruded noticeably from the short hair. He smiled happily at the camera and took another lick from his cone. He was wearing a black-and-white striped t-shirt and black shorts that exposed knobby knees.

Behind the pair, Dani could see the ice cream stand from which the cone must have been purchased. On the sign, a waterfall of cream cascaded into the words Frosty Falls. In the left of the frame she could see the line of customers extending into the parking lot and, inside the little window of the shop, she glimpsed a bored teenager, waiting to take their orders. Something about the scene seemed very familiar, as though she'd seen it before, but she couldn't remember where. She stared at the boy, at the man, and at the shop, trying to focus. She was trying to concentrate on the details of the scene, as Faye had instructed, but somewhere in the distance a dog was barking. Was it Gordie? She didn't think so. She knew Gordie's bark. His was deep and purposeful, usually reserved for canine passersby or brave squirrels that ventured into his yard. This bark was high and persistent, like the yip, yip, yipping of a toy poodle. She tried to focus again on the boy but, as she did, the image on the screen turned black and the words "The End" appeared in white script. Dani was furious. She sat in the dark room, waiting for Kōbō to reappear, but he did not. She began to shout.

"Kōbō? Kōbō where are you? Come back here right this minute!" As she shouted, her seat and then the whole theater began to shake and bounce. She felt water raining down on her face and her eyes flew open.

Inches above her nose, slobber leaked from Gordie's panting mouth. When he saw that she was awake, he began to pace back and forth on the bed. "Gordie," she complained, "get off!" She gave him a light shove and he jumped down off the bed and resumed his pacing on the floor beside her. She wiped the slobber from her cheek. She picked up her cell phone from the bed table and glanced at the time. It was seven minutes after nine. She dropped the phone on the bed next to her and lay back down on the pillow in a futile attempt to pick up where she had left off with the dream. She could not. It was gone. She reached into the drawer of her bedside table and pulled out the pen and notebook that she kept there. She flipped to a fresh page, propped herself up on an elbow and wrote down the dream with as much detail as she could remember. When she'd finished, she swung her legs out from under the comforter and paused to watch Gordie roll over onto his back and kick his legs into the air. She rolled her eyes at him.

"You have a lot of nerve, don't you?" she asked with mock annoyance. "First you wake me up and then you expect me to rub your belly?" Grudgingly, she reached down and did as she was bidden. When he'd had enough, Gordie rolled back over, sprang to his feet and led the way out of the room and down the stairs. Dani fought the urge to lie back down and instead stood up, pulled on her robe and followed him down the steps and into the kitchen.

She'd expected to find Nora still asleep on the couch. Instead, she found her standing in front of the mirror in the bathroom, fully dressed in the clothes she'd worn the day before, applying her makeup. The sweatpants Dani had loaned her the night before were folded and stacked neatly on the arm of the couch, as was the blanket she had used.

"Good morning," Dani said in a still sleepy mutter.

"Morning," Nora replied, never taking her eyes from the mirror.

"I'm surprised you're up so early," she called back. "I'd have thought you'd want to sleep in."

"I can tell you're a person who doesn't have to clock in every day. It's past nine o'clock, that is sleeping in," Nora snorted.

Now that she thought about it, Dani had to concede the point. "I suppose you're right. I guess I have gotten a bit out of touch with that sort of thing. How'd you sleep?"

"Like a rock," she said simply.

Dani smiled, "Four margaritas will do that."

"You'd know," she shot back. "Once the movie started, you were keeping up with me pretty well. How'd you sleep?"

"Unfortunately, the margaritas didn't seem to work for me. I had another dream."

"About Jimmy?" She asked, finally pulling her gaze away from the mirror.

"I'm not sure," she began, "but I don't think so. There was a boy in the dream but he was younger and something about him just seemed—off," she responded slowly, considering each word carefully.

"What do you mean by 'off'?" Nora asked.

"I don't know exactly. The face was different but maybe that's just because the boy in the dream was younger. I suppose it may have just been a younger version of the same kid but it didn't feel like it."

"Right," Nora replied, turning her attention back to the mirror. "So maybe the other male victim?" she suggested. "There was another little boy abducted around the same time, right?"

"Right, Marty Stevens was the other little boy. Or, if we're right and there were other victims, maybe it's one of them. I sort of feel like maybe this victim came before Jimmy, if he was even a victim. Like the crime is older and if I remember correctly, Marty Stevens was the first known victim of the Guardian. So that would make sense."

"What makes you think that the crime you dreamt about last night came before Jimmy?"

"Well, there wasn't really a crime in my dream and it's hard to explain but there was something about the way it was filmed."

"Filmed? What do you mean 'filmed'? We are still talking about a dream, aren't we?"

"Yes and no," Dani responded cryptically.

"Which is it? Yes or no?" Nora persisted, sounding mildly annoyed.

"Well, it was a dream about a film," she began. Referring occasionally to the notes she'd made upon waking, Dani recounted the dream to her friend with as much detail as she could manage. When she'd finished, she looked up at Nora for her reaction.

"Hmmm, OK," Nora began with an expression that suggested she was trying to piece together a jigsaw puzzle. "We know there's a Fanny Lake connection again so they're either trying to bring you up to my aunt's cottage or to Matt's summer place, right?"

Dani seemed confused. "A Fanny Lake connection?" she asked. "What Fanny Lake connection?"

"The Frosty Falls," Nora replied in a matter-of-fact tone that suggested Dani was being very dim not to have thought of it herself. "Remember the little ice cream shop we used to go to during the summers up there? We'd walk up there with your family and my aunt and cousins? I can't believe you don't remember that. By the time we made it back to the cottage, you were always one big sticky mess. You could never lick fast enough to keep up with your cone."

The memories flooded back to Dani now. "Oh my gosh, that's right! How could I have forgotten about the Frosty Falls? I kissed my first boy there. Did you know that?"

"I did *not* know that," Nora made a show of appearing scandalized by the news. "Weren't you like nine years old?"

"I was!" Dani laughed. "I guess you could say I started early. The little boy who stayed in the cottage across the street from yours—I can't remember his name now—walked with us to the Frosty Falls one night and presented me with a bouquet of wildflowers that he'd picked along the way. So I let him kiss me." In telling it now, she blushed and giggled as though it really had been a scandal.

"Well you little hussy!" Nora scolded playfully.

"I know!" Dani laughed. "OK. So I guess that does bring us back to Fanny Lake." She returned her attention to the notebook and jotted a few lines in the margins next to her earlier entry.

"So why did the way it was 'filmed' make you think it preceded the crime with Jimmy?"

Dani doodled absently in the margin of her notebook. "Well, it ..." she began and then stopped again.

"Did you see a date or something that would indicate the time period?" she offered.

"No ... I ...," Dani struggled to put her finger on it. "It's in part, I guess, because of the way it was presented to me, with the old projector."

"But the boys weren't that far apart in age. They had projectors back then and either one could have had their story play out on a projector," she pointed out.

"Yeah," Dani conceded, "that's what I keep thinking. It's not that the boys' age differences were that significant. But when I was shown Jimmy's abduction, they didn't use a projector. It felt like I was watching a current movie filmed about the '70s. This one felt like I was watching an old movie. The hairstyles and clothing were different and ... the ... car," she said very slowly. "I think there was an old car in the dream, in the parking lot."

"A car?" Nora asked, confused. "You said there was an unusual car in the dream about Jimmy as well. Was it the same car?" she asked. "What color was it?"

"Yeah, there was a car in the first dream. I don't think it was the same but I can't remember this one as well so I can't be sure. I'm not sure what kind it was or even what color it was. I only remember seeing a line of people extending into the parking lot and behind them was a car. It seemed like an older car."

"An old car?" Nora said in a voice that suggested she was not feeling hopeful about this newest revelation.

Dani rolled her eyes and shook her head. "I know. I know it's not much to go on."

"A projector dream and an old car? 'Not much' is an understatement," Nora said flatly.

"Maybe Kōbō will show it to me again. I was focused more on the boy."

"And you think the boy was Marty Stevens?"

"Not sure," Dani replied, biting her lip and staring down at the notebook again. "What are your plans for the day?" she asked suddenly.

Nora shrugged. "I don't really have any. Why?"

"Want to go for a drive?"

Gordie had been lying on the floor at their feet but when he heard the question, he bounced up and raced to the side door, where he stopped and stood, his tail wagging furiously. "Gordie, no, no!" Dani called after him. "Not yet, take a break!" She rolled her eyes and Nora laughed.

"Do you want to go for a drive with my dog and I?" Dani began again.

"Sure! Fanny Lake?" she asked.

"Fanny Lake! Does your aunt still have her cottage up there?"

"No such luck," Nora replied. "But it's only a few hours from here. It's half past nine now. If we get on the road within the hour, we'd be up there by early afternoon, we could shop for a while, maybe grab a late lunch and then start back. We'd be back by early evening."

"Sounds like a plan."

"What exactly are you hoping to find up there?" Nora asked cautiously.

"That's the question, isn't it?" Dani frowned. "I really have no idea. What I do know is that Kōbō's trying to tell me something and it seems to involve Fanny Lake. I just feel like I need to go see the place again, to refresh my memory."

"Fair enough," Nora nodded. "Well, unless you want to tour Fanny Lake in your bathrobe, I think you'd better get dressed. While you're doing that, I'll take Gordie into the backyard and see if I can keep him distracted until it's time to go." Nora gave her a playful wink and walked out of the room.

Chapter
X

Four hours later with Gordie happily drooling out her back window and Nora snoozing peacefully beside her, Dani took a left off the M-53. She pulled into the parking lot next to which the Frosty Falls should have been standing. It was not. In its place was the home of dairy royalty in all of its franchised, modernized glory. As she switched off the ignition, Nora awoke and looked around.

"Where are we?" she asked, her voice thick from sleep.

"It's not where we are that concerns me," Dani said, sounding tired and defeated. "It's where we should be."

"OK, I'll bite," Nora said. "Where should we be?"

"Next to the Frosty Falls, but we're not." She got out of the car and glanced around at her surroundings. Nora got out and did the same.

"And you're sure we're in the right spot?" she asked, sounding more alert.

"Yeah, on the corner of Main and Mill Streets, right? The lake we used to go swimming in is down that way," she pointed up the road a bit. "Your Aunt Doris's cottage was back that way," she pointed in the direction from which they'd just come. "I remember that restaurant," she pointed down the block. "The Frosty Falls should be right here. I'm sure of it."

Nora nodded, "You're right. This is where it was. So if not to revisit the Frosty Falls, why would this Kōbō character bring us all the way up here? And are we sure that's what's really going on here?" Nora's tone was cautious.

"What do you mean?" Dani asked defensively.

"Now don't get mad," Nora began, in anticipation of Dani's reaction, "but isn't it possible that it was just a dream about a place you visited as a kid? You said the kid in the dream had ice cream melting in his hand, right? You were always the same way. You said it was like a home movie and wasn't your dad into making home movies back then?"

But Dani was no longer listening. In the distance, a dog was barking. "Do you hear that?" she asked, ignoring Nora's doubts about her dream.

"Do I hear what?" she asked.

"The dog barking?"

"The dog?" She glanced in at Gordie, sitting quietly in the backseat. "What dog? What are you talking about?"

"Will you stay with Gordie? I'll be right back." Dani did not wait for a reply. Leaving the two of them at the car, she made her way across the street in the direction of the barking dog.

"Dani, what are you doing? Where do you think you're going?" Nora called after her.

"Just stay with Gordie," she called back. "I'll just be a minute." A short while later, she stopped and listened again. Because it was already mid-afternoon on a Sunday, and late in the season in any case, the weekend crowds were down to a bare minimum. A group of twenty-somethings drank beer on the patio of a popular rib joint and, in the opposite direction, she saw two elderly ladies leaving a church. Otherwise, the street was deserted. She stood for a long moment listening and just when she thought she should give up and return to the car, the barking started again. Nora's words came back to her, "Isn't it possible that it was just a dream about a place you visited as a kid?" What was she doing? What did she hope to find by chasing down this barking dog—other than a barking dog, of course. "This is insane!" she said to no one in particular. She turned on her heel to go back the way she'd come and as she did, she caught the eye of a young boy with dark hair and a shy smile. He was standing on the sidewalk gazing intently at her.

With a twitch of his index finger, he motioned for her to follow him and he scampered down a gravel side street that led off the main road. As Danielle began to follow, she realized that he was headed in the direction of the barking dog. She followed him at a distance at first, feeling silly and a little concerned that she might frighten the child. The further she went along the gravel road, the louder the barking became. She tried to imagine what type of dog could have such a loud bark and soon decided that it sounded like a puppy, a very energetic puppy. Ahead of her, the road twisted off behind a tall row of lilac bushes. Still several yards away, the boy glanced back over his shoulder, gave her another shy smile and disappeared behind the bushes. She quickened her steps to keep up with him but as she cleared the curve, the boy was nowhere to be seen. She looked from one side of the narrow lane to the other. From behind, she heard him whisper, "Seek him out!" Startled, she spun around. It was as though he'd disappeared into thin air. A chill ran through her and she shifted her weight nervously.

To her left was a white ranch home with burgundy shutters and a long, wooden deck that had been painted the same shade of deep burgundy. Attached by a breezeway was a two-car garage and behind the window of that garage, Dani was amused to find a tan puppy bobbing up and down, her head appearing and disappearing from view in rhythm to her barking. After glancing up at the house, Dani moved slowly across the far side of the drive toward the side entrance of the garage. She peered in the window but the sunlight reflecting off the glass made it nearly impossible to see in. She cupped her hands along the side of her face and pressed her nose to the glass. The first thing she noticed was a car covered by a black tarp in the center of the garage. Along the back of the car on the side nearest the window, the tarp had snagged on the brake light, which stuck out in a sharp point from the back of the vehicle. What immediately caught her eye was the bright orange color of the paint. She pressed her face closer to the window to get a better look but, as she did, snarling, sharp teeth flashed before her eyes. Before she could stop it, a shriek escaped her lips and she stumbled backward onto the gravel drive, the small stones biting into her palms as she braced herself against the fall. She cursed quietly and wiped the gravel from her hands.

"Can I help you with something?" The man's voice was soft and calm but startled her all the same. She stared up at him, feeling as though she'd been captured red-handed in the middle of a bank heist.

"I ummm," she stammered, dusting the dirt from her jeans as she stood.

"Is she yours?" he asked, glancing toward the garage.

"Mine?" Dani, confused, was still thinking of the car.

"I wasn't trying to steal her or anything. I caught her running through the yard this morning and just thought I'd hold her until someone came looking for her. I was going to keep her in the yard but she's quite a jumper. She got over my fence in no time." He smiled at the puppy still bouncing up and down behind the window.

"Oh yeah, quite a jumper," Dani agreed, relieved to have been handed an excuse.

"Is that how she got away from you too?"

Dani stared at him for a moment, searching for a way out of the lie she'd begun. Unfortunately, her mind was blank and the prolonged silence was becoming awkward. "Yep," she said at last, "jumped right out on me."

The man nodded sympathetically. "What's her name?" he asked.

"Her name?" Dani repeated, stalling. "Her name is ummm—Maggie," she threw out the first name to come to mind, that of her niece.

"Maggie! Well that sure is a pretty name!" He smiled amiably. "Didn't remember to bring a leash though, eh?"

Dani stared at her empty hands as though they had betrayed her. "It's in the car," she said slowly. "I heard the barking and was in such a hurry to follow it that I forgot to grab the leash." She was inventing wildly now.

"Oh well," he said, "I can certainly keep her here for a while longer if you'd like to run back and get it. She's got a lot of energy, might be hard to hold onto her without having her on a leash."

"Right," she agreed absently, her mind returning to the car under the tarp. "Mind if I step into the garage and say hello to her first?"

"Oh sure, go right in. It's not locked."

Dani pushed open the door, pressing the puppy back with her foot as she stepped inside. The man followed her in and closed the door behind them. Dani glanced at the closed door and then at the man now standing between her and it. He was more than six feet tall with the strong but somewhat fleshy build of a man who had worked out in his youth but not in the many years since. He had a salt and pepper goatee, cropped close to his sharp chin and wispy salt and pepper hair that was thinning in a circle at the crown. His eyes were the color of coffee beans and his breath smelled vaguely of stale cigars. It occurred to her that his presence between her own position and that of the nearest exit should have made her uneasy but, somehow, it did not. He had such a gentle way about him that she felt immediately at ease.

She turned her gaze to the dog, who was now sniffing her pant legs fervently, her tail wagging wildly. She bent down slightly and offered her hand to the animal, who licked it immediately and looked up at her, panting. The puppy had a slightly square forehead and ears that stood up at the base and drooped slightly at the ends. Dani guessed her to be about six months old, perhaps eight, but no more. She had the build and height of a young boxer, with room still to grow.

"Hey there, Maggie, where've you been?" As Dani greeted her, the dog's ears turned forward and stood straight up, like miniature radar zeroing in on a target. Her expression was nearly human and Dani was half afraid she'd give away the lie. As if to silence her, Dani put a firm hand over her ears and scratched them down into submission. She turned her attention back to the car.

"Are you restoring a car there? A friend of mine likes to restore cars too." She had meant this to sound casual and conversational but to Dani's own ears it sounded nervous and awkward. If the stranger noticed, he gave no indication of it.

"No," he said, shifting his weight from one foot to the other. "I was holding onto it for a friend but …" He let the thought trail off.

"But?" Dani persisted, still trying to sound casual.

"Well, he passed away a while ago and he didn't really leave a will so I've just been holding onto it." His voice was low and distant and he stared uneasily at the car as he spoke.

"My friend just loves the classics. He could probably help you get it ready to sell. He might even be interested in buying it off you. What kind is it anyway?" It took all her will to keep her voice calm and steady as she spoke.

"Oh I don't think I could consider selling it. It's not really mine to sell," he shifted uneasily.

"Is it a Mustang?" she asked, knowing full well that it was not.

"No, no it's not a Mustang," he said. "It's a Volkswagen actually."

"A Volkswagen?" she repeated, genuinely surprised. "It doesn't look like any Volkswagen I've ever seen."

"Well this model always was very unique and they've long ago been discontinued. It's a Karmann Ghia," he said. "They made them back in the '60s and '70s." Dani felt her pulse quicken.

"Oh wow! And it looks like it's in great shape, at least from what I can see under the tarp," she added, hoping to solicit an invitation to see the rest of the vehicle.

"Yeah, it's in good shape," he agreed quietly.

Dani debated for a moment before pressing the issue. "I don't suppose I could see the rest of it?"

He shifted again nervously. "Well, it's a pain to get the cover off and on and it's really not mine to sell."

She was worried that she'd overplayed her hand. "Oh, sure, I understand. I suppose his family wants it back? How long has it been since he passed? By the way, I'm Danielle," she extended her hand to him before adding, "but everyone calls me Dani."

He shook it and said, "I'm Dale. Nice to meet you, Dani. My friend passed away quite a while ago. I don't really keep in touch with the family. I'm not even sure they know that I still have the car."

"Oh, I see. So you want to keep it just for sentimental reasons then?"

He looked at her for a long moment. "You know, I don't mean to be rude but I was just starting to get my lunch ready when you stopped by. Were you going to run and get her leash or do you need a lift back to your car?" He glanced at the door.

"Oh, of course," Dani said apologetically, "I didn't mean to keep you. Why don't I run and get that leash and I'll be back in just a bit, OK?"

"That'd be great," he said, nodding his approval.

Dani gave the dog another pat on the head then slipped past Dale and out the side door. She ran back up the narrow gravel road to Main Street then crossed back over to where Nora stood, looking both relieved and really annoyed.

"Thank God," she began. "Where have you been? I was about to send out a search party."

Dani ignored her. She pulled open the back car door, removed Gordie's leash and collar from his neck and the name tag from the collar. She tossed the name tag onto the front seat then slammed the door, leaving Gordie to stare after her in confusion.

"What kind of car did Craig Miller drive?" she asked Nora.

"What? Why?" Nora glared at her, clearly still annoyed by her earlier disappearance.

"Craig Miller—what kind of car did he drive?"

"An orange one, why?"

Dani rolled her eyes. "An orange what?" she demanded.

"It was a Karmann Ghia. I thought you said you re-searched this case. How could you not know that? It was in all the papers that he drove the same kind of car as …"

But Dani was no longer listening. Once again she was hurrying back toward the little side street, leash and collar in hand.

"Dani, what the …? Where are you going?" Nora shouted after her.

"Watch Gordie for me," she yelled back as she crossed the street.

Nora threw her hands in the air and paced back and forth by the car, staring in at Gordie.

A short while later Dani arrived back at the white and burgundy home of Dale, leash in hand. As she approached, she found him in the yard kneeling on the ground next to the dog, who would apparently be known as Maggie, rub-bing her belly and talking to her quietly.

"I think she's going to miss you," she said, smiling at the pair of them.

"I'm going to miss her too. She's a sweet girl." He stood up and brushed the grass from his knees.

"Well, if you'd like to give me your e-mail, I'd be happy to keep you up-to-date on how she's doing, maybe send you some pictures," she offered hopefully.

"That'd be great, thanks!" He gave Maggie another scratch behind the ears and added, "I'll need a pen and paper. Would you like to come inside and I'll write it down for you?"

Dani hesitated only a moment. "Sure," she said and fol-lowed him inside.

Had she not already met the home's owner, she'd have thought it the home of an elderly woman. The kitchen they entered was outdated but clean and well-organized. The walls were covered with thick, floral wallpaper and the windows were topped with white, lace valances. The cabinets were honey oak as was the floor. She followed him through the kitchen to a living room that was painted a light teal green. A solid oak china cabinet stood in the corner to her left and across the far wall stretched a well-worn sofa in teal green and mauve floral brocade. In front of the sofa was a glass-topped, oak coffee table, and on the wall opposite the china cabinet stood a brick fireplace that had been painted white. The mantel of the fireplace was covered by dusty frames that housed old family photos.

"Make yourself at home," Dale said, smiling affably and waving a hand in the direction of the living room. "I'm just going to run into my office for a moment and get a pen." He smiled at her and then was gone.

Dani approached the white fireplace and glanced from one dusty frame to the next. The first picture was obviously Dale. He seemed a bit younger, a bit fitter and had a bit more hair, but his appearance was not significantly different. He was standing with an elderly woman whose eyes looked very much like his own. More than likely his mother, thought Dani. The next picture showed a group of teenage boys standing around an old model corvette. Next to that was the picture of a lovely, blond woman standing beside the elderly lady that she believed to be Dale's mother. The next showed Dale smiling beside a very old German shepherd. When she reached the last frame, Dani's hand flew to her lips as she stifled a gasp. Although she was much younger in this shot, Dani immediately recognized the motherly figure, but it was the child holding her hand that made her gasp. He was holding an ice cream cone that was clearly melting faster than he could eat it, the cream drizzling in sticky, sweet streams over his fingers. The boy had closely cropped hair but with a cowlick at the crown that made it stand up defiantly. He had freckles on his face and his ears protruded noticeably from the short hair. He smiled happily at the camera as he licked his cone. He was wearing a black and white striped t-shirt and black shorts that exposed knobby knees.

"Oh God, please don't look at that one!"

Dale's voice made Dani leap so far forward that she nearly knocked the frame off the mantel.

"Oh, I'm sorry," Dale began, suppressing a laugh, "I didn't mean to startle you. It's just—I hate that shot. You can see my knobby knees and my hair and ears—that was an awkward time for me, as you can see." His smile was very shy as he glanced toward the old photo.

"Oh my, is that you?" Dani asked, still visibly shaken.

"Yeah, mom and I at the Frosty Falls when I was a kid. We used to walk up there during the summer."

"I think you look adorable," Dani said truthfully.

"Thanks," he smiled again but brushed the compliment aside with a wave of his hand and offered her the piece of paper he was holding. "This is my e-mail address. I'd really appreciate it if you could let me know how Maggie's doing from time-to-time."

"I sure will, thank you." She returned his smile and gave another uneasy glance at the boy in the photo on the mantel. "I hope you don't mind if I ask but when was this photo taken, the year, I mean."

"That photo, hmmm—good question," Dale seemed to consider it a moment. "I must be about eight or nine in that shot so I'd guess it to be 1960, maybe '61." She stared at his expression as he spoke. There was a distant sadness in his eyes. He met her gaze briefly and then looked down at his feet.

"I used to go to the Frosty Falls as a kid but I noticed that it's gone now."

"Oh yeah, that's been years now since the Frosty Falls closed up," he glanced at the leash in her hands. "So you're not from around here then?"

"Vacation rental," she lied quickly. "When I'm not on vacation, I live in Fenton."

Dale nodded and bounced a bit on the balls of his feet. "Yeah, we see a lot of that up here." A silence fell between them and stretched on for an uncomfortably long moment while Dani searched for something more to say. She could think of nothing else.

"Well, I'd better get back," she said, slipping the piece of paper into her pocket. She followed him back into the yard and slid the collar around Maggie's neck. With a wave she bid him farewell and she and Maggie made their way up the gravel road and back to Main Street.

Nora greeted her with an expression that was part relief, part annoyance and part amused astonishment. "What's with the dog?" she asked with a laugh.

Dani tried to speak but her explanation was drowned out by Gordie's excited barking. He was trying frantically to get out of the backseat and, in doing so, left Dani in fear for her car's interior.

"I think we're going to need another leash," she said, shouting above the barking, which was now flowing freely between the two dogs.

"What does that mean? He's coming *with* us? What if Gordie and he don't get along?"

"She," Dani corrected her, as she glanced from one barking animal to the other. "We need another leash," she repeated.

"There's a drugstore on the next block," she pointed up the road. "I'll stay with these two but hurry!"

"You're a good friend." Dani smiled at her gratefully. "I'll explain when I get back." She handed her the leash and hurried up the block. Ten minutes later she returned with a new leash and matching collar, a box of dog treats and two cans of soda. Dani put the new collar and the leash on Gordie and then, with Maggie and Nora standing a few yards away near the curb, pulled him cautiously from the car. After several tense moments of mutual sniffing, he bowed to his new friend and then bounced around her, tail wagging furiously.

"Shall we take them for a walk to seal the deal?" Dani asked.

"Only if you use the time to tell me where you were and how it is that you now have a second dog."

As they walked, Dani did just that. When she had finished her explanation, Nora stared at her in stunned silence.

"Do you really think it's Craig Miller's car?" she asked at last. "What are the odds of that?"

"What other reason could there be for Kōbō to have led me here? That must be his car."

"I'm sorry, Dani, but I'm still struggling with this whole Kōbō thing," she said quietly, her eyes fixed on Gordie as he bobbed happily alongside Maggie.

Dani ignored the remark. "Did the Millers know a local boy named Dale?"

"Dale who?" she asked, her brow furrowed as if attempting to recall.

"There was a name on the mailbox in front of his house. It said "Rizzo." He didn't actually offer his last name, just an e-mail address."

"What's the e-mail address?" she asked.

Dani pulled the slip of paper from her pocket. "Dale49918@outlook.com"

"Did they know someone named Dale? Maybe Dale Rizzo?" Nora repeated the question quietly and bit her lip, shaking her head slowly and then glancing up at Dani. "He was a local kid?" she asked.

"If I had to guess, I'd say he's probably lived in that same house since he was a kid. I think he either still lives there with his mom or, more likely, she passed away and left it to him but I think that's the house he grew up in."

"Was that the kid's name?" she mumbled, more to herself than to Dani. She shook her head again. "Maybe ..." She looked at Dani. "There was a kid that they talked about and I'm pretty sure it was a name like that. Dale or Darren—something like that, but I never met him. He never came around."

"If he didn't come around, why'd they talk about him?"

A sly grin curled around Nora's lips. "You're going to think I'm crazy but I always wondered if he wasn't like a bastard son or something."

"Matt had a bastard son?"

"No," Nora laughed loudly. "Not Matt—their dad. I thought he might have been the bastard son of their father but I'm sure it couldn't be."

"Why would you think that then?"

"Well, *if* this is the same kid that we're talking about—and I can't be sure that it is—Victor Miller would ask Matt and Craig about him. He'd ask how he was doing, was his mother OK, did it seem like they had enough money—things like that. I asked Matt about him once and he just said that he was a friend of the family's but I never heard Victor ask about any other kid like that."

"What makes you think the kid was local to Fanny Lake?"

"Well, the name only came up when we were at the lake and Matt once or twice left me in the cottage alone while he went to 'check on Dale'… or was it Darren? I really can't be sure that was the name."

"Let's assume for the moment that it was …" Dani began.

"Seems to me, you're doing a lot of assuming," Nora interrupted.

Dani shrugged, "I have to start somewhere," she argued. "I really think this Dale is important. Do you really think that it's a coincidence that I saw a picture of a boy in a dream and then met that very same boy the next day?"

"Met that very same boy? Dani, listen to yourself. You don't know that it's the very same boy. You saw a picture of a boy that looks like a kid who only exists in your own mind. Isn't it possible that you're just willing yourself to believe all of this?"

"Why would I?" she asked.

"I don't know, Dani, why would you? Maybe because it's easier to cope with being a psychic than with being a victim of PTSD?"

"Crazy is crazy," Dani snorted, "and it's all in how others perceive you for either of those afflictions—so six of one, half dozen of the other as far as I'm concerned."

Nora looked uncomfortable. "Maybe Kōbō just thought Maggie needed a good home," she said cheerfully. "Speaking of which, what if she already has one? What if her real owner's been out looking for her?"

"When we get home, I'll look into that," she promised. "Believe me, I have no great desire for a second dog but how else was I going to explain peeping into his garage? If her real owner is out there, I'll find him."

"She is a cute one though. You have to admit it."

"I admit to nothing," she declared in a stern voice, casting a sideways glance at the latest addition to their little party.

Chapter XI

By the end of the following week, Dani was still no closer to finding Maggie's *real* owner, despite having contacted every pound, shelter, and veterinary office in the greater Fanny Lake area. She'd even taken the dog into her own vet's office to check for a microchip. None was found. She was slowly coming to realize that she might actually be Maggie's *real* owner. Sitting in her office, staring down at the peaceful pooch sprawled across the rug at her feet, Dani had to admit that it was, perhaps, not the worst thing that could have happened. Far from being jealous of his new sister, Gordie doted on her and would now flatly refuse to go outside until she came along. The three of them had quickly fallen into a new, very comfortable routine.

Professionally, Dani had spent the week working on translations for would-be immigrants from half a dozen different Latin American countries. Prospective newcomers were required to fill out a thick booklet of forms detailing their overall health, legal status, family histories, and arrest records, each of which needed to be translated into English. The government's recent open door policy at the

Texas border had made a significant dent in this part of her business, as the flood of new immigrants had only to make some vague claim of hardship in their native country to be waved through with no further questions asked. It was a prospect that made Dani shudder when she reflected on some of the startling revelations those now neglected documents had previously unearthed. She found herself wishing that she could be as oblivious to the increased dangers of disease, crime, and terrorism as most of the country's citizenry seemed to be.

Although she'd lost a chunk of the personal immigration business, the majority of corporations still sought legitimate visas for legitimate immigrants and that part of her business had, fortunately, kept Dani busy all week.

She'd been so busy, in fact, that she'd had little time to continue her probe into the Guardian murders from thirty-nine years before. She had attempted an online investigation into the infamous orange Karmann Ghia that had been so central to the investigation during the time of the murders. She found no evidence to suggest that it had ever been found. She also attempted to investigate what might have happened to Craig Miller's vehicle, which was known to be the very same make and model as the suspect vehicle. She could find nothing whatsoever online to indicate what might have become of that vehicle either.

In an effort not to appear overly eager, she had not yet contacted Dale. Now, as she glanced from Maggie to the blank e-mail sitting open on her computer monitor, she contemplated how best to approach her first official update. Perhaps, she thought, it would be best to begin with a photo. After all, who could resist such an adorable face? She pulled her small pocket camera from a desk drawer and aimed it at Maggie. In the dimly lit room, the flash deployed automatically, disturbing her subject and creating a picture that was impossibly overexposed. Dani frowned.

"Hey Maggie, want to go outside?" She made the offer in a familiar cadence that made the dog's large ears pop up enthusiastically. Maggie bolted up and made a dash for the hallway, where she met up with Gordie. Together the two animals charged through the kitchen, their claws scraping frantically against the polished wood floors. Dani winced and shook her head. She paused at the back door to slip on her gardening shoes then opened the door and followed the dogs outside.

The cool days of autumn had taken over summer's warmth. Michigan was now moving full speed toward winter and Dani pulled her deep blue, lamb's wool cardigan tight across her body to ward off the late afternoon chill. The leaves were bright on the trees now and the colors were nearly at peak. The first snow had not yet arrived but there had been a light frost on the ground when she awoke that morning, so she knew that it was not far off.

Taking aim with the camera, she snapped a few shots of the two dogs at play and then called Maggie over and commanded her to sit. The clever little dog did so immediately and even gave her brother a reproachful snort when he tried to interrupt her portrait. Dani snapped several more shots. When she was sure she had all she needed, she clipped Maggie's harness to a lead, allowing her full access to the yard but not to the fence that surrounded it. Dani had, unfortunately, discovered very quickly that her own fence, like Dale's, was not tall enough to prevent the dog's escape. Maggie gave her a disgruntled look but then turned to run after a squirrel at the far end of the yard. Dani turned and went back into the house.

In her office, she uploaded the images from the camera, cropped a few of the better shots and attached them to the e-mail. She then sat staring at the blank page for a full ten minutes. More than once she began and then erased a message. "Oh, this is ridiculous," she said in exasperation. She took a deep breath and began to write:

Hello Dale, I hope you're doing well. It was very nice to meet you last week and I wanted to take a moment to thank you again for your assistance in finding Maggie for me. Dani smiled to herself when she realized just how true the statement was. *As promised, I'm sending along some photos. The black dog in the first two shots is my other dog, Gordie. He was also very glad to see Maggie.* There was a long pause as Dani tried to think of a way to bring the conversation around to the car or to Jimmy Prince.

I spoke to my friend earlier this week and he really seemed very interested in the Karmann Ghia. He asked me what year it was but I couldn't really tell him. Do you happen to know the year of the car? He was hoping he might get a chance to see it some time. I certainly wouldn't want to impose on you but I just knew he'd really like that car. It's just up his alley.

How's everything in Fanny Lake? I imagine it must be getting pretty cold up there now. Have you had your first snow yet? Dani could think of nothing more to say, so she tabbed down a few spaces and wrote, *I hope you enjoy the pictures and thanks again for your help with Maggie. Kind Regards, Dani.*

She reread the e-mail and although she was not altogether pleased with it, she could think of nothing better to write and so she sent it with no further modifications. She rose from her desk, grabbed a book from the shelf and a blanket from the closet and plopped on the chaise in her office. The book was a case history of the Guardian murders, which was gruesome but insightful. As she read it, she thought about her dreams. She remembered little Jimmy Prince and the fear she'd felt as he was driven away in that first dream. She thought about the coyotes that had chased her and soon she found herself reaching for the phone. Faye picked up on the first ring.

"Hey! How have you been? I've been wondering about you. I left you a voice mail last week but I hadn't heard back."

"I know, I'm sorry. I've been busy with work. I was wondering though if you might still be willing to help me practice. I don't know if these voices in my head are really telling me anything that I want to hear but I guess I'm ready now to begin listening, or at least, to acknowledge their presence."

"That's great!" Faye seemed genuinely pleased. "I'd suggest that I come by your place. Would that be OK?"

"That'd be perfect," Dani said truthfully. Her experience with Dale and Maggie had helped her to overcome her fear of the voices and the potential stigma that came with them. She was beginning to realize that these voices were meant to guide her, to show her something more important than her own, selfish misgivings and she meant to listen to them, no matter what. "If you wouldn't mind giving me your e-mail address, I'll send you over my home address and the directions." Dani wrote it down and said, "Got it. I'll send that information now. When could you come over?" The two women agreed to meet later that same evening. "Bring your appetite," she said lightly, "I'll order a pizza."

When Faye arrived, Dani greeted her warmly. She felt oddly relieved to be in the presence of someone who understood her unusual affliction. Nora was her friend and she adored her, but Dani was sure that she would always question her assertions about Kōbō and the messages that he was giving her. How could she not? Truth be told, Dani wouldn't believe them herself had she not been forced to live with them.

With Faye, there was no need to explain, nor to pretend. She could speak of the messages and their messenger freely and openly without judgment and Dani had come to appreciate that acceptance more than she could have ever imagined. "I'm so glad you're here. I really need your help," Dani said, as Faye set her purse aside and entered the kitchen. "I had another dream and there's just been so many odd coincidences lately. I hope you don't mind but I really would like to fill you in and get your perspective."

"Absolutely!" Faye agreed enthusiastically. "And here's your first lesson, there's no such thing as coincidence. That only means that your guide chose to remain anonymous."

Dani gave her an odd look but then nodded her understanding. "I've ordered the pizza. It should be here shortly. Would you like something to drink in the meantime?"

"No, don't worry about that. Just tell me, what's happened?" Faye crossed the room and helped herself to a chair at the kitchen table. Her rust-red hair was pulled back in a loose, casual braid. She wore faded jeans and a thick, forest green turtleneck sweater. Her nails were short but well-maintained and polished a deep blood red.

Dani took the seat opposite hers and began telling her first about the Frosty Falls dream and then about her visit to Fanny Lake with Nora (at which point she introduced her to Maggie).

It was then that the dinner arrived. Dani retrieved the pizza, paid the driver, set the plates, and poured the drinks. As she sat back down, Faye sat staring at her for a long moment, her fingers pressed together at the tip of her nose as if in prayer.

"Tell me more about your friend, Nora. You mentioned that she went with you to Fanny Lake, right?"

"Right."

"The last time you spoke to me about her, you said she was hesitant to discuss Jimmy Prince and the Miller family. Do you think that's changed? Does she seem more open to reliving that time in her life now?"

Dani thought for a long moment before she spoke. "I think it's fair to say that she wants to make amends for not doing more then, when it might have saved a life. I don't know though if she's really aware of what that means in a practical sense or if she's really willing to do everything that might be requested of her."

"You need to make her see it through. It's no accident that these messages were brought to you, specifically. You know that, right? Your guide chose to bring these messages to you because you have the contacts and the resources to help interpret them correctly. It's important that you use those resources."

"What do you mean 'use' them?" Dani asked with some apprehension.

"Clearly this is a case that many people for many different reasons would like to see go away. You can't let that happen. There's a reason they brought this challenge to you and you have to see it through."

"I'd like to understand Dale's connection to the Guardian murders. How did he end up with the car and why would they show him to me as a child? Is he a victim or an accomplice?"

"We have no proof that he was ever a victim. Maybe he's one of the coyotes, a predator. Why else would he have the car? If that is the car. Let's not forget, we have no proof of that."

"Well if Dale is a coyote, why would he appear to me as an innocent child in my dream? On the other hand, if he was a victim, then the culprit couldn't possibly be Craig Miller. He'd have been too young." Dani didn't want to think about that possibility. "If it wasn't Craig Miller, then who?" She wasn't sure that she was ready to start back at square one. She realized, with a pang of guilt, just how selfish that thought was.

As if sensing her thoughts, Faye said, "Sometimes—even often times—our guides lead us in a direction that we'd rather not go, but in my experience, if you're smart, you'll go where they tell you to go. They know best and they're trying to help you, sometimes even protect you. You need to have faith in what they're saying."

"And if my guide tells me to wear a tinfoil hat and howl at the moon?"

"Are we back there again so soon?" Faye frowned.

"You're right, sorry. I guess I feel that it's one thing to listen to what my guides are saying and another to do whatever they tell me to do. It's a leap of faith, you know?" What Dani didn't say was that it was a leap of faith she wasn't yet sure she could make.

"It is a leap of faith, and I think it's important to remember that faith is an important element of anything spiritual, but you also have to understand that God gave you a mind of your own to decide right from wrong and to decide for yourself if someone is a worthy guide. Do you really think

Kōbō would have you put on a tinfoil hat and howl at the moon?"

Dani thought about the funny little monk from her dreams and smiled. "Honestly, I wouldn't put anything past him." Faye pretended not to hear. "Alright so then we're back at the beginning. If it's not Craig, then who? He'd have to be older than Dale, I would think, maybe even significantly older and he'd have to have some connection to Dale."

"What about the older guy in the ice cream dream?" Faye asked. "You said that in the actual photo, it was Dale's mother in the shot, right? So why would Kōbō show you someone else in the dream? Who was that?"

"Oh, yeah," Dani agreed, eyes wide, "the ice cream guy. I'd nearly forgotten about him."

"And what about the dream where you were running through the woods? Where do you think you were? Could it have been somewhere near Fanny Lake?"

"I don't know. Could have been …" Dani shrugged. "I honestly don't know."

"In your conversations with Nora, did she have any idea?"

"Not really, no, and if we no longer believe that it's Craig Miller then maybe the whole connection with Nora and the Miller family is irrelevant." Dani had never felt so frustrated.

"I doubt that. There was a reason that she was in that dream. The Millers are somehow relevant here. Maybe it has something to do with the father of that family. He'd be older, did he have a connection to Dale?"

Dani remembered Nora's bastard son theory and felt a renewed sense of hope. "I think so, Nora seemed to think so."

"So did Nora mention any places relative to the Miller family that might be a fit to the place in your dream?"

"Well, she told me that the Millers had a home on Fanny Lake that was in a wooded area, but it didn't have a landing strip. She said they flew into Mackinac but that landing strip didn't have woods near it. She did mention some other island but she'd never been there."

"Did the place in your dream look like an island?"

Dani thought about it a moment. "It may have been I suppose, there was a beach. But if it was, it must have been a fairly big island and I saw only a part of it."

"Did Nora know the name of this other island?"

Dani shook her head. "She said she didn't recall ever hearing a name."

"How many islands are there in Michigan? Have you done a search of it at all?" she asked.

"I haven't," Dani admitted. "I suppose that might be a decent place to begin."

"While you're at it, maybe see if any of them have a coyote population, it might help you narrow it down."

"How would a coyote get onto an island? Can they swim that far?"

"Well, how far is 'that far'? I'm sure some of the islands aren't far off the coast and, besides, in the winter the lakes would freeze over and the wildlife could just walk across."

"Good point," Dani agreed, taking another slice of pizza. "So are you going to teach me some psychic techniques or what?"

"Pizza first, then techniques." Faye helped herself to more pizza and when the meal was over, she demonstrated to Dani a number of deep breathing, meditation, and even yoga exercises intended to prepare her for her nocturnal meetings with Kōbō. When they'd finished, she walked Faye to the side door. Faye grabbed her purse and made Dani promise to call with any updates.

After she'd gone, Dani went into her office, flopped down on her chaise and pulled her laptop from her desk. After signing in, she noticed she had an e-mail from Dale. She clicked it open and began to read.

> *Hello Dani,*
>
> *Thanks so much for the pictures. It's nice to know that Maggie is doing well and that she's happy to be home.*
>
> *As for the car, it's a 1973 Karmann Ghia. As I mentioned, I'm not really planning to sell it but if your friend is ever up this way, just let me know. I'll be glad to show him the car.*
>
> *Thanks Again,*
> *Dale*

She hit reply and began to type:

> *Hello Dale,*
>
> *Thanks so much for the note. My friend and I will be up that way next weekend. Would it be O.K. if we stop by on Saturday? I really appreciate it. If you'd like, I could bring Maggie for a visit as well.*
>
> *Thanks Again,*
> *Dani*

Dani smiled and made a mental note to call Geoff in the morning.

Next, she opened a search engine and browsed for a list of islands in Michigan. As a native Michigander, she was astounded to learn that there were almost one hundred islands in the state. Oh, for crying out loud, she thought, how am I supposed to figure out which one it was? She remembered Faye's suggestion and searched for Michigan islands with a coyote population. The result made her grab for her cell phone.

Chapter
XII

"Coyote *is* the island," Dani practically shouted when Faye answered the call.

"What? Dani I'm barely onto the expressway, what are you talking about?"

"The coyotes aren't *on* the Island—they *are* the island!" she exclaimed. "There's an island in Michigan named Coyote Island! It's off the coast of Lake Huron and I'm sure it's the one. Nora said they were running a camp up there and listen to this," Dani began to read from the article she'd found:

Coyote Island is 3.5 square kilometers in area, more than 2 kilometers wide by 1 kilometer long. The island was purchased in 1972 by socialite Arthur Melden, heir to the immense Melden family fortune and son of former ambassador Brian Edward Melden. In August 1976, a child pornography ring was discovered operating on the island under the guise of a children's day camp called St. Francis Children's Sanctuary. As the proprietor, Melden allegedly flew the boys in his private plane to the island retreat.

Several members of the ring were also charged with first degree criminal sexual conduct for the rape of two boys in the nearby Fanny Lake region. Although no evidence could be found connecting Melden to the Fanny Lake incidents, a warrant was eventually issued for his arrest based on his involvement in the Coyote Island child pornography ring. However, by the time the warrant was issued, Melden had fled the country and all documentation potentially connecting him to the ring had been destroyed.

"Wow! So does the name Arthur Melden mean anything to you relative to the Millers or Dale?" Faye asked. "Have you seen it before in any of the other articles?"

"I haven't, no, but it does seem to me like Nora said something about an Arthur," Dani tried to recall what Nora had said and why the name seemed so familiar. "Right," she said, "Sir Arthur No Name!"

"Sorry?" Faye asked with a laugh.

"She couldn't remember the guy's last name so that's what we were calling him. But she said she thought he owned property on an island up north."

"'Owned property'," Faye snorted, "I guess so."

"Yeah, I don't think she realized that he owned the entire island. She thought he just had a cabin up there or something. I'm going to see what else I can find out about this guy and his island, maybe even make a trip up there to see it. Drive safe, I just wanted to let you know what I'd found out."

"Will do, thanks for letting me know. Good luck!"

After the call, Dani returned to her search engine. She put in the terms "Arthur Melden," "Coyote Island," and "Miller" then hit enter. The search returned only three results but each was a treasure trove. She hesitated only a moment before snatching her cell off the desk again.

"OK. Is this a joke?" Faye answered with feigned exasperation.

"I know, I'm sorry, but I've just found the missing link! Guess who was busted as an accomplice in the Coyote Island child porn ring?"

Faye didn't miss a beat with her reply, "Someone named Miller?"

"Exactly! Craig Miller was busted in connection with the Coyote Island child porn ring in 1976. He was found with eight rolls of film on his person when the police busted the ring."

"So now we're back to Craig Miller. We just have to figure out how Dale is related to it all. Was he ever on Coyote Island?"

"No idea," Dani replied, as she glanced at her watch. "But that's a question for another day. I'm off to bed so, I promise, no more phone calls tonight!"

"I have to say, I'm a little relieved to hear it, but call me tomorrow if you want."

"Will do, bye." Dani clicked off the phone, stood and stretched. At her feet, the two dogs did the same. "Ready to go up?" She followed them up the stairs and into the bedroom.

After Maggie joined the family, a nightly territory war had ensued on the bed with each dog vying for space. After the third such night, Dani had decreed that all dogs must sleep on the floor. Now, grudgingly, each dog chose a side and laid down on the carpeted floor near the bed. Dani slipped out of her clothes and pulled on warm, fleece pajamas then crawled under the covers and turned out the light.

As she began to doze off, Dani had the sensation of falling, as though she'd accidentally stepped off an unseen ledge. She reached out to stop her fall but grabbed only empty air.

Her body jerked in reaction and just as panic took hold, she felt warm limestone beneath her feet and there, in front of her, was Kōbō. "Oh thank goodness! You really frightened me. Sometimes I wish you'd just knock on my door like a normal human being." He smiled at her from his usual seat on the landing and she stepped forward to take the seat opposite his.

"Do I strike you as a 'normal human being'?" he asked.

She laughed, "Good point."

"Eventually, you will be able to hear me in your own mind, even in your waking mind, and you will know that it's me and this beautiful place will no longer be needed."

Dani immediately regretted the complaint. She loved this odd little landing and it made her sad to think she wouldn't be coming back to it.

As if sensing her thoughts Kōbō said, "That's not to say that we can't come back for a visit now and again." He smiled at her warmly.

She smiled in return and asked, "So why are we here today?"

"I wanted to thank you for all your hard work."

She looked confused. "But I haven't …"

"You invited Faye to your home and spent all that time working to know me better and to be able to communicate with me," interrupted Kōbō. "I wanted to say thank you."

"Oh," Dani said, surprised. "You're welcome. If I'm honest though, I didn't really think about that. I guess I was hoping that if I learned how to … ummm," she struggled to find the right words. "I guess I was hoping that if I could learn to hear you better, that maybe I'd be able to understand what happened to Jimmy Prince and the other children."

"A very reasonable assumption," he said with an approving nod.

Dani gave him a stern look. "You know, you're not the easiest person to understand, right?"

"Now you sound like my wife," he said, rolling his eyes at her.

"I didn't think monks could marry."

"I was not always a monk."

"What were you before you were a monk?" she asked.

Kōbō smiled at her playfully. "I had a truly fascinating life—several of them, actually—but this is not the time to discuss that. Now, there is another story that must be told."

"Back to the movie theater?" she asked with a sense of trepidation.

"No, I think not," he said. "Today, I would ask that you simply take a walk."

"A walk?" she repeated.

"Yes. If you take the stairs up," he pointed, indicating the stone staircase that led up from the landing to the top of the cliff, "you will see a path. Please follow the path until you come to the house. There will be only one house. There you will see what I need for you to see," he said.

"I'm afraid," she said honestly. "It's not easy to see all these things."

He looked at her with soft but serious dark eyes and said, in a voice that was not unkind, "So you can imagine how difficult it was to live through them."

Dani nodded in understanding, stood and climbed the stairs. She did not say goodbye to Kōbō for she understood now that he was with her always, even when he could not be seen. As she came to the top of the stairs, she followed a dirt path away from the landing and into a thick grove of olive trees. As she passed through the grove it became a forest and the trees in the forest were no longer olives but pines and maples and oaks. Along the path, needles and acorns bit into the soles of her bare feet. Although the woods were dense, the path through them was well worn and wide enough for two, perhaps even three adults to walk abreast. After what seemed like more than a mile, she saw a clearing ahead. She quickened her pace and as she approached, she could hear voices.

When she reached the clearing, she saw an exquisite home come into view. It was the color of cedar and from the ground level, tinted windows stretched in elegant arches that reflected the towering pines and lake beyond. An atrium of the same tinted glass extended from the front of the house. A deck large enough to accommodate a party of twenty or more extended off the second floor. A blue flagstone path leading away from the home was flanked by hostas, ferns, and astilbes.

A scream to her left pulled Dani's gaze away from the home and down toward the lake. Along the bank, two young boys were cowering from a tall, thin man who looked to be in his mid-thirties. He had horn-rimmed spectacles and his dark hair was closely cropped and parted to one side. Dani thought he looked vaguely familiar. He had a hold on the smaller of the two boys but the child was shoving at the man's legs, obviously trying to knock him off balance. The boy was shouting to his companion, urging him to run. By now, Dani knew that she could have no effect over the characters in these dreams. She'd been made to understand that she was only an observer, not a participant, and so she stood aside passively and watched the scene play out before her.

The second boy finally did run. He followed the edge of the lake to the trail and passed just a few feet in front of where Dani stood, picking up the path and following it back in the direction from which she'd just come. She turned her attention back to the small boy who was still struggling with the man by the lake. In a fit of anger and frustration, the man heaved the young boy off his feet and over his shoulder and then carted him around to the front of the house. Dani padded along after them, following the flagstone path for as long as she could before jumping onto the lawn and running along the side of the huge home. As she turned the corner, she saw the man stuff the child into the backseat of a black sedan, which pulled around and out the long, circular drive. Dani felt the same panic that she'd felt when little Jimmy Prince was driven away in the orange Karmann Ghia. The sedan rounded out behind the thick woods and disappeared from view.

Dani awoke with a start, turned on the light, and fumbled in her bedside table for her notebook and pen. When she'd recorded the dream, she picked up her cell phone from the bedside table and checked the time. It was half past three in the morning. She returned the phone to the table, curled up into the mound of pillows at the head of her bed, and fell back asleep. This time, it was a peaceful, dreamless sleep.

Early the next morning Dani phoned Geoff at the office.

"Aero Core Industries, Geoff Williams speaking."

"Hey Geoff, it's Dani. Sorry to catch you at work but I really need your help."

"Hey Dani! Sure, what do you need?"

"I need for you to pretend to be interested in a car and I need for you to go up north with me, not necessarily in that order."

Geoff laughed. "Come again?"

"It's a long story but I need an excuse to get another look at a car. I couldn't say that I wanted to see it because I've already seen it, sort of. So I told the owner that I had a friend who was interested in it, maybe even interested in buying it."

"Does this have anything to do with your new found *psychic* ability?" Dani winced. "And by the way, I'm not buying a car. Not even for you."

"You talked to Nora?"

"I did. I think she's worried about you and, after this conversation, I think I can see why."

Dani had anticipated this reaction from Geoff. He was sensible to a fault and she had known instinctively that he would never be persuaded to believe in Kōbō or his messages. "Does that mean you won't go with me?"

"To buy a used Karmann Ghia?"

"To *look* at a used Karmann Ghia," she corrected him. "The guy's already told me that he has no interest in selling. You just have to pretend to be very disappointed not to be able to buy it."

"I don't know, Dani," he moaned. She began to regret ever asking him but she could think of no one else. "You don't even know this guy. What if he's some kind of psychopath?"

"I was already in his house—alone—if he were going to do anything, wouldn't he have done it then?"

"I don't know that and neither do you!" Geoff countered.

She ignored the remark. "Would you rather I go alone?" She knew the trap she was setting for him and she knew that it was unfair, but she was determined to get another look at that car.

"No," he said grudgingly. "You know I don't. I'd never forgive myself if anything happened to you."

"So you'll go?"

"When and where?" he asked miserably.

"Saturday, early, I'll come by and pick you up at eight in the morning."

"Eight in the morning? On a Saturday?" he protested. "This little adventure of yours just keeps getting better and better!"

"Well then you'll *really* love this—after we look at the car, I want to take a trip to Coyote Island."

"Where and what is Coyote Island?" Geoff's tone had turned first from concerned to annoyed and was now becoming angry. Dani knew that she was pushing her luck but was unable to stop herself.

"It's an island in Lake Huron, just north of Fanny Lake. It used to be privately held but now it's owned by the state of Michigan. I need to have a look at it."

"Why?" he asked.

"I just do, Geoff," she persisted. "If you don't want to come, you don't have to but I'm going."

"Quit saying that as though I have a choice. You know I'm not letting you go up there alone." Although the gesture was chivalrous, his tone was far from it. Now Dani was becoming annoyed, even though she knew she had no right to be.

"I'll see you at eight on Saturday," she said, then hung up the phone. She set it aside and turned her attention to her in-box. While on the phone, she'd noticed an incoming message out of the corner of her eye. She realized now that it was a response from Dale. She clicked on it.

Good Morning Dani, he wrote. *I'm sorry, but this weekend is no good for me. I'll be in Chicago visiting family.*

"Son of a bitch," Dani cursed so loudly that she startled Gordie, who had been asleep at her feet. She continued reading.

Thanks again for your updates about Maggie. I'm glad to know she's doing well. Take Care, Dale

Dani noticed that he made no further mention of the car or of her interest in seeing it. She decided immediately that she would not mention this note to Geoff until they were well on their way up north. She also began to wonder if letting herself into an unlocked garage while the owner was in Chicago could be legally classified as breaking and entering. How could it be considered *breaking* and entering, she reasoned, if she didn't break anything? Perhaps it was merely trespassing, a simple misdemeanor. It only matters, she thought, if I get caught. "So I won't get caught!" she said to Gordie reasonably. He seemed skeptical.

Chapter XIII

At precisely eight the following Saturday morning, Dani pulled up in front of Geoff's house. As she pushed the car door open, she noticed him coming down from the porch toward her. She pulled the door closed again. He looked sleepy and annoyed. Dani took a deep breath and pressed a button to unlock his door. He had brought along a small cooler that he stuck behind his seat before climbing in next to her. He gave her a weary grin.

"Well, are you ready to do this, Nostradamus?"

"I don't appreciate the sarcasm," she grumbled, "but I do appreciate you coming along." She placed the car in reverse, put her right hand behind his seat and twisted around to see out the back window. She could feel his eyes on her and was acutely aware of the scars on her face. She backed out of the drive and as she returned her gaze toward the front of the car, their eyes met.

"Sorry," he whispered. "I promise, no more sarcasm. I'm just worried about you, Dani. I don't understand your obsession with these dead kids and I don't want to see you following them to the grave."

She lingered there with him for a moment longer, before turning her body forward and slipping the car into drive. "What do you have in that cooler?" she asked, forcing her voice to sound upbeat and nonchalant.

"Orange juice, fruit, and some pop. Want something?" he asked.

"Orange juice sounds good."

He unbuckled his belt and turned around in his seat to retrieve the drinks. He twisted the cap off a plastic bottle of fruit juice and handed it to her, then popped the tab on a can of cola for himself. He buckled himself back into the seat and began to fiddle with the radio until he found a station that he was sure they'd both like. He kept the volume low. "So, remind me again, what kind of car is it that I'm interested in buying?" he asked.

"A 1973 Volkswagen Karmann Ghia."

"Really?" he asked. "I never thought of myself as a Volkswagen guy, but OK. I guess the Karmann Ghia wasn't too bad. And why is this car so important?"

"Jimmy Prince was last seen talking to a guy in front of a bright orange Karmann Ghia and Craig Miller owned the exact same type of car."

"Craig Miller and several thousand other people in this country, right?"

"Maybe," Dani agreed reluctantly, "but how many of those were in the state of Michigan, in the county where Jimmy disappeared, during the time of his disappearance?" she asked. "A very, very small percentage," she continued, before he had a chance to interrupt.

"Alright," he conceded, "I'll give you that but I'm sure Craig Miller was not the only one."

"No, but of that very, very small percentage, how many also had a prior history of molestation charges involving young boys?"

Geoff raised his eyebrows and nodded. "OK, but what evidence do we have to suggest that this Dale person's car is the same car that Craig Miller drove? Not to mention the same car used to abduct Jimmy Prince—other than your dream," he added quickly.

"That's why we have to go back," Dani insisted, as though it were the only logical conclusion to be reached.

"And what? Let's say that this guy was involved in the Guardian murders and has a critical piece of evidence sitting in his garage for nearly forty years. What makes you think he's going to come clean about it now—to you? Why would he? Because some monk in a dream says as much?"

Dani felt a hot flush come over her face and angry tears beginning to sting the back of her eyes.

"Dani, I'm not trying to hurt you but you have to admit that it's far-fetched. It seems out of character that you'd throw yourself into something this … *out there*. Maybe you should speak to someone. You've been under a lot of strain lately."

"Geoff one thing has nothing to do with the other. Why on earth would you say something like that? I wish you'd stayed home." A stifling silence fell between them and they were nearly to Fanny Lake before Geoff spoke again.

"What time is he expecting us?"

Dani had become so engrossed in her own thoughts that she barely heard the question. "Who?" she asked, confused.

"What do you mean 'who'? Dale—what time is he expecting us?"

"Oh, right, he didn't say."

"He didn't say?"

"No, I just told him we'd be in the area and we'd stop by."

"How old is this guy?"

"I don't know. I didn't ask."

"Take a guess," he said, sharply.

"I'd guess early-mid sixties."

"So quite a bit older than you?"

"What does *that* have to do with anything?"

"I'm just wondering. You're going a long way to see this guy again …"

"What the hell, Geoff! Before you thought I was coming up here as some sort of PTSD symptom and now you're accusing me of chasing a guy? I think *you're* the one who needs therapy!"

Geoff's pale skin flushed pink. "I'm just trying to understand this, that's all."

"Your only job here is to keep me company and look at this car with me, that's it." They fell silent again until Dani was pulling through the center of town. As she neared the side street her heart began to pound and her palms began to sweat. She eased the car slowly around the bend in the gravel road and the white and burgundy house came into view. She began to scan the road, wondering where best to park the car when she heard Geoff ask, "Is that him?"

"Who?" she asked.

"What's with you today? Dale. Is that him?" He pointed across the street toward the white house where Dale emerged from the garage carrying a rake and a tall paper bag.

"Oh my God, what's he doing here?" she asked, turning her face from the window and meeting Geoff's surprised gaze.

"What do you mean, 'what's he doing here'? Aren't we meeting with him today?"

Dani pulled past the house, around the block and came back out onto the main road before pulling over. She turned to face Geoff but couldn't bring herself to meet his eyes.

"OK. What's going on?" he asked firmly.

"Well, I asked him if we could come by and see the car," she began.

"Yeah, and what did he say?" he demanded, leaning back in his seat and crossing his arms. He seemed to anticipate her response, which made her feel both relieved and annoyed.

"He said he was going to be in Chicago this weekend," she admitted quietly.

"He tells you that he's not going to be around and, of course, you then plan a trip up here to meet with him?"

"I thought if he were gone, I'd have a chance to sneak into the garage and take a look at the car."

"Sneak in and have a look at it? Dani, that's illegal. You were going to involve me in breaking and entering?"

"Of course not, and it wouldn't be breaking and entering so much as maybe just trespassing."

Geoff waved his hands about theatrically, "Oh well, it's *only* trespassing! What a relief, just a misdemeanor instead of a felony!"

"Oh stop being so dramatic. He's not in Chicago." She frowned. "Why is he not in Chicago?"

"Obviously, he didn't want to see you again."

"Do you think he's dodging me?"

"Isn't it obvious?" he asked with a laugh.

"Son of a bitch!" she cursed, starting the car and easing it back into traffic.

"So that's it? We drove all this way for nothing and now we're just going to turn around and go home?"

"Of course not," replied Dani. "We're going to Coyote Island next, remember?"

"What?!" shouted Geoff. "Dani, are you insane?"

"Geoff, we're right here. We have to keep going up the thumb to see if we can get a glimpse of Coyote Island."

"Why on earth would we need to do that?"

"Well, it's like you said! It would be crazy to come all this way for nothing then just turn around and go home," Dani argued meekly.

"I was thinking we could stop by the outlet mall or grab lunch but driving all the way up the thumb so that we can see a deserted island where a group of perverts molested young boys? That really wasn't my plan for the day, Dani. This is insane!"

The word made Dani wince. "Could we not call it that, please? I just want to get a look at it and we're almost there. I can't believe he lied to me," she complained again, shaking her head in disgust.

"Put yourself in his shoes. Some total stranger loses her dog—or at least tells you a convincing lie about losing her dog ..." Dani winced again, "and the next thing you know she's e-mailing you and trying to invite people over to see your car. Even if he's not involved in these crimes, he'd do well to avoid you but if he is trying to hide something—all the more reason!"

"He could have just told me no."

"He was probably just trying to get out of it politely. How could he have known that he was dealing with some whack job whose back-up plan would be breaking and entering?" Geoff growled.

"First I'm crazy and now I'm a whack job? Is that really what you think of me?" Dani found that she really wanted to know.

"I call them as I see them, Dani, and you have to admit, you've been acting pretty strange lately." She could tell that he was still angry but his tone had softened.

"I'm sorry, honestly. I never meant to pull you into this. I don't know why this is so important to me. I know it would be easier for me to just ignore it and go back to my life as it was before but I just can't stop thinking about little Jimmy and the others. They were just innocent kids until along came a monster and for all these years since, nobody's sticking up for them, for their families. Your sister's younger than you, right?"

"Right."

"How much younger?"

"Five years," his voice had grown quiet.

"So when you were fifteen, if some monster had snatched her off the street and did to her what he did to those little girls back in the '70s?"

He shook his head as if to shake away the thought. "I get it, Dani, I do."

"And then imagine that decades later you had to pay a small fortune just for information about your own sister's brutal murder because you couldn't get anyone to discuss the case with you. You couldn't even get the investigators and the politicians to do you the common courtesy of returning a phone call! Geoff, *somebody* needs to care about this. If that makes me a whack job then I guess I can live with that." Dani was so angry her hands were shaking.

Geoff's head hung low and his voice when he spoke was tight and unnatural. "I'm sorry, Dani. You're right. Someone needs to care. I don't think you're a whack job."

"Thank you," she said. "I appreciate that."

"Breaking and entering would have been pretty weird though, you've got to give me that!" he smiled at her playfully.

She laughed and the tension of the moment melted away, "Yeah, alright. I'll give you that. Maybe that wasn't my best laid plan."

"Do you really think it's necessary to go out to Coyote Island? What do you hope to find out there?" he asked, more seriously.

"It's not that I really expect to *find* anything. It's not about finding something. It's just about trying to see what they saw. To experience what they might have experienced. I can't explain it but I think it would help."

"Dani, no offense meant, but I don't see where walking on that island will help you understand the terror that those poor victims must have suffered."

"No, of course not, but ... look, Geoff, I know you think the psychic stuff is all rubbish and if it weren't going on inside my own head I can promise you that I'd agree. I'm just trying to better understand what they're showing me, that's all."

He nodded and said no more on the subject.

They passed the remainder of the drive talking about lighter subjects: Nora's split from her most recent boyfriend, their own nearly nonexistent love lives, and Geoff's ever-growing boredom with his job. The weather was cool and cloudy, and as they approached the tip of the thumb, the wind off the lake made the temperature cooler still. Along the beach at the very tip of Michigan's thumb they stopped at a diner for lunch. As an apology for the unplanned adventure, Dani again offered to treat.

They took a seat at a bright orange booth and after a short time the waitress arrived. She was a tired, cranky-looking woman and Dani guessed her to be in her mid-fifties. She wore a uniform that was the same bright orange color as the booth. Dani wondered if that might be a contributing factor to the woman's unpleasant attitude. She had long, listless hair pulled back in a ponytail that would have better suited a woman half her age. She brought them two glasses of water in plastic tumblers, set down the menus, and walked away without a word. Dani and Geoff exchanged a look and she stifled a giggle. A few moments later the waitress returned, pad in hand.

"Can I get you something?" she asked unceremoniously.

"Yes, I'll have the cheeseburger platter," Dani replied.

"Fries or onion rings with that?"

"Onion rings, please."

"Something to drink?"

"I'll have a diet, please."

"And for you?" she turned to Geoff.

"I'll have the same only with a root beer."

As the waitress wrote down their orders, Dani said, "Excuse me, do you know where we catch the ferry to Coyote Island?

She looked at Dani as though she'd spoken in some strange, foreign language. "The ferry to Coyote Island? There is no ferry to Coyote Island."

Dani was confused. "So how do we get over there?"

"You don't," she replied flatly.

Dani tried again, "Do you mean to say that we'd have to rent a boat to get onto the island?"

"No," she began, in a tone that suggested she was speaking to someone who was perhaps mentally challenged, "I'm saying there's no way to go to that island. There are too many rocks off the shore to approach it by boat and the landing strip hasn't been used in more than a decade." With that she turned her back on them and went back to the kitchen.

Reluctantly, Dani looked across the table. Geoff's face was buried in the palm of his hand and he was rubbing his forehead as if overcome by a sudden migraine. She was about to apologize when a tall man with a shaved head and thick, brown goatee approached them.

"Excuse me," he said, smiling warmly at Dani, "I didn't mean to eavesdrop but I heard you mention that you were interested in seeing Coyote Island?"

"We are," Dani replied anxiously. "Are you going there?"

"I am," he said, flashing the grin again and extending his hand to her. "Doug Woodmoore, Rainbow Color Tours."

"Danielle Sawyer," she replied, shaking his hand. "This is my friend, Geoff Williams." She motioned to Geoff, who had lifted his head out of his hand. Doug nodded briefly in his direction but did not turn.

"We've got a flight leaving in half an hour if you're interested."

"A flight? You fly to the island?" It was a possibility that she hadn't considered but would welcome, if it would get her to the island.

"No, unfortunately Bess was right about that. The airstrip on that island hasn't been maintained since the '80s. It's too dangerous to land there as it is. But we do fly over it. The colors are peaking this weekend and it's a beautiful view of the island. I can get you pretty low over it if you'd like."

To Dani's mind, the colors this far north were already well past their peak but she didn't argue the point. "Oh, '*over* it'," she repeated, feeling frustrated and disappointed.

"I'm afraid that's the best you'll be able to do short of trying to row a boat out there."

"How far out is it?" she asked hopefully.

"About ten miles."

She glanced at Geoff.

"Forget it," he said in a cold, flat tone that made it clear he would not be persuaded.

"When does the color tour leave again?"

"Half an hour. We've got two others going with us and we'll take a shuttle from here. If you're interested, it's forty dollars per person."

She glanced again at Geoff, her eyes pleading. "I'll treat," she offered.

He rolled his eyes and in a defeated voice said, "Fine."

Dani smiled triumphantly and dug into her purse for the money.

Half an hour later, Dani and Geoff stood out front of the restaurant. Geoff had been in such a rush to eat his cheeseburger platter that he'd dumped ketchup down the front of the cashmere sweater he was wearing and was now muttering under his breath and dabbing at the stain with a wet paper towel from the restroom. Standing with them was an elderly man in a flannel shirt and faded khaki trousers. He was chatting with a boy of about seven or eight. The boy wore blue jeans, an oversized hoodie sweatshirt and a Tiger's baseball cap that nearly hid his flaxen hair.

"Is the plane leaving from here, gramps?" he asked doubtfully, glancing around the nearly deserted parking lot.

"No, of course not, Joey. We're just waiting for Mr. Woodmoore to bring the shuttle around and then we'll go to the airport."

No sooner had he finished the thought than a white minivan pulled in front of them and stopped. On the side of the van, beneath an arching rainbow, the words *Rainbow Color Tours* were emblazoned in a bold, red font. Doug Woodmoore emerged from the driver's side and rushed around to where they stood. He slid the door open for his guests and invited them in with a flourish of his arm. Dani and Geoff pushed past the first row of seats and took their places at the back of the empty van. Young Joey and his grandfather climbed in next. When everyone was in, the tall man with the goatee slammed the side door shut and returned to the driver's seat. He maneuvered the van out of the small lot and back onto the main road.

"We'll be taking off today from the Stone City Air Harbor and will be flying over the entire Pointe Aux Barques area, where the colors are just beginning to peak. Dani rolled her eyes but held her tongue. We will also pass over the lighthouse, Coyote Island, and Turnip Rock. The entire flight will take just under an hour. Is there anyone here who has never flown before?" he asked the group, glancing back at them in the rearview mirror. Little Joey raised his hand.

"And are you excited to try?"

"Yeah!" Joey gave him an enthusiastic thumbs up and his grandfather patted the boy on the back.

"Great! What's your name, son?"

"Mine's Joey, what's yours?"

"You can call me Doug. Did you just eat your lunch, Joey?"

"Yep. I had fish and chips and gramps got me a chocolate milkshake," he smiled up at his grandfather.

"He did, eh? How nice of him." The driver frowned.

After about fifteen minutes, they turned down a dirt side street and Dani could see several hangars and an assortment of small, propeller-style aircraft. The van stopped in front of one such plane that was white with burgundy and blue stripes down either side. The group piled out of the van and Doug approached a second man, who was carrying a clipboard as he walked around the plane.

"Done with preflight?" he asked.

"Just finished," the man with the clipboard replied. "You're good to go."

"OK. Your chariot awaits!" Doug pulled open the door on the small plane and gestured inside. As the guests moved toward it, Doug laid a hand on Dani's shoulder and smiled at her. "Why don't you help me out today and serve as my copilot?"

"Really?" Dani asked with a flirtatious grin. "That'd be great!" Geoff shot her a sharp glare and she returned it with a smug grin.

Seeing the exchange, Doug gave Geoff a friendly pat on the shoulder, "Don't worry, I'll give her right back and meanwhile, you can take this seat right behind hers." Geoff glared at him but said nothing.

They piled into the small plane with Dani taking the seat next to the pilot and Geoff and Joey taking the seats immediately behind theirs, leaving Joey's grandfather relegated to the seat furthest back. They each put on a heavy pair of bulging headphones and pulled the small microphones in front of their mouths. Doug murmured quietly into his microphone and a few moments later the propeller roared to life. The plane taxied down the narrow runway and Dani found herself searching for trees along its border. There were none and Nora's words came back to her, *Who puts an airport in the middle of the woods? Wouldn't you hit the trees with the plane if you did that?* Dani frowned.

As the plane climbed, the hangar and the van grew small beneath them and what was left of the autumn foliage soon came into view. They swooped low over treetops bathed in tones of rusty orange, brilliant red, and warm yellow gold. Dani felt her stomach give a small lurch as the plane dipped down over the historic Pointe Aux Barques lighthouse, a stately, white structure topped with black, circular walkways and a rust-red lightning rod. As they passed overhead, Doug recited some of the history of the structure and the surrounding area, his voice coming through their headphones as his guests peered out the small windows at the landscape below. From there, Dani felt the plane bank west and they headed out along the coastline, flying low enough that Dani could make out little shops along the beach below. This late in the season, there were no boats to be seen on the water, only the white-capped waves and floating dots that she supposed were geese or some other hardy water fowl.

A short while later, the huge rock formation known as Turnip Rock could be seen ahead. The rock island rose precariously from the water's surface like a giant, sedimentary funnel. The narrowest point of the rock's structure was at its base, emerging from the lake's smooth surface. This narrow tip supported a continually expanding breadth of sandstone that rose twenty feet above the water. The enormous formation was topped by trees and vegetation, which were now flecked with the same brilliant autumn colors as the rest of the landscape. Dani wondered how many thousands of years would have to pass before the rock finally toppled over into the lake. The plane banked east and Turnip Rock and the nearby coastline faded from view. They were over the water now and beneath the plane she could see the white caps of the waves forming jagged lines across the dark surface of the lake.

Doug's voice filled her headphones. "Just ahead on your left, you will see Coyote Island. The island has changed hands several times over the years but now is owned by the state of Michigan. You'll notice that there is a landing strip on the north end of the island. Unfortunately, that strip has not been maintained for many years so it is not currently safe for use, although there has been some talk recently of restoring it."

Dani leaned forward and peered out her window. The island was shaped like an enormous comma punctuating the lake in a riotous mix of fall colors. Carved through the island's widest expanse of forest was a landing strip. For a moment, she thought her heart would stop beating. From this vantage point, she could see the airstrip clearly, cutting through the thick mass of trees like a scar through a hairy scalp. The only portion of the airstrip not completely surrounded by trees was the narrow western edge, which must have been the entrance for approaching planes. That edge bordered the rocky shoreline. Dani recognized it in an instant as the airstrip from her dreams and a chill shot through her that had nothing to do with the cool autumn air. Images flashed in her mind of running through dense woods, frightened and cold, desperate for an escape. As she stared out at the endless expanse of Lake Huron, Dani could see the hopelessness of it and she felt tears welling up in her eyes.

"Everything OK?" Doug asked from the seat beside her. "Not feeling air sick, are you?" He gave her a tentative look.

"No, no, I'm fine," Dani replied, forcing a cheerful tone back into her voice as they swooped past the island and it began to fade from view.

"Well you know the problem, don't you?"

Dani shrugged, looking confused.

"You've been neglecting your copilot duties! How about it? Would you care to give her a spin?"

She shook her head fervently. "No, I've never … I don't know how …"

"Oh come on, where's your sense of adventure?" he teased. "It's easy. Come on, I'll walk you through it. Just take the wheel."

Dani put her hands on the butterfly-shaped steering device that protruded from the instrument panel in front of her.

"Now, to make the aircraft climb, you just pull slowly and steadily back on the wheel like this," he demonstrated and the plane climbed slightly. "Then to bring her back down, all you have to do is reverse the motion," again he demonstrated. "Go ahead and give her a try," he said, smiling his encouragement.

Gripping the wheel tightly, Dani pulled it slowly and steadily toward her. The plane began to climb and the sky opened up before her. It was a wonderful feeling and Dani began to relax and let the island's horrible history slip away.

"Careful now," Doug's voice returned in her headphones. "If you climb too high, too fast, you'll stall the engine."

"Oh, gosh, I'm sorry," Dani stammered, and in one, swift movement she shoved the wheel away from her and back to its original position. As she did, the plane lurched downward and Dani could feel her lunch flop uncomfortably in her stomach. Indeed, her whole stomach seemed to flop forward, as though she were on a roller coaster. Behind Doug, little Joey retched violently and for the briefest moment, the remnants of his indulgent lunch seemed to float through the air. Sadly, a moment later, they landed on the very same cashmere sweater that had earlier been the victim of the ketchup stain. The cabin erupted in a storm of swearing, gagging, and tears. Poor Joey was mortified and cried for his grandfather, still buckled in at the back of the plane.

For the next twenty minutes, Dani sat meekly in her co-pilot's seat wishing she had a parachute, Doug mumbled and cursed despite the microphone, little Joey sobbed quietly and not a single passenger paid any attention to the lovely fall foliage. It was a relief to everyone when they finally landed and the foul-smelling guests poured out of the plane and back into the van for the return trip.

Before beginning the three-hour drive home, they stopped at a clothing store and Geoff purchased a thick, fleece sweatshirt, which he changed into immediately. With the putrid-smelling sweater in the trunk, the pair began the long drive home.

Chapter
XIV

As Halloween neared and then passed, the snow began to fall, lightly at first like light tufts of dandruff blowing over the barren landscape then, as winter truly took hold, it came in bitter torrents, piling up in huge mounds along the street and clogging Dani's narrow road. It was during these harsh winter months, when driving in Michigan quite literally became life threatening, that she was grateful to work from home. As the holidays approached, Dani grew busy with all the usual details of the holiday season. Thanksgiving came and went, ushering in weeks of Christmas shopping, wrapping, baking, and celebrating.

Although she continued her casual correspondence with Dale, she made no progress on her plan to see the Karmann Ghia again. She hinted repeatedly about wanting to see it, but it seemed he always had some excuse—a major snowfall had blocked the roads, visitors were expected in from out of town, or he was committed to attend a holiday party. If the excuses were to be believed, the shy man she'd met months before had suddenly become the hottest house guest in the state, an idea that Dani found difficult to believe.

Even more discouraging, it seemed that Kōbō had also abandoned her. After her ill-fated flight with Geoff and Joey, the messages just seemed to stop and she could find no way to reignite her investigation without additional information. On more than one occasion, she pulled the newspaper clipping that she'd saved out of her desk drawer. Lawrence Prince gazed up at her mournfully and the guilt of her inactivity gnawed at her. Throughout the month of December, she'd tell herself that as soon as the holidays were over, she'd take another trip out to see Dale—she'd force him to talk to her, somehow.

But as New Year's Eve came and went and Dani stowed the Christmas decorations for another year, she found her professional life consuming more and more of her time. In the Motor City, the peace and quiet of the annual holiday shutdown is followed almost immediately by the pomp and circumstance of the North American International Auto Show or NAIAS as it was known in the trade publications. Locals simply referred to it as the auto show and it was held each year in Cobo Hall, in the heart of Detroit.

For a full week prior to the main event, industry executives, insiders, and reporters flocked to Detroit to participate in a whole host of conferences, gala parties, and publicity events. One such event was the Global Automotive Congress, an international forum at which executives gave keynote speeches and the automotive elite gathered to discuss such topics as government regulation of fuel economy and the introduction of new technology into existing vehicle designs. For translators and interpreters, like Dani, the congress was a professional windfall.

Unfortunately, Mother Nature had conspired against the event planners by dumping more than a foot of heavy, wet snow on the city on the Sunday night prior to the start of the Congress. As Dani rolled over that Monday morning, she reached out to the window at the head of her bed and pulled back the drapes. A pristine blanket of glittering white snow reflected in the light from the street lamp below.

"Fuck!" she groaned, and let the curtain fall back into place. She pulled the comforter over her head and for a while longer she lay stubbornly in bed, a war raging between her lazy, sleepy self, who was not yet ready to face the snow blower, and her rational, responsible self, who knew that sleeping in any longer would certainly make her late for her first appointment. At last, her responsible self won out and she threw back the comforter and stood to greet the uncomfortably cold morning. Immediately, her lazy self began a new battle and she fought the urge to crawl back into bed. Instead, she went to her dresser and pulled on one pair of thin, nylon socks followed by two of thick wool. Over the socks, she pulled on stretchy, spandex leggings, cotton long johns and finally a pair of thick, denim jeans. She finished with a similar assortment of tops underneath a thick, wool sweater then went down to the kitchen. The dogs, as if sensing the frigid temperatures that awaited them outside, did not follow her.

In the kitchen, she made herself a thermos full of hot cocoa and began to sip it as she stared out the French doors at the pile of snow beyond. When she could delay no longer, she pulled on her heavy winter boots, a knit cap, a scarf and her heaviest winter coat. Lastly, she pulled on tight-fitting gloves that insulated her fingers, but which did not impede their dexterity. Feeling like a tick about to burst, she opened the door and stepped into the wet, crunching drift of snow directly in front of it. Immediately, she sank in up to her knees. She pushed her way through the drift to the garage where she fired up her ancient snow blower and headed out onto the drive.

Forty minutes later with the drive and walkways cleared, Dani showered, dressed in a professional, black pantsuit, put on her normal, thick mask of makeup and headed out. The roads were treacherous and the drive to the posh hotel and casino, where the Congress was being held, took nearly three times as long as usual. Dani arrived embarrassingly late and missed her first session completely. She had contracted with the conference center directly and the surly woman who checked her in made it quite plain that, were it not for the fact that so many of the others had called to cancel rather than face the drive in, she would certainly have been fired. As it was, however, they would allow her to stay and work the rest of the conference.

"How kind of you," Dani grumbled to herself as she walked away. "Allowing me to save your ass from an embarrassing lack of interpreters, you hideous cow!" She continued to mentally berate the woman as she skimmed the paperwork she'd just been given, which included the agenda for her next individual session and the names of everyone who had signed up for the congress itself. One name on that list jumped off the page at her and made her forget all about the surly woman. Halfway down the list of attendees she saw it, *Matthew Miller*. At first, Dani reasoned that it must be a coincidence. It was probably a common name and almost certainly not the same Matthew Miller; although this one, according to her paperwork, was also a Senior V.P. of Purchasing. Probably not a coincidence after all, thought Dani. Faye's words floated through her mind, "there's no such thing as coincidence. That only means your guide chose to remain anonymous."

For the first time since her arrival at the casino, Dani began to pay attention to the other participants gathered in the meeting room around her. Although she knew Matthew Miller's approximate age, she knew precious little else about the monster's elusive brother. Her eyes roamed from one man to the next, eliminating those who looked too old or too young and lingering on those she thought were the most likely candidates. She also noticed that the crowd was much thinner than it normally was for this event and wondered how many of the scheduled attendees had been deterred by the weather. Reluctantly, she gave up the search and headed into an adjoining room to begin her next appointment.

Throughout each seminar and speech, during the seemingly endless panel discussions, and especially during the long coffee breaks, Dani searched the sea of name tags streaming past her with no success. Finally, on the last day of the conference, when Dani still hadn't seen him, she approached a tall, elegant woman at the registration desk.

"Excuse me," she said to the woman whose name, according to the tag on her blouse, was Evelyn. "I noticed on the list of participants that Matthew Miller was scheduled to attend." Dani showed Evelyn the name on her paperwork as she spoke. "He's an old friend from high school," she lied, "and I was hoping to say hello."

Listening to, but not looking at, Dani the woman flipped through the pages of a binder on the table in front of her. She stopped at one and ran her finger down a column of names. "I'm so sorry. I don't show that he ever checked in. Probably the heavy snow," she explained apologetically. "It kept a lot of the scheduled participants away this year. You may want to keep an eye out at the auto show, though, especially the charity preview. Nobody misses the preview, not even during the snowy years." She gave her a polite smile and snapped her binder closed.

"Good to know," Dani said, returning the smile despite her disappointment. "I'll do that."

Although she had received two complimentary passes to the charity preview, an invitation-only cocktail party and media event that marked the official opening of the auto show, she had not intended to use them. She was not dating anyone in particular and so had no one to bring as a guest. More than that, though, cocktail dresses were seldom styled to hide her scars and those that were looked matronly and unflattering. Since the attack, she'd learned to hate shopping for new clothes. She dreaded the fluorescent lights and full-length mirrors. Still, for the chance to confront Matthew Miller, she was willing to endure it.

The last day of the Congress seemed to drag on forever. She'd been assigned to translate for a morbidly fat salesman from Brazil. Dani had not used her Portuguese for more than a year so her skills were rusty and slow. To keep up with his native speaker's pace, she had to lean in and listen very carefully. His breath was foul and he fingered his nose frequently, both of which disgusted her. She was more than a little relieved when the event finally came to a close and she was able to collect her check from the stern woman who had been so anxious to fire her on the first day.

Once at home, Dani popped a slice of leftover pizza into the microwave, picked up the phone, and dialed. Geoff picked up on the second ring.

"Hey Dani, how've you been? Did you have a good Christmas?"

"I did. You?" Dani couldn't help but feel a sense of dread. Normally, she would not hesitate to ask Geoff out, but he was notoriously standoffish when it came to any event that required formal dress, dancing, or small talk of any kind. Had she been inviting him to lunch at The Biscuit or hiking in a state park, she'd have felt confident in his acceptance, but a cocktail party surrounded by executives in black tie was not Geoff's thing and she found herself bracing for the rejection.

"Good, what's up?"

He seemed to be in a hurry. Another bad sign, thought Dani. "Well, there's a function coming up and I was hoping maybe you'd go with me." She felt like she was in high school, asking a boy to a dance. She was annoyed with him for the answer she knew he was about to give and with herself for asking in the first place.

"A *function*?" he repeated skeptically. "What kind of function?"

I knew it, she thought with annoyance. She found herself wishing she'd never called. "It's the Auto Show Charity Preview. It's a cocktail party at Cobo Hall. It's the best way to see the cars—no crowds to push through," she offered hopefully.

"A cocktail party? When is it?"

"Friday evening."

"Oh no, sorry," he said quickly. "This weekend I'm …" he hesitated, "I'm going skiing with a buddy of mine up north," he said finally. "We're driving up after work on Friday."

"Fine," she replied curtly.

"Maybe you should try Nora, she loves that kind of thing."

"Fine," Dani said again with no attempt to soften her tone. "Have fun skiing. Hope you don't break your neck." She ended the call with no further comment but did not set down the phone. She stared at it for a long moment, debating. Although she had considered Nora even before asking Geoff, she couldn't get past the dilemma such an invitation would pose for her. She knew that if she invited Nora and told her about Miller's possible attendance, Nora would never agree to go. If she invited her *without* telling her, Nora would feel that she'd been set up, and perhaps rightly so.

Dani took a deep breath then dialed.

"Hey woman!" Nora answered with her normal boisterous enthusiasm. "How've you been? How's the monk in your head?"

Dani grimaced. "Good. How are things with you? Did you have a good Christmas?"

"I did, thanks. You?"

"Me too. Hey, the reason that I'm calling is, I did some work for the auto show this year and they gave me two complimentary passes to the swanky cocktail party preview thing. Care to come with?" She did not mention Miller but promised herself that if Nora specifically asked, she'd tell her the truth.

"Swanky cocktail party? You bet, I'm there! What are you going to wear?"

Dani sighed heavily. "No idea. You know me, I'm kind of dreading that part of it."

"Oh, come on! You're a beautiful woman, even with the scars. I'm sure we can find you a dress that's just as beautiful. When's the party?"

"Friday night."

"OK. So tomorrow night—mall haul, how about it? I'll meet you up at The Crossing."

The Crossing, Dani knew, was an enormous outlet mall on I-75 between Nora's house and her own. "OK. You're on. Meet you in the food court at six?"

"Super! See you then and don't worry, we'll find you something great!"

Dani hung up the phone and sat stock still for a moment as a wave of guilt flooded over her. If it helps us find the truth, she thought, Nora will forgive me.

Chapter
XV

As they pulled up to Cobo Hall, a valet rushed forward to greet them and take the keys. During their excursion to the mall the previous day, Nora had tried on half a dozen dresses, each more stunning and flattering than the last. She eventually decided on a form-fitting strapless creation by Tadashi Shoji. It was made from a deep gunmetal gray silk that brought out the blue gray of her eyes. On either side, silver metallic paillette details ran from her hips to her bust and highlighted her flawless figure. She paired the frock with metallic, snakeskin D'Orsay pumps with a kitten heel. The young valet's eyes never left her as she stepped out of Dani's car.

On Nora's recommendation, Dani had selected a Monique Lhuillier sheath with a lace bodice and slim, pencil skirt. It had a high, boat neckline and long, lace sleeves that might have appeared matronly were it not for a flesh-toned lining with cutout details that appeared to offer glimpses of smooth, scar-free skin beneath. It hit just at her knee and she'd paired it with fishnet lace, Jimmy Choo pumps that were absurdly high and cost her more than she'd earned during that whole last, dismal day of the automotive Congress. She couldn't bring herself to care though. They were fabulous and made her feel like a queen—a very sexy queen. Standing in Nora's striking shadow, she did not feel as fierce as she might have otherwise, but she did feel more beautiful and confident than she had in a long while. Her scars were fairly well hidden and the dress showed off her trim waist and toned legs. Nora had selected the outfit for her and, as usual, her taste was impeccable.

They entered through the main doors where coat racks with uniformed attendants had been set up to take their wraps. They handed their coats to the attendant and from there were directed onto a waiting elevator that took them up to the main concourse of the show. In every direction, couples in formal wear lingered around shiny new cars parked on revolving platforms. Long-legged models in short, spandex outfits motioned to the vehicles as though they were the grand prize in a game show giveaway. As the two ladies threaded their way through the crowd, their senses were bombarded by pounding music, the smell of sweet treats, and the blinding glare of neon lights bouncing off every surface in the immense exhibition hall. At one display, a giant production robot was posed moving a car door into position. At another, an SUV had been suspended upside down from the ceiling. A few brave souls crossed beneath it but most skirted the perimeter, glancing up at the vehicle over their heads in mild curiosity.

Dani and Nora moved from display to display accepting free gifts where they were offered and using a tiny, plastic knife to cut pieces off a brick of Mackinac Island fudge that they'd bought to share. The sweet-smelling confection was a staple at the auto show and had always been Dani's favorite part of the event.

As a child, she had accompanied her father, a mechanical engineer for one of the Big Three, as the major US car manufacturers were then known, to the auto show every year. She realized years later that the event had been a professional obligation for him but, as he so often did, he had used it as an opportunity to expose his children to the profession that he loved. With the sort of enthusiasm that only a mechanical engineer could have, he'd prattle on about engines and exhaust systems and acceleration. As a young girl, she'd wanted to make her father proud and so she'd listen intently, having no earthly clue what it all meant, but trying desperately to appear as if she did. When she was a teenager, she'd simply nod along, throwing in the occasional "uh-huh" while scoping out the perimeter in search of a fudge shop. Now, as an adult, she'd developed her own appreciation for the unique beauty of a sleek sports car. She had also developed her own professional obligations for attending the event, and she caught herself prattling on to Nora about the introduction of aluminum in place of steel body parts and the headaches it must surely be causing for the line workers and the dealership network alike. She noticed that Nora was nodding along, throwing in the occasional "uh-huh" and pulling chunks of fudge off the brick they were sharing. She smiled to herself.

While standing in front of the Ferrari display, dreaming of a car she'd never own, Dani heard someone calling her name. She turned to find a tall, broad chested, dark-complected man in his mid-thirties making his way through the crowd in her direction. He waved at her. Nora leaned in and whispered, "Nice! Who's that?"

"Married," was all Dani had time to say in response before he was standing in front of them. "Tom, how great to see you!" She gave him a quick hug and then turned with him toward Nora. "Tom, this is my good friend, Nora

Fontana," she gestured in Nora's direction. "Nora, this is Tom Montgomery, one of my translation clients. Tom works for *Auto World Weekly*, it's a trade magazine for the auto industry." Nora shook his hand, smiled at him politely and then turned back to the display without a word to say.

"So, Tom, how's your wife? I'm so sorry, I've forgotten her name. Sarah, is it?"

"It is," he said nodding, "but she's not."

"Sorry?"

"She's not my wife anymore or, at least, she won't be soon enough. We're going through a divorce." Before Dani could form a proper response, Nora had spun on her heel and inserted herself back into the conversation.

"Oh, that's just awful. I'm so sorry to hear it," she cooed sympathetically.

"Uh, yeah, that's just what I was thinking," Dani put in meekly. Tom seemed amused.

"Well, we got married young and it hasn't been working for a while now. The good news is, we don't have kids so it should be a fairly simple divorce, I hope." Nora moved closer. "So have you guys been here long?" he asked.

"Not too long. I have to confess, I'm a little disappointed. Normally you see more of the celebrity bigwigs at the charity preview," Dani remarked, stealing a sideways glance at Nora, who was stealing a sideways glance at Tom.

"They're all down at the hot rod exhibit. I've just come from there myself. Have you been down there yet?"

"No, I didn't know it was going on. Where's that at?"

"It's down on two. Just go to the elevators," he pointed to the far end of the hall, "and take one down to the second floor. They're giving away a motorcycle and there's a big presentation going on so everyone's down there. You can't miss it."

"Why aren't you down there? Not the motorcycle type?" Nora asked with a playful grin.

"Well, I'm not the one covering that area and I didn't feel like fighting the crowd if I could avoid it," he returned the smile.

"Well, we're brave," Dani teased. "We're going to chance it." Nora glared at her from behind Tom's broad shoulders. Dani knew that her flirtatious friend would rather have stayed right where she was but Dani was anxious to look for Matthew Miller and, perhaps just as pressing, she was anxious *not* to play the role of the third wheel for the entire evening. "Let me know if you need any help translating any of this," she called back to Tom, indicating the activity around them with a wave of her hand.

"Will do," he called back. "Good luck down there. Hope you win the bike!"

"Tell me again why we're leaving the cute reporter guy for a crowded motorcycle drawing?" Nora asked unhappily as they made their way to the elevators.

"Because I'm trying to make new business contacts and you were just trying to make the cute reporter guy!"

Nora burst out laughing and smacked Dani with her clutch. "You're awful!"

As they approached the bank of elevators, the doors on one were just beginning to close. "Hold the elevator!" Dani shouted, although the car appeared to be empty. She got to the door with just enough time to stick her foot between the closing panels and pry them back open. Nora was also sprinting for the door and no sooner had Dani pried it open then Nora came piling into the elevator after her. The two were giggling so much that they did not, at first, notice the only other occupant in the car, who was standing alone in the corner nearest the control panel. Nora was the first to notice him and Dani heard the gasp even before she'd seen its origin. She turned and saw the most striking man she'd ever encountered staring back at them. Dani, at first, thought Nora's gasp had been only a woman's natural reaction to the sight of this extraordinarily attractive man.

He wore a tailored worsted wool suit in black with a slight herringbone pattern. Rather than a tie, he wore a mandarin collared tuxedo shirt with smoky gray button covers that reflected the light. The look was at once both classic and unique. His eyes were a deep blue and rimmed heavily with jet black lashes. His full, short hair was the color of autumn wheat, as was the five o'clock shadow that now covered his sharp jawline. His lips were full and sensuous and smiling ever so slightly at Nora.

Dani glanced from the stranger to Nora, who was frozen in place, gaping at him. Dani had never known her to become so unnerved at the sight of a handsome man, not even one as exceptionally handsome as the gentleman standing before them now. He was the first to speak.

"Nora, oh my God, hi!" he greeted her warmly, coming forward to pull her into an embrace. For the first time since their friendship began, Dani felt a pang of jealousy toward her. "How long's it been? What have you been up to?"

As he released her, Nora finally found her voice. "Good," she replied softly, "I'm good, thanks Matt." She emphasized the name and shot Dani a hard glance over his shoulder. The implication was, at first, lost on her. Nora turned to face her friend. "Dani," she said, "this is Matthew Miller." Dani tried unsuccessfully to keep the shock off her face. "Matt," she said, turning back to the man in the expensive suit, "this is my friend, Danielle Sawyer. She's a translator."

"Really? What do you translate?"

"You," Dani replied before she could stop herself.

"Excuse me?" he laughed, flashing his perfect, white teeth.

Dani blushed, "Sorry, I mean I translated an interview that you did for *Auto World Weekly* a while back. My friend, Tom Montgomery, set it up."

"Oh right! So you translate Spanish to English then?"

"Yes, among other languages," she replied, still unsettled by the mere sight of him and the thought of his family history. Although Dani knew that he must be at least five years her senior, he looked ten years her junior.

"This is so odd," Nora said. "I swear I was just thinking of you the other day."

"You were?" He seemed flattered.

"Yeah, Dani and I were just up snowmobiling in the Fanny Lake area," she lied. "It made me think about your family's property up there. Do you still get up to Fanny Lake?" Dani noticed an edge to her voice that seemed almost to be taunting him.

"No," he replied casually, either unaware of the tone or simply unconcerned by it. "We sold off the cottage years ago."

"Oh, that's a shame. Do you know who we ran into up there?" She did not wait for his response. "Dale Rizzo. You knew him, didn't you?" Miller flinched ever so slightly on hearing the name, as if poked by an unseen thorn, but recovered quickly. "Seems to me, he was a friend of your brother's, wasn't he?" Nora continued. "Speaking of which, I heard that your brother passed away. I'm very sorry for your loss." Nora, rather unconvincingly, affected the air of a friend expressing condolences to the bereaved. "That must have been a terrible shock for you."

For just a moment, Miller lost his cool composure, "Thanks, but, of course, that's been years ago now," he replied sharply.

"Why do you suppose he did it?" she persisted, maintaining an expression of innocent concern.

"Oh, who knows with those things," he shrugged. "Everyone has their demons and Craig had more than most."

The elevator doors parted again and without hesitation, Matthew Miller seized the opportunity to escape.

"Great to see you again, Nora," he said with a slight nod of his head. He flashed his beautiful, bright smile at Dani for a second time and added, "Nice to meet you." Dani hated herself for the thrill it still gave her. He slipped through the doors in a heartbeat and was lost in the bustling crowd.

As the elevator doors closed again, Nora spun on her heel and rounded on her friend. "What the hell was *that*?" she snarled.

Dani stared at her, completely caught off guard. "What the hell was what?" she asked.

"Did you know he was going to be here?" she demanded.

Dani remembered, with a pang of guilt, the participants' list that she'd seen with Miller's name on it. She shoved the thought aside. "Here? In this elevator?" she asked, dodging the true intent of the question.

"You know what I mean, Dani," she shouted, her voice beginning to tremble. "Am I supposed to believe that it's just some remarkable coincidence that Matt showed up here, now?"

"Coincidence is simply the end result of a guide choosing to remain anonymous," Dani replied, remembering the explanation Faye had given her during their last meeting.

Nora glared at her. "Do me a favor, keep your psychic bullshit to yourself, okay?"

"Nora, you weren't even my first choice as a guest for this thing. I invited Geoff first. Ask him yourself if you don't believe me. You saw Miller's reaction when we met. I've never met the man before in my life. How would I know he planned to be here?"

Nora's cheeks reddened and she shrugged. "Beats me, you're the one claiming all the psychic connections," she muttered angrily.

"Well, I can't speak for Kōbō but I can assure you that I had no idea that he was here. He sure didn't like hearing Dale's name though, did he?"

She shook her head, "No, he did not. I have to admit, Dani, I think you might be right. I think Dale's the one they used to visit at Fanny Lake. So does that help your investigation somehow?"

"Well, if nothing else, maybe it will finally give me a path to confronting Dale. I've been waiting for some proof that he's involved, other than the dreams. If even the cool and collected Mr. Matthew Miller cracks at the memory of their acquaintance then I'm sure Dale will. He has no pretense at all about him."

The doors parted again and they were back where they'd started. They stepped off the elevator and spied Tom Montgomery, buying a brick of fudge at a nearby stand. Nora looked at Dani beseechingly. Dani had to laugh. "Fine!" she conceded, "seems the guides want you two together."

They spent the rest of the evening snacking on fudge and checking out the newest sports cars. By evening's end, Nora had Tom's number and was sure she'd be seeing him again soon. Dani found herself scanning the huge hall for any sign of Matthew Miller but did not see him again, at least not that evening.

Dani arrived home late from the cocktail party, having dropped Nora off before returning home herself. As she undressed, she thought about their encounter with Matthew Miller. She was now absolutely convinced that Dale Rizzo was an important piece to her puzzle. She was also certain that if she gave him the chance to continue avoiding her, he would. As she slipped into bed, she made her decision. Ready or not, Mr. Rizzo, we're going to talk, she thought as she switched out the light.

As sleep overtook her, Dani found herself at the top of a very familiar stairway. The thought of seeing Kōbō again made Dani feel surprisingly happy. So happy, in fact, that she forgot her usual fear of the narrow steps and so took them two at a time. When she approached her chaise, he was smiling up at her.

"My goodness, you seem very energetic this evening!" Kōbō said by way of a greeting.

"It's nice to see you again. Where have you been?"

"As I told you once before Dani, you don't need to see me to be sure that I am with you. Sometimes, I choose to remain anonymous." He gave her a playful wink.

"So Faye was right?"

He nodded, looking very pleased. "Faye is a very clever woman. I'm glad that you're learning to trust her, and yourself."

"So why have you brought me here tonight?"

"Can you guess why?"

"There's something more that I need to know? Maybe about Dale or Matthew Miller?"

"Both Dale and Matthew are still alive and now you have met them both. Should you have questions for them, you should ask them yourself. What I have to show you tonight has more to do with those who cannot speak for themselves."

For the first time since meeting Kōbō, Dani began to wonder about his sources. "Do you talk to the ones that aren't alive? Jimmy Prince, Marty Stevens, the girls? Do you visit with them like you visit with me?"

"They speak to me. It is not the same as when you and I speak but they do speak to me and I pass the messages along. You will find tonight's message waiting for you at the top of the staircase." He pointed back the way she'd come and she understood herself to be dismissed. Kōbō's answer to Dani's question left her unsettled but she could not have said why. Nevertheless, she did as she was bidden. She rose and climbed the stairs back to the top of the cliff.

At the top of the stairs, she saw that the villa and the wide expanse of gardens in front had transformed into the suburban front yard of a very impressive estate. Directly in front of her was a large, two-tiered fountain that stood in the center of a circular drive. The building itself was austere white stone with arching, tinted windows. An archway to the entrance mirrored the architecture of the windows and was crowned by a massive light fixture that was nearly as tall as Dani. As she approached the entryway, she noticed that the door was ajar. She pushed it open far enough to peer into the beautiful home. Within, the glow of reflective, polished marble was nearly blinding as it shone beneath the light of a crystal chandelier above.

Dani's sleeping mind knew that in Kōbō's dreams, she was only a powerless observer, who was neither seen nor heard. Nevertheless, she felt compelled to observe common courtesies. "Hello?" she called out. "Is anyone home?" As soon as the words escaped her lips, she suddenly realized that she had no idea what she'd do or say if someone were to actually respond. She stood for a moment frozen, praying for silence. She did not receive it. Nor, however, did she receive a direct reply. Instead, what she heard was an argument from somewhere above her current position. She took a deep breath and then a step forward. She closed the door behind her and stepped as quietly as possible across the mosaic floor that covered the foyer. She stole silently up the winding, marble staircase. At the top, she paused again to listen. The voices were louder now and she could make out what they were saying.

"Your actions have brought hell's wrath down on this family and on that of Mr. Melden as well," a very angry male voice was shouting. "Do you think I don't know it was you? Do you think the authorities are so blind that they couldn't figure it out? It's one thing to have a taste for boys, Craig, even young boys so long as the boys, or at least their parents, are willing. But murder? Have you no self-control at all?"

"Oh, and you and Art are going to lecture *me* on self-control now? Is that it? If either of you had any self-control, maybe I wouldn't have a taste for boys at all," a second voice fired back. "Face it, you made me the man I am today!"

The voices were coming from down a hallway on Dani's right. Terrified but determined to get a look at the men who were speaking, Dani crept silently down the hall to the first door on her left, where the voices seemed loudest. She stood with her back to the wall and peered in. What she saw was a large bedroom with stark, white walls and navy blue carpet. Covering the bed was a navy and red plaid bedspread and seated on that was a portly man in his early twenties with a beard and long, unkempt hair. Standing over him was a towering, slender figure with silver hair and broad shoulders. He wore thick glasses and a scowl.

"You're not a man, you're a monster! Don't blame your perversions on me," he was saying, his deep, commanding voice boomed off the walls, although he kept his composure. "The blood of those children is on your hands, not mine."

"Right, it's not blood you prefer to have on your hands, although I'm pretty sure the parents would find your preferences no less perverted," the younger man shot back.

Dani recognized the man on the bed from the many pictures she'd seen of him online and from her own terrifying nightmares. He was Craig Miller.

"I will not stand here and endure such accusations from my own son in my own home," the older man replied. "I've bailed you out before but I will not do it again, not from this."

Craig Miller choked on an angry laugh. "If I go down, you go down. You and Melden and all the rest of your perverted cronies—I'll take every last one of you down with me and you full, fucking well know it!" He was screaming now, his voice thick with hatred for his father. "That's why you'll keep bailing me out!"

His father glared at him for a long moment before he replied. When he spoke again, his voice was ice. "You won't be taking anyone down. If you cannot control yourself, you will leave me no other choice but to control the situation myself." Dani saw him turn to leave through the door where she was listening and an impulse to flee raced through her dreaming mind.

She awoke with a start, feeling disoriented. She remained still and silent, submerged under the comforter, trying to figure out where she was. A moment later, she felt the comforter shift beside her and then a cold nose poked tentatively at her cheek. She smiled to herself then sat up on the pillows. Maggie was standing near her bedside, staring up at her. She bent down to nuzzle the dog's soft head. "I'm OK. Thanks for the concern."

The dog seemed satisfied and returned to her spot on the rug near the bed.

Dani clicked on the light, took the notebook out of her bedside table and recorded the dream. When she'd completed the entry, she clicked off the light, pulled up the covers, and went back to sleep.

Chapter
XVI

The next day, Dani awoke early feeling alert and purposeful. She showered quickly, fed the dogs, and loaded Maggie into the car. The sky, to Dani's great relief, was clear and sunny with temperatures that hovered just above the point of freezing. The snow from the earlier storm had since been cleared from the roads. The clear skies followed her on the long drive to Fanny Lake and, by the early afternoon, she found herself back in front of the burgundy and white ranch home. She knew that if she hesitated, she would be giving her fears and doubts an opportunity to take hold and so she did not. She pulled into the drive, hopped out, and attached a leash to Maggie's collar. Maggie jumped out happily and began to sniff the landscape as Dani pulled her along up to the house.

At the front door, Dani rapped once and then again a few moments later. Out of the corner of her eye, she spied movement in the draperies near the large picture window in the living room. She knocked again, more insistently. Finally she called out, "Dale, I know you're in there and I really need to speak to you." As she raised her hand to knock for a fourth time, the door swung open.

"Dani, what are you doing here! I wasn't expecting you. The house is a mess and I'd really rather not …"

"I need to talk to you about Craig Miller," she said bluntly.

The color washed from Dale's face and he stared at her darkly. "I don't know who you mean …"

"Don't give me that. I spoke to Matthew Miller last night. I know you knew him." Dani's voice was determined.

He stood there, staring at her. His eyes were angry and his mouth was locked in a hard line across his face. Finally, he gestured her into the kitchen where Dani took a seat at the tiny, Formica table. Dale took the seat opposite hers and Maggie laid on the floor between them. Dale reached down and absently stroked her golden coat. The silence grew between them like lava seeping into the crevices of a volcano. Dani let it build. She knew the eruption was inevitable, that it was the result of more than three decades of suppressed truth and that it was not hers to force. Like Nora, Dale had been held hostage all these years by his own shame and embarrassment. He was an explosion waiting to happen and Dani knew that he must come to it on his own.

He raised his eyes, met hers then lowered them again. Nervously, he picked at a bit of ketchup that had dried on the tabletop. He stood, crossed the room, took a half-smoked cigar out of a jar on the counter, flipped on the gas stovetop, and leaned in for a light. A hazy cloud of smoke rose up and veiled his face.

"Is this going to bother you?" he asked, holding up the cigar.

"Not at all," she answered truthfully. "My father smokes them too."

He nodded. "Was it just a coincidence that Maggie ended up here?" he asked, pointing the cigar in the direction of the dog.

"Sorry?" Dani asked, genuinely confused.

"You heard me. Was it just a coincidence that your dog ended up in my garage or was that staged?"

"Staged?" she repeated incredulously. "Dale, you put the dog in your garage. Are you asking me if I trained my dog to run to your specific house and beg you to lock her in your garage?" Dani knew how ridiculous it sounded, they both did. "You know I didn't; but if I'm truthful, I don't think it was a coincidence either. I've come to understand that there are no coincidences. I was brought into your life for a reason, Dale. I'm the excuse you've always wanted but never had to confront this. To let the truth out so that you can get on with your life."

He leaned his head back and blew clouds of gray smoke into the air. He stared at it as he responded. "You make that sound like such a good thing, like it's some kind of relief."

"Isn't it?"

He shrugged. "Whatever else it is, it's the moment I've dreaded, the moment I've avoided most of my life. Don't you see?" he asked, fixing his gaze on her for the first time since her arrival. "There's no small way to do it. It's an all or nothing proposition—for everyone. That's the danger. I can't just divulge what I personally want to divulge. I can't just get myself off the hook, without putting myself and everyone else right back on it."

"You knew Matt Miller, didn't you? And Craig?"

He nodded, returning his gaze to the cigar, now held between his thumb and forefinger. He examined it for a moment, flicked the ash into the sink and put it back in his mouth. When he spoke next, he spoke around it. His words floating out in little gray puffs. "They used to spend their summers up here. They had a huge house out in the woods by the lake. They used to call it 'the cottage'," he choked on a laugh that stuck in his throat. "It was like calling Buckingham Palace a cottage. I knew Matt but really only through Craig. It was really Craig that I knew well. Craig and I were," he paused to take the cigar from his mouth again, "friends. We were friends."

"And did you know Arthur Melden?" she asked, watching his reaction carefully.

He met her gaze for the briefest instant but stared at the floor as he nodded.

It took Dani a moment to work up her nerve before she asked, in a voice that was barely above a whisper, "Dale, did Arthur ever take you to Coyote Island?"

Dale looked at her again for a long, silent moment. She had the sense that he was looking right through her, that he could somehow see the images that Kōbō had shown her.

"No," he said at last. "No, I've never been to Coyote Island."

She was sure he must be lying, attempting to hide a painful truth perhaps. "But you spent time with him?"

"With who? Art Melden?"

She nodded.

"Yeah, I spent time with Art. We both did. He was a friend and colleague of Mr. Miller's—Craig's dad. They sat on boards together, played golf—that sort of thing." He walked to the fridge and pulled it open. "Can I get you something to drink?" Dani shook her head. He pulled out a beer, twisted off the cap, and tossed it in the sink. He took a long sip from the bottle before he spoke again. "Sometimes Mr. Miller would have to leave in a hurry—for work or whatever. When he did, he'd sometimes ask Art to babysit." His tone was bitter.

"He was your babysitter?" Dani asked in disbelief.

"Yeah, you know, like a guardian for us kids while Miller was at work."

A chill ran through Dani and made her skin crawl.

"And he never brought you to his camp on Coyote Island?"

"Who told you about the camp?" He fixed her with an icy stare.

"I read about it on the Internet," she replied sheepishly.

"Ah, the *Internet*," he said the word as though cursing. "Not even the great and powerful Arthur Melden could have controlled that one."

"And he never took you there?" she asked again.

"No, he never took me there. In fact, I don't think he even owned that island back then. That came later. When I knew him, he'd stay at the Miller's cottage when he was in town. It was a huge estate on a secluded lake."

"Did he babysit for you often?"

Dale paced the floor restlessly, like a caged animal searching for a way out. "He only babysat for me a few times, then I stayed away from him."

"Why's that?" she asked.

He shot her a hard look. "If you know about Coyote Island, than I'm sure you already know why."

"Did he hurt you, Dale? Did he … did he …?" she couldn't bring herself to finish the thought aloud. He gave no response but folded his arms tight across his chest and paced, looking for an escape.

"Did he hurt or abuse Craig?"

To this he gave a stiff nod, never breaking stride as he paced across the room.

"Did Craig tell you that?"

Another stiff nod. He paced in quick, tight turns. Abruptly he stopped, turned, and whispered, "I saw it. I was … there. He … I mean, we …" He turned back to his pacing and left the thought trailing after him.

"I'm so sorry. Why didn't you ever tell anyone?"

He snorted and shook his head. "You just don't get it, do you? What makes you think that I didn't? I was a child, after all. Children still believe they'll be defended."

"So you did tell someone?"

He shrugged. "The first few times Melden tried something with me, I was ten. He wasn't blatant. He started out slowly, cautiously." His voice was strangled and so quiet that Dani had to strain to hear. "He'd lift us up to show us something and his hand would linger where it shouldn't have for just a few moments. Or we'd get into some mud the way boys do and need to be washed. It seemed odd to me that I should need a full bath just to clean the mud off my hands but he was the adult, I was the kid. I'd been taught not to question adults and back in those days—it wasn't like it is today."

Dani nodded her understanding.

He stared at his beer, swirling it in the bottle but not really seeing it. "That's the trick. Men like Melden, they start out small to see how a kid will react. If he can get away with small things, he'll build from there because now he knows that he's got a kid that's not going to put up a fight."

Dani thought about her dream. "You don't think Craig's dad was …" It seemed too sick to be possible so she stopped herself, but then took a deep breath and continued anyway, "Do you think he intentionally left you kids with him? Do you think he knew what Melden was?"

Dale's face contorted in a bitter sneer. "I can't say the question hasn't occurred to me. I've heard rumors since then. But I have no way of proving it and I'd certainly hope not." His teeth clenched for a moment before he continued.

"I was over at the Miller cottage once, when Melden was babysitting, and he had these chocolate candies. He invited us to have some. What kid's going to refuse chocolate, right? What we didn't know was, they were filled with tequila. When we had the first one, we didn't want to have any more. They tasted awful to Craig and me, but Melden kept pushing us to try another. He called them an acquired taste," he snorted, "like we understood what that meant. So we had another and then another. Before we knew it, we were laughing like mad and the floor seemed to move under us. It became a kind of game just to stand up. Then I looked over at Melden and he'd taken his pants off. He was standing there with his cock out and he was ..." He glanced up and then began pacing again. "I'd never seen an adult behave like that before. I was horrified. I tried to leave but I couldn't, my balance was all off and I could barely stand, much less run. He said he'd tell my mother that I'd broken into the Miller's liquor cabinet. He said, 'who do you think she'll believe—the drunk little boy or the respected businessman?' He pinned me to the couch and forced it into my mouth. He promised to break my teeth if I got them anywhere near it. It was horrible. I cried the whole time. He kept us there all afternoon. Over and over he'd make me do ..." he took a swig of his beer, "he'd make us do ... things." He stopped pacing at the sink and ran the cold water, splashing it over his face.

"Us? Was Craig there for this?"

He nodded. "Sometimes Melden would come after me, sometimes Craig. The one had to watch the other. Art liked it when the other little boys watched." His face twisted into a sneer. "I found out much later that Art had been abusing Craig for more than a year by then and he was even younger than I was. I think he was maybe eight or nine.

"Finally he locked us in a room. I still don't know where he went, maybe into the basement or some other part of the house, but he left us alone in one of the bedrooms. We were on the second floor so it would have been too high off the ground to jump out of the window safely, but there was a big tree outside the window and Craig knew it well. He pushed open the window, shoved out the screen, and climbed out into the tree. He helped me get out too. We climbed down to the ground and started to run but we were too slow. We were down by the edge of the lake when Melden figured out that we'd escaped and he came after us." He'd been staring into his beer bottle as he spoke but now he glanced up at her.

"In order to get off the property, you either had to follow the driveway down—and there were no trees to obscure the view by the driveway—or you had to find the dirt path that led through the woods next to the lake. That path led back onto the main road. We wanted the cover of the trees so we headed down toward the lake and we were going to follow the curve of the lake back to the woods. But Melden caught up to us. I was crying—terrified—he lunged for us. Craig was a brave little kid, he charged him if you can believe it. Grabbed for his legs and pushed on them to get him off balance. He yelled at me to run." Dale laughed in a way that seemed closer to a groan. "He just kept saying to me, 'Go Dale, I've got him. I'll hold him Dale—run!' I didn't know what to do, so I just ran. I made for that path through the woods, and I ran until I thought my legs would fall off. I finally made it back home and can you guess who was waiting for me there?"

"No!" Dani whispered. "Not …? He didn't go to your house?"

Dale nodded slowly. "He sure did. Craig told me later that the first thing he'd done after I got away was to throw Craig into the car and race over to my house. He knew I'd show up there eventually. By the time I arrived back home, he'd already told my mother that there'd been a horrible 'misunderstanding' and that he'd accidentally frightened me. He told her that I'd broken into Mr. Miller's liquor cabinet and implied that I was drunk and that I'd been giving liquor to Craig. Craig said he just sat there, kind of nodding along. Melden told my mom that I was confused and hysterical. Then he said that he was concerned for my welfare—good Samaritan that he was, you know?" Dale snorted bitterly. "He said he wanted to come over and make sure that I got back safely—said he felt bad that he hadn't kept a closer eye on me. Old Art was a pretty charming guy when he wanted to be and he definitely knew the power of a dollar. He started saying that she shouldn't blame me for *my* bad behavior. He began to tell her about what a bright young man I was and how I deserved a shot at a better life. He mentioned how he was the administrator of a charitable trust set up to help children whose families lacked the means to attend the best colleges. By the time I arrived, he was my mother's new best friend."

Dani felt a cold rage freeze in the pit of her stomach. "I don't understand. I didn't read anything about this incident on the Internet. Didn't they send him to prison? Didn't the police believe your mother?" Dani suspected the truth but she couldn't allow herself to believe it.

He looked at her for a long, silent moment.

"Your mother didn't tell the police, did she?"

He looked down at his beer and swirled it but said nothing.

Dani's rage exploded. "What kind of monster let's a man like that get away when the evidence is staring her in the face?"

"You don't understand, Dani," he began.

"Don't tell me that I don't understand. Since when is it naïve to believe that a mother should defend her son?"

"You don't get it, Dani. You just don't get it. Do you have any idea the sort of money the Melden family has? Art's grandfather was a senator. His father was an ambassador. These people don't have homes, they have *estates*." He shook his head and sipped his beer, looking out the window as he spoke. "When you're a kid, you believe the world is black and white. That bad guys should pay for their crimes and that good mothers should protect their children. As you get older, though, you realize that the world is a complicated place. My mom did what she thought was best for my future at the time and looking back on it now, she was probably right."

"He paid her off?" Dani felt sick.

"I prefer to think of it as settling out of court," he smiled sadly. "Try to see it from my mother's perspective. What would have happened if she had refused to go along with it? If she'd gone ahead and brought it to the police? Men like Arthur Melden *own* the police. They have them in their back pockets. This guy golfs with governors, belongs to the same exclusive clubs as judges and congressmen. He's donated millions to charities and even more to political campaigns. He was never going to fall because a broke, single woman claims he messed with her son. Melden would have waged war on her. He'd have dragged her name through the mud, implied she was a drug addict or a whore or both. In the end, she'd have been disgraced and I'd have been publicly humiliated. At least this way, we always had our home, I got to go to college and money was never an issue. Arthur

Melden never touched me again." His eyes were sad and haunted. "In a way, I got off a lot easier than Craig."

"What happened to Craig?" Dani asked, almost afraid to hear more.

"Craig told his parents what was happening right from the start, almost immediately after his dad first brought the guy home. His mother initially believed him and was outraged but his dad convinced her that Craig was just making it up. He punished him for 'making up lies' about such a well-respected man." Dale snorted his derision.

"Do you think he really believed that? Why would a little boy randomly make up a story like that?"

"Well, either his father knew what Melden really was, and called Craig a liar in order to cover up Melden's crime and his own complacency, or he simply wanted to believe that Craig was lying. I think some parents just don't want to admit that it could have happened to their kid and calling it a lie means it never really happened." He shook his head again. "Mr. Miller told his wife that Craig was an imaginative kid who'd made up a story about a man he didn't like. His mother eventually bought into it. Child abuse of this kind is the ultimate inconvenient truth. No one wants to believe that the rich and noble benefactor is actually a twisted pedophile and nobody wants to hear that their child has already been violated. It's almost better—easier—to convince yourself that it was just a big misunderstanding or a bad dream or whatever. We've seen it even with big-name celebrities. Folks don't want to believe it to be true and with the right enticement—the right story—almost anyone is willing to look the other way. 'Move along now, nothing to see here'," he waved his hand, affecting the air of a traffic cop at the scene of an accident.

"He made Craig apologize to Art. Can you imagine that? Being forced to apologize to your attacker for telling people that you'd been attacked?" Dale shook his head again, staring at the beer bottle in his hands. "Eventually Craig learned that if he brought other little boys over, Art would focus on them instead of him. So he'd go into town and befriend the local kids. That's where I came in."

"Oh my God, that's horrible! And yet you still refer to him as friend? How could you?"

"Well, first of all, I didn't learn the truth until years later and second, he was *eight*! What could you expect? Kids throw each other under the bus all the time to save themselves. At that age, it's just survival, especially with a man like Art Melden. By the time I knew the truth, I knew too much to blame him for it." He shrugged, as though in defeat. "That kind of abuse, combined with that kind of parental betrayal—especially at such a young age—it can really mess a kid up."

"Don't ask me to feel sorry for a man like Craig Miller."

"You said it," responded Dale, giving her a sideways glance, "not me."

She ignored the remark. "What did you say to Craig at the time though? After you came home to find Melden with your mom?"

"We didn't talk about it then. We were both so embarrassed and ashamed. Talking about it would have made it seem real and we didn't want it to be real."

"Did you ever tell your mother what really happened?"

"I was convinced she'd side with him and blame me. That she'd tell me that I was a filthy little boy and a drunk for eating the candies. You have to understand, Art was a well-respected guy in the community and he was an adult, a grown-up." He choked back a bitter little laugh. "If that kind of man tells a ten-year-old that it's all his fault, then it must be true. But I never went back to that house. I'm sure my mother knew something had happened, but we never spoke about it again."

"Did you ever see him again?"

"Art?" he asked.

She nodded.

"He used to show up at community events, local carnivals or fairs, that sort of thing. Once, when I was about fifteen, I was at a community carnival. There was a bathroom in the church and they'd opened it up during the carnival for public use. They had lemonade and cookies and things in the church so it was a bit of a gathering place. I'd gone in to use the bathroom. As I was coming out, Craig was going in. I hadn't seen him in a while and I stopped to say hello. What I didn't realize was that he was at the fair with Art. He walked up behind Craig and saw me. He told Craig to go get him some lemonade and there were people standing all around. Nobody wanted to make a scene," Dale laughed that sad, bitter laugh again. "I can't tell you how much these sickies get away with because nobody wants to make a scene. God forbid, right? Anyway, nobody wanted to make a scene so Craig went for the lemonade and I just stood there, frozen."

"Did he say anything to you?"

"He leaned in, right next to my ear and whispered that he missed me. He told me that he dreamed of touching my body and asked me to come back for a visit some time." Dale spun on his heel and started pacing again, staring at the floor as he moved. He took a long swig of beer before he continued, "Then Craig came back with the lemonade and I got the hell out of there."

"And what about the others? What about Jimmy Prince and Marty Stevens?" asked Dani. "Were they victims of Melden too, or ...?

"I've really struggled with that," he broke in before she could finish. "I've struggled with how to view Art and Craig and even myself. The blood of those kids—it's on all our hands. We didn't stop Arthur Melden. What if we had? What if we'd stopped him before Craig was beyond hope? Or what if I'd stopped Craig before …" He let the thought trail off. He puffed on the cigar he'd been holding then let it fall back into the jar on the counter and swallowed the last of the beer from the bottle. A shroud of regret and shame came over his face. "Craig abducted and killed those kids, I'm nearly certain of it."

"Maybe if your mom had gone to the police, maybe it would have ended there and then."

"Dani, there were who-knows-how-many before me and probably just as many after me. You're still thinking like a child. The world isn't black and white. It's a complicated place and monsters aren't born, they're created. Arthur messed with Craig from such an early age and his father did nothing—really nothing—to stop him or even to minimize the damage. He encouraged Craig to go with him. That really messed him up and I couldn't pretend that I didn't understand."

Dani took a deep, stabilizing breath. "What did you know about the kids? Did you know what Craig was doing as it was happening?"

Dale shook his head slowly. "I knew he'd been arrested for messing with little boys in the past. I begged him to seek help, to talk to someone. I couldn't forgive what he was doing, but I also couldn't forget what we'd been through together. He helped me get away. He stopped what was happening to me but no one ever stopped what was happening to him. I guess I felt guilty. I felt like he'd saved me by sacrificing himself. Then, as he got older, he became the predator that we had both feared as kids."

"Why?" Dani demanded. "I don't understand why."

"I'm not sure that I do either, but I've wondered before if it wasn't maybe a defense mechanism. If you're the predator, you're less likely to become the prey. I think, at least initially, that he found other little boys to offer up as a kind of bait, just so that he'd be left alone and then eventually, it became a way of life. I swear, I never knew he was the Guardian—not really, not for certain."

"But you suspected him, didn't you? I believe you strongly suspected him."

Dale gave her a sad look and nodded, almost impercep-tibly. "Sure I did. I even phoned in an anonymous tip. It was all I could bring myself to do. I couldn't bring myself to come forward—on the record—to the police."

"Why? Dale, you seem like a decent man. Why couldn't you have gone to the police, on the record?"

"You have to understand that, aside from the killing, what he did to those kids is what they did to us," Dale stared at his hands as he spoke. "They didn't stop Art and I didn't believe they would stop Craig."

"Aside from the killing?" Dani felt appalled and made no effort to hide it.

"What I mean to say is, I wish I still had your optimism—your faith in the system. I didn't then and I don't now. They had all kinds of signs and sources pointing to Craig. Did it matter? How many times did they give him a slap on the wrist for molesting kids? He was attached to the mighty Art Melden. They figured out what Art was doing up on Coyote Island. They knew—*knew*—that Melden was involved. Did they slap the cuffs on him right then and there and haul him off to prison? No, of course not. That might offend him! In-stead they waited and debated and finally called him up in advance and let him know that they intended to come and get him. A guy with that kind of money, with private planes at his disposal—what did they think he'd do? Sit around waiting for them to show up? Fuck no! He's going to get the hell out of Dodge and destroy every bit of evidence that they might otherwise have found. He knew it, they knew it—that's why they called and gave him the head's up. And you wonder why I didn't go to the police? I didn't because I know better, Dani. I know how wealth and prominence affect police procedure. People talk about Mr. Miller's wealth but he was nothing compared to Art—just another sell-out parent."

"Like your own?" Dani put in and then immediately regretted it.

His voice when he spoke was choked with anger and pain, "My mother was nothing like Victor Miller. She did what she had to do. She didn't have the pedigree or the credibility to stand up to a man like Art Melden. Victor Miller could have done something—should have done something—and just chose not to."

"Like you could do something now and choose not to?"

He gave her a hurt look. "What does it matter now? It's over."

"It's not over. What about those families? What about the other victims of Arthur and maybe of Craig as well? You know better than anyone that the abused sometimes become the abusers, just as Craig did. How many other monsters must be created before somebody puts a stop to it?"

"What could I do, Dani? Arthur's dead. Craig's dead. Victor Miller's dead. There's nobody left to prosecute."

"But there is still evidence to be uncovered—proof to be found. Who knows how many coconspirators Art and Craig had? How many perverts participated in the child porn ring on that island? How many crooked politicians or cops covered up their crimes? Are you seriously going to try to convince me that there's no one left to prosecute here?" He looked at her but said nothing. "Dale, is that Craig Miller's car in your garage?"

Chapter
XVII

Together, Dale and Dani stood in Dale's garage staring at the covered vehicle before them as if it were a cursed tomb, which, for all practical purposes, it was.

"Do you want me to open it up for you?" he asked.

"No," Dani nearly shouted. "I don't know much about forensics but I know enough to think that we should be trying to preserve whatever we can inside that car. When was the last time you drove it?" Dani asked.

"I've never driven it," Dale replied quickly.

Dani looked at him in disbelief. "You've had this car in your garage this entire time and you've never driven it?"

"Well, it's not really mine to drive."

"Because you don't actually own it legally?"

"Well," he hesitated, "I never said it wasn't legally mine."

"Yes you did," she insisted. "The first time we met you said that it was not yours to sell."

"Well, it's *not* mine to sell. Craig transferred the title over to me before he died but I don't think—in fact, I'm absolutely certain—that he didn't want me to use it or to sell it."

"What then?" asked Dani.

Dale shifted his weight nervously. "He wanted me to hide it, to preserve it."

"To hide it? From the police?" Dani asked.

Dale shook his head. "Toward the end of his life, Craig was convinced that someone was after him. Not the police—someone connected to Melden or his father, I think," he replied. "You have to understand that his crimes were drawing a lot of attention. He risked putting a very public spotlight on the very private lives of some very, very wealthy pedophiles. They wanted him out of the picture, before their crimes became public knowledge. Craig was a man at war with himself. He hated the monster he'd become but he couldn't control himself. It was a compulsion. I think he wanted to be caught, wanted people to know what was going on, so that they'd stop him and maybe Melden and his group of perverts as well. I think the perverts decided not to give him the chance."

"You think Melden murdered Craig? Or maybe his own father?" Dani thought again about the argument from her dream.

"Well, I'm not suggesting that they did it themselves. They'd have people for that but I do think they were ultimately responsible, one of the two anyway."

"You mean someone hired a hitman?" Dani knew that there was conjecture about Miller's alleged suicide but she'd never allowed her imagination to consider the possibility of a hit. "You mean like, with the mob or something?"

Dale nodded. "That's exactly what I mean. He was shot between the eyes. There was no gunpowder residue found on his hands and his hands were *under* the blankets when they found him. How do you shoot yourself between the eyes then set the gun down and put your hands under the blanket—all without getting gunpowder on your hands?"

Dani could only stare at him, mouth gaping.

"Did you hear how they found him?"

"The family lawyer found him, didn't he?"

"The family lawyer found him because his brother called him and told him to go over and check on Craig. A neighbor who knew Matt called to say that the newspapers were piling up at the front door of his parents' house and that no one had seen or heard from Craig in a while. She suggested that he might want to check up on his brother. Their parents were in Italy at the time. Matt claims that he tried to get Craig on the phone and when he didn't pick up, he called the lawyer and asked him to go over and check. Do you have a brother, Dani?"

"Three," she replied.

"If you couldn't get one on the phone, what would you do?"

"I'd go over and check up on him."

"You wouldn't call someone else and tell them to go check on him?"

"No, why would I? I'd want to see for myself that he was OK. I'd want to know what was going on."

"Exactly. Unless, of course, you already knew."

"You think Matt knew? Do you think he was involved?"

He shrugged. "I don't know for certain what Matt knew. It just seems strange to me. I've also wondered how Matt managed to stay clear of Melden. More to the point, I've wondered *if* he managed to steer clear of Melden."

"You think he was abused as well?"

"Again, I can't be sure. One thing I can be sure of and that is that Craig's family would have been anxious to make the whole Guardian connection go away as quickly and quietly as possible. At an absolute minimum, he was a public disgrace and a threat to their standing in the community."

"I think Craig knew that this car could link a lot of people to a lot of criminal activity, and I think he wanted to make sure that happened. I think that's why he left it to me. He had another car so he didn't need it, and if anything happened to him, he wanted to leave behind a way to bring them all down," he stared at his feet as he spoke. "But I let him down. I let them all down. I let my own shame and embarrassment stop me from doing the task he'd left to me, so the car's just been sitting out here."

"But by turning in the car, he'd have linked himself to the crimes as well. Giving up the car meant giving up himself." Dani paced in a slow circle around the car as she spoke, peering in the windows, her hands tucked into her pockets.

"I don't think it mattered to him then and I know it doesn't matter to me now. He's dead, the Guardian murders stopped and his father and Melden went about their horrible little lives. Craig lived a tortured, wretched life and one way or another, it's over now. If this car helps get his story out there, if it helps to expose the monsters—*all* the monsters—then I think that's a good thing. It's long past time that I stopped worrying about what secrets might come out."

"That's wonderful," Dani sighed in relief. "So you're ready to turn it over?"

"Not quite. You have to remember that Craig's brother is still out there. Melden's rich relatives are still there. All those cops and all those politicians who need to hide their own dirty little secrets—or just plain mistakes—are still out there. If we turn over this car, it's just going to become one more dead end in an investigation that's always been littered with them. I don't trust the cops, Dani. I don't trust any of them."

"Lucky for you," she said with a mischievous grin, "I don't plan on taking it to the cops."

He looked at her, confused. "What then?" he asked.

"Have you ever heard of the show *Suspicion?*"

"No."

"It's a true crime show that profiles the prime suspect or suspects in cold case files, and they use their own forensic teams to re-examine the evidence. I've done some translation work for them before and I know the director. I'm sure I can get him to take a look at the case, and I'm absolutely certain he'd be willing to have his own forensics team go through the car. If I can get them to take a look at it, you'll give them access?"

"Absolutely," Dale agreed. "I'll warn you though, don't get your hopes up. Over the years, there have been probably a dozen shows that have profiled this case. Articles have been written and even a few books. You've seen the mountain of Internet articles and blogs about it. All that and nothing's ever come from it."

"They didn't have the car," Dani said, with a forced optimism that she didn't quite feel.

Dale gave her a weak grin and pulled the tarp back up over the car. "Let me know what your director friend says and I'll make the car available when he needs it."

"And yourself?" Dani asked cautiously.

He seemed confused. "Me?"

"Yes, if they want to interview you for the piece, would you be willing to go on the record, publicly, about what you saw and what you know?"

He shifted his weight nervously.

"They'd protect your identity," she put in quickly. "They can put you behind a black screen and electronically manipulate your voice, whatever you need."

He sighed heavily. "No, if I'm going to do this, I'm not going to hide behind some black screen. In for a penny, in for a pound, I guess." He nodded and Dani knew she had him.

"That's great, Dale, really. You're doing the right thing."

He laughed his bitter little laugh and shook his head. "There is no right here, Dani, just varying degrees of wrong."

She ignored that. "I'll send you an e-mail when I have some news, OK?"

He nodded and led her out of the garage and back into the house, where Maggie still lay quietly under the table. She put her back on the leash, leaned forward to give Dale a hug and then started for home.

Chapter
XVIII

First thing the following Monday, Dani phoned her long-time friend and colleague, Lee Calvert.

"Well hey, Dani! I haven't heard from you in a while. How've you been?"

"Good, Lee, and you?"

"Oh, keeping busy. You know how it is. Unfortunately, there seems to be no end to crime. Well, seeing as it's how I make my living, maybe I should be grateful for that but still …"

"To be honest, that's why I was calling," she interrupted. "I was hoping maybe you could help me with an open case. Actually, I was hoping you might be interested in doing a show on it." Despite her bravado in pitching the plan to Dale, her confidence deserted her now and she began to feel like a teenage fan asking for a pop star's autograph.

"Really, what sort of open case?" he asked. Dani could not tell from his tone if he was genuinely interested or merely being polite.

"Well it's a case involving a serial child rapist and killer from the late seventies. There were four known victims here in Michigan and the families have been trying to get a conviction ever since. They've been having an awful time trying to get any cooperation from the folks running the investigation currently …"

"We're not talking about the Guardian murders, are we?" he interrupted.

"Yeah, why?" she asked, feeling her hopes crash even before he began his reply.

"Well that story's been done and done again. It seems like every few years there's a story on that one. The problem is, there's no new evidence to explore. I'm going to have trouble pitching this idea if it's just rehashing what's already been covered." His tone was apologetic but adamant.

"And what if I were to hand you a big piece of new, hard evidence? Would you be tempted to pursue it then?"

"Well alright, now you've got my attention. What have you got?"

"How about the alleged killer's car, relatively untouched since the last time he used it?"

"Be serious," Lee scolded.

"I'm being completely serious. Are you familiar with the case?"

"I am. Who are you calling the alleged killer?"

"Craig Miller. Do you know of him?"

"I do. Are you telling me you've got the orange Karmann Ghia?"

"That's exactly what I'm telling you, Lee."

"How have you verified it?"

Dani's breath caught in her chest. She realized in an instant that she had no real proof at all. "I've met a close friend of Miller's. He … he has it in his garage," she stammered, hoping it would be enough and knowing that it was not.

"But how do you know that it's the very same car?" he persisted.

"Well I just …" Dani was sure this was the end of her plan.

"If you want me to look at this, I'm going to need the VIN number. Get me the VIN number so that I can confirm it and then we can talk, OK?"

"Okay," she agreed with relief.

"I hope you're right about this guy. I'd love to finally wrap that one up," he said. There was an edge to his voice that took Dani by surprise. Lee Calvert was as mild a man as she'd ever met. She couldn't recall a single time when she'd ever seen him get angry or upset. "I interviewed Larry Prince, Jimmy's father, back when it happened. I was working for the *Detroit Daily* at the time. It just ripped my heart out what this crime did to that man's family. I'm sure the same was true for all the families but he'll always be the face that I put to that crime."

"So you were a reporter when that was going on?" she asked.

"Yeah and boy was I green. Let's see … that happened in '77, so I'd have been about twenty at the time. Those crimes were a real wake-up call for me, for all of us. I'm sure that it wasn't the first time that a pervert had snatched kids, but it was the first time I'd ever been involved in something like that. Parents all over the state were in a panic. They had a task force working around the clock. They were even randomly stopping cars, asking the drivers to voluntarily submit to a search, if you can believe that. With all the political correctness these days, you'd never see that happen now but that's how anxious they were to find the guy."

"All that and still they didn't bring it back to Craig Miller? Don't you find that strange? Are you familiar with his arrest record?"

"I am. I know exactly what you're thinking," the edge crept back into his voice.

"I know they had thousands of leads and that their task force was stretched thin. It just seems odd to me that they found the time and the resources to search the cars of innocent people who had no criminal record whatsoever, but they didn't have the staff to pursue a known pedophile working in the next county over, living in the very same county as most of the crimes, who had been implicated specifically in those crimes by someone he knew!" Dani could feel her blood pressure rising.

"Yeah, I know about Grey. They did pursue him after that though, just so you know."

"Who, Grey?" Dani asked, confused.

"Miller. After Grey mentioned him to the cops, they did a lie detector test on Miller and asked him about his involvement."

"You're kidding. What happened?" Dani found that she was holding her breath.

"It came back clean or, at least, that's what they said at the time. So they dropped him as a suspect."

"It came back clean so they dropped him as a suspect?" Dani repeated incredulously. "That's it? Did they look into where he was when the crimes were going on? Did they maybe put a tail on him to see if he tried to interact with kids again beyond that point? If he was a known, admitted pedophile, couldn't they have put him away just on that, on the off chance that it might have stopped more kids from going missing? A clean lie detector test and they decide just to drop it? That's insane! I thought lie detector tests weren't even admissible."

"That's not the worst of it," he replied, his voice heavy and grim. "The lie detector test didn't really come back clean."

"*What*?" Dani caught herself screaming into the phone at poor Lee, who was only the messenger after all.

"Yeah, they had some rookie conduct it, and he read the results wrong but they didn't find that out until years later. They never held him at all for the pedophilia charges. Every time he just got a slap on the wrist—a fine or probation or whatever."

"Doesn't that strike you as odd?"

"Dani, do you know who Arthur Melden is?"

She sighed heavily. "Yes," she replied, in a voice that sounded defeated even to her own ears.

"Are you familiar with *St. Francis Children's Sanctuary*?" He asked.

"I am."

"And do you know the sort of clientele that he entertained there?"

That was a question that Dani hadn't expected. Out of habit, she shrugged, even though he had no way to see. "I dunno, the perverted kind?" she asked.

Gordie walked into the kitchen where she was seated and stared first at Dani and then up at the box of dog biscuits that she kept on top of the refrigerator. He stared back at her for a moment and then back at the treats. When she only returned his stare, unmoving, he gave up and went back into the living room.

"The powerful kind," he corrected her. "*St. Francis Children's Sanctuary* wasn't the only camp of its kind. It wasn't even the only one that Melden created. There were a string of those camps all over the country in the '70s and '80s. They were a cover for child pornography and, worse, child prostitution. There was a big investigation into them down South and when those were busted, the client lists turned up the names of some very elite people. Miller was known to be involved in Melden's camps, and maybe in others as well. No one was ever able to prove in exactly what capacity or to what extent, but he was definitely involved. Personally, I don't think it was an accident that they had a rookie do the lie detector test or that the results came back as they did. In light of all the probation he got for his crimes and the number of times they let him off the hook, I'd expect nothing else."

"What happened to the 'elite people' who were busted down South?"

"As I recall, they blamed it on being stressed out and drunk, as though a few too many beers could make any man want to have sex with a ten-year-old boy! They were given substance abuse counseling."

Dani felt sick. "I don't get this, Lee. I just don't get it. Where's the moral outrage of this country? The desire to protect the children? Wouldn't you expect to see some of that?"

"To tell you the truth, Dani, no."

"What?" Dani couldn't believe her ears.

"Whenever we do a story on child sexual abuse or child prostitution—especially things concerning little boys being used by grown men—we get flooded with complaints. People complain that it's obscene or indecent."

"Well of course it's obscene and indecent. Isn't that the point? Shouldn't we use the media to bring an end to things that are obscene and indecent?"

"I know. I get it. You're preaching to the choir and that's why I'm still interested in your story. But for a lot of folks, seeing a story like this forces them to consider—to confront—a reality that they'd rather avoid. No decent person wants to think about a ten-year-old boy being sodomized by a grown man. It's the sort of image that's disturbing enough that folks just don't want to think about it. It makes a lot of people very uncomfortable."

Kōbō's words came back to her now. "I'm afraid," Dani had complained. "It's not easy to see all these awful things."

"So you can imagine how difficult it was to live through them," had been his response.

Dani understood the revulsion and the fear. Nevertheless, she couldn't allow herself simply to turn away. She knew, as she was sure Lee did, that to do so would condemn even more children to the same horrible fate.

"Thanks again for your help, Lee. I'll get that VIN over to you today and then I'll wait to hear back from you."

"Sounds good, Dani. Nice talking to you."

"You too." She dropped the call and then dialed again.

After several rings, the call passed to voice mail. Dani frowned. "Hello Dale," she said after the beep, "this is Danielle Sawyer. I wanted to let you know that I spoke to my director friend, Lee, and he's definitely interested in doing the show, but he first needs to verify that the car really did belong to Craig Miller, so he's asked me to send him over the VIN number. If you could send me an e-mail with that, I'd appreciate it. Thanks!" She hung up and stood for a moment longer, frowning at the cell phone in her hand. As she stared at it, it began to ring again and startled her so much that she jumped and nearly tossed it into the air. When she realized what had happened, she laughed, pulled herself together and answered the phone.

"Hello?" she answered, suppressing the urge to giggle.

"Hey Dani, it's Nora. Everything OK?"

"Yeah, I'm fine." She cleared her throat and swallowed the giggles. "What's up?"

"Guess who just called me?"

"Tom Montgomery?" Dani guessed.

Nora snorted, "I wish! No, Matthew Miller!"

"Oh my God! How'd he get your number?"

"Who knows? I asked but all he said was, 'I have my sources'. Yeah, I'll bet he does!" There was something in her tone that unnerved Dani but she couldn't quite put her finger on it. "He wants to meet for drinks!" With that, Dani's fears took shape.

"Nora, you can't possibly be considering it."

"Well I'm not talking about *dating* him, if that's what you're thinking. I told you how repulsed I was by his family before, so you can only imagine now!"

Dani felt a rush of relief. "So what then?"

"Well what if he's decided to come forward and tell what he knows? What if he's got information? He may just be looking for a way to tell his story."

Dani was doubtful. "Do you really think there's any chance of that?" she asked, making no attempt to hide her skepticism.

"Well why not? I've felt guilty about it all these years. Maybe he has too. He stopped me from following through with that call up at the cabin, and I really think it's bothered him. He wasn't a bad guy, honestly. He just came from a really screwed-up family and I think now he may be looking for a way to get past all that, just like me. Doesn't he deserve a chance to do the right thing? After all, *he* didn't kill anyone."

Not that we know of anyway, thought Dani, remembering Matt Miller's role in the discovery of Craig's dead body. *"Matt and Craig both knew how to shoot and the old man kept a whole cabinet full of guns in the game room,"* isn't that what Nora had said? She shoved the thought aside. "Do you think it's safe?" she asked, certain she knew what Nora's answer would be.

"I'm sure he won't hurt me. He's not a bad guy," she repeated.

"You shouldn't go alone," Dani warned.

"Well he won't talk in front of anyone else. I need to do this alone."

"Absolutely not," she insisted. "I'm going with you."

"Well alright but you can't let him see you. We're going to that pizza place by my work and you'll have to sit somewhere out of sight and hide behind a menu or something."

Dani thought about the restaurant. It was dimly lit and a seat at the bar would allow her an out of the way vantage point from which to view the entire dining area. "Alright, I'll sit at the bar but if it looks like he's trying to walk you out of the place or if he makes any kind of threatening move, I'm getting you out of there, no arguments," she said firmly.

"Friday night at 6:30."

"I'd rather it be some time during the week. It would give you an easy excuse to slip away early. I saw this guy, Nora. He's more attractive than he has a right to be and the two of you have a history. Best not to tempt fate, don't you think? Pursue Tom, he'll make you happier."

There was a long pause and Nora said, "We've already made plans. It's Friday, 6:30. If you can't make it, I'll understand," her tone was chilly and determined.

I bet you will, thought Dani. "I'll be there," she replied flatly. They made a little small talk in an attempt to heal the conversational breach before giving it up and ending the call.

Dani stood, stretched, and headed back to her office where a full day's worth of tedious legal translations awaited her. No longer did Gordie attempt to follow her into the office. Now he was content to curl up on the couch with his little sister or peer out the large picture window at pedestrians on the street. Every so often, a neighbor would pass by with another dog on a leash, or a squirrel would have the temerity to trespass on the front lawn, and the two would clamber up from the couch and bark raucously at the intruder. As Dani walked back to the office, she stole a glance at the couch, where the two of them were intertwined in a lump, dozing peacefully. It made her wish she could head back to bed herself. She pushed the thought aside and closed the office door behind her.

She powered up the computer and took her seat at the desk, sorting through the pile of work that she'd left there the Friday before, in search of the project with the most imminent deadline. When she found it, she pulled up the corresponding computer file, clicked it open, and began to read. Unfortunately, her mind was not on the work. She found herself reading and rereading the same passages over and over again without really absorbing the words. Finally she closed the file and turned her attention to her e-mail in-box.

A bold number two hovered over the icon and she clicked it hopefully. A moment later she was frowning. Her first new message was a shipment confirmation for a sweater that she'd recently found on clearance, the other was a note from Tom Montgomery thanking her for introducing him to Nora and reminding her to check out his coverage of the Auto Show in the online edition of *Auto World Weekly*. Still no VIN number, she observed. She wondered if she should try Dale again or give him more time. She glanced at the clock in the corner of her computer screen. It was nearly nine thirty. She decided that if she had not heard from Dale by noon, that she would call him again. Until then, she promised herself, she would buckle down and work on her translations.

Half an hour later, having made no real progress at all, she opened an Internet window, clicked on a link in her favorites menu and began to skim through the latest edition of *Auto World Weekly*. The link to Tom's article was halfway down on the home page. The article was a competent, if not entirely interesting, perspective on the displays of the European transplants. She gave it a thorough enough read to allow for a few intelligent comments the next time she saw Tom, then moved on. She clicked on another story about the latest introductions from the Japanese manufacturers. She found it no more interesting than the first. Finally, she clicked on a link entitled, *Domestic Brands Score Big at Detroit Auto Show.*

As the page loaded, Dani was startled to find a very familiar, very handsome face smiling back at her. In a large photo in the center of the page, flanked by his fellow executives, Matthew Miller stood behind a candy-apple-red sports car prototype. She skimmed the article. With the exception of the picture, it was no more interesting than the others. She squinted hard at the picture on the screen, trying to see Miller as the boy Nora had known, the brother of a monstrous pedophile. She could not see the boy he had been, only the slick executive he had become. She wondered what Nora saw when she looked at him now. Had he been this attractive in his youth? Or had his brother's death freed him to be more than he was before, more than he might have been otherwise? What might such a man do to escape the shadow of a monster? The thought left her with an uneasy feeling in the pit of her stomach.

A quiet ding from her computer pulled her back to the present. She glanced around the monitor and found that she had a new e-mail waiting. Clicking on the icon, she felt another wave of disappointment rush over her when she realized that it was not from Dale. Instead, she found a note from Lee confirming that his team was interested in doing the story, provided the prior ownership could be established. She closed the message and glanced again at her clock, not even ten yet, she drummed her fingers restlessly on her desk. Grudgingly, she pulled up her translation and began to work. She stopped three more times during the next two hours to check her e-mail. Finally, at a quarter to twelve, just as she was getting ready to call him again, she received his response:

> *Good Morning Dani,*
>
> *Attached is the VIN number. I believe they will find further proof of my claims in the glove compartment but I remembered what you said about forensics and preserving the car as it is, so I did not open it. If your director friend needs for me to do that, please let me know.*
>
> *See you soon,*
> *Dale*

Dani clicked on the attachment and found a picture of the VIN tag, taken through the glass of the windshield, onto the dash. She forwarded his entire e-mail, including the photo, to Lee with a brief note of thanks for his help and then turned her attention back to her translations. Unfortunately, even after Dale's response, Dani found it difficult to concentrate. She was still tired and more than a little concerned about Nora's upcoming appointment with Matt. Since it was noon, she decided that a quick cat nap might be the perfect solution. She slipped off her shoes and collapsed on the comfy chaise. Within moments, she was fast asleep.

Chapter
XIX

As she entered the dream this time, she found that Kōbō had spared her the climb down the nerve-racking, narrow steps. Instead, she found herself already seated on her chaise, a chilly breeze blowing in from the sea beyond. The sky above was uncharacteristically dark and ominous, as though a storm were approaching. She was so preoccupied by the weather that she'd neglected even to greet her host. Politely, he cleared his throat and awaited her attention.

"Sorry," she said quickly, still trying to steal a glance toward the dark sky. "It's just—I've never seen the sky so dark here. It reminds me of tornado weather. Do they have tornadoes in …" Dani had meant to refer to the place by name when it suddenly occurred to her that she didn't actually know the name of this place. "Do they have tornadoes here?" she asked.

"Even the most peaceful places pass through stormy seasons," he replied.

"True," Dani agreed. She felt she should say more but as she tried to think of something, she was distracted by the roar of an engine overhead. They both sat silently, gazing skyward. A small, private plane broke through the cloud cover and streamed across the sky just above their cliff.

"Where do you suppose he's going?" Kōbō asked.

"I've no idea," Dani replied, feeling suddenly and inexplicably uneasy.

"Don't you think you should find out?" he asked.

She pulled her gaze away from the plane and looked across the landing to where he had been seated, but he was gone and then, in an instant, so was she.

The scene had changed and she found herself sitting in the backseat of a small plane very similar to the one in which she and Geoff had flown during the color tour. She tried to focus on the scene but her head was swimming and her vision blurred. From the front of the plane she could hear men talking but their voices were dull and distant, as though she were hearing them through ears submerged in water. She tried to move but her limbs felt heavy and awkward. She shook her head, trying to clear her mind but it was no use. She looked out the window. Beyond was a muddy gray sky. Below, pine trees dotted a thin stretch of land, surrounded by an enormous body of water. She stared down at her hands and found that they were not her own.

The body that she saw was that of a little boy. He was wearing dark blue, bell bottom pants and bright red snow boots with black spider webs and the face of a superhero emblazoned on the side. The little boy's arms were covered by a puffy winter jacket in the same bright red shade as the boots. She glanced around, hoping to find a mirror that would allow her to get a look at the eyes through which she was being allowed to see. She found none. Instead, in the copilot's seat of the small aircraft, she spied a familiar, bearded face. Dani's sleeping mind recognized the danger and felt the panic. It was the same horrible foreboding that she had experienced as she watched little Jimmy Prince get into the car, the same panic she'd felt as the coyotes rounded on her on the beach. With growing alarm, she discovered that she was just as powerless to protect herself now as she had been then.

She discovered that the young body in which she was trapped could not move. The arms and legs were bound, the senses dulled. She could not see the pilot, who was sitting in a tall seat directly in front of her own. He was chatting and laughing with the bearded monster.

She heard the pilot ask, "How's he doing?"

The monster glanced backward. "Looks like it's wearing off a bit. Should I give him another dose?"

"No," replied the pilot. "The client will enjoy it more if he's awake enough to cooperate and besides, once we get to the island, there will be no one else to see and nowhere for him to run."

The monster gave an approving nod and turned back toward the front of the plane. "Isn't that the island there?" He motioned out the window at the thin strip of land below.

"Yep, just need to circle around before I can set her down."

Understanding filled Dani with dread. She realized in a moment of blind panic what she was meant to see and why Kōbō had brought her here. Somewhere in the corner of her sleeping mind, she knew that for her, Dani, this was just a dream and that she would be allowed to wake and resume her safe life—far from this nightmare; however, she also knew that the scene was truth and that what she was seeing had been one little boy's tormented reality. She wanted to make herself wake up, to flee what she feared was to come, but she felt that to do so would be to abandon this young child. She also felt a morbid curiosity, an overwhelming urge to understand what had happened—no matter how awful. She forced herself to remain calm and to observe.

She glanced around the tiny cabin. The door next to Craig Miller was the color of butter and the ceiling above was ivory. The seats in front of her were also ivory with red piping along the seams. In front of the two men was an instrument panel. Dozens of round gauges and tiny dials were set in a panel that was the same butter yellow as the doors and bordered by red. She thought it surreal that such a horrific scene should be unraveling in such a cheery space. She felt the plane begin to descend. Her stomach lurched, as though she were on the downward spiral of a roller coaster. She knew they'd be on the island soon and, once again, panic gripped her. She choked it back and silently vowed to be the best eyewitness she could be. She felt the plane bounce and brake as they made contact with the landing strip.

On the ground, Miller opened the door and got out. The pilot in front of her did the same, then pushed his vacant seat forward and reached in the back to where she sat. He grabbed her under the arms and lifted her into his own. For the first time, she was able to see him clearly. He was in his late forties or early fifties with salt and pepper hair, neatly trimmed and parted to one side. He wore horn-rimmed spectacles and a dusty blue cardigan sweater over a white oxford shirt. As he held her, she wanted to fight, to flee, but the body in which she was trapped remained bound and paralyzed. Craig Miller emerged from around the front of the plane. "Here, take him for a minute," the older man commanded. "I need my coat." The little boy was passed from one to the other. She could feel the monster's beard against the little boy's cheek. She could smell his acrid breath. Once the pilot's hands were free, the pilot reached back behind his seat, pulled out a black leather jacket and slipped it on. Again the child was passed from one man to the other. As they crossed from the plane to the opposite side of the landing strip, Dani could see the shoreline receding behind them. She saw the blacktop give way to a rocky little beach and scenes from nightmares past rushed through her sleeping mind.

They took a well-worn path into the woods. Tall pines loomed overhead and blotted out the sky. They followed the path for what seemed like a mile or more. Dani could see no homes or permanent structures of any kind. The wilderness stretched on for as far as the eye could see. No sooner had she come to that conclusion, however, than the men stopped abruptly. She was staring over the pilot's shoulder as he carried her, unable to see where they were going. Beside her, she saw Craig Miller bend forward and then she could hear the rustling of leaves and the sound of branches being tossed aside. She heard a sound like the creaking of rusty hinges and as they began to move again, she realized that she was being carried through a metal hatch and down into the earth below.

Beyond the hatch was a structure that seemed like the top half of an enormous white tube, the walls of which circled upward to a low ceiling. Both the walls and the ceiling had the texture of corrugated steel, arching and circling in grooves through the entire length of the long, narrow tunnel. Built-in shelves molded to the curved walls on either side and housed blankets, magazines, camera equipment, work lights, and bottles of beer and alcohol. Individual rooms were defined—but not completely enclosed—by white walls that covered only half the tube, leaving an open entrance through which to pass. She could see room after open room in quick succession down the length of the long bunker.

Again, the child was passed back and forth just long enough for the pilot to remove his coat. Together they passed through the storage space and entered a narrow kitchen with a long, covered card table surrounded by plastic, white lawn chairs. There were built-in shelves in this room as well, but here they were stocked with canned goods, granola bars, bottled water, bread, and sugary snacks. She could hear voices now, men talking and laughing. The pilot passed another half wall and they entered a long room with a narrow leather sofa pushed close against the curving, corrugated wall. Beyond the sofa was a small banquette and opposite the banquette was a black, canvas futon. All the seats were currently occupied by rowdy, drunk men. They cheered loudly when Miller and the pilot entered.

"Hey Art, where ya been? We thought you'd deserted us," one man called from the sofa.

"Who's the cute little trick you brought back?" asked another from the banquette.

"You saving him all for yourself or does everybody get a piece?" hollered a third from the futon.

"Don't worry," the pilot, Art Melden, called as he passed. "You'll get your chance, but his first appointment is reserved for a very special client." Dani was horrified and tried again to escape. It was no use. She was just as powerless to control her surroundings as she was sure the little boy had been.

They passed by a third wall and entered a darkened room where built-in units held long, narrow rows of bunk beds on either side of the space. Haunted eyes stared back at her from nearly every bunk. They walked by them, one by one, and she met each gaze as they passed. Their expressions seemed defeated and resigned to their fates. They looked on her with pity and empathy as the new arrival was carried to the last bunk on the left and tossed up onto the mattress like a sack of potatoes. The pilot pulled a knife from his back pocket and before she had time to panic over his intentions, he'd cut away the ropes binding the little boy's wrists and feet. "Be a good boy now and stay put, understand?" He did not wait for a reply but turned on his heel and walked out of the room, followed closely by Craig Miller. She could hear the other men greet them as they re-entered the room.

"He's a beaut, Art. Where'd you get him?"

"I've recently become his guardian," he said. "His mother isn't well, poor dear, and prefers to stay heavily medicated. Unfortunately, her drug of choice ain't cheap." They all laughed. "I helped her out and persuaded her that she was in no proper state to care for a young child. I have to say, it really wasn't that hard to convince her." They laughed again.

"Do you suppose that cherry's yet to pop?" she heard another voice ask. "How old is he, do you suppose?"

"He's ten and his mother assures me that he's pure as they come. But then, who can trust the word of a heroin-addicted whore? So, of course, I had to check for myself." The drunken men whooped and hollered their approval. "He's the real deal!" he concluded triumphantly.

Dani was grateful that Kōbō had at least spared her *that* part of the experience.

"So who's the big client?" a voice asked.

"Senator Ted Richman's flying in from the East Coast. He's doing some fundraising for the party here in Detroit and he needs a little R&R afterward, so he asked me to set it up. He requested pure and white and let me tell you, that's not easy to come by these days. But for what he's paying, I won't complain! With just this one client, the boy will make up for what I paid the mother."

"I don't know what you're talking about Art," another voice put in. "I see pure, white, tight pieces of ass all over the place by my house."

"I think you mean by your *parents'* house," he chided, "and we've been through this before! You can't use the ones who would be missed. Especially over there in Belle Mead. Over there, you're surrounded by doctors, lawyers, executives … do you have any idea of the shit storm you'd start if you offered up some doctor's kidnapped kid to the senator? You need to use your head, Craig."

Before she could hear Miller's response, a voice in the bunk below hers said, "Hey, Mike, can you see the new kid? Does he look alright?"

She felt a hand reach out from the bunk nearest her head and push lightly on her shoulder. "Hey, kid," he whispered, nudging her again, "you okay?"

She felt the little boy's arms move and slowly, painfully, the child pushed himself up on an elbow and glanced over at the boy named Mike. Backlit as he was, Dani could see that he had a mop of tousled, blond hair that hung to his shoulders. He had full lips, high cheekbones, and dark eyes. He was as pretty as any girl she'd ever seen. The skin on his face was still soft and smooth but his voice had already begun to take on the deeper, bass tones of a grown man. She guessed him to be about fourteen years old. "You okay?" he asked again.

"I feel funny," Dani replied, in the little boy voice that was on loan to her for the duration of the dream.

"That's the drugs," he explained. "They always drug the new kids when they bring them in. That way, if anybody asks, they can just tell them the kid's asleep. It'll wear off soon enough. You're Kevin, right? I heard Art telling the others about you last night. I'm Mike." He gestured to the bed below hers, "That's Diego." Dani nodded to a young, Latino boy who looked to be twelve or thirteen years old.

"Pipe down in there," hollered a drunken voice from the other room.

Mike moved his face very close to Kevin's ear and whispered, "They've got an important client for you tonight. If you want to live to see tomorrow, don't bite unless he asks you to, don't cry, and don't scream. Just try to imagine you're somewhere else—doing anything else—and do whatever they ask you to do without a fight. It hurts the first time but they usually go easy on the cherries, especially the young ones, so it shouldn't be too bad." Dani looked at him through Kevin's eyes, too terror stricken to speak.

For what seemed like an eternity, they sat in the dark, listening to the drunken chatter from the men in the next room. Terrifying images of the torture to come played through her mind. Whether the thoughts were her own or those of the little boy she'd become, Dani could not have said.

From the far end of the bunker she heard the hatch creak open again and a cold gust of wind whirled through the steel tunnel. "Senator Richman!" Melden's voice boomed cordially. "It's so good to see you again. How goes the fundraising?" he asked.

"Brutal, Art, just brutal. I'll tell you, I've been looking forward to this all day."

"Can I get you a drink? Beer maybe?" he asked.

"Scotch would be great if you've got it."

"Of course, please, go on through. I believe you know everybody. Reggie, why don't you move over to the futon and let the senator take the sofa."

The boy named Kevin peered from his bunk back through the tunnel and through his eyes, Dani could see the beer-bellied man named Reggie hop off the sofa and take a seat next to the man on the futon. She saw a tall, slim, dark-haired man enter the room and greet the others.

"Take off your coat," she heard Mike whisper. "He'll be bringing him back here to show you soon and you need to look good. If he doesn't like you, Art will be pissed. Trust me, you don't want to piss off Art." The little boy did as he was told and Dani could feel the arms that were not her own wriggling out of the puffy red jacket and smoothing the white, cotton t-shirt below. The boy had no muscles to speak of, just the wiry, skinny body of a ten-year-old child.

After a while, lights came on in the room and she was temporarily blinded. She felt gruff hands grab the young boy and stand him up in front of the bunk. "Here he is, sir, this is Kevin. Kevin, say hello to the nice gentleman."

"Hello," she heard the little boy's voice chirp out. She saw that the senator had a prominent nose, a heavy brow, and bags under his eyes. She guessed him to be in his early thirties.

"We've got a private suite for the two of you set up right back here," Art said, gesturing to a closed door further down the tube.

The senator walked around little Kevin, appraising him as a farmer might appraise newly acquired livestock. He ran a hand down the length of his pants, lingering over his small backside. Dani felt the child shudder. The senator then moved his hand over Kevin's chest and down between his thighs. The child bolted away. Melden grabbed him and held him firmly in place.

"Listen, boy, I've paid good money for you," Senator Richman's breath smelled of alcohol and his voice was angry and impatient. "I've been looking forward to this all day so this can either be a very special experience for the both of us, or a very painful one for you. If I have to have Art and his friends teach you a lesson, you'll wish I hadn't. Do you understand?"

Little Kevin nodded silently and Melden loosened his grip.

"Don't worry, I don't want to hurt you. We'll have fun, I promise." Dani doubted it. "You're going to be a good boy for me, right?" He nodded as though to prompt the correct response.

The boy nodded along as tears began to fall down his cheeks.

"Big boys don't cry," he whispered ominously. "Remember, you don't want Art to get angry, right?"

He sniffled and tried not to cry.

"Good boy," he said.

Grasping his arm firmly, Art tugged little Kevin along through the tunnel to the "private suite" in the back. Dani could feel his nails gripping the flesh. She felt the boy begin to struggle. Melden's grip tightened until she was sure he would tear into the soft flesh. The struggling subsided and they followed the senator into the dark, private room. "Lights on?" he asked the senator.

"Please," came the response.

She heard a click from behind and the small space flooded with a bright, white light. In the room was a double bed, flanked by the same built-in shelves as she'd seen in the rest of the bunker. Here they were filled with silver tubes, little jars, baby oil, ash trays, bottles of booze, needles, camera equipment, more magazines, and even a small TV. The boy stood stock still in the center of the room, too terrified to move.

The senator began to pull at little Kevin's trousers and Dani heard the door slam shut. Her view of the scene went blank, as though little Kevin had squeezed his eyes shut. Dani tried to force them back open but she had no influence over the dream. As with the others, she was simply along for the ride.

"Now, I've got a very special lollipop for you," she heard the senator say. "But you mustn't bite down on this one, do you understand?"

Dani felt her stomach churn and she was sure the boy would vomit. She felt his mouth being forced open and a sweaty stench filled her nostrils. Kevin pushed him away and she heard the slap land hard across the boy's face. "Now that's not a good start," the senator said angrily. "Let's try again."

Dani bolted awake. She sat up sharply and found both Maggie and Gordie staring at her from the open doorway. She wondered what noise she must have made to cause them to leave their couch and come investigate. She stood up and closed the door in front of them, locking them out. Still dazed from the nightmare, she fumbled through her desk and found some paper and a pen. The still-vivid images hung in her mind. She had no trouble recalling every horrible detail. In truth, she found herself wishing that she could forget them and knowing that she never would.

When she'd finished writing it down, she sat for a long time in the well-lit room, grateful for her familiar surroundings. At the same time, she felt immensely guilty, as though she'd left the young boy to fend for himself by returning to her own time and place. It was a silly thought, she knew, and yet she could not shake it. In an attempt to ease her guilty conscience, she called Faye and recounted the dream to her. Her hands trembled as she recalled the face of the senator and his foul-smelling manhood.

"Do you think it really happened to that poor boy?" asked Dani, afraid to know the answer but unable to avoid the question.

Faye did not reply but instead asked, "Have you tried an Internet search for the senator's name?"

"I haven't," Dani admitted. "I haven't done anything with it yet. I'm still trying to get the images out of my head. Plus, I don't think I want to know the truth."

"I know," Faye replied gently. "But I think the point is that you must ask the questions. We must know the truth."

"I know," Dani conceded. "I just need a little time. Just a day or maybe a few hours—to recover. I want to pretend it didn't happen for just a few hours more before I face the truth." The admission made Dani feel guilty all over again.

"Let me know what you find out. When you're ready, I'd see what you can find on the Internet both about the senator and about that bunker. When you flew over Coyote Island with Geoff, did you see any sign of a bunker? Or a structure of any kind?"

"From the air, the only defining characteristic is the airstrip and even that doesn't look the same. In the dream it looked like well-maintained blacktop. It may have been once, although I doubt it. That's not how it looked when we flew over it. At this point, it just looks like a scar running through the trees. Even in the dream though, the canopy of the trees overhead was thick enough to blot out the sun. I doubt anyone would have known the bunker was there unless they knew just where to look. Anyway, how could they have built a bunker like that on such a remote island? That part of the dream couldn't have been real," she concluded.

"Remember," warned Faye, "you're dealing with a multi-millionaire here. With enough money, nothing's impossible, least of all a long tube in the dirt on a private island."

"A fully furnished tube in the dirt," Dani reminded her.

"You should also keep in mind that for our guides, getting the idea across is more important than relating the exact details. Your dream suggests that there was a hidden location on that island, whether it was a bunker or a cave or some other kind of hidden dwelling, that's not the point. You said the cops busted a child pornography ring on the island. Did they find any kind of hidden dwelling during that bust?"

"I don't know. The article didn't say," Dani replied. "Maybe the cops never found the bunker. Maybe they had a campsite in addition to the bunker that was found during the bust."

"That might be another thing you could investigate further," Faye put in. "But rest for a while. Let me know what you find out," she repeated.

"I will, thanks," Dani said. "I'll talk to you later."

Chapter
XX

The next day, Dani was still struggling to put little Kevin out of her mind when she received a call from Lee.

"I've got great news, Dani," he informed her, after they'd exchanged greetings. "We've confirmed your friend's story. That's definitely Miller's old car." Dani felt both elated and terrified. "We'd like to meet with you both next week. Would Thursday work?"

"Uh, I don't know," Dani stammered. "I'd have to ask him. What time on Thursday were you thinking? Are you going to be filming?"

"No, no, nothing like that," he assured her. "We just want to meet him, get a look at the car and take some notes on how best to proceed. I'll work around his schedule. Why don't you give him a call, since you're the one who found him, and let me know what time works best for him?"

"I will, Lee, thanks. I'll call you back when I know something more."

"This is really great news, Dani. I thought you'd be more excited." He seemed disappointed by her reaction to the news.

How could she explain it to him? "It just feels like …" she let the thought trail off and then began again, "I just find myself wishing that I could turn back time and somehow protect them all." She felt tears stinging at the back of her eyes as the memory of her nightmares washed over her.

Lee's voice was more somber now. "I understand, but we do what we can. We have to play the cards we've been dealt and this one's an ace. Let's enjoy it while we can, okay?" She could tell that he wanted her to be happy and so she played along, for his sake.

"Will do," she said, with feigned conviction. "I'll talk to you soon." She hung up and sighed heavily. After a moment, she dialed and brought the phone back to her ear.

"Hello, Dale," she said when he answered. "I heard back from Lee. They've confirmed the car and they want to come out and talk to you. Are you ready for that?"

"I am." His voice sounded so confident and upbeat that she hardly recognized him. "Are they going to be filming?" he asked, his confidence wavering just a bit.

"No, they just want to talk to you first. They want to come out on Thursday. Will that work for you? They said you can pick the time."

"That's fine. How about four thirty?

"I'll let him know."

"Are you going to be there as well?" he asked quietly.

"That depends, do you want me to be there?"

"It would be nice to have a friendly face there." His voice was just above a whisper, like a shy child asking permission.

"Then I'll be there. I think it's very brave what you're doing."

"It's something that I should have done a long time ago. I need to thank you for finding me, for pushing me. I guess I still don't know exactly how you found me but I'm starting to feel glad that you did. It's starting to feel like a weight being lifted off my shoulders."

Dani thought about Matthew Miller and his father. She thought about the men who had surrounded little Kevin in her dream the night before and about the senator. How many of them were still alive and what would they do to protect their secrets? "Don't thank me yet," she said. "This is the beginning, not the end, of this process."

"I know," he replied. As if sensing her doubts he said, "I'm not naïve to what might happen here, Dani. I've known these people a lot longer than you have, remember? I've known all along what might happen and I'm going into it with my eyes wide open."

"Are you afraid?"

"I've spent my whole life being afraid of these people. It's exhausting. I don't want to do it anymore. Whatever they're going to do to me, let them do it. It's time for this to come out."

"Well then we'll see you on Thursday," she replied, trying to sound upbeat and positive.

Next, and with some trepidation, she called Nora.

"Hey, Dani! What's up?" she asked immediately. Her voice sounded strange and tight, as though she were still on her guard after their last awkward conversation. It was not a good beginning.

"Hey Nora. I wanted to let you know about a development with Dale."

"A development?" she asked, sounding suspicious.

"Yeah, he's agreed to speak with a friend of mine, who is going to do a television show about the Guardian case and

Craig's possible involvement. It's one of those investigative shows that looks into cold case files. They're going to profile Dale on their next program and they're going up to Fanny Lake to interview him."

"Why are you telling me this?" Her voice took on a tone that sounded angry. Was it anger, Dani wondered, or perhaps fear?

"I thought you should know. You were with me when I found Dale and you know Matt. You're going to see him the day after the interview takes place. I just thought you should know," she said again.

"You just thought I should know?" she repeated. "Or did you maybe think you could rope me into an interview as well?"

The truth was that the notion hadn't even occurred to Dani but she didn't say that. Instead she said, "Only you can decide if you're ready for that. It's not for me to push you into anything."

"Right," Nora said, as if trying to cement her own conviction. "I'm not. I'm not ready for that. Matt feels bad for what happened back then. He wants to come clean with what he knows and if I were to go on TV talking about how he covered for Craig …" She left the thought unfinished.

"I'll be honest with you. I don't share your cheery view of Matt Miller but I won't push you to go public with anything if you're not ready. I did want to let you know though, about Dale, I mean. On Thursday, they're just doing a preliminary interview. They'll schedule an actual filming after that."

"I don't need to know any of this. I'm not going to participate in anything like that." Her tone was determined.

"Okay, that's fine. We're still on for Friday though, right?"

She seemed to consider the question for a long moment. "Yes," she said at last, "we're still on."

On the following Thursday, Lee arrived at Dani's home early in the morning. When she opened the door for him, he gave her a quick hug and Dani glanced over his shoulder at the group of people he'd brought along with him. Lee Calvert stood more than six feet tall and had a full head of silvery gray hair. He wore large glasses and had a kind face. After he'd greeted her, he turned and laid a hand on the shoulder of a young woman with jet black hair and eyes to match. She stood no more than five feet tall and next to Lee, she appeared almost like a child.

"Dani, I'd like you to meet my assistant, Elena." The dark-haired girl smiled and nodded. "This is Josh and Mark," Lee indicated two twenty-something guys just behind Elena, both wearing thick, navy blue jumpsuits embroidered with a logo that Dani did not recognize. The pair nodded at her. "And behind them," Lee continued, "is my producer, Christian Tristain."

Chris stepped forward and offered her his hand. "It's a pleasure to meet you, Dani," he said. "I can't thank you enough for giving us this opportunity to bring people the truth about this crime." Lee's producer had the slim build of cyclist with warm, hazel eyes that peered at her through round spectacles. She guessed him to be about her own age and he had a sincere, friendly smile that slid across his face from ear to ear as he greeted her. He had light brown hair and when he spoke, Dani could hear a faint, European accent that she guessed to be German.

She took a step back and invited them all into the house. She made them coffee and pulled together a bag of granola bars, bottled water, and chips to take along for the ride. They discussed her prior conversations with Dale and they went over the questions that they intended to ask him. At this point, they mentioned to Dani that if all went well with this initial interview that they would likely ask to pick up the vehicle that same day and bring it back to their laboratory for testing. "Do you think that's going to be a problem?" Lee asked.

She had the sense that they were afraid of losing their access to the car, as though the whole thing were a prank and Lee and his crew were waiting for the other foot to fall. "I'm sure it won't be a problem. I spoke to him earlier in the week and he seems anxious to move ahead."

The others in the room seemed to breathe a collective sigh of relief. "Super," said Lee approvingly. "Then we're ready to get started whenever you are." As a group, they rose and headed out to the full-sized news van that Lee had brought for the occasion. They piled in and began the long drive up north.

During the drive, Lee and Dani discussed the history of the case. Lee talked about his initial meeting with Lawrence Prince, and Dani told everyone about the widespread panic the crimes had caused in her neighborhood when she was a young girl. It occurred to her that of the half dozen passengers in the van, only she and Lee were both old enough and local enough to have a personal knowledge of the case and the fear it had created in the area. No wonder, she thought, that there has been so little recent activity in this case. Even to the majority of the people in this van, who had been specifically assigned to cover the story, these long-dead children were no more real than photos on an old newspaper. We're going to change that, Dani vowed to herself. We're going to make them understand what happened here. She thought about Dale and worried that the loud, boisterous group might make him feel awkward and shy.

When they pulled into Dale's drive, he came out to greet them, despite the cold temperatures. Dani was relieved to find that he seemed calm and upbeat as they introduced themselves and poured into his tiny living room. He'd put out trays of pastries and fruit for the group to share and Dani reached for one as she, Dale, Lee, and his slim producer took a seat on the couch. The others pulled chairs in from the kitchen and sat opposite them.

"So, Dale," Lee began, "Dani's been telling me a little bit about your situation, but I'm hoping to hear the story from your own perspective first and then we'll draw up some notes on how we want to proceed with the interview for the show. Can we do that?"

Dale glanced nervously around the room at the large group staring back at him.

"Oh, for heaven's sakes!" stammered Lee, "What am I thinking? There's no sense in all of us sitting here. Josh and Mark are our technical consultants. They'll be coordinating with the lab on the car and the forensic testing. Would you mind if they were to head out and take a look at it while we talk?" he asked. The two men rose expectantly.

Dale nodded. "The garage isn't locked. Dani, maybe you could take them out and show them?" He looked at Dani and then gave another nervous glance, this time at Elena still seated opposite the couch.

"Good idea. Elena, could you go with them and take notes for me? Please make sure to note the conditions in the garage and the overall condition of the vehicle. Is it OK if we take some pictures as well?" Lee asked Dale.

Dale nodded again and gave Dani a reassuring smile as she rose to leave.

"If you don't mind," said Chris, "I'd like to have a look as well."

"That'd be great," Lee agreed. "Let me know what you think."

As they headed for the side door, Dani glanced back at the couch.

"They'll be fine," Chris whispered, laying a hand on her shoulder. "Lee's worked with many victims before. He knows how to be discreet." His face was very near her own now and she could smell the masculine, musky scent of his aftershave. She worried that he'd notice her scars, standing as close as he was. She fiddled with her collar, pulling it close around her jawline.

They opened the door and stepped out into the breezeway. Dani pulled her hands up her sleeves to keep off the cold. As they entered the garage, she stepped back toward the far corner and watched as the other four fanned out, surrounded the car, and pulled off the tarp.

Mark got down on his knees near the tailpipe and examined the ground around the rear tires. "He told you he hadn't driven the car at all, is that right?" he asked Dani, sounding skeptical.

"That's what he said, yes," she replied with a shrug.

"We can test the gasoline to confirm," he told Elena, who made a note in a small, leather notebook she was carrying. "The tires are flat on the bottom. No doubt it's been here for a while anyway. I don't see tire tracks leading out of the garage, but I also don't see a real heavy dust build-up."

"Could be he just keeps it swept out," remarked Josh. Mark nodded silently and Elena made more notes in her book. "What about the plate?"

"Still has the old sticker," he observed. "If he has been driving it, he hasn't been doing it legally."

Chris came over to stand beside Dani while the others continued their inspection. "It's pretty amazing that you found this guy. I'm a little unclear on how that happened.

Have you known him all along? Did you know the Miller family?"

Dani shifted her weight uneasily, wondering how she could explain Kōbō and the barking dog. "No, not directly," she replied cautiously. "But my friend's family had a vacation home up here when I was a kid. Our families used to come up here together during the summer."

"Oh, so then it was your friend who knew them?"

Dani nodded, grateful to have found a truthful path without actually having to tell the truth. "She dated one of them. The younger brother, Matt."

"Really?" he asked, sounding intrigued. Dani could see the question forming behind his round spectacles. "Any chance we could interview her for the show as well?"

"I already asked. I was hoping she'd consent to it but I don't think so. As you can imagine, it wasn't the best time in her life and I think she'd rather just forget about it."

"I understand. Do you think you could change her mind?"

Dani laughed. "You're a tenacious one, aren't you?"

"Tenacious?" he repeated. "What is this?"

"Sie sind hartnaeckig," she said with a sly smile.

He looked at her in surprise. "Oh, Sie sprechen deutsch?"

"Ja, Sie sind Deutscher, nicht wahr?"

"Ja, ich bin Deutscher. Ich bin in Magdeburg geboren."

"Oh, also Sie kommen aus den Osten?"

"Kann man nicht das hoeren?" he asked with a sheepish grin.

She laughed, then turned to find the others staring at them in quiet amusement. "Hope I'm not disturbing you, Chris," Mark teased "but might I have a moment of your time over here?"

Chris laid a hand on Dani's shoulder. "Please excuse me a moment," he said and walked over to where Mark was crouched behind the car.

"I'm fairly convinced that he's telling the truth," he said as Chris crouched down beside him. "I don't see any outward signs of it being used. We need to get it into a controlled environment as soon as possible. If he'll let us take it today then that's definitely the way to go."

Chris nodded his agreement. Glancing up at Dani he said, "Dani, could you please go inside and let Dale know that we'd like to take the car today. Could you see if he'll give us his consent for that?"

"Sure thing." She left them to their work and returned back through the breezeway toward the house. Inside she found Dale and Lee in the kitchen sipping beers and smoking cigars. When she entered, they stopped talking and turned to look at her.

"Chris asked me to tell you that he would like to take the car into the lab today. Would that be okay?" she directed the question to Dale.

He glanced at Lee, who gave him a supportive little nod. "Sure, why not?" Dale replied.

"I can't believe you've had it all this time and have never done anything with it," Lee said. "Weren't you ever tempted to use it or at least to open it up and look inside?"

"You have to understand, in my gut I suppose I always had an idea of what happened in that car. I didn't know for sure and I didn't want to know for sure but my suspicions were there. I knew that if I looked inside it—I knew that if *anybody* looked inside it—then I'd have no choice but to deal with it. I should have turned it in right away, I know that. I just couldn't. I used to feel guilty about Craig and his crimes, as if they were mine. So I kept silent. Now I realize that my only real crime *was* the silence."

"What prompted the change?" asked Lee.

He shrugged. "I guess the older I get, the less I feel like carrying around somebody else's baggage. I couldn't control what happened when I was a kid, but I sure as hell intend to control what happens as an adult." He gave Dani a weary smile.

She put her hand over his and gave it a gentle squeeze.

"Okay then," Lee said, his voice taking on a business air. "I'm going to go out and work with the guys to call in the wrecker and bring the car back to the lab. Dale, I'll speak to you on Monday when they're ready to open it up, okay?"

"Yep, I'll talk to you then and thanks for your help with this." The two men shook hands and Lee headed out the side door in the direction of the garage.

"Are you still okay?" Dani asked when they were alone.

"I am," he said, sounding more resolved than convinced. "Of course, it's easy enough to say that now. Ask me again a month *after* the shit has hit the fan instead of a month before and let's see if I still feel the same.

"A month before?" she asked in confusion. "How long does it take to do an interview and pull the show together?"

"Well, according to Lee, it will take at least a month, maybe even *several* months to get all the forensic test results back and they don't even want to begin the interview until then because he'll be asking me to comment on the test results and if we don't know them yet ..." He shrugged and took a sip of his beer.

"A month or even two?" Dani felt very discouraged.

"The case has waited nearly forty years. A couple months more is well worth it if it brings us some solid evidence. I am sorry that I didn't turn it in sooner. Really I am."

She felt a sudden pang of guilt. It had not been her intention to make him feel bad. "No, I know, of course it couldn't have been an easy thing to do. I guess I've watched one too many crime shows. They make it seem like DNA testing can be done while you watch—in a matter of minutes. I guess I'm just disappointed to know the truth."

"They're going to be filming the initial inspection of the car, though, when they open it up. He tells me there's a spot where I can sit and observe. Are you interested?"

"In going with you?" Dani asked.

He nodded. "They're going to open it up on Monday. Lee's supposed to give me a call in the morning and let me know what time exactly. Would you like me to call you?"

"Yes, please. I have to admit, I'm very curious."

"Curiosity is not exactly what I'm feeling, but I do understand what you mean."

"What do you think they'll find?"

He shrugged. "Like I said before, I think Craig meant for them to find evidence in the car and I think that's what they'll find."

"So you're saying you think he *planted* evidence in the car?"

"Well, that makes it sound like he's wrongfully trying to involve an innocent person, and I don't think they'll find that, no. I think—or perhaps I should say that I *hope*—he managed to save some of the items that his old man and Melden would have destroyed, had he not gotten to them first. Look, truthfully, I don't know what Craig knew or didn't know. We'll just have to wait and see, I suppose."

His response left her uneasy.

A short while later, the rumble of a tow truck coming down the small street could be heard from the kitchen. Dani and Dale went to the picture window in the living room and looked out toward the driveway. As they did, the wrecker pulled past the drive, stopped, and began to back up. They turned back to the kitchen and went out through the side door to join the others in the garage, where the main door had already been opened and the guys were directing the driver toward the orange car. A half hour later, through a series of winching maneuvers, they had the car secured onto the flatbed of the truck and they watched as it pulled out of the drive and headed back in the direction of the main road.

"Ready to get started back?" Lee asked the others. A general rumble of agreement went through the group and Dani turned to Dale.

"So you'll call me on Monday?"

"I will." He hugged her briefly and watched as she followed Lee and the others back to the white van.

Chapter
XXI

Late the next afternoon, Dani phoned Nora. For a moment, Dani feared that she would not pick up. The line rang twice, a third time and then, just as she was certain that it would go to voice mail, Nora's voice came on the line sounding rushed and impatient.

"Hello Dani," she said with a sharp bite in her voice.

"Hey Nora, is everything OK?"

"Yeah, it's fine. I'm just rushing to get ready."

"To get ready?" she repeated.

"Yes, for dinner. Are you still coming?"

Dani couldn't help but wonder what answer her friend would have preferred to hear. "Of course," she said firmly.

"Fine," Nora snapped back. "Then why are you acting like you don't know what I'm talking about?"

"Well, I know we're going to dinner. I guess what I don't understand is why you're getting so worked up about getting ready for it. Does it matter how you look for him?"

"Don't give me that shit, Dani. I always spend a lot of time getting ready when I go out. You know that. Don't try to pretend like this is something unusual."

Dani had to concede the point but that concession did not make her feel any better. "We're just going to that pizza place, right? So what are you wearing?"

"If I knew that, I wouldn't be in such a rush. You've got to let me finish getting ready. I'll see you there at 6:30."

"Well, actually, that's why I was calling. I thought you and I should get there early and figure out where we should sit so that I can see you but he won't see me."

"Get there *early?*" she repeated, as though the suggestion was completely ludicrous. "You're telling me this *now?*"

"Well, it only now occurred to me," Dani replied meekly.

"It's almost four o'clock now! How are we supposed to get there early?"

"Don't you live just a few blocks away from the restaurant? I'm not talking about being there hours ahead of time, maybe just a quarter to six or six o'clock!"

"Oh for crying out loud, Dani!"

"What's the big deal? You're not trying to impress him, remember? He's the monster's brother, right? Remember his horrible family?"

"I know, I know," she said impatiently, her voice coming and going over the phone, as though she were looking for something as they spoke. "Fine, I'll meet you at the restaurant at six. Now I have to go." She hung up the phone without waiting for a response.

Dani arrived at the restaurant first. She had dressed simply in a pair of black twill trousers, a heather gray t-shirt and a marled wool, zip-front, ivory cardigan that was knit with a heather gray Nordic pattern throughout. She found a spot at a table by the bar in a dark corner of the little restaurant and watched for Nora.

At ten minutes past six, Nora walked in. The effort she'd put into choosing the best outfit had been time well spent, Dani thought. As always, her appearance was flawless. Her outfit was the perfect mix of casual and dressy and it flattered her in every respect. She wore dark denim, slim-fitting jeans that sat well below her toned belly and accentuated her narrow hips. Medium brown, suede boots covered the jeans to her knees. She wore a crisp, white poplin shirt buttoned to stretch, but not gap, over her firm, full bosom. Over it all she wore a woolen, navy pea coat that fit through the waist and flared ever so slightly over her hips and down to the middle of her thighs. Her jeans were cinched at the waist with a leather belt in the same shade of brown as the boots with a square, brass buckle that glinted beneath the coat when she moved. She'd straightened her dark blond hair so that it hung in soft wisps around her face and shoulders.

As she entered the dark restaurant, she removed the brown aviator sunglasses she'd been wearing against the glare of the snow outside and strode toward where Dani was seated. As she moved, her hair and the navy coat flowed in rhythm to her strides. As always, she radiated a sense of cool confidence and gentlemen's eyes from all over the room sought her out. When she reached the table, she bent down and gave her friend a quick hug. The table in front of Dani's was also vacant and she took the seat nearest to her friend so that the two were seated beside one another without actually being at the same table.

They each gave a nervous glance around the room. Immediately, a waitress approached her. "I'll just have a decaf," she told the woman curtly. The waitress nodded wordlessly and headed back in the direction she'd just come. "Okay," she said in a low mutter without looking in Dani's direction, "where are you going to sit?"

Dani was confused, "Well, I thought I'd just sit here," she said, gesturing to the little, round table at which she sat.

"There?" Nora asked doubtfully. "Then where am I supposed to …" she began to shift her position when she said suddenly, "Turn around!"

Dani swung around so quickly that she slammed her leg into the low wall that ran along the edge of the bar area, separating it from the rest of the restaurant. "Son-of-a-bitch!" Dani cursed quietly.

"Shhh," Nora hissed quickly and then stood to greet the man walking toward her. "Hey, Matt!" she gushed as he approached. Dani did her best to become invisible, cowering near her table, her back to Nora as she greeted the new arrival. As Nora embraced him, Dani stole a peek from behind her menu. Although much more casually dressed, he was every bit as handsome as she remembered. He wore black denim jeans, above well-worn, black leather boots. Under a brown suede jacket he wore a forest green, thermal Henley top, unbuttoned at the collar to show a glimpse of the soft, white cotton t-shirt over which it was layered. His sharp jaw was covered with a light, sandy-brown beard and, unlike Nora, he did not remove his sunglasses when he entered. They were rimmed in tortoise-shell frames and were dark enough to obscure his eyes. As they broke from their embrace, Dani turned back sharply toward her own table.

"Have you ordered yet?" he asked.

As if on cue, the waitress returned to the table and set a cup of decaf down in front of Nora.

"Only the coffee," she explained.

"Can I get you something to drink?" the waitress asked Miller with a warm smile.

"Just water, thanks," he returned her smile as she set a pair of menus in front of them.

"Did you have any trouble finding the place?" Nora asked.

"Not at all. Have you eaten here before? How's the pizza?" he asked, flipping through the menu.

"Good, it's good. Everything here is good, really," she said. To Dani, Nora's voice sounded giggly and unnatural. She wished they hadn't come.

"So what would you recommend? Do you want to split a pizza?"

"Sure, we could do that," she agreed quickly. "Maybe a supreme?"

He nodded and when the waitress returned with his water he handed her back the menus. "We'll split a medium supreme, please." She took the menus and appeared disappointed by the brief interaction, but headed back to the kitchen all the same. "So, what did you think of the auto show?" he asked, returning his attention to Nora.

She shrugged. "It was alright. I have to say, I've never been very impressed by car shows. I guess I'm not much of a car buff."

"So why did you go then?"

"For my friend, she had to go for professional reasons and she didn't want to go alone. I went just to keep her company."

He nodded his understanding, "Ah, so the old wing man bit, is that it?"

She laughed as though the comment were the funniest thing she'd ever heard.

"Oh, brother," mumbled Dani.

Nora cleared her throat loudly, as though to drown her out. "And what about you? Did you enjoy it?" she asked.

"I did. Although, I'm sort of like your friend. Like it or not, I'd have gone for professional reasons. Fortunately, though, I can honestly say that I enjoyed it very much. I am a car guy, as you probably remember."

"I do. What are you doing now?" she asked. "Professionally, I mean."

"I'm in automotive, in purchasing actually, but I'm a senior vice-president now, so it's expected that I come out for that type of thing. And you? What have you been up to? Married with kids?"

Nora laughed lightly, "No, not at all. I've been married twice but I never had children. I work in HR for a staffing company."

"You work in HR? Isn't that all they do in a staffing company is HR?"

She laughed again. Dani was becoming annoyed by her normally serious friend's school girl reactions. "No, of course not! We have accounting, billing, IT—the same as any other firm."

"Ah, of course," he said, nodding.

"And what about you? Are you married?"

"I was," he said. "It didn't work out though."

"Any kids?" she asked.

"We have two daughters, but they live in New York with their mother now."

"Oh, I'm so sorry to hear that!" she cooed sympathetically, just as she had for Tom Montgomery when he announced his divorce. "That must be very difficult for you."

"Well, fortunately, I got my pilot's license years ago and I own a small Cessna that I keep at the airport out in Pontiac so I can fly out to see them whenever I like."

At the mention of the airport, Nora fell silent. The awkward pause in the conversation lingered on for an uncomfortably long time before he spoke again. "You re-member that airport, don't you, Nora? We used to take the plane out of Pontiac whenever we went to Fanny Lake, re-member?" His voice had dropped to an ominous whisper and Dani leaned back in her chair to hear.

Without daring to turn around, Dani guessed that Nora must have nodded for soon he continued. "Do you want to tell me why you and your little friend have been snooping around Fanny Lake? What on earth would bring you back up there after all this time?"

"I told you," Nora explained, her voice a childish squeak. "We went up there snowmobiling."

"When have you ever in your life wanted to go snow-mobiling? How often did I ask you to go while we were up north and you never went once."

"That was a long time ago. I was just a kid," she insisted. "My ex-husband used to love to go. I went with him all the time. Now I go with Dani."

"I don't believe you," he said flatly. "I don't know what you think you're playing at or why you'd want to bring that up after so long, but I'm telling you now, let sleeping dogs lie. It was a long time ago and it's over."

As if remembering her hopes for his great turn-around, Nora began to try to reason with him. "Those families still don't know what happened to their kids though, Matt. Re-member those boys up at the cabin?"

"Of course I remember those boys at the cabin," he snarled. "We were lucky the police couldn't pin down the call then. We got lucky once, let's not press our luck now."

"Don't you ever wonder about it though? What if one of those boys was that Jimmy Prince kid that was missing?"

"What if …?" he began, then stopped himself. "Craig's dead. It does no good to think of that now. You can't change the past. Leave it alone," he commanded.

"But we could set the record straight. We could go to the police and just tell them what we saw. It might bring the family some closure and what harm could it do? Like you said, Craig's dead. Your dad's dead too, they can't hurt you anymore. What harm could it do to tell them what we know?"

"What *we* know?" he repeated with a sneer. "What is it you think you know?"

From her seat behind them, Dani heard Nora wince. Quickly, she reached for the purse at her feet. She pulled it onto her lap and opened it, pulling out her compact and flipping up the tiny mirror inside. Next she pulled out a tube of lipstick and pretended to reapply her makeup as she peered back at them in the mirror. He was holding Nora's hand firmly across the table. Dani could tell it was no romantic gesture. She began to wonder at what point she should intercede. For the moment, Nora did not appear to be in danger, so she returned the mirror to her purse but continued to hold the purse in her lap.

"Nothing," Nora replied. "Just that he had kids up at the cabin."

"Those kids were our cousins. That didn't mean anything. You need to forget it." His voice softened but he did not release her hand.

"Your cousins? They weren't your cousins. If they were your cousins then why …?" She winced again.

"I told you to forget it," he interrupted, his voice becoming hard again. "Do you know what my cousins looked like back then? Because I do. For all you know, he was up there with my cousins. That's what the cops will hear from me if you try to say otherwise." He began to stroke her forearm with his right hand while still holding her hand firmly with his left. When the waitress returned with their pizza, he shot her a sweet smile, as though she'd interrupted a romantic interlude. She set down the pizza, plates, and utensils quickly and walked back toward the kitchen. "Think about it, a woman with your history doesn't need to attract attention to herself over a completely unfounded accusation, right?"

With that, Nora's anger finally flared. "What the hell's that supposed to mean? What 'history'?"

"*Well*," he said slowly, stretching the word out as he spoke it. "You were what? Sixteen? Sneaking up to a private cabin with some random guy for the weekend?"

"It was *during* the weekend, not *for* the weekend and we'd been dating for months. Besides, *nothing happened* and what the hell difference does it make how old I was?"

"Nothing happened? Is that what you think? That's not what people will hear from me if you talk. All I'm saying is that a girl who's willing to go that far, that fast … and you've been divorced twice since? Are you going to tell me that if my investigators were to look into your dating history, they wouldn't find a few skeletons in your closet too?"

Nora flew to her feet, grabbed his water glass and flung the contents into his face. "C'mon, Dani, she growled, we're leaving!"

Dani grabbed her purse, rose and gave him a smug smile as they strode past him out of the restaurant and into the parking lot. "That was fantastic!" she said to Nora as they reached her car.

"I want to talk to those people on the show," she said suddenly. "I don't know what on earth I was thinking to believe he might have changed. I don't know if my information will be of any use or if it proves anything at all but if they'll talk to me, I'll tell them everything I know." The words tumbled from her lips in a frantic rush. "We should go now," she said, stealing a glance back at the entrance to the restaurant. "He'll be pissed and for all we know, he inherited his father's temper!"

Suddenly, Dani remembered the unusual circumstances of the so-called suicide. She remembered that all the Millers were good with guns and a panic swept over her. "Go," she yelled to Nora, who had already climbed behind the wheel of her small sedan. "Don't wait for me!" She watched as Nora drove off before she ran to her own car. She opened her purse and began to dig through it in search of her car keys. Her heart was racing in her chest now and she tried to convince herself that she was being ridiculous. He'd probably gone to the men's room to dry himself off, maybe he'd even stayed to eat the pizza they'd ordered.

Finally, she found her key fob and unlocked the door. As she reached for the handle, she saw the blur of a brown suede sleeve out of the corner of her eye. She began to turn but he was too quick. He seized her arm and swung her around to face him. He loomed over her, his eyes still obscured by the dark sunglasses even though dusk had already fallen. He pressed her against the car, his handsome face still damp and filled with rage. She froze, too frightened to move.

"I don't know what you and that stupid bitch think you're up to," he snarled. "But you tell her this for me, if she goes sticking her nose where it doesn't belong, I'll make sure she lives to regret it. I have a team of lawyers and media pros who will show the world just what a vindictive, spiteful slut she really is."

Dani shoved him off just far enough to plant the pointy toe of her boot squarely between his thighs. He went down like a sack of potatoes, groaning and grabbing himself as she flung open the car door, climbed in and backed out past him. "Now who's the bitch?" she called out at him as she drove past. She left him writhing on the pavement, cupping his manhood as though it might fall off.

Chapter
XXII

Kōbō walked withered and frail beside her as they crossed the grassy lawn of the villa. To Dani, it seemed strange to see him walking around. She had come to think of him as a permanent fixture on the landing, not unlike the marble chaise on which he always sat.

"What are you doing here?" she asked.

"I'm here to escort you, of course, to the press conference." He gave her a satisfied grin and nodded, his jaunty hat bobbing slightly back and forth on his head.

"The press conference? What press conference?" As they walked, she looked around the wide expanse of grass. Little displays were set up everywhere, just as they had been during the auto show, but instead of a cohesive exhibition with a common theme, these displays each seemed to be telling its own, unique story. One looked like a science exhibit with serious men in white lab coats staring into microscopes and twirling flasks of liquid between gloved fingertips. At another, Matt Miller was sitting at a corporate desk, screaming commands into a phone. At a third, she saw Lawrence

Prince having blood drawn. For a moment, Dani feared for his health but something in his expression seemed relieved, almost content and so she moved on. Finally, they arrived at the top of the stairs. On the cliffside landing below, the marble chaises were gone and the entire landing was packed with reporters, all staring out at a small podium at the edge of the landing nearest the sea below. As they climbed down the stairs, a tall, lanky, gray-haired man stepped up to the podium. He had a prominent nose, a heavy brow and bags under his eyes. Despite his advanced age, Dani recognized him immediately.

"Senator Richman," called one of the reporters, "how do you account for your name being tied to the crime?" His question was followed by a rush of comments from the other assembled reporters.

The senator put up a confident hand to silence the crowd before he spoke. "I assure you that I had nothing to do with these horrendous crimes. Obviously, my enemies have set me up to take this fall. As I'm sure you all know, I have always taken a firm stance against crime and have been instrumental in establishing a key tool to aid in that fight. Anyone who fights crime is sure to gain a few enemies. That is certainly at the root of this. Mark my words, my database will lead to the capture of the true criminal here!"

As he spoke, a cell phone somewhere began to ring. First the senator and then the crowd fell silent. Everyone was listening to the persistent cadence of the musical ringtone. All those assembled, including the senator, turned to stare at Dani.

"Answer your damned phone!" the senator growled at her from the podium.

Dani's eyes flew open and she realized that her cell phone was indeed ringing from her bedside table. She fumbled for it in the darkness, knocking off a jar of lotion, which fell painfully onto Maggie's head below. "Hello?" she said, her voice rough with sleep as she brought the phone to her ear.

"Dani? It's Dale. I'm so sorry to wake you but I just got the call from Lee and they're opening the car up this morning. I have to get on the road if I'm going to make it over there in time. Do you want me to come by and pick you up? You're on the way."

She glanced at the time, it was barely six. "Yeah, please. What time do you think you'll be here?"

"Probably nine thirty, if I don't hit traffic, which I might. Lee said he'd hold them off for as long as possible, but it's an independent lab so we have to work with their timetable."

"OK, I'll be ready when you get here." She clicked the phone off and then fought the urge to fall back on her pillow. She reached for her notebook to try and record the dream, but she'd been pulled from it too quickly. She was frustrated to realize that the details were already starting to fade. She could remember that Kōbō had been there, and the senator. It had something to do with reporters and a press conference, didn't it? Why would Kōbō be at a press conference, she wondered, her mind still fuzzy with sleep. She turned on her light and wrote down what little she could remember. She returned the notebook to the drawer and pushed back her comforter. Maggie and Gordie reluctantly rose and followed her out of the room.

At a quarter to eleven, Dale pulled into the drive. "Sorry I'm so late," he apologized, as she pulled open the passenger door and took her seat. "I just called Lee though," he said, waving his cell phone at her, "and he tells me that they're still waiting on one of the technicians so they haven't opened it up yet."

"Well that's good," she said. "Did you get a lot of snow up by you?"

"We did, that's what slowed me down so much. Everywhere I looked there was someone else sliding into a ditch. You folks got a lot less down here than we did out by me."

"I can imagine. I have to be honest, I'd never want to live that far north." He smiled and shrugged but said nothing.

An hour later they arrived at an enormous gray stone building that looked sterile even from the outside. They rushed in to find Lee waiting for them in the lobby. He reached for Dani and gave her a hug then reached past her and shook Dale's hand.

"Good to see you," he said as he greeted him. "Glad you could make it. Okay, as you can imagine, we can't all pile in while they're taking samples from the car, but they have allowed us to film it so we're going to be watching it unfold on a screen in here," he indicated a door off to the side of the lobby. "And if it's alright with you, Dale, we'd like to film your reactions to what you're seeing as it happens, can we do that?"

Dale looked startled. "I guess I didn't realize that you wanted to do that today."

Lee seemed surprised. "Well, we did discuss taping your reactions when we spoke at your house, remember?"

Dale nodded, "Oh, yeah, I remember that. I guess I just didn't realize that you meant right now. It's just … I didn't really dress for it." He held his arms out as if to present himself for inspection.

"Oh, don't worry about that," Lee dismissed him with a wave. "We've got folks here who will do the makeup and your hair, and we'll take a tight enough shot that your clothes won't matter anyway. It'll be fine." He gave him a pat on the shoulder and then held up his index finger, "You'll have to excuse me for just one minute, I want to let them know you're here." With that, he vanished into the adjoining room.

"My hair?" he said quietly, more to himself than to Dani.

She gave his arm a reassuring squeeze, "It'll be fine. Your hair looks fine," she glanced up at his head. "Maybe just a little damp from the snow." He ran his fingers through it and then stopped abruptly as Lee reentered the room.

"Dale, Dani, if I could have you come in here, please?" They followed him through the door and into a huge conference room with a large monitor mounted to the far wall. On either side of the conference room table were large cameras on tripods, microphones, and several computers.

"Dale," Lee began, pointing to a small, elegant blond woman in her mid-forties, "this is Sheila. She's going to be putting some theatrical makeup on you just to take the glare off your skin and to define your features for the cameras. Don't worry," he said, holding up his hands defensively as if to a gunman, "she's not going to make you look like a woman." Dale nodded with a laugh and walked over to shake Sheila's hand. "And this," continued Lee, "is John Prosper. He's going to be interviewing you both for the show and here during this discovery session."

Dale seemed confused. "I thought you were going to do that?"

"Well, no, I'll leave that to John," Lee gestured toward the handsome man he'd just introduced, who smiled broadly, showing off capped, white teeth. "He's our pro in front of the camera. But I'll be present for every one of the interviews. I'll be right here," he assured him.

Dale nodded and a few moments later, he was seated in front of Sheila, a white paper bib tied around his neck, as she applied a heavy coat of flesh toned foundation. "Dani," Lee called to her from across the room, "you can have a seat at the table there. Can I get you anything? Coffee? Tea? Maybe a doughnut?"

"No thanks, Lee," she called back. "I'm fine." She took a seat at the back of the long table and silently observed the bustling, rushing crew as they tested lenses, lighting, and sound levels.

When finally Dale was properly coifed and made up, they settled him in a seat near her own at the far end of the table. Lee pulled out a cell phone and dialed a number. "Hey Mark, we're ready up here whenever you're ready down there. Okay, I'll let them know. Thanks." He powered the phone off and glanced over at them. "The technician we were waiting on arrived just a little before you so they're running late as well. It'll be about ten minutes." They nodded. Lee went to the monitor and turned it on then joined them at the table. On the screen, they could see the Karmann Ghia and a number of technicians in lab coats, face masks, and safety glasses milling around it. After several minutes, a final technician arrived and Dani could hear a microphone clicking on and the murmurs and comments of the assembled group could be heard in the conference room.

"Okay, are we ready to get started?" It was the technician who was last to arrive that was speaking and based on the reaction of the others when he spoke, Dani took him to be a man of some importance. The other technicians murmured their agreement. He approached the driver's side door with gloved hands and tried the handle. It seemed to stick. He tried it again and then a third time with a firmer yank, bracing himself before he pulled. Finally, it creaked open on stiff hinges. The technician stepped away, as if reacting to a strong odor and, for an absurd moment, Dani wondered if there might be a dead body in the car. As he moved, a second technician stood beside him documenting the scene through a series of photos with a very sophisticated-looking digital camera. Dani could hear the camera click, click, clicking and after each shot the technician would peer down at the little monitor on the back of the camera to verify that he had the shot before bringing it back to his face and peering through the viewfinder again. A third technician stood at the ready with a notebook.

"We have a very strong odor of feces and urine coming from the vehicle," the man who had opened the door called out. The woman with the notebook jotted down the observation. He leaned into the car without touching anything and glanced first around and then overhead at the headliner. He pulled his head out, exhaled, and took a deep breath of fresh air. "There's extensive rodent damage to the headliner with both feces and urine visibly present." The photographer moved in to capture the observation with his camera even as the woman captured it in her notebook.

The first man moved back toward the car and called over its roofline to a woman standing opposite him, near the passenger door. "Peggy, why don't you get started over there dusting for prints. If you could, please also check the glove compartment. Tim," he called to a man standing to Peggy's left, "why don't you start working in the backseat and see what you can find." Finally, he turned to his right and spoke to someone off camera. "Becky, I'd ask you to please start working in the trunk if you would." Moments later, the woman named Becky stepped into the shot moving past the camera from left to right to stand in front of the trunk.

"Could you pop it, please, Fred?" she called back to the first man.

Fred crouched down near the steering wheel and pulled a lever. The trunk lid groaned and moved slightly. Becky reached under and pulled it up. "Frank, can you get this, please?" she said to the man with the camera. Before Lee's cameraman could capture whatever she was seeing, the photographer in the lab coat came to Becky's side. Click, check, click, check, click, he shot the scene from several angles, carefully checking each shot in turn.

As she watched, Dani cursed his slow progress and silently wished that he'd move out of the way. No sooner had the thought occurred to her though than Becky called over to another man in a white coat standing off in a far corner of the large lab.

"Pete, could I get a bag over here, please?"

"Large or small?" he asked.

"Large," she replied quickly as she reached with her gloved hand into the trunk. The man known as Pete rushed forward with a large, brown, paper bag and held it open for her.

As Becky turned toward the bag, Dani got her first glimpse of the object in her hand and the glimpse made her gasp. Everyone in the room turned to look at her. She watched in stunned disbelief as the female technician held up a bright red snow boot with black spider webs and the face of a superhero emblazoned on the side, that was stained with a dark, brownish-red substance. The technician placed it in the paper bag and the man holding the bag folded the top down twice and wrote something on a label on the front of the bag.

"Dani, everything okay?" Lee whispered over to her with equal parts concern and curiosity.

"Yeah," she whispered back. "Just shocking to see blood stains on a little boy's boot," she lied. "Assuming those were blood stains," she added quickly.

He nodded and turned his attention back to the monitor.

"Fred, I've got something here," called Peggy from the passenger's side. "Pete, I'm going to need a small bag, please." Fred stood up from where he'd been dusting for fingerprints on the driver's side door and looked across the roofline as Peggy showed him a small, leather book that she'd pulled from the glove compartment. She flipped it open and examined the weathered pages. "Seems to be some sort of ledger or diary. Pete appeared at her side with a small paper bag and she dropped it inside. Again, the man with the bag folded down the top and recorded something on the label. Next, Peggy pulled several small slips of paper out of the glove compartment. "Looks like a registration slip and proof of insurance from 1977," she looked from the papers to Fred and added, "in the name of Craig William Miller." Next to her, Pete opened the first of two small, paper envelopes. She dropped the registration into the first and the proof of insurance card into the second. Again, he jotted notes onto the label on the front of each. "There's a number of stains here and I can see hairs as well," Peggy reported as she examined the interior of the vehicle.

"Same here," agreed Tim from the backseat.

"Let's gather the hairs and fibers into envelopes," Fred instructed the group, "and then for the stains, I say we just cut out the upholstery rather than trying to take swabs. As long as no one needs this car back, it's the most efficient way to make sure we get it all." There was a murmur of mutual agreement and the room became a flurry of activity as the technicians pulled fibers, hairs, and even a dried wad of chewing gum stuck in a wrapper off of the car's upholstery. Dani lost track of the number of times they changed their gloves and by the end, Pete had opened a fresh box of the little paper envelopes used to collect the evidence.

Through it all, Lee's cameras had been trained on Dale. Periodically John would lean over and flash his bright smile at the camera, looking entirely too cheerful for the grim circumstances of their meeting. "Can you tell us what you're feeling as you're watching this scene unfold," was the first question that he'd asked. At the time, Dale had appeared almost startled to hear him speak, as if he'd forgotten that John was still in the room. As the questioning went on, he seemed to become more at ease with the process, his voice trembling only slightly as he answered. He described the experience as both painful and cathartic. Dani felt the exact same way.

Finally, when all the items had been pulled out and collected into bags and envelopes, the team set about cutting the upholstery out of the car so as to test the fluid stains. Even the carpet from the trunk was extracted. As the monitor on the wall went black and the team started to pack up the conference room, Dani rose stiffly and stretched. She and Dale were escorted back through the lobby with the assurance that they would be notified as soon as the results were in, although, they were warned, it would more than likely be at least two months before all the results were available. To Dani, it seemed like a lifetime.

Before he bid them farewell, Dani pulled Lee aside. "I don't know if Chris mentioned it to you but I have a friend who used to know the Millers …"

Before she could finish the thought, Lee interrupted her, "The one with the cottage up north?"

Dani laughed, "So I guess he told you, huh? Yes, the very same and I think she's had a change of heart. I think she's ready to talk about it. Would you still be interested?"

"Absolutely," he said, sounding pleasantly surprised. "Call me next week!"

Chapter
XXIII

The following week it was decided that Nora and Lee would meet at Dani's for dinner to discuss the interview and the types of questions that would be asked. On the day of the dinner, Dani was inexplicably nervous. She'd prepared a lasagna and a salad and was busy cleaning up the kitchen when Lee arrived. She greeted him with a hug and settled him into the living room with a glass of wine and a plate of cheese and crackers while they waited for Nora to arrive. Meanwhile, Dani rushed about the kitchen, cleaning dishes and finishing the food.

Finally, Nora's car pulled into the drive. Dani greeted her at the door and walked her into the living room where Lee was still sipping his wine. He stood to greet her while Dani went to fetch another glass. She stayed in the room only long enough for the two to begin to chat and then went back to the kitchen where she began to set the table, straining to hear what little she could of the conversation going on in the next room.

"So, Dani tells me that you knew Matthew Miller," she heard Lee say.

Nora spoke in much softer tones so her answers floated into the kitchen only in bits and pieces. "We were just kids," she heard her say once and later, "I was in over my head." Finally, she had the table set and the dinner finished. She called them both in to eat.

"So how well did you know Craig?" he asked, as they entered the room.

"Not very well at all, really. He was around, of course. He was Matt's brother so any time I was hanging out at their house or sometimes when we'd go up to the cottage, he'd be there. That's what happened the day I placed the 911 call."

"The day you …?" he looked at Dani, as if for an explanation. Finding none, he looked back at Nora.

"Dani didn't tell you?" she asked, looking from Lee to Dani.

"I didn't want to speak out of turn. I figured I'd just let you get there in your own time and in your own words."

"So you're the caller who hung up before identifying herself? I remember that call. That was you?"

"It was," Nora replied in a voice heavy with guilt. They took their seats at the table and as they ate, Nora recounted the circumstances of her 911 call and told Lee about Matthew Miller's reactions both on that day and during their recent dinner date. Dani informed them both about her encounter with Miller afterward.

"Oh my God, Dani! Why didn't you tell me? I'm so sorry to have put you in that position. I never should have trusted him again. You tried to warn me. I don't know what I was thinking."

"You wanted to believe the best in him. I can't blame you for that. He was born into a messed-up family and, honestly, there was a small part of me that hoped he'd do the right thing too, but some people just aren't created that way, I guess." Nora nodded but said nothing more and so the conversation turned back to the day of the 911 call.

"I remember the caller saying that she didn't get a good look at the boys? So you're not sure Jimmy Prince was among them?" Lee asked.

Nora shook her head as she swallowed a bite of lasagna. A moment later she said, "I couldn't tell you for sure. I only had a momentary glance into the room before Matt and Craig started screaming at each other and the whole scene kind of got out of hand."

"So you got the definite sense that Matt knew Craig shouldn't have been with those kids? That he knew it was a potentially dangerous situation?"

"Oh yeah, definitely. Well any adult with a brain would have seen the problem with it though. They had beer cans all around and some sort of disgusting porn on the television. Plus three guys hanging out with a bunch of kids doing that? The whole thing just wasn't normal, not even for the Millers!"

"So tell me about the other men who were there. You said you knew one of them, right?" Lee had barely touched his lasagna and was staring at Nora with the serious air of the investigative reporter he had once been.

"Right, Michael. I had met his friend Michael before but I didn't know him well, just by sight. He was this tall, skinny, blond kid." Dani thought about her very first dream and the thin boy who had helped lure Jimmy into the car. "He and I were nearly the same age but I only knew him through Craig. He didn't hang around with anyone else that I knew and he and Craig were always hanging around with much younger boys. I'd go into town when we were up north and you'd see him sitting around the pizzeria or at the

Frosty Falls buying cones for young boys. Some of the people we knew talked about how great he was with the local kids, like he was doing them a kindness, but I just always thought it was a little creepy." Dani thought of Dale and of his common bond with Craig. But that was not her story to tell and so she said nothing.

"Did you ever get a last name on Michael?" he asked.

Nora shook her head.

"Would you recognize him if you saw a picture?"

"Maybe," Nora said, "but it would have to be a picture from the right time frame. I only knew him briefly more than thirty years ago. I have no idea what he'd look like now, and I don't know what he looked like when he was younger. But maybe if I saw a picture of what he looked like in the '70s, maybe …"

Lee pulled a small notebook from the pocket of the blazer he was wearing and began to jot down notes. "What about the other man who was in the room that day? Did you get a name on him or would you recognize him if you saw him again? How old was he? Was he white, black? How was he dressed?"

Nora took a deep, weary breath. "He was white, older than Craig I'd say, maybe even in his thirties. It's hard to say about age. I was sixteen. Everyone who can drink looks old to a sixteen-year-old!" The others chuckled. "He had a big beer belly and his hair looked like he never washed it. Honestly, he looked the part of the weird pervert."

"Would you recognize him again if you saw a picture of him?"

Nora shrugged. "Maybe, that's really hard to say. I only saw him that once and very briefly. I remember the gut and the hair but not much else."

"So you see them in there and very quickly Matt reacts to the situation, right? You said he made you leave the house?"

"Yeah, I think he was hoping maybe he'd get me out of there quickly enough to prevent my seeing anything, but I had walked in front of him when we came into the room so by the time he reacted, I'd already gotten a pretty good look. Anyway, he made me leave as soon as he realized what was going on. I didn't go back to the car right away though. I just stepped out the front door, but I left it open. Then I stood there listening."

"And what did you hear?" Lee asked, his pen poised over his notebook.

"Threats. He threatened to tell their dad, threatened to call the cops and have him taken away. He just hurled all these threats at him. I definitely got the sense that Craig's family was fighting to control him and that they were losing that fight. Not just that day, but in general."

"And you convinced Matt to stop and call the police?"

"Well, not exactly." Nora played with her salad as she spoke, pushing the vegetables around the plate. "When we first got into the car afterward, I was pretty upset. I knew that little boy was missing. Hell, by that time everyone in the state knew about the little boy that was missing. He was the fourth victim and the family was very vocal. They were on all the news programs pleading for his safe return. The story was all over the place."

"When I went to the car, I was convinced that I'd seen him sitting in that living room. I insisted that we stop and call the police. At first, Matt agreed; but then as we drove toward town, I mentioned something about the missing kid and how I thought that was him in there. Matt told me that I was crazy, that those were just local kids in the living room. He said to me, 'You know how Craig is, he always hangs around with the local kids.' And that was true enough, I had to admit it. He made it sound like I was overreacting. He said he knew it wasn't right that Craig had beer and porn around kids but that he hadn't heard the kids complaining. He said that there was a big difference between giving a kid a beer and kidnapping or murder. He acted like he couldn't believe I'd suggest that about his brother." Her voice had become thin and tinged with something bordering on hysteria.

"Again, I had to admit that he had a point, right?" She looked at the others for agreement, but when they only stared back at her, she continued. "I was only there for a moment, and for all I know the kids had been threatened not to say anything." Nora seemed to be rehashing the decades-old discussion all over again in her mind. Dani wondered how often she'd had this same argument with herself over the years. "I don't know," Nora continued, "he just made me start to doubt myself. So I calmed down and I think he thought I'd given up on the idea of calling someone. I told him that I hadn't had a chance to use the bathroom at the house and that I had to go. I told him that we should stop at the main grocery store in town so that I could use the bathroom. I knew there was a public phone there."

"So you don't think he believed you'd call and that's why he stopped?"

"I hoped that if I called, I could convince him to go along with it. I really, honestly believed that he wanted to help those kids, so I thought he'd agree to let me make the call."

"But he didn't?" Lee coaxed.

She shook her head, still pushing the untouched salad around her plate. As she spoke, she stared at it, not him. "No, he came over and found me on the phone and threw a fit. Apparently, he never thought I'd actually do it and, by his reaction, I'd say that whatever pity he felt for those boys, it wasn't enough to make him turn against his family."

Lee's voice was soft when he spoke again, "And can I ask why you didn't call the police again when you got home and he wasn't there to stop you?"

Nora dropped her fork and covered her face with her hands. When she took them away, her mascara was smudged and her face was wet with tears. For several moments, she shook her head, unable to speak. Finally she said, "He'd have known it was me and I wasn't ready to ... and then the boy turned up dead in a ditch," she threw up her hands as if in explanation or defeat, Dani wasn't sure which. "I told myself that Matt was right, that it was never that missing boy that I saw that day. I told myself that it was just some harmless escapade with the local kids and that Craig never hurt anyone." Her voice broke and she began to sob, "It was the only way that I could live with myself after…"

Dani was at her side, holding her as she sobbed. Whispering gently to her and rocking her back and forth like a child. After several minutes, Nora regained her composure and used her napkin to fix the damage to her makeup.

Dani took her seat again and Lee leaned in close to Nora. "Thank you," he said. "I know this was difficult for you, but I want to thank you for coming forward. It really does mean a great deal."

"I should have done it then," she said, choking back fresh sobs.

"You were sixteen," he said gently. "But at least you've come forward now. That's what matters." He rose abruptly. "I think that's enough for today. We don't plan to shoot the interviews until after the test results are back, but I'm going to go home and draw up some notes on what we discussed here today. Would it be OK if I called you with some follow-up questions? Maybe you could give me your number?" He offered her his pen and notebook.

Nora accepted them, jotted down her number and handed them back. "Thank you for this, Lee. I know I'm doing the right thing now and that, at least, helps."

He squeezed her hand gently and then stepped around her to where Dani was seated. Dani stood, gave him a hug and walked him to the door. She pulled his heavy coat off a hanger on the wall and handed it to him. "Drive careful," she said, as she closed the door behind him.

When she turned around, Nora was in the living room retrieving her bag. "I'd better get going too."

"Are you going to be OK to drive?" she asked with concern.

Nora nodded. "I'll be fine. I'd love to say it's been fun but …" she shrugged and let the thought trail off. They laughed a feeble little laugh. At the door, she pulled Nora's coat off the hook and handed it to her. She gave her a hug and closed the door behind her. Dani felt exhausted. She put the leftover lasagna away and cleaned up the dishes. Afterward, though it was barely nine thirty, she decided to go to bed.

Her cell phone, unfortunately, had other plans for her. She could hear it ringing from the desk in her office and she reluctantly went in to retrieve it. When she glanced down at the caller ID, she was happy that she had.

"Hey you, what have you been up to?"

"Not much," Geoff replied. "You?"

She moaned wearily, "That's a loaded question."

He laughed. "Really? Want to tell me over lunch tomorrow? I'll treat!"

"Wow! What did I do to deserve that?"

"Let's just say that I've finally forgiven you for my cashmere sweater."

She laughed, "OK, you're on. The Biscuit?"

"Sure, around noon tomorrow okay?"

"See you then." She clicked the phone off but carried it with her upstairs, Maggie and Gordie trailing after.

The next day, Geoff was waiting for her when she arrived at the restaurant. As she approached the table he stood for a quick hug and then returned to his seat. "So, tell me, what's going on. Let's hear the whole, long story!"

She took a deep breath, as if exercising her lungs for the task. "Well—wait, when was the last update? It's been a while, hasn't it?"

"Not since the sweater incident. Like I said, I've only now forgiven you!" He winked at her playfully. "So what's goin' on?"

"Really? It's been that long? Then we'd better order first because this is going to take a while." They ordered and over burgers and fries Dani filled him in on the auto show, the agreement with Lee, the testing of the car, and the dinner with Nora the evening before.

When she was finished, Geoff sat staring at her in stunned silence. Finally he said, "So she really did know something this whole time?"

"Well," Dani shrugged, "she knew he had kids up at that cottage up north and that he and his friends spent way too much time in the company of children. I guess we still don't know conclusively if Jimmy Prince was one of those kids but …" she left the sentence unfinished.

"No matter who the kids are, what kind of freak sits around drinking beer and watching porn with a bunch of twelve-year-olds?"

Dani nodded her agreement as she took another bite of her burger.

"And you say they pulled a bloody boot out of the trunk?"

As he said it, she nearly choked on the burger. She gave him a pained look that had nothing to do with food.

"What is it? What do you know about the boot?"

"I don't think you want to know. It's a Kōbō thing."

He rolled his eyes and said, "You're right, I probably don't want to know but tell me anyway."

She recounted the dream with little Kevin and his red boots. She told him about the senator, about Melden, and about the group of drunken degenerates that surrounded them. She told him about Craig's comments and how Melden had rebuffed him. He listened to it all, his pale eyes fixed on her the entire time.

"Did you ever do an Internet search on the senator?"

"I did. He's still in the Senate but I didn't find anything in any of his profiles to suggest anything unusual. He looks like a pillar of society if you do an Internet search. I mean, I'm not saying I agree with his politics or anything but there's nothing to suggest a pedophile. I start to wonder if I didn't just hear the guy's name on TV and work him into my dream or something."

"Well, I guess we'll see when the test results come back. You'll never be able to do something with the dream alone, but if they have the boot and if your dream was right, then I'd think there'd have to be something on that boot, right? Some kind of DNA evidence or something? Did the Guardian have a victim named Kevin?"

She shook her head. "Not that anyone knows of, but there's always been speculation that there may have been additional victims."

"It's a shame you woke up when you did. You may have seen what happened to him."

"I know. I've felt guilty about that ever since it happened. I can't figure out why Kōbō hasn't brought me back into that dream. Why he hasn't made me see the rest of it."

"Maybe you weren't meant to see it all. Maybe he's trying to shield you from the whole truth. After all, there's nothing you could do for him now. Maybe the boot and the senator's involvement was all that you were meant to see?"

"I hope so. If that were the case, I could let myself off the hook for not staying in it. As it is, I'm finding it hard to forgive myself."

"You shouldn't feel that way, Dani. I'm proud of you. A lot of people would have turned away from this. They'd have written their nightmares off as just that and moved on with their lives."

"It's Dale and Nora who are being brave. All I have to relive are nightmares. They have to relive the reality."

"When do the test results come back?"

"Not soon enough. They tell me it could be months."

"Months? What kind of lab did this guy hire? On the cop shows on TV, the test results are always back before the end of the hour-long show!" He laughed, fully aware of how ridiculous he sounded. He was doing his best to make Dani laugh, and she loved him for it.

"I know, what a bunch of hacks, right?" She smiled back at him, grateful for an excuse to laugh.

They finished their lunch chatting about happier things, and Geoff gave her a long, strong hug as they said their goodbyes. "Call me if the waiting starts to get to you," he said as they parted.

"I may just take you up on that," she called back. She left feeling more upbeat than she had in quite some time.

Over the course of the next several weeks, Dani found herself constantly staring at her cell phone, willing it to ring. When it finally did ring, she would feel her hopes soar only to be irrationally disappointed by all those callers who had nothing to do with the pending test results.

Finally, on a busy Monday morning, when she'd had no time at all to even think about the case, the phone rang from beneath the pile of translation work that littered her desk. When she saw the caller ID, her heart leapt into her throat.

"Hey Lee! What's up?" Dani struggled to keep her voice calm.

"Well, not what you're hoping for, I'm sure. The results aren't in yet, but I've been doing some background searching on the descriptions that Nora gave us, remember? Michael and the pervert with the dirty hair?"

"Oh right," Dani replied, unable to keep the disappointment out of her voice.

"I've got some photos for her to look at. I'll contact her myself, but I just wanted to let you know, seeing as you started this ball rolling."

"Definitely! I appreciate the call. I'd like to be there when she looks at the pictures. Do you want me to call her and set it up?"

"No, that's OK. I'll give her a call and let you know when."

"OK. Thanks, Lee. I'll wait to hear back from you." She clicked off the phone and returned her attention to the pile of paperwork on her desk.

The following Friday Dani and Nora met at Lee's office. He sat them down on an overstuffed, black leather sofa and placed a half-dozen photos on the coffee table in front of them. "Do you recognize any of them?" he asked Nora.

She edged closer to the table and stared down at the photos, glancing at each one in turn. For Dani, such a close examination was unnecessary. Her eyes went immediately to the picture on the far left of the table. At a glance, she recognized the lanky, blond teenager who had helped to lure little Jimmy into the car. She didn't dare mention the dreams to Lee but felt compelled to draw attention to the photo. As she struggled to think of a logical lie, Nora saved her the effort.

Picking up the very same picture, Nora said, "This one. This is Michael. This is just how he looked back then."

Lee gave her an approving nod. He picked up the photo at the opposite end of the table and said, "And this is what he looks like now." The picture was very obviously a mug shot. It was a headshot of a very thin man in his late forties or early fifties with a receding hairline and thick moustache. His cheeks were gaunt and his stare was cold and vacant. "His name is Michael York. He's on parole now but has been in and out of the prison system all his life. He's a known associate of Craig Miller and has already been connected to one of the victims through a DNA match."

"Jimmy Prince?" Dani asked, trying to sound casual.

"No, he was connected to one of the female victims." As he spoke, Lee picked up the first batch of photos and laid down a second. "Do you recognize anyone here?" he asked Nora.

Again, she examined each photo carefully.

Dani leaned in alongside her and gave the first three photos only a cursory glance. When her eyes landed on the fourth photo, they stuck. She recognized him as well, as the man who had given the sofa over to the senator in the bunker. This photo also looked like a mug shot. The man in it appeared in a dirty, white t-shirt. He had a thin mop of greasy, dark hair and dark whiskers covering a weak chin. His skin was tanned and he was grinning at the camera.

As she looked at the line of photos, Nora merely shrugged. "Sorry," she said. "I don't recognize any of them."

Dani snatched the fourth photo up. "Who's this?" she asked, turning over the grainy photo to show Lee. "He looks familiar to me."

Lee gave her an odd look and replied, "That's Reggie Johnson. He was also a known associate of both Miller and York. He's currently serving two concurrent life sentences here in Michigan. Like the other two, he's a known pedophile."

Something in the way Lee was staring at her made Dani nervous. "I'm sure I've seen his picture before—while I was researching the case."

"It's funny you should mention that," he said, a hint of suspicion in his voice. "I looked all over the Internet for a picture of Johnson as he appeared then. I couldn't find one. Not a single one," he repeated slowly. "I had to go back through my own file photos. I got this picture from a neighbor of Johnson's when I was reporting on the case. I don't think it was ever released publicly."

"What are you talking about?" She tried to hide her discomfort as she spoke. "Looks like a run-of-the-mill mug shot to me."

"It does, doesn't it? But it's not. He asked the neighbor to take a head shot of him. He told her he wanted to submit it as a passport photo."

Dani glanced down at the photo again. "A *passport* photo?" she asked incredulously. "Who would want this on their passport?" She hoped he'd find the question funny and that it might convince him to drop the subject.

Unfortunately for Dani, Lee's reporter instincts were not so easily dismissed. He picked up the last photo on the table and showed it to her. "This is his mug shot. This is the photo you will find of him on the Internet."

Dani stared at it a long moment. The two photos looked nothing alike. In the actual mug shot, Johnson appeared much older. His once dark hair had turned as white as snow and had completely receded to show an aging, spotted, bald head. He was much heavier and his once slender nose was now wide and bulbous, as though it had been broken in the years between the two shots. In the police photo, he wore orange prison garb and his gray-green eyes had taken on a wild, angry look. The tanned skin of his youth had been replaced by the sallow, wrinkled skin of a man long incarcerated.

She looked from the photo back to Lee, who seemed to be expecting her to say something. She shrugged, "I guess I must have confused him with someone else."

He continued to hold the picture up for a moment longer before laying it down and sliding it across the table with the others, as a dealer might collect a deck of cards. "So you believe that you saw Michael at the cabin with Craig that day, is that right?" He directed his question to Nora.

"I know I did," she replied confidently. "I knew Michael well enough to recognize him and we made eye contact that day. I saw him and I'm sure he saw me."

"Excellent, and you're willing to say that during the interview? On air?"

Nora seemed to hesitate. She gave a sideways glance to Dani, who nodded her encouragement. "Alright," she said slowly, as if to convince herself. "Yeah, OK."

"Super! I'll be in touch as soon as we have the test results back to set up a time." With that, Lee rose and the ladies rose and departed.

Chapter
XXIV

Dani was stepping gingerly through patches of melting snow and sloppy mud to examine a fat, yellow crocus that had just recently burst into bloom when her cell phone began to ring. She unzipped the pocket of her bulky down parka and pulled the phone to her ear. "Hello?" she answered absently, trying not to slip in the mud.

"Hi Dani, it's Lee. Great news, the first results are finally in!"

The mud and flower forgotten, Dani rushed back toward her front door. "Really? And?"

"It's incredible, that car was a treasure chest. Remember the little book that they took out of the glove compartment?"

"Yeah."

"Craig Miller's prints were all over it but, more importantly, so were Melden's. More than that, we had an expert compare the writing in the book to both Miller and Melden, and it was also a match to Melden. The book was an accounting record of sorts." The grim tone with which he said that made Dani's stomach tighten.

"An accounting record? An accounting of what?"

"Near as we can tell, pornography and prostitution—both of the kiddie kind. It listed client names, transaction dates, and preferred prostitute characteristics like blond, young, butch, or feminine—that sort of thing. It went into all of the transactions in pretty specific detail. Care to take a guess at some of his clients?"

"I couldn't begin to guess. Who?" she asked.

"Well, for starters, Victor Miller."

"You're kidding? So the guy that abused the son was also selling children to the father?"

"If the book is to be believed, yeah."

"Do you have any reason not to believe it?" Dani asked.

"Well, let's remember what Dale said about Craig leaving the car in order to implicate people. It's well-established that there was no love lost between father and son. It's possible that he had Melden include his father's name as a way of implicating him. Although, that would certainly have raised questions from Melden and we have no reason to believe that Melden had an ax to grind with the senior Miller. The book also implicates some pretty important people that have nothing to do with the Millers. Two senators, a congressman, members of the clergy, professors, and doctors—you name it."

"Senators? Which senators?" Dani's breath caught in her chest as she waited to hear the names.

"Senator Charles Burkshire, who retired ten years ago and died just a few months later, and Senator Ted Richman, who is actually still serving. The shit's really going to hit the fan when we reveal *that* one!" Lee reminded Dani of one of her dogs, drooling over a juicy bone.

"They pulled blood and semen stains off the boot and off the interior of the car. They also found small traces of saliva on the back of the driver's seat."

"Saliva on the back of the seat?" Dani asked, confused. "You mean like someone bit the seat?"

Lee tried unsuccessfully to stifle a chuckle. "More than likely, someone was shouting or coughing from the backseat and left saliva deposits on the seat back in front of them."

"Oh, of course." Dani could feel her face reddening.

"They've got the DNA profiles from all the samples taken from the car and now they're working on matching them to something. We've reached out to the family members of the victims for blood samples. Once we have those, we'll know for sure if any of the victims were in that car. They're also doing comparisons to several federal databases. Any current convict serving time in the federal prison system would have their DNA in a database. They've already matched several of the semen stains based on the federal database."

"What about the senator?"

"Well, unless he volunteered it, he wouldn't be in there. Only convicted felons are compelled to give their DNA sample for storage in the federal database. They could try and compel him to give a sample. If he's innocent, I'd think he'd be willing to volunteer one just to clear his name, but I doubt he'll do that. They also found about a dozen hairs in the car, several of them have been identified as canine."

"Dog hairs? Could those help?"

"They could. We know that Craig Miller had two dogs while the murders were going on. Two of the victims also had dogs. According to the guys in the lab, three of the canine hairs are consistent with the type of dog Miller had. One of the hairs was consistent with the dog of the second victim. Obviously, that's circumstantial and you couldn't implicate anyone on that alone but it helps to bolster the other evidence."

"What other evidence?"

"Well, for starters, Miller's semen was all over the backseat of that car."

"How disgusting," Dani remarked as she slipped off her parka and collapsed onto the couch, pulling a throw over her legs.

"That's not the worst of it. Michael York's semen was also found in the car as was that of George Grey and Reggie Johnson."

"Oh my God! What were these people doing in that car? Well, I mean, obviously, I can figure out what they were doing …" Dani stammered. "But were they doing it all together or with each other or …?" She felt her skin crawl at the idea and was embarrassed to be discussing the topic with Lee, a professional colleague.

"It's tough to tell for sure. We're still working through the data. We'll know more once we can tie some of the blood stains to people. Plus, we've got the human hairs that were found in the car. DNA profiles from the human hairs have been linked to Michael York, Craig Miller, and George Grey. We're still working on matching the DNA profiles taken from two other hairs found in the car."

"I thought you said there were twelve total?"

"Some of them came from the same source. Craig Miller, to be more specific. The hairs still had the root attached. It looks like they were ripped from his scalp, perhaps during a struggle."

Dani felt a shiver run through her and pulled the throw up over her chest. "What about the chewing gum?" she asked.

"We've got a DNA profile from it but we haven't been able to match it yet. We'll know more after the family members have given us their samples."

"Didn't they do that before? I mean, as part of the active police investigation?"

Lee hesitated before he replied, "Well, yes, of course, but we're trying to conduct our own investigation, independent from what the police have done. Dale insisted upon it."

"Yeah, he doesn't trust them and I can't say that I blame him, given the history. I think he's afraid they'll come in and shut you folks down if they learn about it."

"I hate to say it but he's probably right. If we have everything recorded and we break the story first, then at least we can be sure the evidence won't go missing later."

"So when do you think you'll have the comparisons completed? Weeks? Months?" Dani held her breath, fearing the worst.

"No, they've already started that process and the comparison samples from the victims' families should be completed by the end of the week. I'll give you a call as soon as we know something more."

"That's great. I look forward to hearing from you, Lee. Thanks again for all your help. By the way, have you spoken to Dale or Nora yet?"

"I did. I hope you don't mind that I took the liberty? I just felt they had a right to be notified right away."

"No, of course not. I appreciate you letting them know. So I'll talk to you soon then, bye." Dani clicked the phone off and had barely a moment to consider what to do next before it began to ring again. She glanced at the caller ID before bringing the receiver to her ear.

"Hi Nora! I hear you've already spoken to Lee?"

"I have. What do you think?" Nora's voice sounded tight and unnatural.

"Well, I think it's good news, right? They recovered lots of evidence and, once we can make the comparison, hopefully it implicates all the right people, right?"

"I guess," she said, sounding unconvinced. "It's just so morbid, like examining a coffin."

Dani didn't know what to say to that. Finally she said, "Well, better to examine it than not, don't you think?"

"Is it?" she asked, almost as though she were posing the question to herself rather than to Dani. "Or are we just waking up all the pain and misery that had finally started to sleep?"

"Do you really think it was sleeping?" Dani asked, feeling defensive and irritated. "I saw you talking to Lee that night over dinner. You didn't seem so at peace with it then. Do you think the families have put this to rest? Do you really think the open questions around this case don't still bother them, Nora? Don't they have a right to the truth?"

"You and your high horse," she muttered. "Don't you ever get tired of the thin air up there?"

"This isn't about me and you know it. I'll help you battle your demons but don't ask me to ignore them. Too many other people are involved."

"Easy for you to say, isn't it? Who are you to decide what I should do with my demons? How'd you like it if I came sniffing around your secrets, prodding at all the skeletons in *your* closet?"

"What the hell are you talking about? Your acting as if you killed those kids yourself. We've been all through this. I thought you were ready to come forward and do the right thing. I thought you wanted to make amends for not coming forward sooner, remember?"

"Did you hear him run down the list of people who could face charges for this, Dani? Senators—convicted felons. Lee said they're probably going to want me to testify against Michael. Would you want to sit in open court and stare into that man's face? Talk about facing your demons—that's not just a metaphor here and, unlike some people, I can't just return to life as usual once the results are in."

Dani could hear the fear in her friend's voice now and was ashamed not to have recognized it sooner. "Nora, I'm sorry, I know this can't be easy for you but you're doing the right thing."

"Oh shut up about 'the right thing', will you?" she snapped. "How the hell do you know what the right thing is in a case like this? Until you can see this from my angle, keep your opinions to yourself!" The phone went dead.

Dani sat staring at it for a long moment. "What the hell did *I* do?" she demanded of Maggie, who had come to sit next to her while she was still on the phone. The dog's ears went up in inquiry and she laid her head sympathetically on Dani's lap. Dani scratched her ears and ran her hand down the length of the dog's golden back, sending up a cloud of fine, golden hairs. "Wow, we really need to brush you!"

Maggie looked up at her with mistrust then slinked off to her dog bed in the corner. Dani brushed the hairs off her hands and jeans and picked up the cell phone. She dialed and a moment later, Dale picked up.

"Hey Dani," he greeted her, sounding weary but not un friendly. "I'll bet I can guess why you're calling."

"I'll bet you can. Are you angry with me too?"

"Angry with you?" he repeated, sounding puzzled. "Why would I be angry with you? Is someone else angry with you?"

"Nora. It seems the reality of it is starting to hit home with her."

"Well, I can't say I blame her for her fears, but I'm surprised they didn't occur to her sooner."

"I'm not sure they didn't," Dani confessed. "I think I just kept convincing her to put them on the back burner. Now they've got nowhere else to go."

"It was bound to happen eventually," Dale said. "Don't beat yourself up about it. You did the right thing and she'll come to see that in time."

"What do you think of the results?" she asked.

"Well, I can't say that I'm really shocked by what I've learned so far. Michael was one of Craig's first real victims. By the time he started abusing Michael, it wasn't about Melden anymore. He never used Michael as bait for Melden, as he had with me. By then he'd developed his own taste for little boys and he'd started abusing them on his own. It wouldn't surprise me to know that he'd abused Michael in the back of that car. Craig never mentioned Reggie Johnson to me. I think they knew each other through Melden. He'd mentioned Grey to me though. Grey had been abused as a kid as well, although not by Melden. Like Craig, he eventually developed his own taste for children. When Craig started abusing kids on his own, I found it a lot more difficult to be around him. I couldn't bring myself to forgive him for that. It was one thing when he was just another kid, trying to escape it himself. But to become the monster we'd both feared … I just couldn't …" His voice had fallen to a whisper.

"I understand. That must have been very difficult for you."

"He'd come by and want to talk from time to time and I'd let him in. I'd tolerate his presence because we had too much history for me to turn him away. But I never wanted to be in that car. I had a pretty good idea about what was happening in there. It turned my stomach."

"Did it surprise you to learn that Victor Miller's name was in the book? Do you think Craig maybe planted it there?"

"Planted it in Melden's own handwriting? Throughout the book? Repeatedly? They didn't just find one lone entry on the back page or something. It was a complete history of transactions and Miller's name appeared repeatedly. Melden would never have set Victor Miller up. Why would he?"

"Maybe Victor Miller found out that his son was being abused and was going to go to the police or something," she suggested.

"Oh c'mon, Dani! That was no secret. There are dates in that book. By the time it was written, Melden's abuse of Craig was ancient history and his dad had been told about it years before. Think about it, what makes more sense? That Victor Miller was a fellow pervert who loaned his kid to Melden in exchange for keeping his secret? Or that Miller was so upset by the abuse allegation that he'd known about for *twenty years* that he suddenly threatened to go to the cops?"

"I see your point," she conceded.

"Did Lee happen to mention to you when they'd have the comparisons completed?"

"No, unfortunately not. He told me that they were already working on them but he couldn't tell me when they expected to have them completed."

"I guess there's nothing left to do but wait."

"It seems so. I'll call you if I hear anything." Dale thanked her and Dani clicked off the phone and set it aside.

Three more painfully slow weeks passed with no further word from Lee. Dani had not spoken to Nora since their argument, although she'd left several voice mail messages. All had gone unanswered. It was not like Nora to carry a grudge and Dani was becoming concerned. Which is why she was relieved when, on the last Monday in April, as she squatted in her front garden bed pulling away the prior year's dead growth, she looked up to see Nora's car pulling into her drive.

Her friend looked beautiful, as always, in a slim-fitting pantsuit and patent leather pumps. She had obviously come straight from work. "I hope you don't mind. I know I should have called first," she said, as she stepped out of the car.

Dani stood, muddy to the knees, her work gloves covered in dirt. "No, it's OK," Dani replied. She knew that it was time to let the argument go and that it was past time they were back on speaking terms; yet, she couldn't help feeling angry that she'd been made to wait so long for an apology.

"I know it's past time that I forgive you," Nora said, striding gingerly across the muddy lawn toward her friend.

"Past time that *you* forgive *me*?" she hadn't meant to raise her voice but she drew stares from her neighbor across the street nonetheless. "You should forgive me for what exactly? Allowing myself to be hung up on in the middle of a conversation?" Dani gestured angrily with her hands as she spoke, incidentally flinging mud and bits of dried leaves in the direction of Nora's lovely suit.

Nora stepped away, brushing them off. " 'In the middle of a conversation?' Don't you mean in the middle of yet another one of your sermons on morality and doing the right thing?"

"Oh don't give me that bullshit," she snapped, waving her hands and flinging more mud in Nora's direction. "I didn't say anything and you know it. You were just looking for someone to yell at and I was a convenient target!"

"Didn't say anything?" she repeated incredulously. "Do you really think …," Nora's rant was interrupted by the ring of her cell phone. Glaring at Dani as though the interruption were her fault, Nora pulled the phone from the pocket of her blazer and glanced down at the caller ID. Her eyes softened at once. "Oh my God, it's Lee! He must have the results."

Dani pulled off her muddy gloves and tossed them aside. "Come on in the house. Well, answer it first, then let's go in the house!" Their anger forgotten, the two women rushed inside and set the phone on the kitchen table between them. Nora pushed a button and Lee's voice filled the small room.

"Nora, it's Lee. Is everything OK?"

"Yes, sorry, I was just coming into the house when you called. I'm at Dani's house. She's right here with me."

"Hi Lee," Dani called out to the phone on the table.

"Well this is perfect then. I'm glad I have you both on the line for this. As you've probably guessed, we've got the comparison results back and it's amazing! We've got 'em!" he said, his cool reporter demeanor abandoned for the moment. "We've got 'em all and then some! Let's start with the boot. That's my personal favorite. The blood on the boot didn't trace back to any of the known victims. It was a match to a little boy who was reported missing in 1974 by the name of Kevin Sowers. His blood was also found on the car's interior." Dani winced at the words. She knew it was unrealistic but she'd been holding out hope that little Kevin had somehow escaped the fate of the others. "He was reported missing by his maternal grandmother, Nellie Sowers. The boy's mother was a heroin addict who died five years after he went missing. The grandmother was the boy's primary guardian because the mother had been busted so many times for possession and apparently no one knew who the father was."

"The grandmother is still alive, she's eighty-nine now, and we brought her in to see if she recognized the boot. I don't mind telling you that she brought me to tears that day. She'd given the little boy the boots and a matching jacket as a birthday gift just a week before he went missing. She said that she'd allowed her daughter to take Kevin for the weekend. Apparently, she'd just come out of a month in a rehab clinic and the grandmother wanted to encourage her, to reward her for the effort. The time with her son was supposed to be the reward. Nellie was convinced she'd turned a corner in her treatment, blah, blah, blah," Lee's voice was cold and bitter. "Anyway, a week went by and the daughter never brought little Kevin back home. After several attempts to contact them, the grandmother gave up and phoned him in as a missing child. That was the last anyone had heard of Kevin until now."

"Why on earth would that be your favorite part of the test results," Dani asked, obviously shaken by the story.

"Well, let's be clear. The evidence was never going to paint a pretty picture, and my best hope was that it would provide us with clues to the identity of some of the perverts associated with these pedophile rings. And *that* is why this is my favorite piece of evidence, because little Kevin's DNA wasn't the only profile found on that boot. Mixed with his blood was the semen of another individual."

"The senator's?" Dani blurted. She hadn't meant to say it. She hadn't meant to say anything, but she suddenly found that she couldn't wait another moment to learn the truth.

"How in the hell could you know that?" asked Lee, astonished.

"Well, you seemed so anxious to tie him into this after you saw his name in the book. It was just a natural conclusion," Dani lied. "But I thought you said his DNA would only be in the database if he'd been convicted. How on earth did you convince him to give you a sample of his DNA?"

"That's the best part," remarked Lee on the other end of the phone. "We didn't have to! Turns out, the good senator headed up a committee to encourage voluntary submissions to the NDIS here in the United States. As a publicity stunt during an election year, he very publicly volunteered his own sample back in the mid-'90s. It was meant to encourage others to do the same. So we didn't even need to ask permission, his DNA was on file!"

"Sorry," Nora interrupted, looking slightly embarrassed, "I'm not following you. What exactly is the NDIS?"

"Oh, sorry, it's the National DNA Index System. It's a national database through which the authorities collect the DNA of convicted criminals and that of anyone, like the senator, who wishes to volunteer a sample. So now we've got his semen mixed with Kevin's blood on the boot. We've got him, ladies, I'm sure of it." Dani had never heard Lee sound so excited.

"What about the other samples?" Nora asked.

"Well two of the human hairs matched Jimmy Prince, as did the saliva on the back of the driver's seat. The third hair was a match to the second victim, the little girl who was shot. The saliva in the gum matched Marty Stevens. We also found the fingerprints of all three on the interior of the doors. Only the third victim does not appear to have been in that car, but the police have tied her to Reggie Johnson's car based on an earlier DNA match and we can definitely place him with Craig Miller. They were known associates."

There was a long, silent moment as the women digested the information they'd just been given. Finally Nora spoke, "So now what?"

"So now we break the story," Lee replied, sounding more than a little pleased. "We need to get both you and Dale in here for an interview. I'll text you the address. Can you come in tomorrow?"

Dani held her breath, afraid Nora might back out after all. But she need not have worried.

"Yep," Nora replied quickly. "What time? It's not at your office?"

"No, we'll be filming at an offsite location in Detroit. Come in as soon as you get off work. I'll see you there. Also, and I don't know if I mentioned this to you earlier, I won't be conducting the actual interview on camera. That will be John Prosper."

"Oh, I love that guy! I've seen him before on your show. I'm a big fan!" Nora gushed, suddenly sounding like a giddy teenager.

Dani rolled her eyes. "Lee, what about Dale?" she asked.

"He's coming in first thing tomorrow. We'll see you tomorrow then, Nora."

"See you then. Thanks, Lee. Oh hey, Lee? Mind if Dani comes along?"

"Not at all, bring her along. We'll set her up off camera."

"Thanks, Lee! See you tomorrow."

Chapter
XXV

The next day Dani was awoken again at the break of dawn by her cell phone ringing from her night table. She reached across and pulled it to her ear. "Hello?" she murmured sleepily.

"Hey Dani, sorry to call you so early. I'm getting ready to go to this interview and I'm getting a little nervous about it. I talked to Lee and he said you were planning to come in for Nora's interview?"

Dani smiled in the still dark bedroom. "Yes, would you like me to come for yours too?"

"Would you mind? I know it's early." Dale's voice was apologetic and shy.

"Not at all! When will you be here?"

"I'm just leaving the house, maybe three hours?"

"OK. I'll see you then. Drive careful!" She threw back the comforter and headed downstairs, followed closely by her furry companions.

Nearly three hours later she was dressed in deep indigo skinny jeans, an ivory cashmere turtleneck, and a matching quilted wool, three-button blazer that flattered her slim figure. As Dale pulled up, she pulled a pair of tall, leather riding boots on over her jeans, grabbed her bag, and headed out to the car to meet him.

Behind the steering wheel, he was a bundle of nerves. He reached across and gave her a quick hug as she took a seat beside him. "I really am sorry to drag you out so early, but I just can't seem to keep my nerves in check. Suddenly the idea of going in front of God and everyone to talk about Craig, Melden—everything, it just seems so overwhelming!"

She turned in the passenger seat to stare at his profile. "I understand, Dale. But today you're not going to be saying it to God and everyone. You'll be saying it to John, to Lee, and to me—and that's it. You know Lee and me, so John will be the only stranger and even he's not a complete stranger, you've met him before, right?" She was trying to sound supportive, she gave his arm a gentle squeeze as she spoke and did her best to hide her own apprehension. "We've been all over what you'll talk about and John will lead you through it again during the interview. All you have to do is tell your own story in your own words."

As they pulled out of Dani's subdivision, the GPS guided them in the direction of I-75. "So where are we going exactly?" she asked.

"Believe it or not, they're filming it at some warehouse near Eastern Market."

"A warehouse? When I see it on TV, it always looks like it's at someone's house. I always thought they came to your house to do the interview."

"Ah, the magic of television!" Dale gave her a wink.

"If this weren't so nerve-racking, I might think it was fun."

"Yeah, I start feeling that way too, until I remember what I have to do and what we'll be discussing." She gave his arm another firm squeeze as they turned off Grange Hall onto the expressway.

An hour later they arrived in front of a massive red brick building. The four-story structure was lined with windows from the ground floor to the roofline. They pulled up to the curb, approached the meter and dropped in as many coins as they could come up with between the two of them and then entered the warehouse through a side door.

Inside, the building was a vast, vacant space divided only by rows of steel support beams. Wooden pallets were stacked against the wall nearest the entrance and voices echoed back to them from a small office in the far corner. Near the office, a crew of workers were setting up theatrical lights. "I think that's where we need to be," Dale whispered, as if hoping, somehow, to remain unseen.

Dani led him confidently across the polished concrete floor, her boots click-clacking to the rhythm of her strides, effectively eliminating any hope of a silent approach. They entered the small office to find Lee and John huddled around a laptop computer, reviewing background footage they'd recently shot of Fanny Lake, Belle Mead, and Coyote Island. Dani's boots clicked to a stop behind them and Lee glanced around to greet them. "Good morning! Did you find the place okay?"

"We did, thanks." Dani found herself speaking to his back, as he had already returned his attention to the footage on the screen.

"I prefer that first shot," he said to John, pointing toward a thumbnail on the screen. "Give me one minute to get them settled and I'll be right back." He glanced at his watch. "It's getting late though, we should think about getting you into makeup." He gave John a firm pat on the shoulder to drive home his point then turned his attention to the new arrivals.

"Okay, so I'm going to have you follow me," he said, leading them back through the office door and out to where the crew had set up three large, square fixtures that now cast a bright, white pool of light down on two wooden dining chairs, each facing the other and spaced about two feet apart. Several yards to the left of the chairs and in the shadow of the bright lights stood a very ordinary-looking card table piled high with a computer monitor, manila file folders, camera equipment, and electrical cords falling in a tangle from every direction around the temporary work space. Lee placed a hand on Dani's back and guided her to a folding chair that had been set up just beyond the card table. She set her bag down beside the chair and took her seat. As she did, she noticed that the monitor on the card table was showing a live video feed of the currently empty chairs in the middle of the pool of light.

"Dale," he said, leading him past the chairs and toward another temporary work space that had been set up near the office, "you remember Sheila, don't you?" The small, blond woman greeted Dale as if he were an old friend.

Dani had to laugh as she watched Dale sitting uncomfortably in a chair as Sheila fussed with his makeup. A short while later, Lee pulled up a second folding chair near her own. "So just to let you know how this will play out," he explained, "we're going to start the show with a review of all the families and the crimes. We've lined up some of the original footage from back in the '70s, some of the photos and John will do a voice-over explanation of the original investigation." Dani, who was familiar with the show's format and had watched it many times before, nodded along, imagining the scenes as he spoke. "We'll film a very extensive interview with Dale today and then we're going to pick and choose segments from that interview to work into the final show. We're going to use his material to set the scene for the pedophilia and then later as we explore the car and the evidence." He took a sip of coffee before continuing. "Then we've got Nora coming in for her interview this afternoon and we'll be using her material as background for the Miller family and to set up the 911 call."

"Oh my gosh, I'm so glad you mentioned that," Dani said, startled. "I meant to call Nora and let her know that I came in with Dale. She's going to have to meet me here."

"John should be about done with the office," he said, pointing back to where John was still sitting in front of the laptop. "You can call from in there. Might be quieter for you."

"Thanks," she said, pulling her cell from her purse. As she walked back to the office, she flipped from one screen to the next on her cell.

"Didn't your mother ever tell you that you should look to where you are going?" Dani heard a familiar, accented voice and looked up just in time to avoid a collision.

"Oh my goodness, Chris, hi!" Her face flushed a scarlet red and Chris Tristain gave her a warm, teasing smile. "Sorry, I was rushing and not paying any attention."

"I see this. It is a surprise to see you. You must be here for the interview, right?"

"Yes, the interview. Well, interviews actually, I'll be staying for Nora's as well."

"Oh, that's great. It's nice that you are here to support your friends. If you'll excuse me, I have to make sure that we're set up but I'll see you again shortly." He smiled and brushed past her, his aftershave floating pleasantly back to her as he walked away. A moment later, John followed him out and joined the others at the chairs under the bright lights. Standing in the office, Dani dialed and held the phone to her ear as she glanced out the door at the activity going on in front of the cameras. She frowned when the call passed to voice mail.

"Hello Nora, this is Dani. I wanted to let you know that Dale called me this morning and asked me to come in for his interview as well so I'm already here. I'll meet you here later. I'm going to need to turn my volume off while they're filming so maybe send me a text and let me know that you got this, 'kay? Thanks!" She clicked off the phone and stood at the door for a long moment watching Chris and Lee position Dale in the chair at the center of the bright lights, his body language clearly illustrating his discomfort. At the same moment, John Prosper, the handsome, confident reporter scheduled to conduct the interview, strode into the light and took his seat opposite Dale. The two painted a portrait of polar opposites.

Dani switched her phone to vibrate and slipped back quietly to her seat. Lee had moved his seat up near the monitor and was soon joined by Chris. The two stared quietly at the monitor as the cameraman and reporter readied the shot. As the interview began, Dani found herself staring more often at the tiny monitor just in front of her instead of at the much larger, live scene going on just beyond it. Initially, Dale's responses were short and abrupt, as though he were being drilled by a prosecuting attorney. As the interview progressed, however, he seemed to relax and his answers became more conversational. Dani recalled the day he'd first confided the truth to her in his kitchen. Now, sitting bolt upright in the center of the glaring stage lights, he divulged his secrets to the world. At times, she could sense him fighting the temptation to get up and pace. He squirmed as though his seat were made of needles. She squirmed in her seat as well, flinching at his memories, wincing in empathy for his pain and his shame. When it was over, she felt as though she'd gone over Niagara Falls in a barrel. Her muscles ached from the tension and she was exhausted. She realized with dismay that she suddenly had a splitting headache, but she shoved it all aside and greeted him with a supportive hug when he joined her at the little card table.

"Good job!" she congratulated him enthusiastically. "How do you feel?"

"Exhausted but relieved. It's nice to have it over with," he replied quietly, as though afraid the others might overhear and take offense.

"Well you did a great job and it's so great that you were willing to do this, that you were brave enough to tell the story."

He had only enough time to shrug before Lee and Chris had joined them, shaking Dale's hand and patting his back, thanking him for his time and effort. Lee told him that they'd be in touch soon and then turned his attention back to the little monitor, where Chris was already reviewing the interview frame by frame.

"I should get going," Dale said as he slipped on his jacket. "You're staying for Nora's interview, aren't you?"

"I am. I'd like to go grab some lunch though before she gets here. What about you? Are you hungry?"

"Starving, actually! Want to go grab something to eat? I can drive and then drop you off before I start back."

"You're on!" Dani picked up her purse and made the mistake of letting the others know that they were heading out to grab a bite to eat. Fifteen minutes later, armed with half a dozen takeout orders, the two left for a nearby deli.

An hour later, Dani returned alone with a sack full of sandwiches to dole out to the hungry crew.

"How's it going?" she asked Lee and Chris as they reviewed the footage.

"Well, I won't say he's a natural but I think we can make it work." Lee turned his face away from the monitor just long enough to give her a confident little nod.

For several hours Dani distracted herself with games on her cell, as the crew set up for the second interview and reviewed the first.

Finally, at half past six in the evening, Nora hurried in looking rushed, flushed, and, as ever, beautiful. "I'm so sorry it took me so long. Traffic coming into the city was a nightmare! I'd never want to work in the city. How do the people here deal with so much traffic?" she complained, giving her coat and purse to Dani before joining Lee by the chairs in the center of the bright pool of light.

"No worries," Lee assured her. "We've had plenty to do wrapping up the piece we did with Dale this morning."

"Oh right! How'd it go?" she asked. She gave the lights and chairs a nervous glance, as though she were the second patient in line for an experimental surgery.

"Not bad and I'm sure you'll be even better!" Lee escorted her to the makeup table and introduced her to Sheila before returning to where Dani sat, still playing games on her phone. She glanced up at him as he approached. "How are you holding up?" he asked.

Dani smiled. "I think I'll make it. How's she doing?" she inclined her head in the direction of the makeup table.

"Little nervous but she'll be OK. I'm sure."

Twenty minutes later Nora sat under the bright lights opposite John Prosper. Unlike Dale, Nora was immediately at ease. She spoke with cool confidence about Matthew Miller and their brief romance. She talked about Craig Miller's talent for trouble and his family's struggle to control him. Lastly, she spoke about the 911 call itself and her quick glimpse of the boys at the Miller home on Fanny Lake. For the first time since the interview began, her composure fled and she broke into tears. The camera turned to Prosper, who waited patiently. His eyes held a carefully planned look of empathetic concern.

When the interview was over, she returned to the card table where Dani was seated. For a while, she hovered over Chris's shoulder as he reviewed the footage. Dani was exhausted and anxious to get home. She handed Nora her coat and purse and stood to leave. "Are we going?" Nora asked, never taking her eyes off Chris's monitor.

"Aren't we?" Dani replied. "I've been here all day. I need to get home and you're my ride."

Reluctantly, she pulled her eyes away from the screen and pulled on her coat.

"The show's scheduled to air the week after next," Lee informed them, as he walked them back across the warehouse to the exit. "I'll be in touch if we need anything more."

"Thanks for all your help, Lee." Dani gave him a hug and the two ladies waved goodbye to the crew.

"The week after next," Nora repeated quietly. "Two more weeks to enjoy my life as it is before everything changes."

"Oh, come on," Dani said, putting an arm around her shoulder as they walked toward the car, "it won't be as bad as all that." But Dani knew the truth. They both did.

Chapter
XXVI

On the day of the broadcast, Dale, Dani, and Nora gathered together at Dani's home in front of her TV. She had set out snacks and finger foods as though they were preparing to watch the big game instead of a morbid rehashing of a decades-old murder mystery. Her guests were as jittery as hens at a slaughterhouse, and Dani had no idea what to say or do to calm their nerves.

"I wish they hadn't conducted that interview in a warehouse," Nora complained, as Dani reentered the living room carrying a platter full of hot wings. "It felt creepy and the lighting was horrible."

"At least you didn't have to be there at the crack of dawn," Dani put in. "Poor Dale had to be on the road at five in the morning!"

"I didn't mind," he added quietly, taking a wing from the tray.

"It's starting, it's starting," Nora squealed. "Turn it up!"

Dani turned up the volume with the remote and took a seat between the other two. It was the first time any of them had seen the footage fully compiled, including images taken from the original police investigation. The first half of the show was spent reviewing the victims' profiles, the crime scene photos, and the background of each of the chief suspects. As the second half began, Nora made her first appearance, confidently answering the reporter's questions about her relationship to the Miller family and her involvement in the 911 call.

"Oh my God," she moaned when her image first appeared on the screen. "Do I really look that heavy? I look huge!"

"You do not," Dani assured her. "Besides, they say the camera adds ten pounds. That's just ..." she rushed for something comforting to say, "... that's just camera weight!"

"*Camera* weight?" Nora repeated with annoyance. "What the hell does that mean?"

"Shhhh, I'm on!" Dale waved a dismissive hand at the two chattering women and everyone's attention returned to the screen. Dani was shocked by his on-screen appearance. Through her closer acquaintance with him, Dani had come to think of Dale as a gentle giant. Despite his outwardly tough appearance, she had come to know him as a shy, amiable individual. That was not, however, how he came across on-screen. In the finished piece, he seemed simply tough. He looked out of place in the suit and tie that he'd worn and his shyness came across as indifference. Dani shifted uncomfortably on the couch, wondering if the others could see it too.

Fortunately, they cut quickly from scenes of his interview to scenes of the vehicle itself and the evidence they'd pulled from it. The audio from Dale's interview now provided the commentary, streaming over the images of the bloody boot, the leather diary, the chewing gum, and the stained interior of the old car.

During the show's last segment, Dale was interviewed about the abuse that both he and Craig Miller had endured at the hands of millionaire philanthropist Arthur Melden and about their shared belief that important people wanted Craig Miller silenced for good. As a compelling climax to the episode, John Prosper revealed the potential involvement of Senator Ted Richman based on his DNA profile found at the scene. "Calls to the senator's office were not returned," concluded Mr. Prosper in a well-rehearsed, grim tone.

As the credits rolled, Dani sensed a collective sigh of relief and yet for a long moment, no one spoke. Finally, she asked, "Well, what did you think?" She glanced first at Nora and then at Dale.

"I can't believe I really went on television and said that," Dale whispered, more to himself than to Dani. He seemed at once both terrified and relieved. Dani noticed that his hands were trembling as he spoke. She put her own over his to steady them and he gave her a grateful smile.

"What about you, Nora?" she asked, turning to look at her friend.

"I wonder if Matthew saw it."

It annoyed Dani that Nora was still so concerned with Matthew Miller's opinion of her. She wondered how her intelligent, confident friend could still have energy to waste on a man like Miller. "What do you care what he thinks?" she asked, unable to stifle her irritation.

"What do I care? Dani, think about it. This guy's probably got a whole fleet of lawyers and I just went on national television and slandered his brother. His father's name was found in Melden's little book of perverts! I'd have to be an idiot not to care what he thinks! You just don't get it, do you?"

A sudden flush of shame reddened Dani's face. "It's not slander if it's true," she murmured meekly.

"Truth is in the eye of the beholder. You don't think his lawyers could prove his own version of the truth for the right price? Damn it, Dani! When will you grow up?"

"When will I grow up? You're the one hiding from the truth for almost forty years!" Dani hadn't realized until that very moment just how annoyed she'd become by everyone's persistent suggestions that she was being naïve. Something deep within her finally snapped. "Please explain to me why it's childish to expect personal accountability from an adult woman, Nora? When this whole thing first came up you ..."

Her tirade was interrupted when first her phone, then Dale's, and finally Nora's all began to ring as one. Dani pulled hers off the coffee table but before she could answer it, Nora jumped up from the seat beside her, phone in hand.

"It's him," she said, as though Jack the Ripper had just entered the room. "What do I do?"

"Don't answer it," Dale and Dani responded in unison and then exchanged a look of mild amusement. "Jinx, you owe me a Coke," she added playfully.

Nora rolled her eyes and turned on her heel for the coat closet. "I cannot believe you. I've got a pissed-off maniac calling me and you're playing children's games!"

"Oh come on, Nora! It's a jinx. Who doesn't call jinx when there's a jinx? Getting angry isn't going to help anyone!" Nora stormed past her and a moment later she heard the side door slam. Dani turned back to Dale, feeling both annoyed and ashamed.

"She'll cool off," he said. "Just give her some time. I understand what she's going through and it's tough."

"Who called you?" she asked, glancing down at the cell phone still in his hand.

"Lee. He probably just wanted to see if we watched. You?" he asked, indicating her phone.

"My friend, Faye," she replied with a glance at the caller ID. "She must have seen it. Do you think I should try to stop Nora?"

"Give her a day or two." He stood and stretched. "I should get going. I've got a long drive back."

"Well thanks for coming over and let me know if you hear anything more about the case." She pulled his coat out of the closet and held it up for him as he slipped it on. "Drive careful and send me a text when you get home, okay?" She walked him through the kitchen.

"Will do, mother" he teased, as he pulled the side door open and stepped out into the chilly spring evening.

Once he'd gone, Dani opened the door that led to the upstairs and the two dogs came piling out, tails wagging furiously as they scrambled for the back door. She pulled it open and watched them trip one over the other in their haste to get outside. As she watched them run around the yard, she heard her cell phone go off again. She picked it up and glanced at the caller ID.

"Hey Geoff," she said as she brought it to her ear. "I knew it would be you. I take it you were watching?"

"I was. I just talked to Nora. She seems pretty upset."

Dani frowned. "I know. We had an argument and she stormed out. Dale thinks she just needs to cool off."

"Oh does he?" Geoff's voice took on a hostile edge. "Well how nice for him. Dani, how do you know this Miller guy's not going to come after her? If your theory is correct, his brother was a serial killer. How can you be so calm?"

"His brother was a serial killer, that doesn't mean he is. He's gone this long without killing anyone!"

"That we know of," he protested.

"She's fine. She's going to be just fine." Dani fought back a nagging doubt that fluttered around in the pit of her stomach.

"I hope so, for your sake as well as hers. How are you doing? Do you still feel like you did the right thing?"

"What did I do? They're the ones who did the interview."

"You're kidding, right?" he said sharply.

"I didn't mean it like that. I know I'm responsible for getting them into this but I, I mean, I wasn't on television tonight. I'm not the one worrying about how I looked or if anyone will recognize me."

"Matthew Miller would recognize you. Nora told me about your run-in at the pizza place. What's to stop him from coming after you too?"

There was silence for a long moment before a bark from the French doors made Dani jump. She laughed and stepped over to open the door.

"What's so funny? Dani, this is no joke." Geoff's voice was stern and concerned.

"No, it was just … the dog barked. Oh, never mind. Look, I know it's serious but it'll be fine. Really, stop worrying. The killer's dead. Nobody's coming after anyone. Look, I'm exhausted. I'll call you next week."

Two hours later with the food put away and the dishes done, Dani led the dogs upstairs. The dogs each took a spot on the rug and Dani changed into a nightshirt, pulled a book off a shelf, and settled under her down comforter. Almost immediately, she began to drift off.

She found herself barefoot in her nightshirt on the warm stone steps of the elaborate villa. In front of her was emerald green grass leading to the azure blue of the ocean beyond. The sky was bright and the sun was hot. Magenta Bougainvillea tumbled down from the rooftop above and

Dani passed beneath them as she started out for the cliff side. When she reached the landing, she found Kōbō smoking peacefully on his marble chaise, staring out at the ocean below. He smiled up at her and gestured toward the seat opposite his own.

She crossed the landing and sat down, carefully gathering the tails of the flannel nightshirt modestly around her legs. "It's good to see you," she began. "I suppose you know about the interviews?"

He seemed amused by that. "If you know, then I know," he reminded her.

"Oh right, I guess so," she laughed. "My friend, Geoff, is worried that Miller will come after Nora but I think that's silly. What do you think?"

He frowned. "What you know, I know and what you feel, I feel. Let's not pretend that you're not worried about her too. Nevertheless, Matthew Miller is not his brother. I do not believe he will harm your friend, not physically anyway."

"What does *that* mean?" she demanded, unable to keep the panic out of her voice.

"It means that your friend is a strong woman and she will survive, as will you. They've done what they needed to do, Dani. Take comfort in that and help them through it. That is all that is left to do now."

"They did what they needed to do because of me," Dani muttered. "If I hadn't interfered …"

"You give yourself too much credit," he replied reproachfully. "You are only the translator here, remember that. The message was always for them and it was always their responsibility to answer that call. You are not responsible for the message, only for its delivery."

For a moment, Dani felt as though she'd been slapped but she dared not say so. "So now what?" she asked, more sharply than she'd intended.

"So now life goes on. Those with a debt to pay will be made to pay it and those owed peace will receive it, in whatever small measure possible."

"And me?" she asked, thinking about her life before Kōbō.

"I've got a few more people who would like to speak to you. Will you be ready to hear them now?"

She thought about the voices on the other side of death's barrier. She imagined a distant room where Kōbō sat chatting with ghosts over tea and the image made her laugh.

"Will I ever hear from Jimmy again?" she asked.

He seemed confused by the question. "What makes you think you have ever heard from Jimmy?" he asked.

"Well, it's just … all the messages I've been receiving. One of the other Guardian victims then? Or Kevin?"

"The other children were not in the bunker that night and little Kevin never took a picture of Dale and his mother at the Frosty Falls," he replied.

"But I don't …?"

"You really should answer your phone," he said, pointing to Dani's chaise.

She glanced around and found her cell phone ringing on the chaise next to her. She picked it up but did not answer it and then turned to find that he'd gone.

Chapter
XXVII

She awoke with a start in the dim morning light. Her cell was on the night table but it wasn't ringing. She reached over and checked it all the same. The clock on her home screen told her it was not yet eight-thirty and her call log told her she'd already missed three calls. She laid back on her pillows and hit the speed dial for her voice mail. She closed her eyes and fought to stay awake as the first message began to play.

"Good morning, Dani, it's Lee. I wanted to let you know that we've already heard from the Guardian Task Force. That's the police task force that's still investigating the Guardian murders. They're pressing for our cooperation but, of course, Dale doesn't trust them. Anyway, just trying to keep you in the loop. I'll call later."

She deleted that message and listened to the next. "Dani, it's Nora. You would *not* believe what's going on over here. I've got lawyers calling and reporters … there's a news van parked across the street from my house. Matt's called me four times. I can't keep ignoring him. Call me, will you? I'm sorry I got angry last night but I need to talk to you. Bye."

She deleted that message and listened to the last. "Hi Dani, this is Faye. I tried calling you after the interview but couldn't get you. I'm just calling to see how you're doing. Let me know if I can do anything to help! Bye." Dani deleted that one as well and set the phone down on the bed next to her. She rolled over and stuffed her head under the down pillows. Just as she was about to drift off, the phone rang again. Reluctantly, she sat up and checked the caller ID.

"Good morning, Dale," she answered sleepily

"Good morning. I hope I didn't wake you."

"It's OK. I had to get up anyway. Is everything OK? You sound a little ... I don't know ... excited maybe?"

"When you do get up, switch on your television and you'll see why I'm excited. Our story is all over the news!"

"What? What station? What news?" she asked, throwing back the comforter and dashing past the dogs and down the stairs.

"Any news, any station," he said. "I'm watching Wake Up, America but there are a few different shows running stories on it."

"Wake Up, America? What channel is that?" she asked, fumbling with the remote.

"Twelve, at least it's twelve here where I am."

Dani found the station and watched as a mob of reporters surrounded Senator Ted Richman as he was walking toward his car. She found herself wondering if the senator had seen the show the night before or if he'd simply woken up to the hysteria.

"Senator," she heard a reporter call out, "how do you account for your DNA on that young boy's boot?" The senator gave no reply.

Another reporter called out, "Senator, any idea how your semen ended up on that boot? The victim's blood was also found on it. Any comment, senator?" Again, the senator gave no reply but rushed past, his bodyguards pushing through the throng of reporters toward a black sedan waiting at the curb. The shot turned to a smartly dressed news anchor seated behind a large, black desk.

"Now as we mentioned, the evidence implicating Senator Richman was found in a vehicle that at the time belonged to this man," she said, as a picture of Craig Miller appeared onscreen. "Craig Miller was the son of a prominent auto executive in the 1970s. His brother, Matthew Miller, followed in his father's footsteps and is now the senior vice-president of North American Purchasing in his father's old company." The scene changed to show Matthew Miller leaving his home also followed by a pack of ravenous reporters. Like Richman, Miller gave no reply to the many questions being hurled after him but ducked into his car and drove off.

The camera shot returned to the smartly dressed woman behind the desk who said, "With more on this story here is our chief correspondent, Dan Rawley. Dan, what more can you tell us on this incredible story?"

The scene changed to show a slim, well-built man in his twenties standing alongside a middle-aged man with silver-gray hair. "Well Heather, as you know, another astonishing revelation in this story recently came from Matthew Miller's ex-girlfriend, who claims that while on a romantic weekend getaway, Miller took her here," he paused for a moment and waved a hand to indicate the home in front of which he was standing. "This is the Millers' former estate near the peaceful town of Fanny Lake, Michigan. I am joined today by the home's current owner, Dr. Gary Klinger. Dr. Klinger, as you know, Nora Fontana, the ex-girlfriend of Matthew Miller, claims that she saw alleged serial killer,

Craig Miller, her then-boyfriend's brother, in what is now your living room, plying young boys with alcohol and watching pornographic movies. It is believed that one of the victims, little Jimmy Prince, may have been one of the boys in your home that day. What is your reaction to that news? Did you have any idea?"

"Well, Dan, we'd heard rumors about this, of course. There have been rumors about it for years but no one from law enforcement had ever confirmed it to us."

"So your home has never been searched for any DNA evidence? Have they ever tried, for example, searching the air ducts to the home for any evidence that may still exist?"

"No, they have not."

"And why do you suppose that is? Would you be willing to cooperate with investigators should they choose to do that?"

"Absolutely," the good doctor said quickly. "I couldn't tell you why they haven't, only that no one has ever approached us about it."

"Thank you, Dr. Klinger. Heather, back to you."

Dani realized that she was still holding the phone to her ear. "Dale, you still there? Sorry, I didn't mean to keep you on the line."

"No, that's OK. I'm just sitting here, watching. If I'm talking to you on the phone than the others can't call me."

"The others?" she asked, thinking of the voice mail she'd received from Nora.

"You wouldn't believe the calls I'm getting. Reporters wanting to do follow-up interviews, lawyers wanting to defend me, like they think the cops will come after me. Then there's the lawyers who are offering to help me sue Melden's estate, and then a whole host of other calls just from nut jobs of all kinds, calling me a pervert and a child killer and you name it." His voice sounded tight and unnatural as he spoke.

"I'm so sorry, Dale. I know this can't be easy for you."

"It's not but I don't blame you. It was the right thing to do and if it helps to uncover the truth here, it'll have been worth it. At a minimum, maybe that pervert senator will be forced to resign."

"Forced to resign? I think they should lock him in prison and throw away the key," Dani shot back.

"That'll never happen. It should, but it won't. That's just not the world we live in."

Dani frowned and then the scene on the screen made her heart jump into her throat. "Oh my God, it's …"

"Nora," Dale breathed, finishing her thought. On the television screen, Nora was running from her home to her car parked on the curb, a swarm of reporters following after her.

Dani heard a reporter say, "Ms. Fontana, Matthew Miller has alleged that you are nothing more than a jilted girlfriend trying to settle a decades-old score with his family. What is your reaction to that?" Nora shot the reporter a look to kill before pulling away from the curb and disappearing down the street.

"What? Miller's trying to say she's just a pissed-off ex-girl-friend?" Dani couldn't believe how ridiculous it sounded.

"Apparently so, yeah. They know that if they can dis-credit her, then her part of the story goes away. A lot of people are asking why she waited so long to come forward if the story's true. Why wouldn't she have spoken up years ago? He's making it sound like she just made it up now because she heard about the car."

"You understand why she didn't say anything sooner, don't you Dale?"

"I do, of course. But I'm not your average American viewer. Any time you have an ex-girlfriend, you're always going to have someone saying it's just sour grapes. It's the nature of the beast."

Dani felt an almost overwhelming surge of guilt rise up like bile through her throat. "Nora told me that she had news vans parked in front of her house, do you?"

"Oh yeah. The cops have been over here trying to direct traffic because the news vans have clogged up the streets. You know, you get a little town like Fanny Lake thrown into the spotlight like this, it's bound to cause problems. The cops want to talk to me as well. I've got a lawyer coming over later. We're going in together to talk to them."

"What are you doing until then? Do you just ignore the reporters when you drive past or are you talking to them? I mean, I haven't seen you on the news report yet."

"I haven't left the house yet. I'll have to eventually, of course, but I guess I'm hoping they'll just give up and go home before then."

"I don't think that's likely to happen," she said quietly, almost apologetically.

"I know, but a man can hope, can't he?"

"Do you want me to bring you something? Groceries maybe?"

"What? And have them start chasing after you? Never. I don't want you to be any more involved than you have to be. You need to stay as far away from this as you can get."

"I can't just stay here, insulated from everything while you and Nora ..."

"Yes you can," he cut her off. "And you should, can you imagine the fodder it will give them if a beautiful woman who also just happens to be connected to Nora Fontana, the jilted ex-girlfriend, starts bringing me groceries? You'll ruin whatever credibility we have."

Dani shifted uncomfortably. "But what's the big deal? You live in Fanny Lake, we vacationed there, the Millers vacationed there. There's a perfectly logical explanation for the connection."

"Nothing here is perfectly logical, Dani. Least of all your connection to me. I'm still not sure I even understand it. How did you …"

A new development on the television report spared Dani the need to reply, "Look, it's the senator again. Looks like he's ready to give a statement."

On the screen, the lanky, now gray-haired Senator Ted Richman stood behind a podium and raised a commanding hand into the air to silence the chatter of the reporters. "There has been an allegation made," he began, "that I was somehow involved in the disappearance and subsequent death of Kevin Sowers. I can only say that this is a completely ridiculous allegation. I have never known anyone by that name and certainly would never hurt a defenseless child. These allegations are absolutely unfounded," he declared with theatrical certainty.

Hands went up through the crowd. "Senator," began one reporter, "how do you account for your DNA being found on the bloody boot?"

"I don't claim to be a scientist but I can tell you for a certainty that DNA is not a perfect science and that there have been mistakes made in the past during such investigations. I'm confident that when the folks at a qualified FBI lab take a look at this evidence, that then we will get to the bottom of this tragic misunderstanding."

"So now he's going to try to discredit the lab?" Dani couldn't believe what she was hearing.

"What other option does he have? It's his only hope. Fortunately, that lab has done a great deal of work in the past for other police units with other cases. If they allow the senator to trash the lab's reputation, they'd have to reopen all those other investigations. It'd be a PR nightmare. Lee and I chose that particular lab very, very carefully. They've got a very solid reputation." Dani could hear from his voice that he was very pleased with himself at that moment, and rightly so in her mind.

"But didn't he just trash it right there? The implication's been made."

"The implication's been made that the FBI lab would find something different but my guess is, they won't. The powers that be are going to let Richman take the fall. They're going to have to, we've backed them into a tight enough corner. At least, I hope we have."

Following the Richman segment, a series of commercials came on. "I should get going," Dani said. "I've got a pile of paperwork up to my chest waiting for me in the office. Are you going to be OK? Maybe you could just switch your cell off to block the calls?" Another wave of guilt washed over her as she thought about Dale cowering in his home, hiding out from reporters.

"I'll be fine," he said quietly, his voice taking on an ease and peace that Dani never would have expected. "The worst is behind me."

Dani wasn't so sure, but she kept her doubts to herself. "Do you regret it? Coming forward, I mean?"

"Not at all. This kind of pedophilia, Dani, it's like an outbreak of a deadly disease. It's like Ebola or the Black Plague. If we're ever going to stop the spread, we first need to trace it back to the source. Only when we do that can we get a measure of the scope of it. Only then can we track down all the known carriers of the disease. If we can track down the carriers, we can stop the spread and help the victims. It's the only way, and I should have had the guts to do it forty years ago. Who knows how many new victims are out there now because of my cowardice? And how many new carriers?"

"You can't blame yourself, Dale, you ..."

"Why not? Don't let me off the hook, Dani. Don't let anyone off the hook who knows something and could come forward but doesn't. It's about being a responsible adult. It's about protecting other children from facing the same fate."

Dani could think of no further argument and so she said simply, "Call me if I can do anything to help, okay?"

"I will. Thanks for everything."

"Wait, Dale?" Dani blurted out. She was remembering something from her dream the night before. Something that had been needling at her.

"Yes?" Dale asked.

"Remember that photo on your mantel? The one of you and your mother at the Frosty Falls?"

"Yes."

"I don't suppose you remember who took that photo, do you?" She was oddly nervous. In the pit of her stomach, she was sure she knew the answer. In the back of her mind, she hoped she was wrong.

"Sure I do," he said in a tone that made Dani uneasy. "Our friendly, neighborhood serial killer, Craig Miller. He'd gotten his very first camera from his mother earlier that week, as a birthday gift. He was taking pictures of everything that day and he asked if he could take a picture of my mom and me. The shot turned out so well, we had it framed. I've kept it all these years to remind me of the boy he was, rather than the monster he became. Why do you ask?"

On the other side of the phone, Dani felt as though she'd turned to stone. "Nothing," she replied, her voice sounding choked and unnatural in her own ears. "Just something a friend said to me last night."

"You have to remember that he wasn't always a monster, Dani. I won't deny that he became one and I won't say it wasn't his fault. We're all responsible for our own actions, as well as for our lack of them," the shame crept back into his voice, strangling the words as he spoke them. "But monsters aren't born, they're created and Craig certainly wasn't the only monster mixed up in all this."

"You mean like Grey and Reggie Johnson," she said.

"I mean like any child who has ever been a victim of prolonged abuse at the hands of men like Arthur Melden or Craig Miller. The abuse itself is the disease, Dani, and it spreads. Nobody's quite sure why, and it doesn't happen every time, but it's been proven to happen time and again, the victims become the abusers."

Dani thought about the other children she'd seen through little Kevin's eyes, Diego and Mike. She thought about the other children on the other bunks, those whose names she'd never learned, the haunted eyes that had stared back at her. Where were they now, she wondered. Had they all been killed? Or had some of them survived and, if so, had they become carriers of the same, awful disease? She couldn't imagine young Mike as a pedophile but then she thought of the young boy who had fought off Arthur Melden so that his friend could escape. She could never have imagined that young boy as a pedophile either and yet …

"You still there?" she heard Dale's voice ask.

She shook the images from her mind. "I am. Sorry, I drifted off for a minute. How did you avoid that fate, Dale? How is it that you didn't become a carrier?"

"I don't think anyone knows for certain how the victim becomes the monster and why some kids escape that fate but if I had to guess, I'd say it's because I had a mother who loved me and who made sure that I never went near that guy again."

"But she …" Dani began.

"She took his money? Yes, she did. But she used that money to help me get a college education, to make sure that I always had a roof over my head and because she knew that there was nothing she could do to change what had already happened. Unlike some of these poor kids, I had a mother who accepted the payment as an apology for what had already happened and not as a down payment for future services."

Dani shifted uncomfortably, trying to blot out the images that his words brought to mind. "Let me know if you need anything, okay?" she offered meekly.

"Will do," he said, and the line went dead.

Over the course of the next several months, news stories and scandalous theories surrounding the case popped up like mushrooms in a damp field. One awful story put forward by Arthur Melden's estate portrayed Dale as a financial fortune hunter who forged the notebook and planted it in the car. Another salacious story profiled the many loves of Nora Fontana. Even poor Tom Montgomery was tangled up in that one, complicating his still-pending divorce. When the story broke, Dani was certain that she'd seen the last of him as a translation client. To her surprise, however, he seemed to take it in stride and even stuck by Nora through the worst of the media attention.

On a more positive note, Lee reported back to Dani on thousands of new leads in the case, not the least of which came from a former member of Senator Richman's security staff who claimed that while on a fundraising tour through

Michigan, the senator had made an unscheduled stop on a private island for what he said was a hunting trip with the island's then-owner, Arthur Melden. The curious thing, said the bodyguard, was that the senator had never been known to hunt and hadn't even brought a gun. During the visit to the island, the bodyguard had been required to stand guard in the freezing cold for hours outside a submerged bunker that the senator claimed was a hunting blind. "It wasn't like any hunting blind I've ever seen," he'd said in one interview, "and I've been a hunter for forty years. If he was hunting anything in there, it sure wasn't deer."

Perhaps even more damning was his claim that a man matching Craig Miller's description was also present at the bunker that day. According to the bodyguard, he had shared a smoke with the man he identified as Miller while standing guard for the senator outside the bunker. He recalled Miller being angry and feeling slighted by something Melden had said earlier that same day. He could not comment on the content of that original conversation, however. When asked why he had not come forward sooner, he explained that as a bodyguard to politicians, one sees many things and that discretion is an important part of any security job. "But had I known what he was up to in that bunker …" he'd said in one interview, "If I'd thought for a moment that he was hurting someone's little boy … I have kids of my own …"

The mountain of new evidence grew daily. Victims and witnesses came forward to tell their tales of abuse at the hands of Arthur Melden, Craig Miller, George Grey, and Reggie Johnson. Michael York, who had been arrested again for armed robbery, even offered to tell his story for a reduced sentence on the robbery charge.

By mid-summer, the FBI had announced a formal investigation into the involvement of Senator Ted Richman in the disappearance and presumed death of Kevin Sowers.

As Dale had predicted, he was forced to resign. The FBI also announced that it would be working with the Guardian Task Force to search both the former home of the Miller family at Fanny Lake as well as Coyote Island, which was currently owned by the State of Michigan. Perhaps most shocking of all was a third announcement by the FBI declaring that they were reopening the file on Craig Miller's alleged suicide, based on witness accounts that he feared for his life prior to his death.

On the day of that last announcement, Dani was having lunch with Faye in a sports bar in Fenton. The news broke over the big screen above their table, the reporter's words scrolling across the bottom of the screen as he spoke, the volume muted. "Are you sorry that you got involved?" Faye asked Dani as they watched the screen.

She seemed to consider the question for a moment before answering. "No, not really, although it still infuriates me that I had Craig Miller in my head all that time."

"You did not, you had Kōbō in your head. As you will always have Kōbō in your head."

"Still, he was getting his messages from that monster. I thought I was helping little Jimmy Prince and instead …" Dani grabbed for the beer she was drinking and let the thought trail off.

"You *were* helping little Jimmy Prince. Why should it matter where the information came from? Think of Dale, he wasn't entirely innocent. In a way, wasn't he just a messenger sent to you by Craig Miller?"

The suggestion offended Dani and she made no effort to hide it, "That's ridiculous. Dale was a *victim* and don't tell me that Craig Miller was as well. Dale was a voice for the good."

"Victim or no, why did he say that Craig Miller left him the car?"

Dani couldn't bring herself to answer the question.

"Because Craig Miller knew people were after him," Faye continued. "He wanted that car to be discovered. He knew what it would prove and it did prove it, so what's your complaint?"

"My complaint is that I feel like I gave him some sort of redemption. I feel like I helped little Jimmy's killer!" Dani complained more loudly than she should have in the crowded restaurant. Diners nearby shot uncomfortable stares in her direction.

Faye put her hand over Dani's and gave it a gentle squeeze. "Think of it this way, if a killer came to you and wanted to confess his crimes. If he came to you and said, 'I'm guilty and I want the world to know it', would you listen?"

"Of course," Dani replied immediately, shrugging her shoulders lightly.

"Then what's the problem?" Faye gave her a sly smile.

"No fair," Dani complained quietly, "you tricked me."

Faye popped a fry into her mouth with a smug grin. "Have you heard anything more from Kōbō since?"

"Not yet, but I'm sure he won't stay away long." Dani was surprised to realize just how much she looked forward to his return.